BEWARE THE DOG

JUNKYARD DOGS 1

DOMINIQUE MONDESIR

Copyright © 2021 by Dominique Mondesir

All rights reserved.

No part of this book may be reproduced in any form or by any electronic or mechanical means, including information storage and retrieval systems, without written permission from the author, except for the use of brief quotations in a book review.

This is a work of fiction. Any similarity to actual persons, living or dead, or actual events, is purely coincidental

For my family without their support none of this would be possible.
Thanks to Cheynne Edmonton for the amazing cover art as always info@standoutcovers.com
And lastly thanks to my proof readers Martin Ohearn and Brandon Sommerville for making this book readable.
To my Grandmother, I hope you never read this.

1

The only thing I could taste was the nylon rope placed in my mouth to stop me from talking.

It pulled against the corners of my mouth, cutting into it. The more I moved the more it rubbed the skin raw.

I hardly noticed it, as metallic-smelling smoke filled my nostrils and whirled around me like mist; my eyes tried not to focus on the bodies that lay unmoving around me. I tried to avert my eyes from their twisted and mangled forms, but it felt impossible to do so.

I willed my eyes to stop but they had a life of their own.

Their gaze crept towards the pools of blood. The discarded guns. The impossibly large holes in the middles of foreheads.

All for what?

They had been told what would happen if they resisted, if they fought back, but they refused to listen. All for the company. A company they didn't own, a company they only worked for and that paid their wages, yet their unwavering loyalty to said company that hardly gave two fucks about if they lived or died was maddening.

They should have just surrendered.

Footsteps coming towards me forced me to lift my snot-filled face up; they thundered against the floors of the ship, disturbing the eerie peace that had come over it. I squinted my eyes trying to penetrate the smoke and I couldn't see anything till he was right in front of me, appearing like a ghost out of thin air.

He had dark skin and a bald head with a tattoo of a gun target just above his temple. A short goatee speckled with a few grey hairs covered his chin; tinted shades covered his eyes. Beads and bracelets hung from his forearms as he stood in front of me and looked into my soul.

"'I fell in love with a hooker who robbed me of my soul. I fell in love with a hooker who robbed me of my sight. I fell in love with a hooker because she was the only woman for me. I fell in love with a hooker till the only thing I had was two packs of cigarettes and thirty dollars on me.'

"That song," said the newcomer, "was my father's favourite, from a band called Junk Yard Dogs. It was a band he loved more than me, it was a band he saw more than me, and it was a band that meant everything to him. One day I grew the balls to ask him why, and you know what he said, amigo?"

I shook my head from side to side, fearful of the answer.

"Because, boyo! That song represents life. No truer words have ever been sung in no song. Then he passed out on the sofa, drunk off his ass."

I looked at him not knowing what to say. Hell, I couldn't say much anyway seeing as how rope filled my mouth.

"I bet you're wondering why we hijacked your fine ship here?"

The thought had crossed my mind.

"It's simple, you have something we want and we have something you want."

My eyebrows raised in confusion. These assholes had nothing I could want.

"Oh, I can see in your eyes you don't believe us. But we have the most important thing you value... your life."

The canine-filled smile he sent my way told me everything I needed to know. I was in a world of shit with no way out. How was I going to survive this?

2

What a thundercunt!

I sat in a chair that poked the small of my back as if it were robbing me of all the money I possessed; more chairs like it were positioned around a large conference room that appeared to stretch for miles. Motivational posters hung on the drab white walls and coffee stains covered the glass table in front of me.

I worked for one of the largest corporations in the galaxy, so you would think they could afford basic shit like a cleaner, to make sure the conference table was clear of marks and a fresh lick of paint on the walls to improve morale, but no, apparently the year's earnings had been below what we were expecting, although the directors still got their yearly bonus.

"Listen, people, this year's figures aren't what we expect here at Xcorp; the overall margin is down one point five percent from last year and the board is chewing my ass because of it. Our shareholders expect year on year—"

The person who was speaking was Gregory Goodwin.

Balding on the top, although in his early thirties with an ever-growing spare tire around his middle, Gregory was the poster boy for the company.

"I don't care if you dimwits have to stay all night, but I will get these financial figures back on my desk, by close of play tomorrow."

A tentative hand rose from the table. "Yes, Trina?"

"It's my youngest's birthday today and I promised him—"

"I do not give a fuck if a family member is dying of cancer, I do not give a fuck if you only have a day to live, and I especially do not give a fuck about some snot-nosed brat who doesn't give a shit if you're at his birthday or not, as long as he has the latest toys. Everyone works until the job is done!"

Like I said, thundercunt.

"Oh, stop crying like a weak bitch, Trina, we all have to make sacrifices for the company. You think I got to where I am by not giving my all? I worked through birthdays, holidays, weddings and deaths, to get to where I am today, and you can too if you just put the extra effort in."

It was the same speech he always gave when he wanted to motivate us. But most of us saw it for what it was, a half-ass excuse for him to get away with the bullshit he always got away with.

"Are we at least going to get paid for the overtime we do for once?" asked Nick, a small Asian man with curly black hair.

"I'm afraid not," Gregory said, trying to look apologetic. "You know how it has been."

That was it! That was his explanation for Xcorp's yet again not paying us for all the hard work we'd had to put in over the last six months. It wasn't even an explanation; it was just... more bureaucratic bullshit we had to swallow with a smile.

"Right, I think that's about it for today's meeting," Gregory said, dusting down his pinstripe Armani suit. "Oh, before I forget, Quinton, you'll need to take a short trip off-world to one of our space stations and deliver something for me. The board asked me, but I couldn't do that date as it conflicted with an important appointment I had."

"When is the trip booked for?" I asked, looking up surprised.

"In two days."

I opened my mouth to say something but he cut me off. "That isn't a problem is it?"

I shook my head softly from side to side and lowered my gaze to the floor.

"Glad to hear it," he said, walking out without a backward glance at the boardroom.

I stepped out of the entrance doors of the Xcorp office building and allowed a heavy sigh to escape my lips; I looked at the computer glass covering a small portion of my forearm and shook my head.

It had gone past midnight.

I checked to see if there were any missed calls or messages from my wife, but there were none. Swiping the computer off, I pulled up the collars of my tatted full-length jacket and began to walk home. The night air was chilly to the skin but at least it wasn't raining.

The night lights of New-London, so named after World

War 3, were dazzling to the tourist and first-timers whose feet touched its soil. But that soon wore off after the first week where they were conned out of everything they owned, the constant rainfall soaked them to the bone and the price of everything was triple what they normally would pay back home.

I continued until I came to a transport tube, which ferried commuters through tubes that crisscrossed over the New-London sky, through buildings, water, and even underground, and grimaced at the length of the line. Even at this time of night, the queue to get on was still ridiculously long.

A face I recognised from work was waiting in line for his turn to get on. Burying my head deeper into my coat and lowering my gaze I continued on by.

The walk would do me some good anyway and clear my head from those numbers I had to stare at, while Gregory was nowhere to be seen. He no doubt had left shortly after the meeting and gone home, to his trophy wife and two model kids.

I continued walking until I stopped in front of what was once London Bridge; broken in two it lay across the Thames like some disused toy.

A relic from a bygone era.

WW3 had taken everyone by surprise in the early 2020s; tensions had been mounting amongst European countries and the United Kingdom, plus what was once America had its own issues amongst its people triggering a civil war, which the Chinese and North Korea saw as the perfect time to attack America.

The devastation that followed almost killed the planet, making war between countries illegal. There was still crime. There was still murder. But now only on a smaller scale.

After the dust settled and the tempers lessened everyone did their best to make Earth a safer, better place. They fought against pollution; they did their best to save the forests, but off-world was a different matter.

Like wars before it, WW3 advanced technology at a breakneck speed. Computers got faster, weapons got more advanced, and the power of interstellar travel was birthed. Ships that could travel faster than light grew from the ashes of war, and humanity used them to populate planets in and beyond our solar system.

Out there in space, anything went, with the world government doing its best to police vast areas between colonised planets, but it was a losing battle.

Space was too vast.

People too greedy.

London Bridge and monuments like it were left as a constant reminder of what human nature could lead to, and it had worked up to a point, but as the days slowly slipped into years and the years into decades and the decades into centuries, nothing had really changed.

Yes, there hadn't been a war since, but like the saying went, there was always more than one way to skin a cat.

"Quinton? Quinton Blake?" came a voice from behind me.

I turned around and from the shadows of a building, a man approached me. His movement was rat-like, head constantly shifting to the left and right; the faded black hooded top he wore shrouded most of his face in darkness, making me take a hesitant step back.

I looked around and to my dismay found the streets deserted. It would be my luck: the one time London Bridge is deserted is the time I get killed by some junkie.

I wasn't sure if I should run. This man knew my name, but why approach me like this?

"Do I know you?" I asked, trying to get a look under his hood.

"You did once, but some time has passed since then."

He stopped in front of me and lowered his hood. Sore-covered lips greeted me in a smile below sunken grey lifeless eyes; wisps of patchy brown hair sat upon a head which looked more bone than flesh. I stared into a face waiting for some recollection but failed to find any.

"It's John," he said in a whisper, "John Brown."

My mouth opened in shock as I stared at the person who was once my best friend. We had gone to school together, then university, but had parted ways sometime in Uni. We were inseparable. Both from small middle-class families, boys whose own siblings were vastly older than they were, we bonded over our love of cartoons and video games.

"Long time no see, John," I said.

"I would say you look good, Quinton," he said, looking me up and down, "but I would be lying. I see you don't hit the gym as much anymore; you used to love that exercise shit."

"Yeah, well, what with my career and family..."

"You remember the bitch you used to date in Uni? It was shortly after we stopped hanging out as much, what was her name?"

"Claire Rogers."

"That's the one," he said clicking his fingers. "My god, she had you under the thumb, there wasn't a thing you wouldn't do for her. You were like a little lovesick puppy always running after her, always doing what she said. Between you and me I heard she was sleeping behind your back. I wonder whatever happened to her."

"I married her," I said in a dead voice.

"Oh, err...." John scratched his arm while he looked off uncomfortably into the distance. "Congratulations, I guess."

"Anyway, John, it was good to see you—"

"Got any kids?"

"Two."

"Right. Right."

"Anyway, like I was saying—"

"My folks passed away, you know," he said, taking a step forward. I could smell a faint odour of stale alcohol and tobacco on his breath.

"Yeah, they passed away a few years back. Got sick and never recovered; if I could afford the medical treatment they would still be alive today. After Uni, I went travelling—you know, I wanted to see the ruins, explore sights—but I fell in love with a bastard of a man who took me for everything I had. Scuba diving instructor—how cliché can you get?"

"Yeah, I remember you saying you wanted to. Ever go off-world?"

"Nah, got as far as the Galapagos Islands—well, what's left of them—before I was taken for a fool. The next stop would have been Mars."

"Well... that's life, I guess," I said weakly.

"Yeah, I guess it is," he said, taking another step forward. "Not. like you, ay? You had your head screwed on right. A's in school. 'A' student in Uni. Never put a foot wrong. Got recruited by Xcorp, the largest company there is, right out of Uni. You must be living the dream."

"Yeah... yeah, I guess," I said with a shrug. "Anyway, I gotta be going, before the old ball and chain wonders where I got to."

I turned to leave but as his hand clamped on my shoulder, I know it would not be that easy. It never was with John.

I turned back around and the rotting smell of his gums washed over me, forcing me to take a hurried step back.

"Listen, man, I've fallen on hard times and I could do with some help—"

"John, let go of me!"

"Man, you don't know how hard it's been living on these streets. Going from hand to mouth. Always struggling. Always trying to survive. It's been easy for you!"

John always had a problem. One of the reasons we stopped hanging out was his love for drugs. I partied like everyone in Uni, smoking a bit of weed here doing a bit of ecstasy there, but that was never enough for John. He always wanted more. From coke to heroin, to even the new shit like T12.

"John," I said, taking his hand off my shoulder, "you've got a problem; you've always had a problem. Since we were kids you always had to push further; nothing was ever enough for you. I put in the hard work to get to where I am, hours of study, hours of sacrifice, when you didn't. I couldn't help you then, and I sure as hell can't help you now. You need to get some help and I'm not the person who can give it to you."

I walked away, but he called out to me.

"That's it, walk away, Mr Never Breaks The Rules! I just tried living a little, is that so much to ask for? I may be an addict but at least I'm not dead inside, living a life I hate—I can see it in your eyes!"

I kept my head down and kept on walking. What the hell would he know? How did he even find me anyway?

Running footsteps forced me to turn around just as John grabbed me once again by the lapels of my jacket.

"Look, I'm sorry, man," he said in a raspy voice. "I'm sorry, I just need a little dough to tide me over. Not much.

Just something to keep the edge off, you know? Just something to help me sleep."

"Get the fuck off—"

"I'll suck it!"

"What?" I demanded, pushing him off me in disgust.

"I'll suck it, I'll suck it like it's never been sucked before. I know you've always wondered what it's like to be with another—"

I pushed him hard in the chest with everything I had, knocking him to the ground. He looked up at me with a hunger that turned my stomach.

"For the love of God, John, get some damn help."

I turned around again, but it was a mistake. Something heavy and metal hit me in the back of the head, forcing a cry from my throat as I dropped to my knees. I protected my head with my arms as another blow rained down from above; I curled in upon myself as a kick knocked the wind from my lungs.

"I tried to be nice, but you didn't want to listen, did you? All you suit-wearing bastards are all the same. Only caring about the bottom line," said John as his boot made contact with my ribs once again.

"What would you know about suffering, Quinton?"

Another boot made contact forcing me to whimper.

"Look where all your hard work has gotten you! Face-down in the gutter!"

I felt his hands invade my pockets and I tried to fight him off, but I just wanted it to be over, just wanted the beating to stop.

He placed his mouth against my ear, till all I could smell was poor decisions and regret. "The difference between us has always been, I'm willing to take what's mine and you're not."

I could hear the rustling of my money in his hand as the edges of my vision began to turn black.

"Where's all your hard work got you now?" he asked as I fell into unconsciousness.

3

I woke up to something wet hitting me in the face. Lifting a hand to shield my eyes I opened them to find it was still night, but now it was raining. Getting to a sitting position, I passed my hand to the back of my pounding head where it came away red and sticky.

People walked around me as if I was an inanimate object to be ignored. I got up shakily to my feet and wrapped my arms around myself as a shiver swept through me. Looking down I found out why.

Shoes gone.

Jacket missing.

Wallet nowhere to be found.

John had cleaned me out. I shook my head and looked down at my computer still attached to my forearm. No doubt he would have taken that too if they weren't all DNA coded so only the owner could use them. I checked the time and found less than an hour had passed.

Head down, feet squelching against the damp leaves that stuck to them, I made my way home.

The rain hadn't let up but only increased as my house came into view. Bought when Claire and I didn't have much money, it was a standard three-bed house slotted in suburbia.

I walked past similar houses with better paint jobs, nicer lights, and the latest robotic gardeners who tended to every detail of their homeowner's lawn. Then I stopped in front of our house and looked up.

Most of the lights on the front of our porch were out; a few flickered like dying stars, but they only highlighted the fading paint job and the overgrown weeds that needed to be cut. I walked forward and cussed as I stubbed my toe on cutting shears left across the pathway. Picking them up I threw them to one side.

I had asked my sons to do the gardening, but one quick look at the state of the grass and weeds surrounding me told me they hadn't even bothered to start.

Shaking my head, I opened the front door to find it was unlocked and walked on through. The eerie glow from chargers and electronics on standby gave me enough room to manoeuvre without knocking anything over, taking the stairs two at a time; I walked past my sons' room to see the tell tale glow of a screen still on; opening the door I was greeted by both my sons sat in front of the TV watching something animated and gruesome.

Blood splattered the screen, capturing their attention.

"Sun, Rise, what are you two doing up?"

Sun was my older and Rise my younger. Sun, Rise. Two idiotic names my wife had chosen because names associated with nature were the "in" thing at the time. I had suggested something a little less out there, but by the time I had come back from picking up diapers, she had already registered the names.

They were twelve and ten. I sometimes wondered if they were mine.

"Boys, I asked you a question!"

"For fuck's sake, Quinton. Can't you see we're watching something?" Sun said, pointing to the screen.

"Don't—"

"Why don't you go bother Claire—can't you see we're doing shit?" Rise said.

"How many times have I told you boys its Mum and Dad?"

"Well, 'Mum'," Sun said with air quotes, "says labels hold you back from your true destiny. The government imposes labels on us to hold us back."

I rolled my eyes and held back my response; I was too tired for this shit. My head felt like it was splitting in two and my feet were killing me.

I closed the door without saying another word.

"Limp dick asshole," I heard one of them say through the door.

I made my way to the bathroom and washed as quickly as I could. As the blood swirled down the drain I tried to muster up some kind of anger, some sort of rage, but all I felt was hollow inside. After washing myself off I walked into my bedroom to find it cold and empty.

The bed was still unslept in.

The clothes I had washed and folded were still resting at the bottom of the bed.

Throwing the covers back I got into bed and rechecked my computer, to see if I had any missed calls or messages but I had missed none.

I thought about calling Claire, to see where she was but

this wasn't the first time she had stayed out late with her friends, nor would it be the last, and it would only cause an argument if she picked up—one I didn't think my head could take.

Shutting my eyes once more I drifted off till my computer buzzed on my arm signalling a message. I opened it with blurry eyes and groaned when I read what it said.

Quinton,

Gregory. I know I said I needed you to fly out in two days but something came up in head office, so I'm afraid I'll need you to fly out first thing in the morning. I know it's short notice but we've all got to do our best to keep this beast afloat.

Get your shit packed and ready for the morning.

I closed the computer and lay back down uttering the thousandth sigh of the day and closed my eyes.

The alarm woke me up all too early. I dragged myself out of bed, feeling like a sack of shit.

Water. Packed. Dressed.

And I was out the door before the sun had even risen. I didn't have to get the boys ready for school because they were off for the summer, but I still wanted to get in touch with Claire and let her know I wouldn't be around for the next few days. Plus she would need to get in before the boys woke up, so there was someone there to look after them.

I tried ringing her but didn't have much luck. At the nearest transport tube I paid the fee for the journey to the space station and settled in my one-person see-through pod. They came in varying sizes depending on use, but they all had the same interior.

Clean and temperature-controlled with glass all around, they were one of the few ways to travel through the city.

The use of cars had been outlawed in all major cities hundreds of years ago, with only the rich and famous having enough money to afford them, or keep them running. They used them on the roads outside the city which had once been teeming with metal life, roads that had cars bumper to bumper; now the only thing that travelled on them were electric public transport vehicles and the occasional rich asshole who used the roads as his personal track.

I tried to settle my head back on the headrest of the chair but the bump that had grown at the back of it, from last night's beating, made me wince and lift my head back up.

A buzzing on my forearm made me look at my computer, Claire's name flashed across the screen forcing me to take a slow intake of breath.

Calm. Calm. Calm.

That was what I reminded myself as I swiped the screen to receive the call. Claire's makeup-smudged face with heavily laden eyes greeted me.

"What?" she demanded.

"Hi, I didn't see you—"

"I was out with the girls. I told you this more than once this week that I will be spending some time with my friends. If you listened more then you would have known that."

"Are you—"

"Yes, I'm sure! God, sometimes it's like speaking to a brick wall with you."

I took another deep breath and said, "I'm sorry, I must have misheard. I know this is last minute and I'm sorry to do this to you, but I have to go off-world for a work meeting for the next couple of days. I'm on my way to the space station now, so the boys will need looking after."

"For fuck's sake, Quinton! I had plans for the next few days. You know what tomorrow is, right?"

"Your birthday," I mumbled.

"Yeah, my birthday, and I had plans with friends. Now I have to blow that out of the water to look after your kids, the same kids you're never around to spend any time with. They hardly know who their father is with the amount of time you spend in your office. If I didn't know better, I would say you're sleeping with your secretary, but just thinking about that makes me laugh, it's so unlikely."

I gritted my teeth and took two more deep breaths. There had been offers. There had been longing looks and too-long touches on the shoulder, but I had halted them all for the same family who thought so little of me.

"Honey, we've been through this. If I keep putting in the hours then the promotion is mine, plus some of the bills are late and with you not working at the moment—"

"So this is my fault, is it?" she asked, eyes flashing in anger.

"Of course not, I know the stress of work makes your anxiety flare up and I would never put that mental strain on you. Can you just make sure everything is looked after while I'm away?"

Silence on the other end while she looked at me with a layer of disgust she barely concealed.

"Whatever," and with that, the line went dead leaving me staring at a blank screen.

4

The journey was shorter than I expected. I woke myself up with a snort and looked out the window at the approaching space station, where metal sprouted from the ground like roots from a tree and twisted into individual launching pads for the spaceships that rested on them. Light reflected off the glass from the signal towers and temporarily blinded me while we made our descent.

Each major city had their own space station for incoming and outgoing flights for trips off-world, not that you technically needed it as ships could land anywhere they pleased, but for the sake of safety and regulation all ships wishing to land on Earth had to go through one of these stations, for multiple scans and debriefings.

It stopped fugitives, also known as jumpers, coming in and going out.

My pod landed with a soft hiss and I entered the fray with the other weary morning travellers; creased suits and ruffled hair were easy to spot as it seemed I wasn't the only one who had a rushed morning, with little to no sleep.

Many commuters who surrounded me worked off-world in the nearest colonies such as Mars; a handful of hours there, a couple of energy drinks when you arrived and a handful of hours back and you had made another commute for one of the big corporations.

I moved towards my gate queue and got stopped by a man in a grey suit and bags under his eyes that you could hide children underneath. "You Quinton Blake?" he asked, looking me up and down before looking at a picture projected from his forearm.

"Yeah," I answered uneasily.

"Mr Goodwin said to give you this," he replied, handing me a small antique data-stick. I held it up to my eye and then looked back at him in confusion. These were out of date before I was a kid.

"What does Gregory want me to do with this?"

"This is what you need to deliver to our sister station when you arrive."

"I have the files I need to deliver," I said tapping the computer on my forearm. "I don't know if this is some kind of joke, but I can't deliver this to our sister station when I arrive there. I'll be a laughingstock. Does this thing even work still?"

Grey Suit threw his hands up in the air in frustration and said, "Gregory said you weren't too bright, but I didn't think he'd use such an idiot. All you have to do is hand the data-stick over to the head of our sister station when you arrive, then they'll pat you on that little behind of yours, tell you what a great job you did, and push you on your way."

I looked at the data-stick then back at him, confusion overlaying my gaze, but I kept my objections to myself. If this was what Gregory wanted to get delivered, then who was I to say different? If I was in any luck I would be back on

Earth a lot sooner than I thought. I pocketed the stick and gave him a small nod and went on my way.

I rounded a corner to my terminal, and a pretty female Space Station employee stopped me in my tracks and pulled me to one side.

"Mr Blake, I presume?" she asked with a tilt of the head.

"Err, yes."

"Follow me this way please," she said.

I stood watching her, shrinking back at a loss for what to do; if I missed my flight then it would be my ass but I was more worried about how this woman knew my name and what she wanted from me. Biting my lip I glanced nervously at my watch then chased after her. After finally catching up I said, "Where are we going?"

"To your flight gate, of course, Mr Blake," she said, all smiles and graceful nods.

I rechecked my holographic and looked back to where we had come from. "But gate 6 is that way."

"Ahh, I see the confusion now," she said with another far too pleasant smile. "You obviously missed the email with your updated itinerary. Xcorp, as you well know, has several of its own private space-faring vessels, which it uses to courier its most important members of staff. You shall be taking such a vessel today, to get you to your destination."

My mouth opened and closed while I slowed my walk. "But, but, you must be mistaken—that's not me. I'm just about middle management, and that's stretching it."

"Well, someone in head office must think you're special, because this is Xcorp's newest vessel," she said, pointing to a ship I could see parked on a landing bay through the glass.

Jet black and mean looking, it was all angles. Two thruster engines that could swallow a grown elephant whole without it touching its sides powered it from the rear.

Plasma cannons, lasers, ion blasters and city-destroying photon missiles sat on every available space, giving the ship more weaponry than a military vessel.

"Are we going to war?" I asked, but she just gave me one of those smiles, which was beginning to get on my nerves. "Look, I don't know what's going on here but you must have the wrong person. I am on a simple business trip—"

"Are you or are you not one Quinton Blake?"

I nodded.

"Then this is your ship and it is waiting for you to board."

I looked at her with growing frustration that swelled in the pit of my stomach like a dormant volcano that refused to erupt. Biting the inside of my cheek I nodded my head and allowed her to lead me the rest of the way. Basic tiled floors gave way to checked marble, and the faint sounds of classical music floated on the air as waitresses served cocktails to men in twenty-grand suits. Everyone spoke in hushed tones in case they broke the tranquillity of the environment, I looked down at my own crumpled suit and frowned, suddenly feeling very out of place.

More than one raised eyebrow and discerning look was sent my way.

I passed my hand over the creases but it only made it worse; giving up in a huff I continued on and we reached my gate.

"Just walk on through and someone shall meet you on the other side, Mr Blake," she said with another infuriating smile.

I nodded and walked on through, clutching my travel bag to my chest. This had to be wrong. There must have been a mix-up like you saw in all those terrible movies when two people with the same name somehow swap lives. I looked hastily over my shoulder for my doppelgänger but found no one there.

Don't be stupid!

Who would want to change lives with you?

This is just a simple mistake made by head office, or worse, some sick prank Gregory has somehow managed to pull off. That's all this is, I told myself, not believing one word of it.

Finally exiting the tunnel gate I approached the ship cargo door and was met by a woman dressed in a white blouse with the Xcorp logo on it and a black pencil skirt. She had brunette locks pulled into a fashionable bun and dark red lips. She smiled my way as I approached.

"Ah, Mr Blake, so glad you could make it today. If you'll please follow me this way, I shall show you to your seat."

"Err, I think there's been a mistake—" I began, but she didn't wait to hear the rest of what I had to say, as she was already making her way inside the ship.

I followed with a sigh and entered the ship through the cargo bay doors. An array of combat gear littered the floor. Everything from plasma guns, pistols and ammo to body armour sat in racks around the walls of the cargo bay. I noticed rucksacks lined in a corner, each one with different logos or symbol stitched on it. One was of a lion with an eyepatch and a crown, another was an octopus holding guns in each one of its limbs; there was even one with what appeared to be Little Red Riding Hood with an Uzi in each hand, riding a wolf.

We made our way through the halls of the ship, our feet echoing on the polished metal, passing room after room. I wondered what was inside but the woman I followed kept up a brisk pace until we came to an opened door. I stepped through into a room twice the length of the entire first floor of my house.

I shook my head slowly correcting myself. This wasn't a room, this was an apartment.

"This first room is what the brochures would call your relaxation area, but to you and me it's your living room," said the woman walking past me.

Simple but elegant brown leather chairs matched the oak wood panelling that lined the floors, a holograph screen floated in the centre of the room with the Xcorp logo on it, a glass table with a miniature waterfall dominated the centre of the room.

"Through here," she said, walking over to a door on her left, "is your master bedroom—an en-suite, if you're feeling too lazy to use the shower in your bathroom, which is down the hall."

I stood mouth agape while I took in the four-poster bed with silk sheets.

"The door on your right is your office if you need to do any work, and I believe that's it," said the brunette, hands clasped in front of her.

I took in my surroundings and remembered to close my mouth as I turned to face her. "What is all this?"

"This is how the senior members of office travel, Mr Blake; normally all this would be for Mr Goodwin, but as you're taking his place you get to enjoy some of the perks if only for a brief time."

"I.... thank you, I didn't catch your name."

Her head jolted back in shock before the first genuine smile I had seen all day graced her lips. "You've never done this before, have you?" she asked, gesturing around the room.

"No, why do you ask?"

"It's because you're the first person to ask me my name; normally people like me are just part of the furniture."

I nodded my head as she walked away. She turned back towards me and I caught a glimpse of what appeared to be a fox-like tattoo on her right shoulder through the white blouse she wore. "My name's Paige, Mr—"

"You can call me Quinton," I said, cutting her off, "and it's a pleasure to meet you, Paige. What's your tattoo of?" I asked, pointing to her shoulder.

"It's nothing," she said hurriedly, covering her shoulder with her left hand before rushing out the way we came.

Nice one, dickhead.

The only genuine person who has shown you any sort of kindness and you chase them away. I swivelled on my heel and took in my surroundings, rubbing my hands with a smile. I walked towards the fridge and pulled it open to be greeted by bottles of Dom Perignon.

Well, when in Rome.

5

I could smell smoke—was I dreaming?

I turned over in my goose down bedding and dug myself deeper under the sheets and pillows wrapped around me; I hadn't known comfort like this since I had wasted thousands on a honeymoon, which was short-lived because Claire had discovered she was pregnant with our eldest and had wanted to go back home.

It didn't matter that it was the first vacation I had had in ten years, it didn't matter I had worked sixteen-hour days non-stop for nearly a year, none of it mattered.

Claire had wanted to go home so home we went.

I coughed lightly clearing my throat and tried to welcome the embrace of sleep, when another bout of coughing came upon me, I tried to clear my throat but this only made it worse. Slapping my hand against my chest, I forced myself up to my elbows.

Wait.... I took a sniff of the air and leapt out of bed.

That was smoke I could smell. "Lights!" I said, waiting for the room lights to come on but nothing happened, I said it again but they just weren't responding. I ambled forward and slammed my shin into one of the wooden posters of the bed; hopping on one leg I swore under my breath as I tried to get my bearings.

Being unfamiliar with the layout of the room I needed some light if I wanted my shins to see me through the night; clicking my fingers I woke my computer on my forearm up and switched on the light bulb feature, which acted as a mini torch.

Faint wisps of smoke curled around my legs as the light illuminated the room. Walking out of the bedroom I made it into the lounge, where the smoke was the thickest. I grabbed a towel off the table and wrapped it over my face, having seen a movie where the lead character had said it helped against smoke. I had no idea if it was true or not, but what harm could it do?

As I followed the smoke through the apartment it got stronger at the entrance, I took a hesitant step back and contemplated what I should do. If there was a fire behind the door, then the last thing I should do was open it, but if I didn't try to escape the apartment, then I would slowly choke to death and die.

Burnt to death or choked to death.

Suffocation or cremation.

I could feel the seconds tick by as I paced back and forth before the door. Finally, throwing my hands up in the air I moved forward and opened the door—well, I tried to but it wouldn't budge. I waved my hands in front of the door like an asshole;, nothing happened. I pressed the emergency button next to it to force it open and I could hear the gears turning as they tried to do their job but the door only opened a couple of inches then halted.

Gritting my teeth in frustration, I looked around the room for something to pry it open and came upon an expensive-looking metal art sculpture sitting on a desk. Grabbing it by the base I jammed it into the gap of the door and began working it back and forth.

The muscles in my arms strained as the gears in the doors ground loudly together. Finally, they gave way enough that I could slip through the gap I had created.

I stumbled forward into the hallway and sprawled along the floor.

Getting back up to my feet, I tried to see what had caused me to fall, and I hurried backwards until I smacked against the opposite wall.

A dead body.

Blood coated the floor around it, with my footsteps imprinted in the blood like a prehistoric creature's paw print left in tar.

The body was of a man with blond hair who wore combat fatigues. He had a hole through the centre of his head that I could see all the way through; apart from that there didn't appear to be any other wounds.

I inched closer and tapped his shoe with my foot. I didn't know what I expected to happen but I did it again, just in case this was some sick joke.

Nothing happened.

He was murdered outside my door! What if someone thought I was the murderer?

I looked around for the murder weapon but failed to find one; I took another step back and wiped my feet along the floor. Surely no one would think I did this?

I would just explain if anyone asked. They would believe me. Why wouldn't they? What did I have to gain from doing this? I... I—

My chest grew tighter by the second as my breaths became shallower. About to wipe my hands over my face I stopped, as they had become coated in blood. Looking for something to wipe them on I glanced down at my body and realised I was naked except for a pair of boxers I had worn to bed. I made my way back towards my room when a shout to my left grabbed my attention. I lifted my arm and projected light, so I could see further down the hall, but the smoke made visibility poor.

Cussing my bad luck I thought of what to do.

I could return to my room and hide while I waited out whatever was happening, but that meant a lack of anywhere to run if the wrong person turned up at my door. The killer was still at large and with no weapons to defend myself I would be a sitting duck.

Another shout.

This one sounded like a command.

Looking back longingly at my room, I picked up the metal artwork I had used to open the door and crept forward.

That's it, dickhead! Walk towards the shouting.

I stopped every so often and scanned my surroundings; doors to rooms that looked similar to mine were open. Someone had ransacked the rooms leaving clothes and broken glass on the floor.

I continued until I heard a sound up ahead. When I doubled my grip on the metal art piece its weight gave me confidence as I leaned against the wall and waited.

Footsteps approached me.

I waited for a second or two and came around the corner I was hiding behind with the art piece lifted above my head. A roar of anger escaped my lips.

I didn't get far as a calloused hand grabbed me round the throat and threw me against the wall, and then the barrel of a gun was placed under my chin.

My eyes bulged as my feet dangled off the floor.

"What kind of fucking moron tries to sneak up on someone when they're lit up like a Christmas tree, from the light they're holding?"

I tried to respond, but the only thing that came out was a gargle. He released my throat and I slid down to the floor, coughing and spluttering. I rubbed my neck and slowly got up to my feet.

"Are you the killer?"

He narrowed his eyes and looked at me as if I was the world's biggest idiot. "Who would ask someone that? But better yet, why would I tell you the truth if I was?"

"I dunno," I said with a shrug. "Thought it was better to just get it out in the open. Save us both some time."

"No, I'm not the killer but you are in extreme danger from whoever is. Do you have any weapons..." he began to say, but trailed off when he took in my attire.

"What? I was sleeping, I normally sleep in the nude so I would call this a bonus. Do you know what the killer wants or who they are?"

"No, Quinton, we don't."

"How do you know my name?"

A scream from down the hall behind us snapped our heads in that direction. A quick burst of gunfire followed it.

"It doesn't matter how I know your name, all that matters now is—hey! You need to listen to me," he said, forcing me to pull my eyes away from the sounds.

"What I need you to do is go back to your room and find somewhere safe to hide. Can you do that for me? Somewhere like the closet or bathroom? This will all blow over soon and we'll be on our way."

I looked into his eyes and I wanted to believe him, really I did, but I could see the lie in his eyes as much as he could see the fear in mine. He turned his head back towards the way we heard gunfire and I saw Little Red Riding Hood atop a wolf, with an Uzi in each hand, tattooed on his neck. It was the same logo I had seen on the rucksacks in the cargo hold when I had first entered the ship.

"Who are you and what are you doing on this flight? This should be a simple delivery mission; instead, I am surrounded by what I can only guess are soldiers."

"Mercenaries actually," he said, turning back to face me.

"What?"

"Yeah, they hired us to protect this flight."

"Fat load of good you've done doing that!"

"Keep your voice down," he said, lifting a hand to cover my mouth. "I want you to make your way towards your rooms and hide somewhere safe. When it's safe I'll come and get you."

I moved towards the direction of my room, but a blast of gunfire lit up the hallway ahead of me halting me in my tracks.

The merc got in front of me and lifted his gun into the air, scanning the area ahead of him.

Without warning, he let off three quick rounds from his rifle that made my ears ring. I staggered back and worked my mouth open and closed while he scanned the area with one closed eye.

"You could have shot a friend—shouldn't you radio to see if it's one of your teammates?"

"No point, they're all dead."

I looked at him in shock while I recalled how many rucksacks I'd counted on the way in.

"What do you mean they're all dead? Who is attacking us?"

"It means what it means, and if I knew that then I wouldn't be sitting here with you."

Another flash of gunfire and the metal ceiling above us pinged as bullets bounced off it.

The merc dropped to his stomach and grabbed my shirt on the way down, so I followed him. Flat on the floor, I lay next to him as he sighted down his scope and let off another round.

"I think I got the bastard," he said in a low voice, slowly getting up to one knee. He kept his sights on whatever he could see up ahead, then slowly stood.

"This whole thing stinks," he said, scanning the passage behind us before moving forward. "They hired me and my team to protect this ship. From what or from whom, they never gave us that information. All we knew is, we had to accompany this ship to and from its destination. Me and the boys thought this was the easiest gig yet until someone drugged us.

"When we woke up, we found the pilot's throat slit and all our gear damaged or missing. Lucky some of the boys are paranoid fuckers and always hide a stash of weapons away, I feel bad for teasing them about it—if it wasn't for those guns then we would be all dead right about now."

"Xcorp hired you?" I asked in disbelief.

"Yeah."

"But that makes no sense—"

He waved a hand in front of me for silence as a shape took form in the smoke. He inched forward; I trailed behind him until we saw what it was.

A body crucified against the wall.

The man wore combat fatigues similar to the merc's; the latter was now walking forward with a look of fire in his eyes. I could see the muscles in his jaw grind back and forth while he kept on inching forward.

"I think we should—"

I began but never got to finish my sentence as a body dropped from the ceiling duct behind us. I half turned but was shoved out of the way as metal flashed in the air and blood sprayed behind it. The merc fired a shot but the person ducked low and swept their blades up in an arc taking the merc's hand clean off.

It and the gun fell to the floor with a clatter.

He opened his mouth to scream, but two blades penetrated the sides of his neck before a sound could leave his mouth. He dropped to his knees, the light slowly fading from his eyes, and then fell face-first on the floor, leaving me alone with the attacker.

I ran, but was tripped and came crashing down to the floor. Turning around I looked up at a familiar face that smiled down on me.

"I hope I didn't spoil the trip too much for you, Quinton, but you have something I need," said Paige.

6

My mouth gagged, hands bound behind my back, I wasn't going anywhere.

I would love to say I gave Paige a struggle, but the simple fact was, she easily overpowered with a few well-placed kicks and punches to the legs and body that had me gasping for breath.

I was then dragged kicking and screaming to the lounge area for the residents of the ship; sofas and coffee tables with everything from board games to inbuilt entertainment systems surrounded us.

I even spotted VR helmets and chairs for people who liked to game.

I took it all in and tried my best to avoid the newest feature to the room: blood.

Blood coated the walls and floors as bodies lay scattered about the room, all lying prone in the last moments of how they died. Some were slumped against the wall, some were sprawled face down over chairs, some gave off the smell of urine or excrement, as their bodies had given out in their last dying moments.

Paige tied and gagged me, then she sat opposite me while she cleaned her knives. Blackish-grey, the knife and handle were made out of one piece of steel, which had patterns along the whole blade that reminded me of running water.

"Beautiful, aren't they?" she asked, lifting one blade up to the lights. "They are both from the tenth century and made from Damascus steel; the steel is named after the city of Damascus, which was the capital city of Syria. I love these blades. They keep their edge no matter what they have to go through or cut. They say technology has figured out how to make sharper, harder, more resilient blades, but who knew how to make blades better than the very people whose lives depended on it?

"Yes, anyone can create a blade now with all the technology we have now, but the need for it isn't the same. This blade is made out of necessity. The blade of the future is made for art."

I stared at her wide-eyed and gave her a nod, feeling foolish immediately after I had done it.

She went back to cleaning her blades and allowed the silence to once again envelop us. She cleaned her blades with a focus and passion I had rarely seen, working in the office. It was a look that spoke of love and care.

"I'm sorry," she whispered.

She looked me in the eye and smiled faintly before turning her attention back to her work. "Things got a little messy and out of control. After I drugged the mercenaries I had planned for it to be a simple task of collecting you and what we came for and then making our way to our ship. I didn't expect the mercenaries to wake up so soon, or for them to have a secret stash of weapons hidden away somewhere.

"I was hoping I could complete this task injuring no one, but that idea soon flew out of the window after they fired the first shots."

What was she expecting to happen?

We were on board a ship full of mercenaries who had been hired to protect the ship and its cargo and they had tried to do their job, while she drugged them, damaged their gear and tried to get away. They were simply doing their job and if that meant shooting at her then so be it, I just didn't know what would now happen to me, or why she wanted me so badly.

Footsteps echoed through the ship and made me look up as a man with dark skin and a bald head entered the room. He had a short goatee speckled with grey hairs and a tattoo of a gun target near his temple. Another man, who wore a black shirt and a clerical collar, followed in his footsteps. A ginger mop of hair gave way to a great brushy ginger beard.

"What the hell, you two!" said the ginger man, in a heavy Irish accent. "You killed everyone before Sodom and Gomorrah got their chance to have some fun." He tapped together a pair of pistols that had Christian crosses etched into the handles. "This bunch of sinners were pretty overdue for their time with the Lord, I believe." He looked around the room and gave a dismissive snort. "Bunch of fuck wizards."

The man with the bald head and dark skin walked towards me and slightly lowered the tinted glasses that covered his eyes.

"'I fell in love with a hooker who robbed me of my soul. I fell in love with a hooker who robbed me of my sight. I fell in love with a hooker because she was the only woman for me. I fell in love with a hooker till the only thing I had was two packs of cigarettes and thirty dollars on me.'

"That song," said the newcomer, "was my daddy's favourite, from a band called Junk Yard Dogs. It was a band he loved more than me, it was a band he saw more than me, and it was a band that meant everything to him. One day I grew the balls to ask him why, and you know what he said, amigo?"

I shook my head from side to side, fearful of the answer.

"Because, boyo! That song represents life. No truer words have ever been sung in no song. Then he passed out on the sofa, drunk off his lazy ass."

I said nothing as all I could see was my fearful reflection in the lens of his shades.

"I bet you're wondering why we hijacked your fine ship here? It's simple really, you have something we want and we have something you want."

I said nothing as my eyes roamed over the three figures in the room. I could feel my pulse quicken as I did my best to slow it.

"Oh, I can see in your eyes you don't believe us, boyo. But we have the most important thing you value... your life," he said with a smile that reminded me of a rabid dog.

"Now if you would be so kind as to escort us to your room," he said, lifting me off the floor, "and Poppy, I think we can lose the gag and bonds, don't you?

"It's not like our friend here has any place to run to."

They escorted me to my room and the only thing making a sound was our feet on the metal floor; I tried desperately to think of somehow to escape, but nothing came to mind without me being filled with bullets or the sharp end of a blade.

How did this happen?

I was just a simple office drone who was told what to do and worked until I was told not to. What did these people think I had that could profit them in any way? I just hoped after I gave them what they wanted they would leave me alone. Then it was only a case of trying to send out an SOS for help.

We entered my room, and I turned back to the man I assumed was their leader. "What now?"

"We want what they gave you to deliver to your sister station," he said with a grin.

"Why?"

"Don't concern yourself with that; all you need to know is your life depends on it, boyo. Now, where is it?"

I walked through my lounge and entered my bedroom where my luggage was kept. Eyeing my crumpled business suit I quickly got dressed, not wanting to be killed in my underwear, and searched through my luggage until I picked up the old data-stick. Weighing it in my hand, I gripped it until my knuckles went white.

"What's taking you so long, you knob jockey?" came an Irish voice.

I straightened up and took a deep breath as I walked back out. All three looked at me expectantly while I stopped in front of them. My palms began to sweat as I saw hands tapping ever so slightly on weapon handles. These people had shown a ruthlessness that scared the shit out of me, but I needed to do something, anything so they kept me alive.

"How do I know once I give you this then you won't kill me?"

"You don't, fuckface," said Irish.

"Look, Quinton," said the woman, walking forward, "I didn't want to use violence on this trip, that's why I drugged those trigger-happy goons, but sometimes your best plans never work out how you want them to. I promise you once you hand over the data-stick then we shall be on our way. You have my word."

I looked into those beautiful eyes of hers and wanted to believe her. They were warm, inviting, trustworthy, but an image of a severed hand dropping to the floor jumped out at me and forced me to take a step backwards.

I wouldn't be another victim.

In one swift movement I placed the data-stick in my mouth and swallowed.

"No!" came the anguished shout of Irish as he rushed forward and grabbed me by the throat. "You stupid motherfucker! We were willing to let you go, but now you've fucked up! Ya think swallowing what we want will save you? I'll just cut it outta you."

"Willis, no!"

"Why not?" Willis said, hand still choking me.

"Because," she said, stepping forward, "I gave him my word I wouldn't hurt him if he gave us what we want, and I always keep my word. Now let him go, or we shall have a problem."

"Are you stupid? He didn't give us shit—"

"If you want the data-stick—" I croaked as the lack of blood to my brain made me dizzy, "then you'll have to take me with you."

"I still say we cut him open," Willis said.

"And I said—"

"Poppy! Willis! Enough," said the crew's leader, bringing the room to silence. He walked forward and tapped Willis on the shoulder. The ginger asshole didn't move, staring me down for a second or two, but a deep inhale of breath from their leader made him step back.

Their leader came to a stop in front of me and looked me in the eye.

I fought with everything I had to not look away. "Well, boyo, I like your cojones. If you're up for a little adventure then we'll take you with us, but you may come to regret it."

I already was.

7

I stared at the walls of my quarters, mind numb and body cold.

They had escorted me onto their ship after I had swallowed the data-stick, and dumped me into a room that was a big step down from my last living quarters. Gone were the multiple rooms and instead I had one room just big enough for me to stretch my arms out in, gone were the silk sheets and goose feather filled pillows; instead I had a bed pushed up against the wall that wasn't big enough for a child. It came with an itchy blanket and lumpy pillow, which I was sure I had seen move.

I tilted my head back and tried to close my eyes but all I could see were images of blood, vacant eyes and mangled limbs.

They offered me food as the days passed but I refused to eat, only drinking the water they gave me. I wasn't on a hunger strike, but whenever I ate anything I would throw it back up. Maybe I was still in shock from the blood bath I had witnessed. Maybe I felt some sense of guilt for causing the death of those men. Maybe....

A knock on the door interrupted my thoughts. "Come in."

The door slid open to reveal Paige aka Poppy. She smiled at me as she walked inside and looked for somewhere to sit, but as the only thing in the room was my bed and bag, she opted to sit next to me on the bed. A tingle swept through me as our knees touched, but I pushed it down as the images of her handiwork popped up in my mind.

"Sooo," she said, drawing out the word, "how you doing?"

I gave her a raised eyebrow as my hands swept over my surroundings. "I couldn't be better. My life has really improved after running into you folks. I feel like I'm on top of the world."

"Fair point; stupid question I suppose."

We settled back into silence while she fidgeted with her fingers; I looked at her out of the corner of my eye and I saw a tattoo on her right shoulder, the same one I had glimpsed through her shirt when I had first met her. It felt like a decade had passed since then. The tattoo was of a graceful white nine-tailed fox with piercing green eyes.

"José asked me to come here, he's our crew leader who you met, because Willis is threatening to storm in here and force his arm down your throat so he can get the data-stick. José would rather wait till you.... pass it out," she said going red in the face, "and I agree with him but Willis has the patience of a terrier on coke, so I'm here to make sure he leaves you alone and offer you a tour of our fine ship, *The Kennel*."

She got up and offered me her hand, which I took hesitantly, allowing her to lift me to my feet. "My name's Poppy Palmer. I normally use a different name while working undercover."

I followed her out of the ship and allowed my eyes to adjust to the sights I had failed to see upon arrival.

The ship had a rusted antique feel to it, which was also homely at the same time. Tarnished walls surrounded me and every so often we would pass a wall with Bible passages written in chalk. I stopped in front of one that read:

"'Peace I leave with you; my peace I give to you. I do not give you as the world gives. Do not let your hearts be troubled and do not be afraid.'"

"That's Willis's doing," Poppy said, standing next to me.

"Is he a priest?" I asked in disbelief.

"He's... complicated. Well, I guess we all are in one way or another, but yes, he used to be a priest then something changed. Something—well, it's not for me to say really. But you'll find these all over the walls on the ship; I think it gives it character."

I wouldn't agree with her on that point, but finding out Willis was a priest or used to be was amazing. The World Government had outlawed Christianity and other religions after WW3. Although there had been outrage and there had been demonstrations to prevent the laws from being passed, the destruction of modern war had broken people's spirits and wills. The Earth was near collapse and differences like religion had to be put aside, as a World Government was created amongst the ten strongest countries across the globe, which all shared power equally.

Each country had an appointed representative who sat on the council and backed the interests of their countries and the surrounding nations as best as they could. It was far from a perfect situation, but it was better than the alternative. But even in the past, they had said only the elite few controlled things in the shadows; now they were just doing it out in the open.

We continued past walls with wires hanging out of sockets and pieces of machinery piled in corners.

"Your ship sure has a... lived-in feel to it," I said, trying to choose my words wisely.

Poppy tilted her head back and the sweetest sound escaped her lips, which caused my heart to skip a beat. It was warm and gentle all at the same time.

"Sorry," I said, realising she had spoken.

"I said, it's not the sexiest ship to be on or the newest. But the old girl does what we ask her to do, nothing more, nothing less."

A faint waft of herbs and spices tickled the hairs of my nose causing my head to turn left. Poppy eyed my reaction with a smile and changed direction. I followed her and the further we walked, the stronger the smells got; it wasn't only herbs and spices I could smell anymore, the smell of meat being char-grilled made me salivate and the sound of fat popping and cooking was like music to my ears as we finally came upon an open canteen.

A large industrial stove and cooker rested against the back wall of the canteen, with an open charcoal grill placed next to it on the same wall. A ten-foot-long counter with herbs and spices and cooking utensils stood some way from the stove and grill, and behind that stood a bear of a man.

Six foot four with a mixture of fat and muscle, his brown complexion and dark locks gave way to a smile as he saw us approach. He lifted one giant paw of a hand and pushed back his locks as he placed down the knife he was holding in the other.

"What do we have there then?" he asked in an accent hard to place.

"Tuari, this is Quinton Blake," Poppy said, pointing my way. "I would love to tell you his last name, Quinton, but it's a secret he won't even divulge with us, because we have a sweepstakes going amongst the crew as to what nationality or origin his fat ass is from. We have bets ranging from Greek to Mexican and anywhere in between."

"Hey! Less of the fat—you know I have a thyroid problem!"

"Sure," Poppy said with an eye roll. "It wouldn't be because of all the cakes you've been baking?"

"You know what they say, never trust a skinny chef," he replied.

I stood back and looked at Tuari and could see her point: it was hard to place his origins and the accent switched ever so slightly from word to word. "That accent of yours is fake, and I'll bet your name isn't even Tuari."

There was silence as the pair shared a look broken by Tuari slapping the table in laughter. "Ha, I like this one! I like this one. Maybe my name is Tuari, maybe it's not. Maybe I was born on the beautiful beach of Balos in Crete," he said, voice and accent changing ever so slightly, "maybe I was born in the city of Tehran in Iran," he said, voice changing again, "or maybe I was born in San Miguel De Allende in Mexico," he finished with a smile, voice flowing seamlessly into a Mexican accent.

I couldn't help but smile at the big man's infectious personality. He resumed chopping and threw over his shoulder some herbs that fell onto the meat he was cooking on the grill behind him. He spun around and pressed the herbs onto the meat, which caused flames to flicker and dance in the air. Picking a piece of meat up from the grill he passed it over to me. I took it and bit into it without a second thought, juice running down my chin; the smoky flavour wasn't so overpowering that it overrode the herbs on it.

"So I hear you have something we want, wee boyo,"

Tuari said, accent once again changing, "something people will kill over. Something precious. And it's stuck in that wee belly of yours. Now I know that Strawberry Fruitcake Willis would love to take it by force, but there is more than one way to skin a cat.

"For instance, there are certain herbs and spices one could eat which would cause the person to lose control of their bowels. Forcing them on the toilet till nothing is left, then they would be so weak to resist it would be a simple case of pushing them aside while one sieved for gold."

I stopped eating and looked at the piece of meat he had given me, a feeling of dread settling in my stomach as I wiped my face clean.

Nobody spoke as I inspected the meat closer. Shit, what was I going to do? I could already feel my legs going weak and—

Both Poppy and Tuari exploded in laughter as they watched a range of expressions cross my face. Tuari handed another piece of cooked meat to Poppy, who ate it with relish, licking her fingers clean after she was done.

"Don't worry, hombre, I would never plan to harm you. Not yet," he said, eyes turning cold and forcing me to take a step back, "not yet."

Poppy manoeuvred me back the way we came, passing more closed doors and junctions, till we came to an open door that smelled like a brewery and had soft hymn music playing in the background.

"Damn," Poppy muttered under her breath as we neared the door, "just keep moving and—"

"Who looks to seek past the door of judgement?" came a voice from inside the room.

I slowed down and looked inside to see a room converted into some sort of holy shrine. Pictures of Jesus, biblical imagery and crosses covered the walls. A small altar rested against one back wall, with open candles along its edge; a small canister emitting scented smoke rested in its centre.

"Willis Moor! How many times has José asked you not to keep open flames going in your room? You remember the last time you fell asleep and we had to drag your drunk naked ass out, before you died of smoke inhalation."

Willis sat crossed-legged on the floor, beer bottles around him as he took another sip from a bottle in his hand. He was naked except for his underwear. Lean muscle covered his body; whereas Tuari was built like a bear, Willis had the body of a cat. Multiple scars covered his body. I looked away as he caught me looking.

"I want those out by the time I get back."

"Only the Lord can instruct me on what—"

"If not I'll tell José the toilets need cleaning again. I'm sure he can think of someone to give the task to."

"There are special places in hell for people like you! Hell! Where your spine is ripped through your ass, and your legs are broken and remade and broken—"

"Let's go," Poppy said, leading the way as Willis's rant continued. "Once he gets started, he'll be at it all night."

I followed her along corridors and past hallways till we reached a large double set of doors, with two deep claw marks gouged into the metal.

"That's what you get for agreeing to deliver bear hybrids to Mars, from a planet which has only been colonised for ten years," she said with a shudder as I inspected them. "The place was a hellhole. Spiders the size of pit bulls and ants the size of spiders."

She continued forward and the doors slid open allowing us on the bridge of the ship.

"And this is the bridge," Poppy said with a smile. "You're bound to find someone here or in the canteen no matter the time. Anyway, I think there's someone who wants to speak to you. I'll leave you to it."

She exited the way she came and I walked forward hesitantly until I saw the crown of a dark brown head.

"Don't stand there all day, boyo," came the gruff voice.

I looked behind me and bit the inside of my cheek. Was I safe? If they wanted to do anything to me they would have done so already, surely?

Making up my mind I took another few steps forward until I was standing in front of José. He indicated for me to take a seat next to him.

Tinted blue shades looked my way, while he took a puff on a cigar.

He said nothing as he surveyed me like a puzzle to be solved, or prey to be stalked and killed.

"I don't believe I've properly introduced myself, my name is José Battle and this is my crew; we like to call ourselves the Junk Yard Dogs or JYD for short.

"We specialize in the collection and delivery of most things. I guess you could say we are a courier company.... in a sense."

I gave him a look of disbelief but kept my thoughts to myself. If he wanted to act like his business was legit or right then who was I to burst his bubble? All I saw were a group of hired killers. Through all the smiles and jokes, and easygoing nature, I still couldn't unsee what I saw back on the Xcorp ship.

"I know this situation is not ideal but you have no one to blame but yourself; if you had done as we had asked then you would be safe and sound back at home, instead of with us."

"You expect me to believe I wouldn't have ended up like the others on the ship?"

José lowered his glasses and gave me a pitying look before raising them back up. "The others were a threat. You are not. The others knew what they were signing up for and they were well paid for it. Do not pity or mourn a soldier who goes into battle willingly, because it is his destiny and choice to do so.

"Instead pity the innocent victim who can do nothing but watch and stare while choices are made for them, even though they do not want them to be."

"Sometimes life makes victims out of us, no matter what we do."

"It is interesting you think so, amigo," he said, as he got up to his feet and walked to the viewing screen with a smile.

"No matter how many times I see it, it always makes me smile. Home."

I turned to the screen and saw what appeared to be a small planet slightly bigger than Earth's moon appear on the screen. Terraformed for human living, I supposed; I just hoped it wouldn't be my final resting place.

8

We landed on the planet and docked on one of the large grey circular platforms that acted as a docking station. Descending to the surface I didn't know what to expect, but it certainly wasn't an area that resembled a dilapidated downtown.

It didn't have the pristine and polished look of a New York skyline, or the reserved elegance of the city of Rome.

No.

Instead, it looked like a street worker who smoked forty a day and was on her last legs but couldn't give up the game because she knew nothing else.

Dirty grey buildings gave way to dirtier streets and every street corner looked like it ended in an alleyway a thief would dream of. As I stared at the location the crew had brought me to, a wave of despair overcame me.

This was where dreams came to die. This was where my body would turn to dust; I would never see my kids again, I would never get to lie in my bed. This was where it would all end.

"What do you think?" Poppy asked, coming to rest next to my shoulder.

I looked over the city, lost for words.

"Stunning, isn't it? As the saying goes, if you can make it here you can make it anywhere. Safe Haven has been our home since the crew formed, and the borough of Paradise Lost is where we reside.

"The planet isn't controlled by any government or ruling body, but the gangs that populate the planet have a sort of alliance. Like cats trying their best not to start a fight."

"Everything works and everyone gets on," José said, coming to stand next to us, "as long as you don't show weakness. This is more of a jungle than New York ever was. You say the wrong thing, you're dead. You do the wrong thing, you're dead. You offend the wrong person, you're dead."

"How do you survive then?" I asked around the lump in my throat.

"By doing and saying the right thing, amigo."

"But more importantly," Poppy said, giving me an elbow nudge, "by not being weak."

"God, I hate this shit hole," Willis shouted from the rear. "Fire and brimstone shall plague this borough destroying it where judgement shall be passed on the—"

"Will you shut the hell up, you pubic-faced ginger idiot? What do you all say we head to The Office for a drink? I'm feeling thirsty after all my hard work," Tuari said.

"Your hard work! You did nothing but stay on the ship, while the rest of us did all the heavy lifting!" Willis said.

"I helped—who told you where your guns were kept after you mislaid them?"

"You mean after I spent half an hour looking for them, I know it was you that hid them and I'll be getting—"

"A drink in The Office sounds like honey to my ears,"

José said, cutting them off before the argument could escalate further. "First round's on me."

The Office turned out to be nothing more than a rundown old shack with more bullet holes along its front walls than a wall used for an army firing-squad line. Dirty windows that you couldn't see into made up a section of the front and peeling paint made up the rest.

The Office sign stood above the door with a necktie hanging down from the O that looked suspiciously like a noose.

We walked in and were greeted by smoke, the stale smell of beer and regret.

Bodies lay slumped over tables; the only thing indicating they were alive were the small snot bubbles that formed around their noses. Others sat in corners shrouded by the darkness, sipping at their drinks and eyeing us with interest.

We walked through the wooden tables and chairs bolted to the floor and made our way towards a bar that looked out of place from the rest of the room. Polished black marble graced its top, and red and black paint so new you could almost smell it covered the wood at the base. A fine gold trim ran its way down the edges of the bar.

Tuari approached the bar slowly, walking up and down its length before taking a step back and letting out a loud whistle. "How much did this beauty cost you, Jerry?"

A bartender who had been ducked down behind the bar popped his head up and waved his arms furiously in our direction. Short with a slight paunch at the front, he had a great brushy moustache that made up for the lack of hair on his head.

"Oh no you fuckers don't!" he shouted, still waving his arms in our direction, "You lot are still barred after the last bloody mess you left me with. Gordon Bennett! It took me a week to get those bloodstains off the ceiling, a whole week! And I am not buying a new bar, this is my fourth one this year!"

"Four bars isn't bad going; I suspect all busy establishments like yours change the décor frequently," said Tuari innocently.

"This is only the second month of the year!"

"Well, it makes the place look fresh, but if you ask me I don't know why you keep on getting new bars; it's not like you've updated the rest of this place," Tuari said, hand sweeping over the room.

"The pond-scum who drinks in here could sit on the floor and still be happy, but I refuse to lean or serve on a dirty bar. I spend most of my day behind this worktop so I want the best."

"Jerry, give me my usual," Willis said, walking past the bartender and leaning against the bar.

Jerry looked among the crew and lifted his eyes to the sky as he saw the battle of kicking them out would be more trouble than it was worth.

"My friends call me Jerry, it's Mr Jones to you," he said in an English accent as he stepped behind the bar.

He poured a large pint of Guinness for Willis, an Amaretto and coke for Poppy, a double Jameson on ice for José, and a pink gin and lemonade for Tuari.

"What you having?" Poppy asked over her shoulder.

"I'm okay," I said with a small shake of my head, which got a round of boos from the crew. "Okay, I'll have pink gin and lemonade." Which got a small nod from Tuari.

Poppy handed me my drink as Willis argued with Jerry.

"What is this, you helmet! The prices are almost triple what they used to be."

"I need to cover my cost somehow; black marble isn't cheap," Jerry said, stroking the worktop surface.

"But still, Jerry, we're loyal customers, surely you could —" Tuari began before Jerry cut him off.

"If the prices are too high, then you could always go to the... Oh, that's right," Jerry said with a smirk, "I'm the only boozer in this part of town, so you can either put up, shut up, or piss off."

The crew looked at one another before they raised their drinks in the air with a shout and downed them in one.

Happy hour had begun.

9

The drinks had continued to flow one after the next, and the bar had grown busier and busier with each passing hour. Upon closer inspection the bar was bigger than it first appeared, with the shadows being pushed to the edges as my eyes got accustomed to the gloom.

The place could hold three hundred people easy, with another two floors above the one I was in. The second floor acted as a dance floor and they had converted the top into a rooftop terrace for the sightseers among us.

As the drinks flowed I tried my best to sip what I could and spill the rest.

This was my chance for freedom.

I eyed the crew every so often as they drank more and more, keeping my options open as to what I would do. It was easier to get lost in the crowd that surrounded us, but whenever I wandered too far, one of them would always appear next to my shoulder in deep conversation with someone next to me. After trying to mingle a few times I grew fed up and returned to the bar.

I would allow the night to drag on before I attempted my escape. The way the drinks kept coming and how they put them away, it wouldn't be long before most of them would be seeing two of me anyway.

Then, I would try to make my escape and look for an outbound ship to get the fuck out of here.

If I couldn't find a ship, I would call Xcorp and inform them of my location and hide out in the city till help arrived.

"Poppy for your thoughts," said a voice next to me.

I looked over into Poppy's smiling face and mustered up a half-hearted smile. Her cheeks were flushed and red and her hair had come undone out of her bun to cascade over her shoulders.

"How is this the only bar in the borough?" I asked Poppy.

She let out a sigh and passed her fingers through her hair before answering, "This is the only bar in this section of the borough."

"What do you mean?"

She pulled a napkin from the bartop and placed it in front of us, then drew a circle and wrote Safe Haven above it. "The planet Safe Haven is divided into four sections or boroughs if you like; each borough is controlled by a criminal organisation that runs their borough with an iron fist. Smaller crime organisations or gangs can also operate in any of the four boroughs, but they will get taxed on anything they make or earn.

"Think of it as an agent's cut off the top," Poppy said with a wink. "Now,, any of the four major organisations who control their borough can get toppled any time and someone new can take over; when that happens it's best to lie low and get out of town because things turn into a bloodbath—it's not happened for a few years but like dormant volcano I can feel tensions brewing."

"Who controls the borough we are in now?"

"The Hammer and Sickle, run by Lady Isabella Ivanov. She's... a fearsome woman but like everyone, she has her fair share of enemies."

I nodded my head while I looked at the drawing. "This doesn't explain why this is the only bar in this part of town."

"Oh, that's simple. Jerry torched the rest," Poppy said, knocking back her drink.

I looked at her in shock, which made her laugh.

"Jerry is being overdramatic, there are other places to drink, but I wouldn't call them bars and I wouldn't venture in there alone, not if you wanted to live."

The night continued on and the drinks kept on coming. The crew, now dispersed amongst the heaving crowd, had left me alone at the bar with Poppy, whose head was resting on the bar top, one hand gripping her drink like an eagle keeping hold of its catch.

"Poppy, you want another?" I asked, but all I received back was a grunt.

This was my chance. Getting up slowly from my seat I scanned the area around me and found the coast was clear. If I headed straight for the front door now I would be caught; the only option I had was to head to the toilets and try to make an escape from there. I laughed at how stupid the plan was, but I had seen it work in movies hundreds of times and some part of that had to be true.

Working my way through the crowd I tried to keep my movements as natural as possible until I got to a door and made my way through.

I made my way up a flight of rickety wooden stairs until I came to a landing. The male toilets were to my right. The coast was empty, so I decided to move while I had the chance. As I entered the toilets an overpowering aroma of piss and shit hit the back of my throat causing me to gag.

The smell stung my eyes as I used a hand to cover my mouth.

I checked the stalls and nearly threw up at what I saw. Toilets without seats occupied all the stalls, with shit smeared along the back walls of more than one.

"Fucking animals," I muttered as I found the last one empty.

I made my way to the only window in the room and worked it back and forth; dirt and grime had sealed it shut over the years but I could feel it coming loose under my onslaught.

The door to the toilet opened and I let go of the handle of the window and moved to the sinks, keeping my gaze on my hand as I opened the taps.

Brown rusty water splashed over my hands as the guy behind me took a piss. I grimaced as the water touched my hands but kept the act up.

Footsteps echoed through the room as he stood next to me and turned on a tap.

"Are we supposed to clean our hands in this?" he said.

"Yeah, I know, right?" I said with a shrug.

He was a man of Chinese descent, who wore a black suit and had golden beads around his wrist.

He caught me looking and sent a smile my way. Two golden canines flashed in the gloomy light.

"I saw you hanging with the JYD crew, you a new member or something?"

I stared at him in puzzlement, not fully understanding the question.

"José Battle's crew, the Junk Yard Dogs."

"Oh, sorry, I must have had too much to drink. Yeah, I joined their crew not long ago; I'm still very much the new guy."

He turned his tap off and dried his hands on his trousers. "So what is it you do for them?"

"This and that, you know," I said with a shrug, trying to end this conversation as quickly as possible.

"I see, I see," he said, still drying his hands on his legs.

An unwelcome silence stretched out before us while we locked eyes. I didn't know what he wanted but he was making me feel unwelcome.

"How about I get you a drink," he said, nodding towards the door.

"Nah I'm all good. Thing is, I've got this stain on my hand that won't come off," I said, turning back to the sink. "Maybe I'll catch you downstairs."

"No problem," he said.

I heard the door open and close behind me and breathed a sigh of relief as I lifted my head up, only to see him staring at me in the mirror.

What the—

He rushed towards me and locked his arms around my neck from behind, getting me in a rear naked choke. The squeeze and pressure was unbearable as my hands clawed at his face. I heard him hiss in pain as one of my fingernails raked across his eyeball, but he refused to release his grip, only squeezing tighter.

Black spots were forming in my vision, the darkness in my peripheral vision was slowly closing in; I had to do something. Forcing my head back violently, I felt my skull connect with his nose.

He grunted in pain and released his hold slightly, which

allowed me to lift his arm up from my neck to in front of my mouth, where I bit him with everything I had.

The grunt turned into a scream and he pushed me away.

I spun on my heel and faced him, spitting out hair and blood onto the filthy toilet floor.

"What do you want?" I demanded in shock.

"Just what's on your person, Mr Blake."

I stared at him in shock allowing his words to sink in. "What do you mean?"

"Let's not piss about here, I know full well who you are and why you were taken by JYD. The word on the street is The Lady will give them a huge payout for the information you have, but here's the thing, The Lady is a cold ruthless bitch who will pay anyone as long as she gets what she wants.

"Plus, if I take less than the price she's willing to pay the Junk Yard Dogs, then I'll be in her favour."

Who was this lady and why was she so interested in the information I had on my data-stick? Was she going to use it to manipulate the stock markets? Or was there something deeper going on here I was missing?

The Lady.

Realisation slapped me in the face as I added two and two together—Lady Isabella Ivanov.

She controlled this borough; she was to be feared; and she was the one that wanted what I had. To survive I would need to make it out of this borough and into the next, before my face became too recognisable.

He came at me again and I threw my best punch his way, which slapped against his cheek, sound ringing out through the toilet. He stopped in his tracks and looked at me in confusion.

"What, what, what was that?" he said in disbelief.

"A punch!"

He looked at me again then threw his head back in laughter. The sound wounded my pride more than any punch or kick thrown ever could. Holding his stomach he rested one hand on his knee while the sound poured from his mouth.

"You," he said, pointing towards me, between bouts of laughter, "are so fucked. If that's your best line of defence then shit, dude, you aren't gonna last long in this city, even if I didn't come along. Everyone here is a killer, bounty hunter, hired gun, gang member, crook, thief, pimp or worse.

"Shit, growing up here I saw my grandmother knife a man through the throat. Life here is tough, salaryman. But I'll tell you what, you hand me the information you have and I'll let you—"

I didn't wait for him to finish as my leg sprung up and kicked him square in the balls. His eyes bulged and I threw another punch, this one catching him in the side of the ear. He toppled forward and I threw a knee his way that caught his chin by luck more than anything else. I turned on my heel and ran for the door but something grabbed my leg causing me to trip and fall.

My face hit the wet floor with a thud, and it was all I could do not to be sick as the smell of urine invaded my nostrils. My hand pressed into something soft and squidgy as I tried to get up, but my leg was caught. Looking back I saw my attacker had gripped one leg; kicking back with the other I caught him in the face but he refused to let go. I kicked again and again until he grabbed my other foot with his free hand and dragged me towards him.

He got on top of me and hammer-fisted me in the nose. The pain was unlike anything I had ever felt before. My eyes watered and I tried to squirm out from underneath him, but I received another blow for my trouble.

If this was what being hit felt like you could keep it.

Never being in a fight in my life, much less being hit in the face, my body panicked, not knowing what to do. I tried to breathe but his weight crushed the oxygen out of my lungs; every time I shifted he shifted his weight. Another blow clipped me in the side of my ear causing a ringing sound to occur.

His fist crashed into my eye socket forcing me to scream out in pain.

I felt his weight shift off me but it didn't matter.

Vision blurry, ears ringing, I curled up upon myself trying to fight the pain that swept through my body.

"How pathetic can you be, dude?" said a voice above me. "I must admit the kick hurt, but if that's all you got then I'm doing you a favour by killing you now."

His boot connected with my ribs forcing another cry of pain out of my lungs.

"Where's the information?"

I said nothing but still grunted for air.

"Where's the information?" he asked, following it up with another kick.

My ribs were on fire, it was hard for me to breathe, and I saw nothing but blurred shapes when I looked up. To say I was taking an ass whipping was an understatement. I tried to roll to my knees but a kick up the ass landed me back on my face.

I didn't deserve this!

I had done nothing wrong. I just wanted to work, pay off my bills and maybe take a holiday once in a while. If my wife and kids said thank you in the process, then it was a bonus, but apart from that I didn't ask for much.

So why was the universe taking a giant dump all over me?

"Look, you're going to tell me what I want to know sooner or later because you're not used to this. This life, what you're feeling, it must feel foreign to you, alien, I get it. But let me help you. Just tell me what I want to know, then this all stops, what do you say?"

My vision cleared and I looked into his eyes, and I could tell he was lying. I didn't know how I knew, but I just did. As soon as I gave him what he wanted, then he would leave me to die on this floor.

"Fuck you!"

I didn't know where it came from; I didn't know why I said it but it felt like the right thing to do. Even though it was probably the last thing I would ever do.

"Fine," he said, pulling out a flick knife from his back pocket. "It looks like I'm going to have to start getting creative."

I saw my reflection briefly in the metal of the blade as it descended towards me, and I did the only thing that came to mind.

I screamed.

10

I shut my eyes and screamed waiting for the end to come; and through the chaos I heard a single cough.

I slowly opened my eyes and saw that my attacker was halfway towards me but had stopped and was looking up. I swivelled my head till I could get a better viewpoint and looked into the disappointed gaze of José.

"No, please," he said, taking a pull on his cigar, "don't let me stop the fun, amigos—continue, continue."

My attacker slowly stood up from where he was and wiped a hand under his bleeding nose. "José," he said with a nod.

"Arun."

They both regarded each other with smiles that didn't reach their eyes.

"I know you're not trying to muscle in on my job now, Arun, because if you were, then there would be unfortunate consequences for your actions. We're not out in space anymore, amigo, you know there're rules to this shit. Rules we must all adhere to when in this borough."

"Bah, what rules? They're more like guidelines."

José took a step forward.

"It wasn't even a thing, José, just a small misunderstanding. Now if you excuse me, I'll be on my way."

He stepped over me and made his way to the door that José was standing in front of. José didn't move, his eyes never left Arun's face.

Arun licked his lips and moved from side to side, switchblade still in his hand.

With a nod, José moved to the side and allowed him to pass. The door closed with a slam bringing silence once again to the toilet.

"Aren't you tired of lying in piss and shit all day?"

"I think one of my ribs is broken," I grunted, holding my side.

"Get up, we've got to go," José said, with a hint of irritation in his voice.

I didn't respond. Fuck him and the self-righteous horse he rode in on. If it weren't for him then I wouldn't be in this mess; I would be making my way back home, to normal, instead of being stuck on some godforsaken planet with the scum of the galaxy. Who was he to look down his nose at me?

I got up to my feet and looked his way, urine running down my forehead.

"You done?" he asked, taking another pull on his cigar.

I didn't respond but straightened up as best as I could.

"Good, because that weasel shitbag Arun runs with the Laughing Hyenas and if we don't get out of here before he calls for backup, then there's going to be carnage."

I rolled my eyes at the gang's name. It felt like I was in some *West Side Story* play.

I followed him out the door and back down the stairs, as he spoke into the computer at his wrist. We entered the chaos of the bar, where the rest of the crew were already waiting for us.

"What did this rusty trombone do now?" Willis asked, pint of Guinness still in his hand.

"Nice to see you too, Willis," I said dryly.

"He ran into Arun upstairs," José said nonchalantly.

"Shit," Willis said.

"I still don't see what the big problem is," I said.

"Arun and his gang the Laughing Hyenas," Poppy said, "are what we call in the business scavengers. They wait for a crew or gang to complete a mission, and then they swoop in and take their kill. The reason gangs like his exist is because they normally sell what they take to the original buyer for half the price, and the buyer doesn't care if the original crew that was commissioned for the job completes it or not, as long as they get what they want."

"My heart bleeds for you," I said.

"Hey!" Willis said, slapping me on the head. "they don't take captives and they always leave a mess. You're lucky you ran into good God-fearing folk like us."

"Where's Tuari?" José asked.

"Getting the transport ready," Poppy answered.

"How's everyone doing for firepower?" José asked.

Poppy held up her hands, which had four knives in each; Willis banged the handles of his pistols together and gave José a manic grin; José pulled out two revolvers as big as his forearms and checked they were fully loaded.

Poppy handed me a knife and I held it as if it was a poisonous snake. "What the hell am I meant to do with this?"

"Defend yourself."

I looked at them as if they had all grown two heads. "Knives and pistols?" I stuttered in disbelief. "Don't you have plasma weapons, ion cannons or at least something bulletproof?"

They returned the same look I had given them.

"Listen, *chico*," José said, cigar hanging from the corner of his mouth, "those types of weapons are expensive as shit to buy, expensive as shit to maintain, and expensive as shit to refuel. Bullets are cheap and there isn't much that can go wrong with a pistol.

"Now come on, let's get out of here before Arun's friends turn up."

We navigated our way through the crowds, the crew alert, watching their surroundings with the keen eyes of professionals. Where was the drunken state they had been in less than ten minutes ago? Were they faking? To lure me into a fake sense of security? How had José known where I was? Better yet, how long had he been outside the door waiting to intervene while I got seven kinds of shit kicked out of me?

We moved through the crowd like sharks through a shoal and I breathed a sigh of relief as the exit came into view.

It was short-lived.

The glass along the walls shattered as canisters trailing smoke entered the bar.

"Get down!" José shouted as he pushed me to the floor, while bullets quickly followed the canisters that had entered.

Hands over my head, I was swallowed up by the chaos that erupted around me. Glasses broke, people screamed and shouted, and the sound of gunfire filled the air. I had never heard a gun go off before; I thought it would sound like fireworks—stupid, I know—but as I huddled under the weak fleshy protection of my arms they didn't sound like any firework I had ever heard.

They sounded like death.

"You have to move!"

I heard the command but I refused to get up from where I lay. The floor was safe. The floor was comfortable. The floor was my friend.

A pair of rough calloused hands grabbed me by the arms and lifted me up. José shook me from side to side forcing me to focus on his face.

"If you lie on the floor like a victim, then you shall become a victim—now move!"

We hurried through the crowd, ducking and dodging as best we could as pieces of glass and bits of mortar flew in the air around us. Bodies flew past us riddled with bullets, slamming against the wall. They left a trail of red as they slid down to the floor, vacant eyes staring at me accusingly.

I could see the exit we were aiming for. Up ahead, a rusty door with a flickering emergency exit sign called out like a siren.

I doubled my pace, rushing towards the door, but a hand yanked me back as a hail of bullets peppered the floor in front of the door. Before I knew it, I was pulled along and thrown over the bar's counter where I landed with a thump.

"Glad you could join us," Poppy said with a smile.

I scrambled backwards pressing my back against the bar counter as I looked to my right and left.

Poppy, situated to my left, gave me a cheeky smile and a wave, while Willis at my right merely grunted in my direction. Jerry the bartender was next to Poppy, shotgun in hand.

"You witless cockroach motherfuckers better believe you're paying for the repairs to my bar," Jerry said, clutching his gun with a death-grip. "I am sick of this shit! All I ever wanted was to open up a nice bar, a place where the intellectual can come and have a drink or two, a place where I could chat about politics, art, the finer things in life.

"Instead, I have moronic conversations like which celebrity you would sleep with or what's the dirtiest thing you think she's ever done! I'm sick of this shit."

"To be fair, Jerry," Willis said, taking a sip of his pint of Guinness, "this is what happens when you burn, threaten or kill the other competition. When this is the only watering hole in the borough, then people will flock to it like the disciples flocked to Jesus in his time of need."

Jerry narrowed his eyes as he looked Willis's way. "That's your sixth pint... You've only paid for three."

Another round of gunfire saved Willis from giving a response as it blasted chunks off the marble top, creating a cloud of fine dust that fell onto Jerry's shoulders.

"Motherfuckers!" Jerry yelled, jumping up and firing back at our would-be attackers.

Willis pulled him back down as a wave of bullets blasted the area he was standing in front of.

"Count my debt as paid up," Willis said, nodding to the bullet-ridden wall.

The bullets stopped flying and the only thing that could be heard was the moans and groans from the wounded. I turned towards Poppy, about to say something, but she placed a finger to her lips and slowly shook her head.

"Where's José?" I mouthed.

She gave me a shrug as footsteps echoed through the bar. I clutched the knife I was holding tighter, hoping it would act as a talisman to ward off evil.

"To those of you still alive!" a voice from the bar called.

"We do not wish to kill any more of you, but we shall unless we get what we want."

Nobody responded while boots crunched glass underfoot.

"We are looking for one Quinton Blake. Hand him over and we shall leave this shithole you call a bar at once."

My face paled and lost all feeling as I looked into Poppy's eyes. The voice that spoke wasn't Arun's, so who wanted to kill me now?

I tapped the handle of the knife against my forehead, as bile tried to force its way up my throat.

This was not happening.

This was not happening.

This—

"What do you want with him?" José said from somewhere in the bar.

"That is none of your concern."

"You came in here, fire upon us indiscriminately, demand something from us, but do not tell us the reason why. That, my amigo, is just plain rude. This borough may be filled with the scum of the galaxy but at least we buy someone a drink before we fill them full of holes."

I looked to either side of me and could see Willis and Poppy edge further and further away from me.

Were they leaving me to die?

"Find him," said the newcomer. "Kill the rest!"

As the words left his mouth Jerry and Willis popped up and fired at our attackers. The sound of gunfire was deafening as the attackers returned fire. I placed my hands over my head and hunkered down as a body flew over the top of the bar and crash-landed at my feet. He groaned as he tried to get up, defiance and anger radiating from his eyes.

I sat there frozen as thoughts of what to do swirled around my mind.

His hand inched towards his pistol and still, I stayed there staring at him.

I had to move or he would shoot me. I held the knife tighter in my hand while he got his bearings and raised his gun my way.

A flash of silver appeared and sliced his throat, spraying me with blood. Wide-eyed with blood on my face I slowly turned and looked into the face of Poppy, who regarded me with caution. She said something but it didn't register. I could see her lips move but it was like the world was on mute.

She slapped me in the face hard. Hard enough for my ears to start ringing.

"You need to move!" she said, shouting in my face.

She pointed over my shoulder forcing me to turn. Glass covered the floor and bullets blasted the wall above.

"I'm not crawling through that shit!"

"If you don't you die."

I couldn't argue with that. But where I was sitting appeared a lot safer than crawling over glass and under bullets.

I turned and looked back towards Poppy; her eyes were urging me on. Turning back around I gritted my teeth before I felt a hand on my shoulder. "You can do this," she said.

I nodded as I scampered forward. Glass cut into my hands and knees and bullets broke bottles apart overhead causing them to fall upon my shoulders. I just wanted to go home! I shouldn't be here. This was just a misunderstanding.

These thoughts rattled around my brain before I finally came to the end of the bar and peeked around it.

The scene was chaos.

What I saw appeared to be out of a cheesy action flick.

Bodies lay on the floor riddled with holes, their open eyes reflecting the last emotions they had. I stared into those eyes and felt sick. Sick? I was glad they were dead and I was still alive.

Blood mixed with spent bullet casing covered the floor as José hid behind a stone pillar and took potshots at anyone stupid enough to show themselves. Willis and Jerry were nowhere to be seen as Poppy tapped me lightly on the shoulder.

"When I say so, I want to you make a move for the exit," she said.

I said nothing but simply nodded.

"Whenever you boys are ready!" she yelled over my shoulder.

I saw José nod before leaning his back against the pillar protecting his life. He reloaded his revolvers, closed his eyes and whispered something to himself before swinging back into the open and shouting, "Now!"

Willis and Jerry popped up themselves from their hiding places and began firing, as Poppy leapt onto the bar top and somersaulted into the air. She landed with her legs around the neck of one of the attackers and stabbed him in the eyes with her knives. I could hear his screams over the gunfire.

I watched in amazement as she moved like a snake. Wherever her knives flashed blood would follow.

She rolled under another attacker's wild swing and stabbed him in the groin; with a twist and a yank she pulled out her blade. She didn't wait to see if her opponents were dead before she moved. She was that confident in her skills as a murderer. Willis and José gave covering fire. Each shot they made counted; they were ruthless in their effectiveness, no bullet was wasted, no shot was made in haste.

"Go!" Poppy yelled as she stabbed another man in the neck.

I didn't have to be told twice as I leapt to my feet and began making my way towards the exit. "There he is!" shouted a voice behind me.

I turned around and saw who had spoken.

Salt and pepper hair cut into a buzz cut, with a crooked nose broken on more than one occasion, he stared my way. Like his men, he wore combat fatigues, but unlike his men, he stood tall and proud amongst the raging battle that whirled around him, almost as if he was immune to damage.

His rigid finger still pointed my way as his grey soulless eyes bored into mine.

A smoke canister detonated in the centre of the room and he was engulfed in smoke and vanished from my view. I kept looking his way till someone bundled me off and pushed me out of the door; I tried to fight them off until I got a slap in the face and saw that it was Poppy who had pushed me through the door.

"We need to get going, dumbass!" Willis said, slamming the door closed behind José and sticking a small square metallic device over the door handle.

An electric muscle car fashioned in the styling of a 1969 Ford Mustang slid in front of us kicking up a dirt cloud into the air. Tuari was behind the wheel pressing on the horn for us to get going.

I took one last look behind me at the door as I was dragged and pushed towards the vehicle; we jumped inside and before the door had been closed we were already pulling away at speed.

"What did you place on the door?" I asked Willis.

He smiled in my direction, teeth flashing in the gloom. "A little present."

I looked back towards the bar as an explosion tore through the bar exit that we had come through, sending flames shooting up into the sky and illuminating the night sky in a fiery red blaze.

"Jerry's gonna be pissed!" Tuari said, looking back in the rearview mirror.

"It ain't the first time we've blown up his bar and I doubt it'll be the last," José said, to sounds of laughter.

I looked around me and just stared.

I was in the company of a bunch of psychopaths!

11

The silent motor of the muscle car pushed us along through the surrounding traffic. We overtook cars that got in our way and bullied others that didn't get the hint. Soft sounds of instrumental chill music whispered through the speakers putting me slightly at ease, I looked out the window at the passing lights, which looked like fireflies caught in a jar, and wondered how my life had gotten to where it currently was.

Things like this didn't happen to people like me. I had already mapped my life out. My life...

I shook my head and took in the surroundings of the borough. So far I hadn't seen any natural vegetation or any signs of wildlife, it had just been one crumpled tower block after another, one half-finished apartment block, or a hotel with scantily clad women leaning against its walls waving halfheartedly at any car which passed by.

As the car did its best to smooth out the bumps and potholes in the road, I leaned my head back against the headrest and allowed a yawn to escape my lips.

"It's the adrenaline dump," Poppy whispered in my ear.

"Huh?"

"The adrenaline from the gunfight you have just been in—it affects each one in different ways, but one of the main things it does is make you tired, weary. Your body and mind have just been through a major trauma so are trying to cope with it as best as it can. Some of us," she said, nodding to Willis and José, who were snoring, "sleep it off, others like me just replay the events again and again in our minds, wondering what we could have done differently."

I nodded my head and tried to fight the mouth-stretching yawn that escaped me.

"Just let your body relax, it knows what to do."

I snorted and shook my head. "This may be normal to you," I whispered back at her, "but this to me, is, is..." I sighed as words failed me.

"I can't believe you imagined your life turning out how it has."

"No. I didn't imagine being kidnapped against my will and—"

"No, I'm not talking about that. I've watched you, Quinton, it's our duty to watch every one of our jobs before we do them, casing the joint so to speak, and I've watched you from afar, I've watched your life. It's one of misery. Any blind fool can see you go to a job you hate, you are in a loveless marriage to a woman who doesn't respect you, even your own children hate you, and through it all, I wonder why."

"Why what?" I said breathlessly.

"Why would someone put themselves through that?"

"Because of duty, because it's the right thing to do, because it's what a man does for his family."

She said nothing but only got closer to me, wrapping her arms around me and burying her face in my neck with a sigh. Even though the words had left my mouth and I knew they were the right thing to say, they still felt like a lie to me. A lie I had told myself repeatedly time and time again.

Whenever the bills came in late and I was the only one holding a job.

Whenever I would get home to a cold empty house.

Whenever I would get home to a cold empty bed.

Those words, that line, had kept me going because if I didn't repeat them to myself daily then I would go mad. I would blow my brains out and embrace death with a smile on my face.

Did that make me selfish?

Did that make me less of a man?

I just wanted to be happy.

"There must have been some dream you wanted when you were growing up, some vision or life plan you had for yourself that didn't involve a nine to five and a retirement plan," she said softly in my ear, making the hair on the side of my neck stand up.

"There was once... but the dream has long since died a horrible death," I muttered under my breath.

"Being in a life or death situation for anyone isn't normal, no matter how many times you encounter it; you may think it gets easy but it never does."

The car kept on eating up the miles and I returned to staring out the mirror, my thoughts muddy like a puddle splashed in by a child. Poppy's soft breathing on my neck deepened as sleep slowly took her. "I wanted to dance and soar like a graceful bird-of-paradise," she said, each word getting softer and softer, "just dance and dance, until my worries and troubles went away."

And with that sleep quickly took us both.

12

I opened my eyes as I felt the motion of the car come to a stop; I looked out the window and saw we were parked in what appeared to be a back alley. Grey brick walls surrounded the car on both sides. I wrinkled my nose as the stench from the alley worked its way past the glass windows.

Willis and Tuari had already made their way out of the car, their doors closing with a soft hiss behind them.

Sat in the front passenger seat José unclipped his seatbelt and turned to look at me, eyes hidden behind red lenses I didn't need to see them to read the concern that laced his features; he turned his gaze to the softly snoozing Poppy, who was still asleep on my shoulder, and his lips drew back into a fine line.

"You're a grown-ass man, so I don't need to give you this advice but I feel the need to anyway. I would watch how you handle this situation," he said, nodding to Poppy. "I can guarantee you, Necktie, she isn't like any other woman you've ever met or been involved with before, so tread carefully otherwise it could end up badly for you."

"You mean it could end up worse than being kidnapped against my will?"

José gave me one of his toothy grins. "By all means, my amigo, you're free to go any time you want, but I doubt you'll last five minutes out there. Those men that hit Jerry's bar weren't part of Arun's crew, which makes me think we have multiple players after your *culo*. I know every two-bit crew in this godforsaken borough, and I've never seen those men before. The way they moved, the way they fired, makes me think they're military or even mercenaries."

I thought back to the mercenaries stationed on my ship and shuddered inwardly. What if they thought I had something to do with the deaths of their men? What if they thought I had done a runner and I was trying to sell whatever was on that stupid stick to the highest bidder?

What if they were out for revenge?

Shit! I had to get in contact with Gregory, my boss, and let him know where I was and what had happened. From there, Xcorp could decide on the best course of action and try to get me out of this mess in one piece.

"Anyway, my statement still stands: if you want to leave then be my guest, but I would take my advice about her," he said, nodding Poppy's way.

"Thank for the advice, but I'm happily married with kids."

José said nothing as he stared at me for a minute or two. "Funny, for a man who's happily married with kids, this is the first time you've bought them up."

I stared at his back while he exited the car and swallowed the anger that wanted to explode from the pit of my stomach. Taking a deep breath I lightly tapped Poppy on the shoulder and watched as she slowly opened her eyes.

Despite myself, I couldn't help but stare as her eyes fluttered open and she smiled my way.

My eyes traced the lines of her curves as she stretched like a cat, her breast straining against the fabric of her shirt.

"What?" she asked softly.

"Er... what? Nothing. I mean, we have arrived," I said hastily, trying to make a quick exit out of the car but failing horribly as I got caught up in the seatbelt that restrained me. She laughed at my predicament before unclipping me and stepping out of the car to follow the rest of the crew.

Focus, man!

I told myself that as I exited the car and followed them. They were still my captors; they were still murderers, and I had to figure out a way to ditch them before it got too late. It was only a matter of time before the data-stick passed through my gut, and then I would no longer be needed by them.

I sidestepped rubbish that littered the floor and bumped into Poppy, who gave me a smile and pointed to a brown wooden door with peeling paint. "This is our safe-house for the next twenty-four hours until we can figure something out."

I ran a hand over the bullet holes in the wall beside me and took in the dilapidated door a strong breeze could knock off, and looked at her in confusion, "You said safe-house, right? As in safe to be in?"

"Trust me," she said.

Willis, José, and Tuari had already made their way inside as I followed her. She held the door open for me and I couldn't see anything as I stepped inside and smashed my face on something solid.

"Fuck!"

"Sorry," came Poppy's voice from behind me, "I forgot to say to you not to walk forward,"

I couldn't see a thing in front of me until my eyes adjusted to the gloom, and a door made of solid steel materialised in front of me. I waited until Poppy closed the other door behind us causing darkness to descend upon us, until a light flickered from above. The sudden illumination from it felt like I had stepped into the sun.

"Please identify yourself," came a voice from the speakers.

"Poppy Palmer."

"Voice recognised. Question, what do you fear the most?"

Poppy didn't respond as the seconds ticked away. As I was about to speak she cut me off: "I fear myself."

"Answer accepted: welcome, Miss Palmer."

The door swung opened revealing a hallway that wouldn't be out of place in any family home. It took me by surprise, but what surprised me the most was the bowing AI robot that stood in front of us, dressed in a butler's uniform. No AI machine could be modelled after the human form anymore. No silicone flesh-like coating, no human-like features.

A soft light metal casing covered its skeletal form, with a speaker for a mouth and scanners for eyes. The World Government had set laws in place after WW3, banning countries from replicating lifelike human AIs and also placing a limit on how intelligent they could be. During the war, they had been used to great effect, with one AI machine being able to kill hundreds of men in a matter of hours. The AIs were growing smarter and stronger every day.

It gave humanity a fright, and it was one of the key elements to a call for a ceasefire during the war.

"Hi, Geoffrey," Poppy said, patting the bot on the shoulder. "This is Quinton, he's going to be our guest for a few days; treat him as if he was one of us."

"Certainly, madam, should I also tidy up after him as well?" said Geoffrey in a British accent.

"As long as you don't wipe his ass like you do Willis," Tuari said from somewhere in the house.

"That was one time, you cock-gobbler! And it was because I damaged my hands after that stupid prank you pulled! Remember, the one with the hot potato?" Willis shouted from somewhere in the house.

"I would have thought you would have found it funny, what with you liking potatoes and—"

"I already told you!" screamed Willis from the top of his lungs. "Not all Irish live and die on fucking potatoes."

"Well, this could go on all day," said Geoffrey dryly. "Would you like to follow me, sir?"

I gave Geoffrey a second look as I tilted my head to the side but he was already on the move; I looked back at Poppy, who gave me a wink and a smile as she walked past me. Doing as I was told, I followed Geoffrey up a couple flights of stairs till we got to the top floor. He pushed opened a door that led into a low-ceilinged room with a spare bed in one corner and a wardrobe in the other.

"I'm afraid 'guests' get to stay in the attic," Geoffrey said, turning to me. "It's not all doom and gloom though, you have your own bathroom through that door, although there's no running hot water and the flush on the toilet sometimes doesn't work, but apart from that this could be a penthouse suite in any serial-killer motel you would happen to stay at.

"I would say make yourself at home but…. it appears sir is travelling light."

"Yes, most of my things are still on the ship *The Kennel*."

"If this is a long stay, I would suggest sir get it before he begins to smell. Hygiene is of utmost importance."

"Yes, I, you're right," I said, feeling at a loss for what to say.

Geoffrey gave me a nod then turned and exited the way he came. "Oh, one more thing, sir, if at any time you hear what sounds like a fire alarm I assure you it's not; the best thing you can do is arm yourself with the nearest weapon available and make for the exits."

"Right," I said, watching him leave.

I walked towards the nearest window and pulled back the curtains to find it bricked over. On further inspection they all were. With little means to escape and the only door leading out of this place being controlled by voice recognition, I knew I was in for the long haul.

13

I tried to fall asleep but between the scratchy blanket and the spring poking me in the back, sleep evaded me. After the hundredth time tossing and turning, I finally got up to my feet and just sat on my bed.

Sat on my bed and thought about my life.

What was I going to do? Escape seemed as impossible as flying back home without a ship, but I somehow had to figure out how to escape the clutches of this crew and survive long enough that the other two crews didn't kill me first.

I had to admit being with the Junk Yard Dogs was an adventure, something that had put a bit of sparkle into my life, but I couldn't help feel this was all just smoke and mirrors to allow me to drop my guard, so they could get what they wanted.

Shaking my head, I got up and opened my door as quietly as I could. Making my way down the first flight of stairs I heard hymn music coming out of a door to my right; flickering shadows danced under the door and told me to move on. I waited till I was sure no one was coming out of the room before I moved off again and made my way down another flight of stairs.

I slowed my descent as I heard the unmistakable tones of José.

"You sure this thing ain't gonna blow up in our faces?"

I made my footsteps as light as possible, holding my breath as a floorboard creaked underneath me.

Shit.

I held my breath waiting to be found, but when no one came to investigate, I slightly relaxed and continued downward.

"I know this is a big payoff for everyone involved but right now, you have other shit to worry about. Arun from the Laughing Hyenas tried to jump him in the toilets and some military slash mercenary cats tried their best to use our brains to redecorate Jerry's bar The Office.

"I thought this a simple mission?" asked José.

I couldn't hear any response from the person José was talking to, which could only mean he was on a phone call. Phones had gone the way of every other gadget with the rapidly increased need for human technology. Why have a phone when everyone had a personal computer attached to their wrist that could do the job just as well and more? The only downside was they could be hacked and monitored, which gave rebirth to mobile phones in the underground market.

Disposable mobile phones or burners as they were called on the underground gave the user a level of security that computers didn't. They were cheap to buy, easy to use, and disposable.

"Listen, *mi Señora*," I know you have huge plans in play here—

"Come on, the borough's been going crazy with rumours

concerning you, and what you're planning, I can still remember the last war that ravaged these streets, but if you're involved in what I've been hearing is going to happen, then me and my crew what no part in it. We're runners, smugglers, collectors.

"We ain't hitmen."

I continued to creep until I was only inches away from the door; I tried to steady my breathing as I rubbed my sweaty palms down my leg.

"Also it appears you have a leak in your organisation. Someone told Arun and his goons we were collecting the data-stick, and where they could likely find us, so I would be careful right now who you trust."

As the conversation came to an end I had turned and was walking back upstairs when José's voice caught my attention.

"By the way, what plans do you have for this *niño* after you get what you want?"

A chill went through my spine as I stopped in my tracks, while two people casually discussed my fate.

"Good, because I have plans of my own that involve him, plans I don't think he'll like. We'll see you tomorrow at the meeting point."

José fell silent and it left me contemplating my brief future and how I was going to escape before tomorrow's meeting.

14

A knock on the door woke me up from my deathlike state, I ran a hand over my heavily laden eyes and looked around in panic when I noticed the room I was in wasn't my bedroom; it took another second or two till the events of the last few days finally caught up with me.

I must have finally fallen asleep last night.

Another knock at the door, this one louder, forced me to groan under my hand as I got up to my feet and dragged myself towards my door. Yanking it open, I was greeted by a hot pot of coffee and a plate full of waffles with a side of bacon.

"Morning, sleepyhead," Poppy said, beaming from ear to ear. "I thought you would like something to eat, as we ate nothing last night."

I eyed the plate suspiciously, not wanting to take it, but my stomach rumbled despite my best efforts not to look interested.

"Thank you," I said taking the plate of waffles, "but you can keep that devil's piss known as coffee, I can't stand the stuff."

"Oh," Poppy said with a shy smile, "I thought it was only me who thought that way about coffee. I wasn't going to bring you any but Willis said only real men drink it."

"Willis is an ass," I said, sitting back on my bed and using my knees as a table. Butter dripped down the stack as I cut into them and took a mouthful.

I closed my eyes as the taste washed over me.

I hadn't realised how hungry I was until I began eating.

"God, these are good, Tuari sure can cook."

"Actually I made them," she said, flicking a strand of hair behind her ear.

"Oh."

I kept my gaze on her as she blushed and looked away from me. Not knowing what to say I nodded and mumbled, "Thank you."

The only sounds heard were from my knife and fork as I kept on eating, not knowing and really not caring if this meal was poisoned or not.

"This is fantastic, Pop, I didn't know you knew how to cook, I thought the only chef on the crew was Tuari."

She looked at me sideways, brows furrowed in confusion.

"What?" I asked.

"Why did you call me Pop?"

"I don't know, sometimes people call other people nicknames because they're friends or because they're close or because... It just felt right."

"Hmm," she said, looking up at the ceiling and repeating the name to herself, "Pop, I like it. It sounds... interesting."

"I'm glad. So," I asked, dragging out the word, "how did you come to be part of the crew?"

"They found me."

I didn't know what to say, so I nodded and kept on eating allowing the silence to lengthen.

"Yes, they found me and gave me a place to stay, a place to call home and a place where I felt like I have a family. My life hasn't always been easy; there were times..." She dipped her head as a faraway look appeared behind her eyes.

I said nothing, fork halfway to my mouth.

"There were times," she said, lifting her head up and giving me a weak smile, "when all I thought about was suicide. All I thought about was how easy it would be to end it all, but then like a guardian angel José plucked me from the trash and gave me a purpose, something to live for, some reason to keep ongoing."

"And that purpose was to kill, steal, and smuggle for money?"

She looked at me sharply, the first sign of true irritation I had seen on her face towards me since we had met.

"You give away the most precious thing you have, your time, for minimum wage and a noose around your neck and you look down at me as if I'm nothing. I work for the things that are honest to me, that mean the most to me, that I would live and die for.

"I may be a killer but at least I'm honest as to who I am."

She backed away from me and turned her back walking towards the door.

I had upset her, she whom I had seen kill men with nothing but a knife and her body. She hadn't shown emotion while in the process, no anger, no hate, no regret. It appeared like she was just a factory worker on an assembly line who needed to get the job done.

That in itself scared me more than anything.

But despite all that I still felt bad.

Bad for upsetting this woman I had only known less than a handful of days, and I didn't know why.

"After you're done, José says you need to get ready, we're going to see The Lady."

15

I was back in the car and although I'd been rested, mounting tension in the pit of my stomach I couldn't quite shake had replaced it. I had heard enough about The Lady to know she was the main reason I was in this mess, the main reason why my life had been turned upside down and everyone in the galaxy appeared to either want to kill me, torture me or question me.

I neither wanted to meet her or be in her presence, but I no longer had a choice.

I thought back to my home and my family and wondered if I would ever see them again, wondered if Xcorp had reported me missing to the authorities. Was my name on all the news channels? Would I even warrant front-page news?

I doubted it.

I had done nothing remarkable in my life, anything noteworthy. I had just kept my head down and kept on chugging away in the vain hope it would get me one step further up the ladder, one step closer to that glorious retirement I kept on telling myself would come the more hours I put in and the more time I gave away; but life, as I was finding out, sometimes loved kicking you when you were down, and I hadn't been more down than this.

I gritted my teeth and clenched my fist as we drove past one run-down building after the next. Although the sun had arisen it did nothing to improve the view we drove past; instead it highlighted its flaws, its blemishes, whereas the darkness covered it up like make-up on a black eye on a housewife.

"Where's Poppy?" I asked José, who was in the backseat next to me.

He looked my way and gave me a shrug; I took the hint and returned my attention to the passing buildings and oddities that swept past my window, allowing the time to simply pass me by.

"You're real quiet back there, ass-face," Willis said over his shoulder. "Thought you would be happy to be on the move, happy to finally get this over and done with."

I said nothing but just continued to look out the window.

"I know you thought you were clever swallowing the data-stick, but what goes in must come out and we know it hasn't left your system yet, so we'll just hand you over to The Lady and she shall get it out of you one way or the other. I heard she is a patient woman, and she always gets what she wants, so I wouldn't count on trying to outsmart her. To be the number one crew in the borough of Paradise Lost takes something you don't need in controlling the other boroughs; it takes a level of evil that would make even the devil shiver.

"Although this planet is no bigger than a moon with boroughs in jungles and mountain ranges, this borough is different. This borough is ground zero. It's where everyone starts off. People think getting to the top and staying up that fucker is the hardest part of the journey, but it's the fighting at the bottom with the rest of the crabs, maggots and worms, all trying to pull you down while you climb to the top, that's where the real fighting takes place.

"The other crews in Paradise Lost treated The Lady like a joke when she first came on the scene, but that soon changed when the bodies started to pile up. Not much scares me, but The Lady is a demon from the greatest depths of hell.

"I just hope I get the chance to send her there one day."

I let out a snort and rolled my eyes, which caused Willis to snap his head around.

"Something I said funny?"

"Everything you say is funny, you mad Irish bastard," Tuari said in the driver's seat next to him, "which I am surprised at because how anyone can understand a thing you're saying is beyond me."

"I ain't talking to you, shitbreath, I'm talking to know-it-all back there," Willis said, pointing my way. "You got something to say or something you wanna say, just come right out and say it."

I bit my lip and kept staring out the window, fingers drumming against my knee.

"Thought so—"

"I thought the Christian faith took issue with little things like murder, kidnapping, stealing, and being an all-round piece of shit! If I'm not wrong, they even had a list of commandments that stated something to that effect.

"You, being a practising Christian, would know that, but it seems, Willis, you have ignored all the core principles of your faith and are only using it when it best suits you. Fuck anyone else! As long as the paddy here gets his pint of Guinness and gets to be judge, jury and executioner." I was breathing heavily now, the tension I was feeling loosening my tongue.

"What I find funny, Willis, is you think you're so different from the people you think so little of, but you and they are one and the same. I don't know if you think you're going to Valhalla or Eden or whatever it's called, but I can assure you, you aren't."

Silence came upon the car as Willis' jaw worked from side to side. Tuari drove eyes forward, not taking them from the road; José, who sat next to me, had his head turned to the window.

I knew Willis expected me to avert my gaze from his, but I would not give the asshole the pleasure. They needed me alive until I got to The Lady, so I knew he would not kill me, although it didn't mean he couldn't hurt me.

"It's called heaven, the place where all the good souls are destined to go," he said before turning back around.

Was that it?

After all the bullshit I had expected him to say his response left me feeling empty and angrier than ever.

"And another thing—" I began but was cut short as something slammed into the back of us, forcing my head forward into the headrest in front of me.

A flash of white flared across my vision and there was a faint ringing in my ears as I grabbed the back of my neck in pain. The world returned in thunderous colour and sound. Someone was shouting and it took me a second to realise it was Willis.

"Who do these herpes-covered sons of whores think they're dealing with!"

I looked behind us and could see a blacked-out van right up our ass. They sped up again and barrelled into us causing the car to fishtail. Tuari wrestled control of the vehicle, righting it back the right way just as a second blacked-out van pulled up alongside us. The glint of firearms got my attention causing my heart to skip a beat.

"Guns! Guns! Guns," I shouted, pointing out the vehicle.

"Yes, we know, dickhead, we've got them too," Willis said, pulling out his pistols. "It seems like Sodom and Gomorrah get to have some fun."

"Put these in your ears," José said, handing me a pair of earbuds, I looked at them in confusion before looking back at him. "We're in a confined space about to shoot firearms—you work it out," he said.

I did as instructed and was taken aback as the sound around me dimmed. It was like being underwater. The panic was still there, but I could take in the frantic nature of what was happening around me, if at a much lower volume. It made everything easier to deal with.

A gun appeared in front of my face as the window next to me slid down. I saw the muzzle flash and felt the vibration go through my chest as the van next to us tried to swerve out of the way.

Something pinged above my head and the next thing I knew my head was being pushed down towards my knees.

Another few explosive rounds went off above my head before they allowed me to resurface.

"Tuari! Get us outta Dodge, hombre," I heard someone shout, but couldn't figure out who.

The car was launched forward as Tuari pushed it to its limits. Cars swerved out of our way and sounded their horns, as many had to come to an emergency stop in fear of colliding with us. The back window shattered as we took a straight and shot through an intersection.

I closed my eyes waiting for another vehicle to T-bone us, but when the jarring sensation of metal on metal never came I opened my eyes and saw we had made it safely across. The only difference now was, Willis was hanging out the window firing his pistols at the vehicles chasing us.

He pulled his head back in as the door mirror on his side was blasted off the car door.

"I got a glimpse of one of the shooters," Willis yelled, reloading his pistols. "It's the Laughing Hyenas. I can't see Arun anywhere, but I know that cock weasel must be in one of the vans. He wouldn't miss an opportunity to rub our faces in it."

José reloaded his revolvers slowly as he nodded his head. "It appears he has chosen to make his move."

"He's probably still pissed off because of the job we stole from him on Mars," Tuari said, turning the steering wheel hard left.

"Or," Willis said before firing a shot out the window, "he's probably pissed at us because you left a dozen boxes of bees on his ship."

"I thought you would like the prank with the bees, what with you being a Christian and all."

"You're thinking of locusts, idiot!"

We took another hard turn as one of the vans pulled up beside us. The door on its side slid open revealing Arun's smug face as he levelled a shotgun towards us and fired. Once again I was pushed down towards my knees as buckshot exploded around me. Lifting my head up again I yelled in surprise, as Arun was right next to my door and was pulling it open.

I grabbed the handle on my side with both hands as the door was yanked open and tried to pull it back closed with all my might. Arun hung onto the handle on the outside and tried his best to keep it open. I strained with all my might and inch by inch the door came back towards me.

Arun's face appeared within arm's reach, snarl plastered on his lips.

He reached for a pistol tucked in the waistband of his jeans and I did the only thing that came to mind.

I punched him.

He blinked at me in surprise until I punched him again, his snarl now turning into a grimace.

About to punch him again I turned my head just in time to see a motorbike coming towards us. Letting go of the handle caused the door to swing out, catching Arun full in the face. The bike tried to stop, but it was no use as he crashed into the open door taking it clean off its hinges.

Door and bike went one way, rider went the other, as I stared into the door-shaped hole now on my side of the car.

Thrown back into his van, Arun rested amongst a tangle of limbs he tried to extract himself from.

José pushed me forcefully back as he sighted down his revolver, took careful aim and fired. The rear wheel of the van exploded and caused the van to fishtail as the driver tried to fight the steering wheel back for control but failed. Arun's eyes widened in panic as the van spun out of control then flipped and rolled.

I leaned out of the door opening and stared back in wonder as the van finally come to a stop onto its roof, wheels still spinning.

"Bye, Arun," said Willis.

We continued down the road at speed, my body trying to relax but unable to; something was wrong.

"Hold on," I said, looking around the car, "wasn't there another van—"

That was the last thing I remembered as the remaining van slammed into the side José was on and flipped our car into the air.

16

I woke to the sound of birds.

My head felt heavy and shaken, like it had been in a tumble drier.

I moved my fingers around and felt what I thought was grass beneath my palms, but that wasn't right because I hadn't seen a patch of grass anywhere in this forsaken city.

One side of my face felt cold as I tried to open my eyes but all I saw was green. Shifting my head to the side I got a better view of my surroundings. I had landed in what appeared to be a patch of grass, with ill-looking trees surrounding me. I got up to my hands and knees and rolled over onto my back.

I was alive.

I was alive!

I couldn't remember much of what happened after the van had struck us, only that I had somehow been thrown from the car's open door and had landed in safety.

I moved my limbs anticipating pain at every flex and turn but with a sigh of relief not finding any. Something ran into my eye causing it to sting; wiping it away my hands came back bloody. I touched my forehead tentatively, wincing as my hands touched a lump that tried to double as another head.

If I was thrown from the car, then where is it?

The sound of movement to my far left answered my question. The patch of grass I was on was on a slope that came to rest at a river some hundred feet below me. The car belonging to the Junk Yard Dogs was upside down, resting at the bottom of it, wheels still spinning.

I looked up as I heard movement above me and saw the van that had rammed into us, come to a rolling stop on the road above me. Keeping my body low to the ground, I turned my head back down the ravine and saw movement in the shadows of the car.

This was my chance to escape.

I wouldn't get another opportunity like this one.

Keeping my body as close to the ground as I could I crawled away, forcing my body to move with all the speed I could muster.

It had taken me hours to walk along roads and alleyways so I wasn't seen, until I felt somewhat safe. I had run for the first half an hour—well, when I say run it was more of a five-minute sprint that turned into a jog, which turned into me dragging my legs behind me while I coughed up all the bad food and drink I had eaten since I left college. I had always promised myself I would get back in shape but life had kept getting in my way, or so I told myself.

I leaned against a wall and planned my next move.

I was on a foreign planet in a foreign city, with no

money, food, drink, friends or any way to contact anyone that I loved.

I slowly slumped to my knees as the weight of my situation piled on me. What was I going to do? I couldn't trust anyone, as everyone was out for my blood, and I couldn't show my face anywhere public or I would get noticed.

I needed to gain someone's computer as they had taken mine off my wrist after they took me hostage. It would be the only way to get a message to my family, the only way to get rescued, but the real answer was how would I acquire one, as everyone's computer was DNA coded to only work for them.

A glint on the ground drew my eye to an object on the alleyway floor,

Bending to pick it up I saw it was a shard of glass. Weighing it in my hand I gripped onto it and closed my eyes at the thought of what I was about to do.

The sun had set and pushed long shadows into nothing but darkness. My heart was in my mouth as I waited at the edge of a corner for someone to pass by; my palms were sweaty and the shard of glass in my hand kept on slipping out of my grip. I tried to close my eyes and steady my breathing but it still didn't slow my heart rate down; things had gone from bad to worse once I had gotten on that Xcorp ship and they would not get any better.

People passed me by who were too tall, too big, too muscular or too mean-looking.

I didn't know the target I had in mind, but I needed to overpower them easily and quickly. I kept my face in the shadows, biting the inside of my cheek, while I waited.

Shit!
Come on. Come on.
My lower back poured out enough sweat to cause my shirt to stick to it. I unloosened my tie and pulled at my shirt trying to get my body to cool down.

I saw someone walk past me who looked about my height and I walked towards them until they stopped and turned around.

A mop of grey hair covered most of his eyes, "What the fuck do you think you're doing?"

"I, errr, I wasn't doing anything," I said hastily, taking a few steps back, "I was just walking."

He took a step closer to me and I held up one palm in an unthreatening manner.

"Well, it looks to me you were about to jump me, Necktie," he said, spitting out the last word in disgust.

"Nah, you got it all wrong. I wouldn't dream of doing anything like that, it's just I need to message—"

"What's in your hand!"

I hid the shard of glass behind my back and gave him a shrug.

"You trying to play me, cocksucker?" he said, taking another step closer.

"I would never dream of it, sir, but you see I'm in a bit of a predicament. I need help making a call—"

I stopped mid-sentence as I noticed a laughing hyena with blood dripping out of its mouth tattooed on the back of his hand; I licked my lips as I tried to get my thoughts in order.

"You need to make a call because?"

I tried to think of what to say without giving much away, but the words failed me.

"Don't worry about it," I said, turning and beginning to

walk away, but I didn't get far as a hand landed on my shoulder.

"Don't I know you?" he said behind me.

"Nah, don't think so," I said, trying to shrug his hand off and walk away, but found I couldn't as he redoubled his grip.

"Yeah, I know you, you're that corporate dickhead my crew's been looking for, Arun's gonna give me a fat bonus for bringing you in."

I spun around and struck him with my elbow across the side of his face; the blow was messy and uncoordinated, but it got the desired effect of getting him to let me go. He leapt for me, but I struck him again with a punch that sunk into his eye with a sickening crunch. He staggered backwards, hand going to his eye, and I knew he wouldn't let me go unless I put him away.

He came for me again and I was ready for it. When I lowered my head he slammed his nose into my forehead; the sound of his nose breaking turned my stomach but I kept up the attack, hitting him with windmill punches wherever I could.

I had hoped my onslaught would subdue my opponent but I was wrong.

He took a step back and smiled at me with bloodied teeth.

Shit.

"You really ain't from around here, are you?"

I said nothing as I looked to my left and right for a way out.

"You're like a lost little lamb stranded in the big bad wilderness with no way to get home, with no shepherd to look after you and no flock to take care of you. It's a shame you'll probably die here, so far from home, but the universe doesn't give a fuck about you and it never will."

He spat in my face, which took me by surprise, as he ran towards me and tackled me to the ground, his hands wrapped around my throat fingers digging into my flesh as I tried to fight him off but failed. The corners of my vision darkened as I grew light-headed. I struck his face, but each blow became weaker and weaker the longer he held onto me; I turned my face to the side and a flash of light caught my eye. I grabbed onto it and stabbed him in the shoulder with the shard of glass, causing him to yowl in pain as he tried to roll away. I stabbed him again and again, this time catching him in the leg and arm; he crawled away and I got up and walked after him. He didn't get far as I stamped on his leg, which caused him to scream in pain once again.

"Unlock your computer," I told him in a hiss.

"Fuck you!"

I stamped on his leg again and was alarmed at the amount of blood pouring out of it.

"If you don't do as I say then I won't be able to call for help, as it looks like you're about to bleed out."

He looked at his leg, face already going pale, and pressed his finger against his computer; I grabbed his wrist and used his forefinger to quickly type out a message to Claire and hit send. I didn't have time to call her and I didn't know if she would pick up, but this way she would get my SOS for help no matter what. I looked at the sleek glass of the computer, which was more of a fashion accessory than anything else, as you could get ones that projected their screens in mid-air, and thought of my next move.

Who else should I call or what else should I do while I had access to the galactic web?

Still pondering the question I frowned in confusion as

the screen went dead, and shook my attacker's wrist to bring it back alive. It remained blank as I looked down at him in annoyance and saw his vacant stare looking at me.

I dropped the limb and jumped back.

"Hey, you OK?"

I crept forward and nudged him with my foot but didn't get any response.

Shit. Shit. Shit.

This wasn't how this was supposed to go. I only wanted to scare someone into letting me use their device so I could get some help; now I had a corpse at my feet. Coming closer I nudged him again before I knelt down and touched his neck not knowing what I would find, but seeing it in the movies enough times, hoping that it would cure him of what was wrong.

His skin still felt warm, but he was definitely dead.

A sound behind me made me turn around. A man was in the mouth of the alleyway looking at me.

"Can, can, can you give me a hand? My friend has fallen and I need to get him some help."

"Yeah, sure," came the reply as feet approached me.

I kept my face away from the stranger and began walking towards him. "Just keep him company, I'm gonna get some help," I said, passing him by, my face still half turned away from him.

I kept on walking keeping my pace steady until I heard a shout behind me. "Hey, stop! This man's—"

I didn't wait to hear the rest of what he had to say before I tucked my head down and ran for my life out of the alleyway as fast as I could.

17

It was raining.
I was cold.
I was wet.
I was starving and that was the least of my problems.

The cold I felt had nothing to do with the rain falling on my face and everything to do with the image of the lifeless face I kept seeing wherever I looked. It haunted me.

The people who passed me in the street looked like him. The people who sat at restaurant tables looked like him. The people who huddled in the alleyways for warmth looked like him.

I couldn't get away no matter where I was.

I ran and ran and ran after the incident happened. Even when my chest hurt and I found it hard to breathe, even when my legs screamed in pain, I just kept on moving, because to stop would be to review what I had just done.

I don't know how far I went.

All I know is I kept on moving until weariness took over my body.

I sat with my back slumped against the wall and just

allowed the pitter-patter of the raindrops to fall onto my shoulders.

I killed a man.
I killed a man.
I killed a man.

I repeated the words over and over again in my head, while I hugged my arms to my body. Once again I asked how had life gotten so messed up.

I buried my head in my knees and shivered as the rain made its way down my back. I had always tried to do the right thing. Always stayed inside the lines and never went off-script. I had my life all planned out for me.

Go to school. Get a good job. Get married and have friends. Retire.

But somewhere along those lines things blurred, and I hated my job with a passion almost as much as I hated my home life. It became a battle of staying late at a job I didn't want to do, so I didn't spend time at a home I didn't want to go to. In those self-hate-filled days, I dreamed of escaping it all. I dreamed of travelling and doing the one thing I truly loved.

Painting.

It was a passion that grew from learning about one of my favourite painters of all time, Caravaggio. The bad boy painter of his era defied everyone from the Pope to the public. He cared little for what critics said and lived his life on his own terms. Growing up I would read about his exploits and dream it was me fighting in duels and bedding the models I painted.

But as I grew older and my skills didn't match my dreams, the crushing weight of life destroyed those dreams for me.

I believed I was good, good enough to live the dream I

wanted, but my parents—one an accountant, the other a lawyer—thought it would be better if I placed my efforts elsewhere.

I chuckled to myself.

If only they could see me now. See how doing the right thing, the accepted thing, and not placing my efforts into dreams had gotten me where I was today.

I killed a man.

There was that thought again, I tried to shake it but couldn't.

Every time I had a moment of peace it would pop into my head with such clarity it hurt. I hugged my knees and did the only thing I could think of; I cried. I cried for the unfairness of it all; I cried for the craziness of it all; I cried because it was the only thing I could think to do, the only thing that really made any sense.

So I cried and cried while the rain washed away my tears.

I didn't know how long I spent on the cockroach-covered ground of the alleyway, but I knew it was long enough for one of its many occupants to throw a waterproof blanket over me. I couldn't remember anyone doing it so I must have dozed off through the night. I knew I couldn't stay in this spot forever because I had sent instructions to Claire where to send help to pick me up, so I had to move.

I slowly got up from the ground and gritted my teeth as stiff joints popped back in place, and cold muscles tried their best to move me.

I looked up towards the sky and let out a sigh, as I made my way towards my pickup point.

The journey took me longer than I expected, as I got lost on numerous occasions and had to ask for directions. Finally getting to where I wanted to be I stood across the road from The Office in a darkened alleyway and waited.

I felt bad for Jerry as I looked at the damage the bar had taken. Windows gone. Sign half hanging off. There was not much left of the burnt building that was once Jerry's pride and joy, yet repair work had already begun to take place on the building. Rickety scaffolding that would pass no safety codes back home covered the building, and there were piles of wood and materials stacked up in front of it.

Work on the bar had appeared to stop for the night, with the odd customer walking up to it and raising their hands in shock and anger when they realised their local watering hole would not be open for the next few weeks.

In the past, before WW3, most of the manual jobs in construction and labour had been done by capable AIs, but as the war broke out and AIs were used to hunt, kill and spread terror their presence amongst the public was never the same.

They became a victim of their own success.

Placed in folklore, music and movies their image became one of horror. They were used to scare little kids into doing their chores; they were always the bad guys.

They became the enemy.

Even now, hundreds of years later, when they could have fixed Jerry's property in a matter of hours, their use was still shunned.

That's why it had been a shock to find one in the company of the Junk Yard Dogs. Such a valuable piece of tech would be worth millions, even though the AI butler wasn't as sophisticated as the ones used for war.

There had always been rumours about AIs still existing

after what had now become known as the Dissemble, where all the world's governments had tried to wipe them off the face of the Earth, but like humans the AIs had intelligence and with that intelligence came a need to survive and adapt no matter what.

I stayed in the shadows for a few more hours until something caught my eye.

A man I never thought I would see again took a seat in a dirty little café situated on the same road as The Office. He looked at the table in front of him in disgust before clicking his fingers at an annoyed waitress who had passed him by. She stared daggers at him as he placed an order before he waved her away dismissively.

I sunk back further in the shadows unsure of what to do.

I had asked for help, but I had thought it would come in the form of some lawman I could trust on this crooked planet, or a friendly face. Not the face of someone who turned my stomach cold.

I paced back and forth while I watched him take the order he had placed.

Porcelain cup on a saucer with a teabag placed at its side so he could dunk it in at his leisure, he worked on the computer on his wrist for a few minutes while he allowed the tea to brew before he took a sip.

I could see his wet lips smacking from here in that disgusting manner he loved to affect, which would always irritate me.

Closing my eyes and taking a deep breath, I walked out of the shadows and up to him, where I pulled out a chair and sat opposite him.

"Hello, Gregory, long time no see."

18

Gregory said nothing as he looked at me over the rim of his cup. Slurping loudly he placed the cup back on the saucer and his nose wrinkled in disgust as he leaned back. "I see you're keeping well."

I looked down at myself and realised for the first time how I looked.

Dirt covered the bottom of my trousers and was splattered across most of my body, a large rip along my shirt showed parts of my stomach and my tie had darkened spots on it I could only assume were blood.

I looked like I had lived on the streets all my life and I was sure I didn't smell too pretty either.

"I could be better," I said, straightening my tie.

He nodded and slid the menu my way.

I picked it up and could already feel my mouth water as I scanned through what it offered. Getting the attention of the waitress, who took a step back when she saw my appearance, I placed an order for a large beef and bacon burger with all the trimmings along with a milkshake.

Gregory continued to sip at his tea while he stared at me.

Neither of us said anything while we watched the foot traffic pass us, and waited for my meal to arrive.

After some time had passed the waitress delivered my meal to me at arm's length as if I were a rabid dog, then quickly scuttled away.

I dove into my meal without shame and savoured every bite I took. Juices ran down my chin and into my beard but I cared little. I bit off chunk after chunk and kept on going till there was nothing left of the burger. Sitting back with a sigh I burped loudly and closed my eyes as my body filled with warmth.

"Better?" Gregory asked.

I nodded.

"So what happened out there? One minute I get a message saying you've boarded the ship and everything is running smoothly, the next thing I know I'm getting messages from the space station saying you never arrived.

"If it weren't for the simple fact we picked up a distress signal from your ship, then we would have never known you were taken."

I picked a fry from my plate and dunked it in my shake and bit into it, not quite looking at him. Where to begin? So much had happened in such a short time that I didn't think I could compress it into words.

"I... things have been kind of fucked since I got onto the ship you booked for me, really fucked up. A female who belonged to a crew called the Junk Yard Dogs infiltrated the ship. She poisoned the guards and mercenaries you hired with some sort of sleeping agent. It didn't quite take as she expected and they woke up earlier than she wanted them to.

"A fight ensued, I was captured, I was brought to this planet, another fight ensued, I was taken to a safe house then in transportation leaving the safe house the crew and I were attacked. Which brings us to here."

Gregory leaned back in his chair and took another sip of his tea while he allowed what I told him to sink in.

"There appear to be a lot of missing parts to your story."

"I gave you the Cliff Notes version."

"How did you get a message out?"

An image of a bloodied face jumped out at me from my subconscious, which made me shiver. "I... borrowed someone's device."

Gregory looked around in confusion as he took in our surroundings. "Someone from this area allowed you to borrow their computer without asking anything for doing so?"

"Don't judge a book by its cover; there are some good people who call this place home."

"If you say so. Anyway, I am pleased you're safe and sound, the board is pleased you're safe and sound. We are lucky this whole mess hasn't reached the press. They would have a field day and our shareholders would have a heart attack before they began pulling their funds from our company.

"Hopefully this whole thing can get resolved with little to no fuss."

"With little or no fuss," I said, voice rising with each word. "People died—"

"Keep your voice down," Gregory hissed my way, looking around us.

"People died. Lots of people. That ship was left in a wreck. People have died on this planet. We can't just brush that under the carpet and act like nothing happened."

"Why not? We paid the mercenaries killed on the ship to do a job, and they knew the risk that job entailed. So did the other members of the crew. In regards to the people killed on this planet, it is none of our concern. The company is only worried about the well-being of its property."

Only worried about the well-being of its property.

Those words rebounded in my head as I took another fry and tried to force it down past the bile that was rising in my throat.

"Now, on to more important business, are you still in possession of the item I gave you?"

"I—it's hidden."

"Hidden? What do you mean it's hidden? Is it safe?" Gregory said, leaning forward.

"Why is it so important? What does it contain that makes everyone I encounter want it? People are killing for it."

"What's on the data-stick is of no importance to you. You were only tasked with delivering the item, something that you have failed to do, so you are in no position to ask questions that are, frankly, above your pay grade.

"The only thing you should be concerned about is whether or not the data-stick is safe, because if it is not, then your career within this company is finished."

"Career! You think I care about some dogshit career? Didn't you hear what I said? People have died trying to get this thing and you're not going to tell me what this is all about?"

"Like I said," Gregory said, spreading his hands wide, "the information is above—"

"You knew they took me before I told you—how?"

"We didn't find your body on the ship with the rest of the corpses."

"How did you get here so quick?"

Gregory scratched his neck before he took another sip of

his tea. "Your wife Claire notified us as soon as she received the message. We had to inform her of what took place, naturally, once we suspected they kidnapped you. There are company protocols in place for this sort of thing, in case your kidnappers sent a ransom to your loved ones."

"That still doesn't explain how you got here so fast—"

"Do you have the stick on you?" Gregory said, cutting me off.

"You didn't answer my question."

He said nothing as his eyes darted behind me; I turned around and saw to my horror a face I thought I had escaped. Combat fatigues hugged his muscular frame, as he passed a hand through his salt and pepper buzz-cut hair. Coming to a stop in front of me, he clamped his hands down upon my shoulders and greeted me with a smile.

It was the same man who had attacked The Office, the same military-dressed prick who had nearly killed me while he was shooting up the bar.

I looked to my right and left and saw that my exits were blocked.

"Hello, my friend, long time no see."

19

Brick walls surrounded me on all sides as I shuffled in the wicker chair I was tied to. Feet bound together, hands bound behind my back, my body shivered as I tried to get comfortable. Water dripped from corners of the walls and moss grew from different sections, as I tried to roll my shoulders back and forth to rid them of the tension that coursed through them.

I chuckled to myself as I shook my head. I sure as shit didn't see this coming.

I had thought all my troubles would be over; that once I had sent the message to Claire everything would be OK—but how wrong I was. It appeared my troubles were just starting, and I didn't see a way out of this mess. I no longer knew who I could trust, which meant I no longer knew who I could turn to for help.

Which made escape, or the prospect of escape, as likely as me flying to the nearest moon.

A steel door slid open in front of me and Gregory strode in holding a cup and saucer, while the goon who had shot up The Office carried a chair behind him. The goon placed the chair six feet away from me, and Gregory took his seat there with a flourish.

He looked me over before taking a sip from his cup and placing it back on the saucer.

"Where are my clothes?"

He ignored me and continued to sip from his cup.

"I take it you like to talk to men tied up and naked. I'm surprised, Gregory, I didn't take you for that kind of man."

"I had hoped it wouldn't come to this," he said, shaking his head sadly, "I had hoped you would have delivered the data-stick as promised to the space station and then once done, you would now be back in your office doing whatever menial task we set you.

"Instead, you were captured through no fault of your own, but nevertheless, you were captured, which placed a major risk on me, the board and the company just to recover what you lost."

"Recover what you lost? You mean by having this asshole next to you shoot up the bar I was in, nearly killing me and everyone in it?"

Gregory looked up at the man next to him and shrugged.

"Mr X's methods are... extreme, but he gets results. The board has decided it was safer to terminate any threat to the business, which involved you. I battled for your cause, you understand? Because your dear wife would have been so upset, but they refused to listen to me."

I looked into his eyes and couldn't believe what he was saying, but there was something else there I couldn't decipher.

"Mr X?" I said with a raised eyebrow. "What are we in? A Bond movie?"

"My real name is of no concern to you, maggot!"

"I'm hearing that a lot lately, must be something I've done."

Gregory sighed as he stretched his neck out and rolled his eyes. "This is getting tedious! You will tell us where you have kept the data-stick, otherwise we will be forced to hurt you."

"What makes you think I'll tell you anything? After I've told you what you need to know, you'll just kill me."

"If you tell us then your death will be painless. If you don't, then Mr X here shall torture you till you beg and plead for mercy, then he will torture you some more, then depending on how he feels, he may keep on torturing you or he may give you the death you so desperately want. Either way, it doesn't really matter to me."

"You're different from how you are in the office. Where are all the motivational speeches? Where are the threats? Where is the dickhead boss I so know and love?"

Gregory shrugged and drained the cup he was holding, before he fixed me with his gaze. "That's just a mask I have to wear for the office, someone I must be to climb the ever-growing ladder of success.

"Inside I am as dead as you. I really don't care if you live or die but without the data-stick I won't be able to pay my bills, I won't be able to afford the lifestyle I've come accustomed to, I won't be able to retire in another ten years. If I lose the data-stick I'll be like you, worthless, because no other company will touch me with a barge pole after Xcorp spreads the word about me."

He got up from his chair and walked away, handmade Italian leather shoes tapping against the stone floor.

"It could have been you here instead of me, I hope you remember that."

He turned around to face me and shook his head. "No, it

couldn't. The reason you got on the ship instead of me was because I knew it was likely to get attacked. That's why those mercenaries were on board; I heard wind of something taking place and I chose not to risk my life. Also it was Claire's birthday, which I couldn't have missed."

"What does my wife have to do with this?"

Gregory laughed as he looked at me as if I was the world's biggest idiot. "Did it never occur to you that your wife was sleeping around? The late nights, the unanswered calls, the cold marriage?"

It had but I would never admit that to him.

"Claire and I have been seeing each other for years; she's my mistress. My bit on the side. My cheap thrills when my wife won't put out. She does things I would never dream of asking my wife. Filthy things. In all honesty, I wanted to get rid of her years ago, but she fell pregnant with our first son and then threatened to go to my wife, which I couldn't have. After the second came along I knew I had to keep her sweet."

"But we all have sacrifices we have to make in this life."

"No, my sons," I said in a hoarse whisper.

"Trust me, I've taken the tests; both those little bastards are mine, unfortunately. Wish they won't but hey, what you going to do?" he said, turning back around and leaving the same way he came.

"No, my sons," I whispered once more as one of Mr X's fists smashed me in the face.

20

I could lie to you and tell you I stood firm. That I held my tongue like a man and showed no emotion. That I withdrew within myself like one of those Buddhist monks who had set themselves on fire and simply accepted their fate.

But that would be a lie.

I felt pain, oh, I felt it alright; my head bucked and snapped back as Mr X's fist drove into the fleshy parts of my body, as he punched my face, punched my liver, punched my stomach. I did the best I could in holding back my grunts of pain, but as time went on those grunts became louder and louder until they turned into screams. I tried to hold back the pain I was feeling by biting my lip until it bled, but Mr X was an expert in delivering punishment.

He was an artist and I his canvas.

When I thought the pain couldn't get any worse he proved me wrong.

Dragging over a small square table with a chipped metal top, he unrolled a canvas bag on top of it and zipped it open. I didn't want to look at what was inside but I couldn't help myself. Light from the shitty overhead bulbs reflected off something metal.

One by one he slowly pulled out his instruments of joy.

Hammers, saws, clippers, needles, metal clamps… and on and on it went.

"You know, maggot," he said drawing a needle across the metal table so it made me wince, "all this is unnecessary. The hammers, the metal clamps, the knives, all used by amateurs. You can make most people talk by using your own two fists; there are certain body parts you can attack just with these," he showed me his hands, "that can do all the damage you need.

"These are just for a bit of show. People like your boss don't trust people like me when we say we don't need all this shit, so we have to bring it along so we look like we know what we're talking about. But honestly, it's not needed."

"Does that," I worked a loose tooth out of my mouth and spat it on the floor, "does that mean you won't be using them?"

"Oh no, no, I have to show these devices have been used otherwise I may not get paid and he may not believe the information you gave me is correct."

I looked at him in disbelief.

"I know. Fucked-up world we live in when you can't even trust the word of your torturer."

Without warning, he slammed the needle he had into the meaty part of my shoulder, which forced a primal scream out of my body that left me feeling light-headed.

I dry heaved, taking in big gulps of air while I tried not to look at the piece of metal sticking out of my shoulder. My shoulder felt like it was on fire.

"That's it, breathe. Come on, breathe. Stay with me," he said, getting within inches of my face.

I tried to do as he said as the pain slowed to a dull ache.

"See, that's another problem with most people who do my job. They rush it. Always trying to get the information out as quick as possible so they can get paid and get laid. But I always say, maggot, if you can't enjoy your work then what's the point?"

He delivered another punch to my solar plexus, which caused me to gasp for breath.

"Please, stop, I—"

Another needle to the other shoulder made me push myself violently backwards so I and the chair collapsed back. I hit my head on the floor and saw white dots but it did nothing to take away the pain coursing through my shoulder.

"Cunt!" I said as I kicked and bucked on the floor, trying to distract myself from anything other than the pain.

"Pardon?"

Mr X grabbed the chair I was tied to by the seat and pulled me back up so I could face him. His salt and pepper hair was sleek with sweat and excitement. I could see nothing but his crooked nose, which pissed me off just staring at it. Oh, how I wanted to break it again.

"I'm sorry," I said panting heavily, "I'm sorry, that word should never be used. Never, ever, never." I shook my sweaty face from side to side. "I should have called you a thundercunt or a shitcunt, or a—"

He slammed a needle into the meaty part of my thigh, which nearly caused me to bite my tongue off.

"I'm sorry, I'm sorry, I didn't mean that, honestly I didn't, but has anyone ever told you that your nose looks like a bent cock?"

He smiled at me and I knew I was in trouble. It made me shiver for what was about to happen, but I was tired of being someone's plaything, tired of not having the strength to stand up to myself. When he punched me once, twice, three times in the dick I blacked out.

I don't know how long I was out for, but it was long enough for him to slap me in the face.

"Hey, hey, sleeping beauty, wake up, we're only getting started, sweetheart."

My head moved back and forth and I tried to focus on his face, which went in and out of focus.

"Are you back with us, sleeping beauty?"

I mumbled something through the pain that wasn't even recognisable to my own ears.

"How does it feel to know your life is just one big cliché?"

"What do you mean?" I asked.

"I mean, you were in a job you hate, a dead marriage, kids you were raising who weren't yours and your boss was fucking your wife!" Laughter poured from his mouth that felt like acid on my skin, "I mean how more cliché and pathetic can you get? The only thing you need to finish this shitty story you call a life is two disappointed pushy parents who always wanted you to do better but you never could.

"Man, your life sucks a fat phallus. I don't know how you didn't resist the temptation to blow your own brains out."

I said nothing as I hung my head in shame at his words.

Had my life been that predictable? That easy to read? Didn't I have more to offer? More to give?

I had dreams; I wanted to do things, achieve things, but life had gotten in the way, I kept telling myself, and I had to be responsible. I couldn't become the artist I wanted and also support two kids and a wife. I couldn't take the risk of trying to make a name for myself in the art scene while my family suffered.

But maybe all those thoughts were just excuses because I was too scared.

Too scared to act. Too scared to do. Too scared to live.

They say revelations happen to you in the weirdest places and mine had come to me bound naked to a wicker chair in a room I knew I would die in.

I smirked through the pain then smiled, then chuckled, then laughed. I laughed and laughed until my stomach hurt and tears ran down my face.

"What the hell are you laughing at, maggot?"

"Just my life, it's funny when you think about it."

"Funny, huh? Well, here's something to laugh about." He punched me repeatedly in the dick until I blacked out one more time. I came to with him tapping me on the face.

"Ain't you... going to ask your question?"

"What question is that?" he asked.

"Where I kept the data-stick?"

He was so close to me all I could see was his dead lifeless eyes and smell his foul coffee breath.

"I guess, but I'm having so much fun I don't want it to end so soon. But okay, maggot, I'll bite—where is the stick?"

"It's somewhere where I would like you to stick your nose."

He looked at me and smirked before punching me in the gut; I doubled over in pain while my stomach rumbled.

"No, no," I said, chin on my chest, "honestly it's somewhere I know you would love to root around in, it's got lots of hidden—"

Another punch to the gut that caused me to stamp my feet in pain.

"OK, OK, wait, wait, I'll tell you where it is—I swallowed—"

He punched me again with a three-piece combination

that had me bring up blood; it was ejected from my mouth with force and landed on his shoe.

"I'm trying to tell you what you need to know, you dickhead!"

"Fine, tell me."

"It's in my ass."

He looked at me sideways and gave me a raised eyebrow.

"I swear to you! It's in my ass!"

A swift front kick to the stomach brought up more blood.

"You think this is funny, Necktie? You think this is a laughing matter? Well, let me show you how we treat clowns."

What he did next... there were no words for the amount for pain that coursed through my body. Taking a needle from the metal table behind him he shoved it under one of my nails. The pain was all-consuming. It wrapped me in a blanket and refused to let go.

I nearly lost my voice as I screamed at the top of my lungs, then did something I hadn't done since I was a child.

I shat myself.

Nose wrinkled in disgust, Mr X took a step back from me and stared down his crooked nose at me. "Did you, did you, did you just shit yourself?"

My head hung down on my chest. No longer caring, no longer wanting to continue on, I could hear his voice but it sounded far away as the pain turned down the volume around me.

"I, I swallowed it," I said just above a whisper.

"What?" he asked, getting closer to me.

"I....said, I swallowed it. When taken." The words alone left me breathless as I felt hands lift my chin up.

He stared into my face, then his eyes travelled down as he looked at the mess I had made of the floor.

"You can fuck right off, maggot! If you think I'm digging in shit to look for some stupid data-stick you swallowed, you'll just have to get your hands dirty and see if you can find what Gregory wants, because there isn't a hope in hell he pays me enough to look through shit."

A knife appeared in his hands and he cut the rope that bound my hands and legs together.

I didn't move. All I could feel was pain.

"Hey!" he said, kicking me in the shin. "It's time for you to get up and get to work, this thing won't find itself."

I still didn't move, eyes half-closed, as he approached me and grabbed me roughly by the chin.

"I said—"

I moved with a speed and strength I didn't know I still had. It was born from the simple act of survival. From the fact that if I didn't move now, then my fate would be sealed, that once again a decision would be made for me as to how I lived and ultimately how I died.

My hand darted forward and I embedded the finger with the needle sticking out of it in his eye up to the knuckle.

His mouth formed a small O of surprise as I grabbed the back of his head and kept on pushing my finger forward until it couldn't go any further.

I had expected him to struggle, to fight back, but he didn't. He stared at me in surprise as if I had turned into a mystical creature before his very eyes and he couldn't believe what he was seeing.

I kept hold of the back of his head while I gritted my teeth like a pit bull locking onto its prey.

I locked eyes with his one remaining good eye and I refused to look away until the light from it faded. Pulling my finger out of his eye socket with a wet suction-like noise I allowed his body to fall to the floor.

 I looked behind me at the mess I had created and knew what I had to do before I escaped. It wasn't something I was looking forward to.

21

I pressed my body against a wall as I tried to focus on the task ahead.

I had gone through the trouble of recovering the data-stick, not a job I wanted to repeat in a hurry, and now I had it on me. I had re-clothed myself in Mr X's combat fatigues and although a couple of sizes too big, they were better than trying to escape this place bare-ass naked.

I didn't know where I was.

After I was kidnapped by Gregory, he had bundled me in a car and we had travelled through the back streets of Paradise Lost until we had reached this building. In a lot of ways, I was thankful he hadn't taken me on board a ship or to some other far-flung planet, which would have made escaping next to impossible.

The pain from the beating I had endured was still hot and sharp, but I did my best to put it in the back of my mind. Getting my wounds treated and wallowing in self-pity would come later; now I needed to get out of here before they found me.

I peeked around the corner of the wall I was leaning

against and ran as fast as I could forward, which resulted in a zombie-like shuffle, probably no faster than power walking.

I heard footsteps up ahead before I saw who was making them.

I halted in my tracks and pressed my body against a corner out of sight, waiting for whoever was coming to pass me by. I clutched a hammer I had taken from Mr X's torture supplies and allowed the weight of it to calm my nerves.

"How long do we have to stay on this shithole?" said one voice that sounded like gravel.

"Not sure," replied another voice, which was high and whiny, "but the sooner we get off this planet the better. It feels like you can catch something, just by looking at the girls here; every idiot walking the streets is either crazy, a psychopath, or some criminal.

"You know Drew got stabbed by some meth-head yesterday because, and I quote, he smelled like the devil's ring piece and no man should continue living who smelled like that."

Laughter echoed along the corridor as the footsteps got closer.

"Serves him right for trying to help the dirty fucker in the first place," said Gravel Voice.

"Speaking of something smelling like a ring piece, what is that smell?" asked High And Whiny.

"What? I can't smell anything."

"You can't smell that?" said High and Whiny. "It smells like someone took a shit in this corridor."

"Could just be the sewer from outside; Gregory complained about the drains overflowing. And it looks like there was a group of homeless sleeping in the alleyway out back."

"Yeah, yeah, maybe. God, I hate this—"

A shaven head appeared in front of me and I reacted before any thought passed between my ears; swinging the hammer down with all my strength I hit his skull with a loud crack that caused the person in front of me to stumble forward. I swing again and grimaced as blood squirted on my face.

The person I attacked fell to the floor in a heap as a shout of panic went up beside him.

"Fuck!" screamed Gravel Voice, who stared at me in panic.

I didn't give him time to think as I rushed forward and swung the hammer his way.

He ducked underneath it, causing me to hit the wall he stood in front of, taking a chunk out of it. I swung back around and slowly made my way towards him, backing him up step by step. He stared at me wide-eyed; I could smell the fear on him.

I enjoyed it. For once I was the predator and he was the prey.

"Hey, man, look, I don't know what the hell is going on here but I was just brought on as security—whatever fucked-up shit they did to you was none of my doing."

As he spoke his hand continued to move towards the computer on his wrist. "Stop that."

He nodded his head as if he had heard but his hand kept on drifting towards its target.

"I said stop that!"

I rushed forward and took another swing at his head, but he ducked low and dropped for my hips, rugby tackling me to the ground. His shoulder knocked the wind from my lungs as he landed on top of me.

His hands wrapped around my throat and squeezed as I

looked for my hammer. I caught it out of the corner of my eye, and I tried to reach for it but it was too far away. Once again my vision was going black in what had been less than a few hours. I looked up and could see his smug face looking down on me.

The same smug expression Gregory had given me.

The same smug expression Mr X had given me.

And it pissed me off.

I had come too far to die like this, to allow this hired killer to stop me in my tracks. Pulling my feet close to me I hip bumped him off me and got to my feet in a wild panic. He tried to follow me up but I kneed him in the face, shattering his nose upon impact.

He grabbed for me, but I slapped his hands out of the way and grabbed the back of his head and repeatedly drove my knee into his face until it became numb. I allowed him to drop to the floor and walked over and bent down and picked up the hammer I had dropped. Lifting it up I slapped the hammer against my palm as I turned around and walked back toward him.

His face was a mess of blood and broken bone.

He was still breathing. Bloody snot bubbles grew out of his nose and popped over his mouth.

I looked down at him and lifted the hammer but hesitated; I drew my arm further back prepared to deliver the killing blow but something in my gut stopped me. Allowing my arm to drop to my side, I turned away just as an alarm sounded throughout the building.

Red light flashed along the ceiling as the alarm grew louder and louder.

Not wasting another moment I ran forward taking one corner after the next. I could now hear shouts mixed with the sound of the alarm. As I slipped on something on the floor and collided with a wall, my shoulder struck it first, causing me to bite down on the pain that I felt. Pushing off it, I turned as I heard footsteps behind me.

"Stop!"

A man dressed in fatigues sprinted towards me. I did the only thing I could think of and swung the hammer his way; he lifted his arms to defend himself, but the hammer broke through his defences and cracked him on the jaw, dropping him to the floor.

I didn't wait to see if he would get up but spun on my heel and sprinted forward, taking more lefts and rights until I saw an emergency exit up ahead. Head low I sprinted forward and barrelled into it, bursting it open.

The frosty night air hit me in the face, waking me up as I ran down a flight of rusty metal stairs and found myself in an alleyway. One way lead to a dead end, the other appeared to lead to a main street. Not wasting any time I ran forward and found myself on a road with electric cars speeding past. I turned left without thinking and just kept running, jogging, walking and stumbling forward—whatever I needed to do to create distance between myself and the building I had been in.

I didn't know how long I walked for, but it was long enough for me to begin to relax, long enough for the stress to disappear from my shoulders, long enough for me to stop looking over my shoulder, long enough for me to feel like I had escaped.

That is, until I felt a hand land on my shoulder and I turned around to come face to face with an officer of the law.

22

My back and ass ached from sitting on the hardest metal chair I had ever come across; the wounds from my shoulder, knee, face and everywhere else I had been inflicted with damage throbbed and stung with every movement I took. Most of my wounds had stopped openly bleeding, but now they just oozed, which was a lot more worrying.

I tried to move my body to get comfortable but handcuffs secured me to a table that hindered my movement.

I rubbed my itchy ear against my shoulder and looked around the small room I was in. Grey walls gave away to a dirty carpeted floor that could have been any colour once but was now just beige, a two-way mirrored wall was to my left and an empty chair sat in front of me. I looked up towards each top corner of the room and found that they were empty of surveillance equipment.

A door before me opened and a man dressed in a grey suit, with matching tie that had a ketchup stain on it, made his way towards me. Bushy brown moustache covered his top lip, a mop of brown hair covered his head. He had the weight and bearing of someone who looked like a sergeant.

He dropped a brown file in one hand on the desk in front of me, while he ate a hot dog with all the trimmings with the other. He pulled out the chair opposite me and placed himself in it, while he continued to eat.

"God damn, Jerry knows how to make a good hot dog and serve a fine beer," he said, finishing his meal and licking his fingers clean.

"Jerry, the owner of The Office?"

"The very same."

Who would have thought Jerry had so many fingers in so many pies?

"Well, Mr...?"

"I would rather not say until I have a lawyer present."

"Whoa, whoa, whoa. Let's not start throwing the L-word around, shall we, let's just back up a minute and go through the events which led to you being here."

"I would rather have a lawyer represent—"

"Listen, take my advice, all the lawyers in this borough are shit and a lawyer from another borough won't touch this case, even if they got to sleep with Miss Paradise Lost. This is such a slam-dunk case, I don't know why my officer even brought you to me," he said, opening up the paper file in front of me, which left a greasy mark on the files.

"Who even uses paper anymore?"

"A police force network is constantly hacked, then the information gathered from that hack is leaked to the public, sensitive information. Information about a certain high-ranking officer in certain poses taken for his lover, a lover his wife knew nothing about and is still looking for her piece of flesh, although he already told her he had certain urges and if she just tried to—" He cut himself off and shook his head.

"Anyway, that is not important. What is important is the state we found you in."

I gave him a blank stare not allowing any emotion to register on my face.

"One of my officers found you covered in blood and shit carrying a bloody hammer with fragments of bone and hair flecking the metal. Which isn't a first in this borough, far from it. What is a first is that you offered yourself up with no resistance, nor did you try to flee, which is strange indeed."

"The reason I offered myself to your officer is because I am not guilty of anything."

"Is that so?" he said, drawing out the last word.

Eventually he broke his own silence: "Everyone is guilty of something in this cesspit of a borough; there is a reason they named this planet Safe Haven after all."

"Like I said, I am not guilty of anything."

"Then how do you explain carrying a bloody hammer?"

"Found it."

"Really?"

"Yes."

"We are doing tests now on the hammer and on the blood samples taken from your clothes and I would bet my retirement saving they both match. Which means the weapon was in your possession when it was used to create such a mess, that or you were in the vicinity when said weapon was being used. So would you like to try again and tell me what you did with the hammer?"

"Can I please see my lawyer now?"

He shook his head. "How about an easier question, what's your name?"

I stared at him while he chewed the ends of his moustache in frustration. I wanted to tell him who I was and where I had come from, but who would believe me?

I had already killed two men, plus maybe a third, and I had the might of Xcorp trying to kill me and every gang in this city wanting to take me to see The Lady.

I couldn't trust anyone.

Not my wife.

Not my boss.

Not the company I had given up so much of my life for.

"My name is Officer Hank Phillips and I want to help you, but I can't do that if you don't help me," he said with a smile.

"Get me a lawyer and I'll give you all the help you want."

He shook his head and threw across the table a picture of me entering Jerry's bar.

"Is this you entering Jerry's bar the night it got destroyed?"

I shrugged my shoulders.

He threw another picture across the table of me exiting from the back, while the building was on flames.

"It was a busy night that night; many people were at Jerry's bar. What's your point?"

He shook his head and showed me another picture, this one of a dead man whose face had been caved in by a blunt object.

"Do you recognise this man?"

"Who would?" I replied, pointing to the picture. "His face is all fucked up."

"What about this man?" he said, throwing another picture my way, which showed another dead body with its skull cracked in.

"Or this man, or this man, or this man."

He kept throwing photographs my way, till I was

drowning in a sea of battered murdered faces. I studied each one in turn, trying to find out some clues as to what they had done to deserve such a fate.

"Look, I don't—" I began but was interrupted by a knock on the door.

"Come in," said Officer Phillips.

A man dressed in uniform hurried up to us and whispered something in Officer Phillips's ear, which caused a smile to break out on his lips.

"You sure?" he asked.

The officer gave him a nod and walked out the way he came.

"Well, it seems we shall not be needing any help from you after all," he said with a shark-like smile. "Forensics have matched your hammer with ten different murder victims, that we couldn't solve the cases on."

I stared at him open-mouthed not knowing what to say.

How could this be? Yes, I had killed people, but it was only to escape. To survive. The pictures of these men he showed me appeared to be weeks if not months old. My gut rumbled as I sensed a black hole opening up beneath my feet.

"I... I, I didn't do this," I stammered.

"Well evidence doesn't lie," he said, giving me a shrug as he placed the pictures back in the brown paper file.

"But I didn't do this! Those pictures look weeks or months old and I haven't been on this planet that long."

"Well, that's too bad for you, isn't it?" he said, getting up. "Now if you were affiliated with one of the crews in the borough, maybe we could have worked something out but as it stands, you have no money, no influence and no friends. So I'm sorry to say, you'll be going away for the rest of your life."

The crooked bastard was trying to shake me down.

"You can't do this! This isn't how the law works."

He placed both his hands down on the table and gave me a look that caused my spine to shiver.

"I guess you haven't realised we do things differently here in Safe Haven. Money talks and power rules and you, my friend, have neither."

He walked to the door and tapped on it lightly. Two officers came in through the door and took up positions beside me as one of them unlocked my handcuffs from the table. They lifted me up to my feet and dragged me away.

It couldn't end like this! I had escaped death more times than I could count and they would sentence me for crimes I didn't commit, just because I didn't have friends this asshole feared.

"Wait, wait, wait!" I said, struggling against their restraints. "Hear me out—have you heard of the Junk Yard Dogs?"

"What about them?" Officer Phillips said, bored expression plastered on his face.

"If you speak to them, I'm sure we can sort this out. Just get in touch with José and all this will go away."

"Ha, those broke bums don't have the capital it will take to get you out of this. Take him away."

"No, wait, wait. Listen to me! José is doing a job for The Lady. You know of The Lady, right, of course you do. Well, he is in the process of completing a job for her and I'm integral to those plans. Now I don't know about you, but I would hate to ruin the plans of The Lady. To say that she may not take too kindly to anyone who gets in the way of those plans is an understatement."

My lungs hurt as I spilled out my words without taking a breath. The officers who had been dragging me out of the room had stopped as they looked between me and Officer Phillips. I couldn't read his thoughts but I could see the cogs turning as he calculated how best this could profit him.

"All I know is, José would pay a hefty sum to see me returned, and the person who returned me would also be in The Lady's good graces."

He stroked his chin while he chewed the ends of his moustache. "Take him away while I make some calls. Put him in cell H."

"You sure, sir?" one of the men holding me said.

"Absolutely," Officer Phillips said with a smile.

23

Something banging against the metal bars of my cell woke me. Opening my eyes I looked around me, shocked I had fallen asleep standing up. My cell was big enough for a child-size bed that took up ninety percent of the room and a metal bowl that acted as a toilet.

The bed was been occupied by one Killer Mike.

Mike was an interesting character who never spoke but merely stared at me. The name was tattooed across his neck with a blade dripping with blood underneath it. Whenever I moved his eyes would follow me like a dog waiting for its owner to throw their stick. I had taken a place against the far wall, as far away from him as I could, and I watched him as he watched me. I must have fallen asleep at some point because waking up now, I saw he still stared at me as he had done hours prior.

"Time for you to go," said the guard who had banged against the bars.

I looked at him in relief.

"You're lucky to be alive if I'm honest; old Mike here

doesn't like sharing his cell with others. You see the dark stain on the wall behind you?"

I turned around and noticed a large dark stain where the back of my head had been.

"Well, that's the brain matter left after old Mike here smashed his last cellmate's head against the wall; he must have really liked you."

I watched the cell door open before me with a feeling of relief. Walking forward I stopped and turned to Mike. "Thank you."

His eyes widened in surprise, and then he gave me the slightest of nods.

I turned back around and allowed the officer to escort me through the building until we reached a set of double doors, which brought us to the front of the building.

"Your ride's over there," said the officer, gesturing to a smoky grey electric car that had been fashioned after a 1967 Ford Mustang.

I allowed a sigh to escape my lips as I made the walk to the car. My eyes darted left to right looking for a means to escape but I was tired.

Tired and fed up of being chased, beaten, tortured and lied to.

I just wanted to lay my head down on a soft pillow and dream away my problems. Every step I took towards the car hurt, my muscles and bones creaked and popped as I tried my best to get my body working properly.

"Look who it isn't!" said Willis as he leaned out of the back window of the car.

I stopped next to the car and saw expressions on faces that ranged from anger, disappointment and worry to amusement.

"Thanks for helping us out after the car crashed," Willis

continued, getting out of the car and poking me in the chest. "I see you had time to save your ass, but no time to fucking help us out."

"Help save you! You! The people who kidnapped me against my will. You! The people who ruined my life so I can never go back to what it used to be. Why the should I help you assholes when this is your fault?"

"Oh, here we go again. Bringing up old shit! Get over it. What has happened has happened, but it was pretty unchristian of you to leave us like that.

"If it weren't for my quick thinking and cat-like reflexes then that dick weasel Arun would have had us for sure."

"Errr—quick thinking and cat-like reflexes?" Tuari said, stroking his chin. "You mean praying to your God and trying not to shit yourself?"

"I was praying for God to give me the strength to lift your fat ass up, while you were half-dazed and slumped over the steering wheel."

"I was faking," Tuari whispered to me not so subtly behind his hand.

"You what!" said Willis.

"And the fart I gave when you pushed my ass out of the window... intentional," Tuari said, whispering the last word.

Willis's face went red as his hands clutched and unclutched at his sides. "My. Mouth. Was. Open."

Tuari burst into laughter as Willis chased him around the car park. Tuari was surprisingly nimble for a man of his size.

"So," José said, yellow-tinted glasses showing me my reflection, "you look like shit, and smell like it too."

"Thanks."

"I can see you've been through some shit, but at least you're alive and kicking, hombre."

I nodded my head not knowing what to say.

"What you did back at the car crash was pretty messed up, my man. Pretty messed up and selfish. How many times have we saved your life since and you just left us like that? If you want to stay in this crew then there are a few rules you must adhere to. First—"

"Hold up," I said, lifting my hand in the air to stop him, "who said anything about wanting to join your crew?"

José tilted his head to the side as Poppy giggled behind her hand while she leaned against the car.

"You were in jail and you called us to get your bitch ass out; you have nowhere to go, and nowhere to stay. If you had someone from the civilian world you could rely on then they would be here already, but seeing as you don't, you called us to come to the rescue.

"We had to pay a lot of money to that corrupt cop in there so we could get you out, more money than normal because he knows we have a deal with The Lady, a deal you told him about, so now we are out of pocket before the job has even been completed. Which means you now owe us, and seeing as you don't have any money to pay us back, you'll have to work it off till the debt is cleared."

"Will this do?" I said, pulling the data-stick out of my back pocket.

José pulled out a handkerchief from his breast pocket and used it to cover his hands before he took the stick from me. "I know where this has been," he said, putting the stick up to the light.

"You sure this is the data-stick Xcorp gave you to deliver?"

"I'm sure, trust me I'm sure."

He continued to inspect the stick before wrapping it in the handkerchief and passing it to Poppy.

"Why now, *mi amigo*, after all this time," he said, Spanish accent rolling over me, "did you decide to give this up? After everything we went through? I was sure I would have to get the ginger man to cut you open to get it."

I thought back to waking up in a cold bed and making sure the children I thought were mine were looked after because their mother wasn't home. I thought about how I worked my ass off in a job that offered me very little, for a company now trying to kill me because I might affect their bottom line by a fraction of a percent. I thought about the emotionless words of Gregory, and how he cared very little if I lived or died, but worse of all I thought about the beating I had taken and how my body still screamed with every movement I made.

"I've... it doesn't matter. But will that do, will the stick be enough to clear my debt?"

"It's a start," José said, smiling my way, as he whistled for Tuari and Willis to get back in the car, before he jumped in the passenger's front seat. With a roar, the engine from the car started and we took off without saying another word.

24

We were back in the car and speeding along the highway, Tuari was riding with José next to him up front, Willis was to my right with Poppy sitting to my left in the back.

We sat in silence as we sped past cars on the road, cutting some off, overtaking others. The view outside the car window offered me nothing but derelict buildings with people's clothes hanging outside the windows to dry. Hustlers and pimps stood on street corners and eyeballed everyone who stared their way for too long.

"Are all the boroughs like this?" I asked.

"No," Tuari said, tugging on the steering wheel sharply, "Paradise Lost is where the bottom feeders live, the people who are desperately trying to make a living. The other boroughs are all different, each one unique in its own way and offering services only they can provide. Paradise Lost, for example, is where the best alcohol is made and where the best rats can be employed to find out any information you want.

"The Jungle, on the other hand, is the best borough to

get fresh produce from, but they also deal in chemical weapons, poisons, dirty bombs and technology; if you want something made they are the people you go to."

"If Paradise Lost is such a shithole then why run your base of operations here?"

"Because, *mi amigo*," José said, lighting a cigar, "everything comes through the streets of The Lost first, before it makes its way towards the other boroughs. The other boroughs may be nicer, but I would rather see an invasion than hear about it third hand."

"Plus this is our home," said Poppy, "and there's no place like home."

José looked at the computer attached to his wrist as a flashing light was emitted from it. He pressed a finger to his lips for silence and tapped its surface.

"*Hola*, I hear you've been having a lot of problems lately," said a voice that purred like a tigress through the speakers.

"You could say something like that, but it's nothing my crew haven't dealt with before; it's just another day in the office. Fools will always try their luck, that's what fools do."

"Indeed."

I felt an irrational grip of fear as I listened to that voice. It spoke of danger and violence at a moment's notice, yet you would beg and plead to just keep listening to it.

"I've had a few... issues of my own, I've had to deal with—"

"Do you need any help?" José asked.

"I thank you for the offer, but you know better than to ask me that. My men are more than able to take care of any problems which arise, no matter how small or large." What sounded like a distant scream could be heard in the background, but it was cut off abruptly.

"Sometimes people forget how I got to this position, just

like when the waters of the seas are tranquil people so quickly forget the devastating power of its waves, or the monsters that lurk underneath its surface."

"Until they are reminded again," José said, blowing a smoke ring out of the window.

"Until they are reminded again," said the voice over the speaker. "I know we had an arrangement to meet up at our normal spot, but I'm afraid things have changed. Eyes are all over Paradise Lost, so I shall send you the coordinates to a new location. I'm afraid it's off-world but this is the safest option for both of us."

"I understand. Send over the information and I shall see you soon."

"It shall be my pleasure," said the voice before the line went dead.

"Tuari, change of plans. Take us to *The Kennel*; it appears we are going for a little trip," José, said leaning back in his chair as a smile lingered on his lips.

I was back on the JYD's ship, *The Kennel*, and was eating alone in the canteen. I was eating the leftover bouillabaisse meal Tuari had made; it tasted delicious and did its best to fill the hole in my soul.

I had been disinfected, washed, bandaged and taken care of by Poppy, who even gave me something for the pain as my body tried its best to heal. But what I saw. What I had done. I didn't know if I would ever recover from it; I felt like a different person. It was hard to explain but...

Footsteps interrupted my flow of thoughts and then José sat opposite me with two glassfuls of brown liquid in ice, with a cigar dangling from the corner of his mouth. He slid one glass across the table to me, then picked up his own and held it in the air. I did the same to mine and toasted him.

"Well, amigo, you sure have had seven kinds of shit kicked out of you, haven't you?"

"Feels like ten," I said, taking a sip from the glass and finding it was in fact spice rum. I took another sip and nodded my head in appreciation.

We sipped at our glasses neither saying anything while we allowed the silence to fill the space between us.

José was wearing a sleeveless bomber jacket that showed off his muscular arms; bracelets adorned both his wrists and a tattoo of a German shepherd that looked like it was on steroids graced his shoulder.

He caught me staring at it and smiled. "The dog breed is called a Kuchi or Afghan shepherd. It was a breed used by the nomadic peoples of that region to protect their caravans and livestock; it always resonated with me."

I nodded my head as I studied the tattoo. "Did you always want to do this?"

"What?"

"Be an outlaw?"

The tinted blue glasses he wore stopped me from seeing his eyes but he looked off into the distance while he sipped at his drink. Some time passed and I didn't think he would answer me, or worse, I had offended him, but he put down his drink and turned my way.

"I used to be like you. I had a cubicle job that paid me just enough, like some *puta*, so I could save up and go on pointless vacations and buy shit I didn't need, but I never made enough to make a difference in my life. I even had a wife. We were trying for a baby but she miscarried and I spent more time trying to fill the gap that grew between us with pointless shit but, as every smart man knows, that never really solves the problem.

"Until one day my boss said the wrong thing and I just snapped. I then saw everything for what it was, a lie. I didn't want to believe it; I had lived my entire life trying to be better than my padre, trying to not hate my life as much as he hated his, but in the end, I ended up on the same road travelling towards the same destination."

"So breaking the law is the answer to a happy life?" I said with a raised eyebrow.

He laughed into his drink as he took another sip.

"The answer to a happy life? I wish I knew the answer; I think many men wish the same. The only thing I can say is, what I do now makes me happy, what I do now gives me freedom. It may not be freedom or happiness to someone else, but it is freedom and happiness to me.

"I know you see us as monsters, killers, thieves, wild lawless crazy motherfuckers, but there is a beauty in that also. A beauty few men will ever know."

I sipped at my drink and watched him as he puffed on his cigar; he enjoyed every pull he took, content in the simple joy of smoking a fine cigar. I finished my meal and leaned back enjoying the comfort of having a full stomach in what felt like an age.

"After I left you my former boss Gregory captured me. He wanted to know where the data-stick was; he had that asshole who shot up Jerry's bar do this to me," I said, gesturing to my body. "I never told him where it was, but certain things happened during my short time as a hostage that have made going back to my old life impossible, I don't think I can ever live a normal life again—what with Xcorp now wanting me dead so they can tie up any loose ends."

José got up from where he sat and walked over to a

cupboard in the canteen. He pulled it open and rummaged inside till he pulled out a bottle of spiced rum, then walked back to our table. He topped up my glass and his before toasting me once again.

"How did that old normal life treat you?" he asked.

I was about to reply "well", but it would have been a lie.

"It treated me like shit if I'm honest. Before they tortured me I found out—" I shook my head and looked off into the distance. "It just sucks knowing everything I thought was true was a lie."

"That it does, that it does. But now you have another chance at a new life. This life can be dangerous—there is no pension, retirement is an afterthought and ninety percent of the people you meet will want to kill you—but in exchange, you get a family who will always have your back and a family who will never lie to you."

I looked back at him, taken aback, before asking, "Are you offering me a job?"

He burst into laughter, head tilted back as he slapped the table in front of us. I quickly followed suit not knowing if it was the drink or the very idea that had me in stitches.

"I think you would have had enough of that for one lifetime, no? No, I'm not offering you a job but a place on the crew. A place to call your home, as one man gave me a very long time ago."

I thought over the opportunity he was offering me. On the one hand it sounded like the adventure of a lifetime; on the other, part of me still yearned for my family, a family that wasn't mine but a family nevertheless.

"Look, I don't need an answer right away; just think it over. But there are a few rules we adhere to on this ship.

"Number one, whatever the crew makes the crew shares, no matter if the job was your idea or not.

"Number two, no stealing.

"Number three, no lying.

"Number four, we all get to vote on decisions that impact the crew.

"And number five, try and keep your shit clean, but that rule is more of a guideline than anything else."

He got up from the table and downed the contents of his glass in one and left me to my thoughts.

25

I had somehow found my room after many false attempts; the alcohol was hitting me hard because of the pain medicine Poppy had given me for the beating I had taken. Finally, standing in front of my door I waited for it to slide open only to find that it was already occupied: Poppy sat on my bed, sad smile plastered over her face.

I said nothing as I knocked my shoes off and half stumbled, half fell onto the bed next to her.

I closed my eyes and allowed the soft mattress to take away some of my aches and pains.

"How do you get over it?"

"Get over what?" she asked, her voice sounding far away.

"Get over their faces, the images that won't just go away. No matter what I do, I keep seeing their bloody battered faces. They won't leave me alone. Whenever I think I'm about to have a good night's sleep they appear again, just staring, not saying anything. Always just staring."

Poppy pulled herself up beside me and lifted my head till it rested in her lap. She stroked my hair while tears ran down my cheeks.

I allowed the words to pour from my soul, as I closed my eyes against the flow of tears.

"And the craziest thing is, that isn't the worst thing that happened to me that day; I also found out my wife has been sleeping with my boss for years and the two kids I raised as my own aren't mine but his. My entire life has been one big lie.

"I've wasted so many hours, so many opportunities, so many—"

She kissed me then. Kissed me full on the lips till she stole my breath away. It was the first fragment of peace I had felt in a long time. I can't remember how long we stayed like that, but it was long enough for the voices to quieten down and go away. Long enough for my tears to dry away.

Long enough for me to feel like the person I had been ten years ago.

She parted from me and hovered above my face; her dark hair cascaded around us creating a little protective shield for our faces to hide under.

"Some faces you forget, some faces you remember, some you regret, others you take great joy in knowing they are no longer alive and the universe is a better place without them.

"I wish I could make it go away, I wish I could stop the pain, but it's just something you must learn to deal with, something that time will partially heal but mostly won't.

"After a while, it will just become part of you. The only advice I can give you is to never enjoy it.

"Never enjoy the kill. Let it be what it is, but don't seek it out. Otherwise you'll go mad looking for reasons why you do what you do."

"Like Willis?" I whispered.

She kissed me on the lips and only smiled; I tried to

return the gesture but it felt like my face was straining against an immovable object.

"Does it make me a monster, that part of me won't miss them?"

"No, it makes you human," she said, kissing me again.

"My wife and I had stopped loving each other before we got married. The kids... I always tried to connect with them, but they always felt like strangers to me; now I know why. I will never see them again, will I?"

"José isn't a tyrant; you can come and go as you please when we haven't got a mission on, but I think it's for the best you bury the hatchet while you can. Your enemies may use them to get to you; the further you're away from them the best thing it is for everyone all around."

I nodded my head at her words and drunk in the beauty that was her eyes; they made my heart skip a beat. She leaned in to kiss me again but I pushed her gently back.

"Why are you doing this?" I asked. "You barely know me."

"That's a silly question. How can you explain why your favourite colour is red or why you prefer one flavour of ice-cream over the other? You just do. In this life, time is short, and you learn to act on gut instinct. Now let me see what I can do about those nightmares of yours," she said, leaning towards me.

26

I could see movements through the fog and darkness. I squinted through it and tried to get a better idea of what I was seeing. I moved forward and stretched out my hands but it was so dark I couldn't even see them in front of my face. I continued forward confident now that I could see something in the darkness; I didn't know how long I walked for but I tripped over something and fell forward.

I looked back. Overhead lights picked out a body on the floor.

The lights didn't diminish the darkness around me, only highlighted the body in all its glory. Dressed in fatigues it lay on its front. I took a step forward but needn't have bothered; I knew who it belonged to. Salt and pepper hair was cut into a buzz cut. I willed my feet to stop moving but they paid me no attention, I didn't want to see what was on the face-down side; I didn't want to know what the picture looked like. But like disobedient children, they kept on moving forward of their own accord.

I stood over the body, and legs that didn't listen to me

bent down. I screamed for my arms to stop but they moved away from my trunk and slowly turned the body over.

I tried to close my eyes but it was useless.

I looked down and took in the sight before me. The face of Mr X was motionless, peaceful. Eyes closed, he appeared to be at peace wherever he was. There was no tension in his forehead, there was no vein pulsing along the side of his head.

He appeared younger than I remembered. Without the tension causing lines on his face, we could have been the same age. I moved one hand slowly towards his face and tried to jump back as his hand shot up and caught my wrist.

I tried to pull it away but it was a wasted effort.

His eyes opened.

One was nothing but a hollowed-out hole; the other, grey and lifeless, looked into my soul. We stayed trapped in that embrace until his lips pulled into a slow smile. Rotten teeth sent foul breath washing over me.

"Well, well, look who it isn't, maggot. Come to gloat?"

I said nothing as I tried to pull away.

"I'll bet your little bitch ass has. Come to gloat because you think you've killed the big bad wolf of the story—but that couldn't be further from the truth, could it?

"You have done nothing but delay the inevitable."

"What... what... what do you mean?" I stammered.

"Wha... wha... what do you mean?" he said, mocking me with a grin. "You sound like a bitch! A bitch who's about to get everything that's coming to him. You think Xcorp will let you get away with their shit and they won't come looking for you? Then you're a bigger fool than I took you for. They'll kill you and those little friends you've made. If that asshole Gregory doesn't do it then some other manager will; it's not when, it's just a matter of how and where."

I stared into his face, sweat pouring down the small of my back.

"But, I, I didn't do anything! I didn't ask for this!" I said, pleading.

"Stop being such a pussy. I didn't ask for any of this, oh why me, why do bad things always happen to bad people, blah, blah, blah. You know what we would do to little bitches like you in the army?" he said, eye gleaming my way. "We'd make you put on a dress then let you get a running head start before the boys would chase you down and once they caught you, oh boy! There was no telling what could happen, or what could end up where, if you catch my drift."

"Fuck you!"

"That's more like it," he said, grinning my way. "That's the fire you'll need if you want to survive what's coming, because believe me, there's a shit storm heading your way that you'd better be prepared for because if you ain't, you'd better start picking out a pretty dress to wear to the prom, maggot."

27

I woke up in my bed covered in sweat.

I looked around in a panic as the unfamiliar surroundings of the ship took me by surprise; I had been expecting to wake up in my bed back home, but after a few seconds had passed the realisation of where I was sunk in. I saw my crumpled clothes spread out across the floor and then I remembered there should have been someone else in the bed with me.

I felt the cold side of the bed where Poppy had been and frowned. The only evidence we had slept together were a few strands of dark hair left on the pillow. Lying back down, I let out the heavy sigh trapped in my chest and stared at the ceiling.

What the hell was I doing?

I was still married... well, not in spirit, thought or feeling, but on paper, I was married. Married to a woman who couldn't give two shits about me but still married. Who informed my boss of my location so he could kill me.

What did I know about the woman who I had just slept with? I knew her name was Poppy Palmer and she was a smuggler-come-pirate- come-outlaw, who was handy with a knife and who moved like a dancer. Not necessary the type of woman you would take home to your mother or the qualities you would look for in a wife, but who was I to judge what was good partner or wife material? I didn't have the best track record in that department.

But apart from the murder and the kidnapping, she was a kind person—well, to me anyway—and had never shown me anything but care and tenderness.

But maybe that was a trap itself; hadn't José warned me about getting too close?

I throw my hands over my face and groaned as the hopelessness of the situation finally dawned on me.

Didn't I have enough problems without adding to my list of troubles romances with women who could kill me without breaking a sweat?

I got up to my feet and groaned, as my limbs had grown stiff; I stretched my arms over my hand and sighed as my joints popped. Looking back at my bed I knew I wouldn't go back to sleep no matter what I did, so grabbing some fresh clothes out of my bag I threw them on and made my way out of my room.

I looked left to right and walked right, as I hadn't been down that part of the ship yet; I ran my hands over scorch marks that appeared to be made by weapons fire, and bullets holes that had peppered the metal of the walls and left them full of holes.

Water dripped from overhead pipes and buckets collected what had become too big a problem to ignore.

I continued on, allowing my feet to take me where they would, and took another right and left, till the corridors became darker and less well lit and maintained and the damage to the walls more intense. I stopped as I came across an immense door marked with more bullet holes than I could count, and a large bull's-eye target painted in the middle of it.

I looked behind me before looking back at the door, uncertain what it would yield. Biting the inside of my cheek I shrugged and walked forward as it slid open.

The thunderous roar of gunfire pounded my ears, forcing me to cover them up as I took in the scene around me. The room I was in was as large as a football field and had been converted into a gun range; sandbanks dotted the far end with different targets at varying distances spread out across the shooting range.

Willis stood with his back towards me and fired at different-sized targets that flew across the field; the targets moved and dipped like insects, never staying still for too long and making a clean shot that much harder. Willis fired off his pistols rapidly, hitting nine out of every ten targets he aimed for before reloading another magazine and firing again.

He moved like a well-oiled machine. No movement was wasted, no effort was exaggerated. He pointed, shot, reloaded.

I don't know how long I watched him for but I wanted to leave before he caught sight of me. Slowly backing away I got within a couple of feet of the door before the sounds of the pistols stopped and I heard his voice like an angry terrier calling out to me.

"Oi, fuckface! What are you doing staring at my ass?"

"I wasn't staring at your ass, I was just watching you work."

"Yeah, yeah, I've heard that line before. Just don't get no ideas," he said, pointing his pistols towards me, "or I'll blow your dick off."

"I'll keep that in mind," I said, slowly backing away.

"Where are you going?"

"I just thought you would like some alone time. It looked like you didn't want to be disturbed."

"Ahh, bollocks to that, come over here," he said, waving his hand towards me, gun still in hand.

I suppressed the urge to sigh and did as he said, hoping this would be over quicker than I expected it would be. The closer I got the more overpowering the smell of gunpowder was, till it was the only thing I could smell. He looked me up and down and tapped his finger against his lip.

"I take it you've never fired a gun?"

I shook my head.

He didn't hide his disappointment. "Figures. Seeing as you're a newbie I think its best if you start with the Springfield XDM 9mm. It's an easy-to-use gun with triple safety guards and little recoil, so even kids can practice with them and not get hurt," he said, walking off and unlocking a metal cabinet fixed to the wall. Racks upon racks of guns greeted my sight as he ran his fingers along the shelves and picked a handgun from the rack.

"Originally made in Karlovac, Croatia, it's an old gun, which means spare parts are cheap as shit, and it's so easy to use and fire that even a dickhead like you can use it," he said, handing it my way.

The matte black pistol felt awkward in my hands.

"You know, you should really get into motivational speaking, maybe at schools, unemployment centres," I said, pointing the gun away from me and at the floor.

"It's no use pointing it down there, cockface! Aim up and fire at the targets; all of them are stationary so it should be easier for you."

I did as I was told and fired off as many rounds as quickly as I could. I expected a bigger recoil from the gun than the one I got; the firing of it was smooth but also nerve-racking. But despite all that I couldn't help but smile. This was exhilarating.

It was over before I knew it. Gun shaking in my hands I looked at the targets to see if I had hit any.

"Did I hit any?"

"No."

"You sure?" I asked.

"Not unless you count the sandbanks, the ceiling and the walls as threats," Willis said, taking the gun from my hand and reloading it again. Once done he handed it back to me and got in close.

"Look, all the movie bullshit you see where the hero is pointing his gun sideways and firing from the hip and doing forward rolls and backflips is all bullshit. All it takes to be a good shooter is a few simple things."

"Such as?"

"Well, if you shut up, I'll tell you, cupcake."

I looked at him with a side-eye and waited for him to continue.

"How you hold a gun has everything to do with your ability to manage the recoil; the better you manage it the more well-aimed shots you can fire. Know the targets, identify if they're a threat, and fire. Hesitation kills. Better to be sorry than dead. Which takes us onto trigger management. Don't finger-bang the trigger like it's the end of prom, apply steady pressure. And lastly, remember to breathe. Breathing eases tension, which makes any task more simple."

I looked at him dumbfounded.

He rolled his eyes with a sigh. "Grip, breathe, aim, press. Just remember that."

I looked at the targets and the face of Mr X appeared

again in my mind's eye. Shaking my head I handed the gun back to Willis. "I don't think I can—"

"It is better to be a warrior in a garden than a gardener in a war. If you don't want what happened to you to happen again this is the best way to ensure that.

"Forty-five percent of these rat-fuckers you meet are just wannabe hard men with a drug addiction who can barely keep their gun straight; the other forty-five are just as scared as you and would rather not be there."

"What about the ten percent?" I asked, looking at him worried.

"Run."

He pointed to the targets once more and I tried, again and again, to do as he had told me. I don't know how much time passed but it was enough for me to know I wasn't getting any better. As the last bullet was fired and the silence stretched on until I began to fidget, I finally turned to him and said, "What?"

He pinched the bridge of his nose and let out an aggravated sigh.

"In all my God-given years, I have never seen anyone who can't shoot worth a shit less than you. I mean you are offensively bad, to the point where I think it's better if you don't even carry a gun because your crew may be in more danger than the enemy. But that isn't really an option, so I have one more idea."

He went back to the racks of guns and knelt down till he was on his hands and knees and crawled forward, moving boxes and tools about till he found what he was looking for and wiggled back out. In his hands was a rusty metal case about thirty-five inches in length. Writing was engraved on the top of the box, which Willis slowly ran a hand over.

"'For the one in authority is God's servant for your good.

But if you do wrong, be afraid, for rulers do not bear the sword for no reason. They are God's servants, agents of wrath to bring punishment on the wrongdoer.'"

He unlocked the case and held it open before me.

Velvet coated the inside of the case and inside rested a custom-built sawn-off shotgun. The barrel had a copper-gold finish to it, which blended into the light wood handle. The head of a snarling dog was engraved in a small emblem.

It was the most beautiful piece of destruction I had ever seen.

I went to pick it up but hesitated, looking up at Willis, who gave me a slight nod.

My hands trembled slightly as I picked it up and clutched it in both hands. The weight felt right.

"This baby was something I designed myself, but... it never felt right in my hands; it was too messy, not precise enough, not fast enough, but I loved it too much to get rid of it. It takes normal shotgun shells and explosive shells I made for that extra kick. There is a loading mechanism in the handle where the shells are kept and this loads a greater number of shells than your standard shotgun.

"I named it The Peacemaker."

I ran my hand along the barrel and smiled.

"How do I fire it?"

"Point and shoot. It ain't rocket science."

I did as he said and aimed for one of the targets. My finger about to press the trigger, he yelled at me causing me to jump.

"Not like that. Not unless you want to blow your thumb off. Remember, the barrel is shorter than a normal shotgun, so your grip has to be further back."

"Just a word of warning, it may not be the best idea to cause the person holding a gun to jump."

He ignored my comment and nodded to the targets in front of us. I walked slightly forward doing as he had instructed me to do. I focused on the target in front of me, but his voice cut through my thoughts.

"Just point and fire! This fucker ain't about precision."

I pointed and pulled and was thrown off my feet as an explosive roar escaped the end of the barrel.

White dots appeared in front of my eyes as I sat up and rubbed the back of my head. Laughter was coming from the side of me as Willis slapped his thigh and stomped his feet in merriment while he held his sides. Tears streaked down his cheeks and collected in his ginger beard as he mimicked me shooting the shotgun.

I got to my feet with a groan and made my way towards him.

"What the fuck was that?" I demanded, anger filling my cheeks.

"God almighty, that shit was beyond funny."

"How is this gun meant to be any good for me if it will always dump me on my ass when I use it?"

Willis took a few deep breaths while he collected himself. "I completely forgot I had left explosive shells in it. That's why the kickback was so strong. You may need to hit the gym and practise firing with the explosive shells more but the normal shells shouldn't be anywhere as strong."

"Explosive shells...." I said, turning towards the targets on the firing range and feeling my mouth hang open.

In front of me lay nothing but destruction.

The targets closet to me now lay unrecognisable on the floor; the pellets in the shell had sprayed out and destroyed everything in front of me. Further afield I could see other damage where the shrapnel of the damaged targets had penetrated other targets. I looked down at the shotgun still clutched in my hands and marvelled at the destructive power it held.

"Loaded with explosive shells this thing can blow a hole in a two-to-three-inch thick metal door no problem; use it against vehicles, armoured combatives, or any motherfucker you want to make sure the authorities can never identify. Like I said, you will need to put on some muscle if you ever want to use it properly, but we have a gym out back so I would start hitting the weights if I were you.

"Now pass it over," he said, hand open.

I gave him the gun and he emptied the fiery red shells carefully and replaced them with white ones.

"Red is for explosive, white is standard. Now do as I showed you before," he said, handing me back the gun and programming a new set of targets to appear on the firing range.

I positioned myself as before and this time planted my feet as I steadied myself for the recoil to come. I squeezed the trigger and watched as the target before me blew apart. The recoil wasn't as strong. The damage wasn't as total. But damn, it felt good.

I squeezed and squeezed the trigger, blowing apart anything that appeared in front of me; the target started to move but it mattered little. All I had to do was point in its relative direction and the shotgun did the rest.

I kept on shooting until spent shells littered the floor around me and sweat coated my back.

"Think that's enough for one day," Willis said, checking the time on his watch. "Come back here and practise as much as you want, because the more you do, the more that thing in your hands will save your life."

I replaced the shotgun back in its case and smiled.

The Peacemaker.

The name had sounded corny to my ears at first but I had grown to like it.

"Do you think I have what it takes to become the ten percent you were talking about?" I asked him jokingly,

Willis said nothing as he tidied up; his eyes didn't meet mine as he checked and rechecked his pistols.

"I mean—"

He looked up at me then and I tried not to take a step back as I saw in his eyes the insanity he was trying to control. It was terrifying to behold. It spoke of a man who had done things that would always haunt him no matter what he did; it spoke of a man who had lost his mind, found it and wasn't too sure if he wanted it back.

It spoke of demons.

"The ten percent are my people."

It was all he said before he walked away from me, but it conveyed enough that I prayed I never came across one of his own.

28

I had stayed for some time in the firing range after Willis had left and just allowed what he had told me stink in.

Now, making my way back towards my room, I had gotten lost amongst the myriad of corridors of the ship. A small seed of panic was developing in my stomach, but I knew whatever happened I would come across someone eventually; if worst came to worst I would have to shout for help.

I took another left and saw a large pair of double doors before me, which I knew would take me to the bridge. I hoped I would find someone there because it was time I swallowed my pride and just asked for directions.

Entering the bridge, it took my eyes time to adjust to the dim lighting as I made my way further inside. I scanned the room and saw José's black dome-like head just visible over the top of the chair. I made my way towards him and saw that he was staring at a cluster of holographic images displayed in the air in front of him.

"What's your take on this, boyo?" he said, zooming in on a few of the holographic pictures.

Each picture depicted a ship—no, on closer inspection I saw it was, in fact, different ships that had been captured at different time intervals all leading up to the last few hours. The hull and outline of each ship were slightly different, but all were sleeker looking than *The Kennel* and appeared to have more firepower, judging by the cannons and gun turrets that covered each ship's outer surface.

"It appears to be different ships photographed at differently timed intervals. All are slightly different in body image but all have one thing in common, weapons. Apart from that, I'm not sure what you want me to say," I said with a shrug.

He tapped his chin and threw his hands out so the images moved away from him and enlarged.

"All these images were taken just after we left Safe Haven. All the ships pictured here have been captured by our sensors. They all have a few things in common—when they notice we've detected their presence they flee, they all have similar weaponry, and you can follow the trail of pictures all the way back to a few hours after we departed Safe Haven."

"If it was the same ship, I would say we're being followed but you can clearly see each ship is slightly different," I said, pointing to the images.

"What if it was done on purpose?"

"What do you mean?" I said, looking at him confused.

"I mean what if it's the same ship just disguised to look different," he said, thick Spanish accent coating the words.

"Well, it could, but I mean how—"

The ship lurched underneath my feet causing me to slam into the console I was in front of; I braced myself against it and held on for dear life as the ship rocked back and forth. I steadied myself and looked towards José, who still sat calmly in his captain's chair.

"What the fuck was that!" I yelled, walking towards him.

I didn't get an answer as the bridge doors opened and Willis, Poppy and Tuari made their way through the doors.

"That," said José, pushing his red-tinted glasses up his nose, "was the surprise attack from the *coños* who have been following us since we left Safe Haven. All hands on deck! Let's see if we can't make these motherfuckers pay before we shake them off our tail. Tuari take over from the autopilot, Willis weapons, Poppy surveillance, Quinton…" he said, looking my way, "stay out of the way and don't get hurt."

"What?" I asked, affronted.

"Have you ever been in a space dogfight before?"

I shook my head.

"Then shut your whore mouth," Willis shouted from where he sat, "and watch and learn. Newbie here has been on the ship five minutes and he already thinks he knows his elbow from his asshole."

"Just watch," José said, "watch and learn. Hopefully, this won't be your last time in a situation like this."

"You never know though," Tuari said with a laugh. "Our Luck's been pretty good lately; it's about time it ran out."

I looked at him as the colour drained from my face and all he did was smile.

"We have a battleship class ship on our rear; I can detect ion cannons, plasma cannons, lasers and numerous other forms of weaponry on her. She appears to be keeping a safe distance from us while she targets our engines," Poppy said, fingers dancing in the air in front of her.

"Tuari, how far out are we from our targeted destination?" José asked.

"A little over an hour."

José said nothing as he tapped his finger against his chin.

"Incoming hail," Poppy said, looking over her shoulder.

"Well, it would be rude not to answer it," Tuari said before José could respond.

An image flickered across the bridge viewing screen before it settled onto a picture of Gregory's face; his expressionless gaze scanned everyone on the bridge before settling on me. A slight smirk curled the corners of his lips before he nodded his head.

"Can I speak to one José Battle?" he asked.

"I am him."

Gregory turned his attention towards José and said nothing as he studied the man before him.

"Hmm, interesting, I expected something different. Nevertheless, you are in possession of property that belongs to the Xcorp organisation, and as such I have come to recover it. If you hand it over willingly and peacefully nothing shall happen to you or your crew; if you do not then I shall be forced to destroy it and cut our losses."

José said nothing as he looked towards me then slowly turned to Gregory. "What about our boy here?" he said, pointing towards me.

"I am afraid we shall be taking him as well."

"You see, that's where we may have a problem," José said, wolf-like smile appearing on his lips. "You said 'nothing shall happen to your crew' and as of right now Quinton here is part of my crew, so would you like to re-negotiate and come back with a better offer?"

Gregory said nothing as he stared at José, I saw the mask crack ever so slightly as he bit the inside of his cheek, then it was renewed again. A blank, almost bored expression washed across his face.

"I am afraid Xcorp doesn't make deals with pirates; we have a zero-tolerance policy regarding such matters."

José gave him an "I don't really give a fuck" shrug, which only caused Gregory to bite the inside of his cheek even harder.

"Look, mate," Willis said, "what's your name?"

"Gregory Goodwin."

"Fuck me," Willis said rolling his eyes. "I have never met a Gregory who wasn't a complete and utter cunt," he said to the room before addressing, my former boss: "Look, Gregory, we ain't giving up the goods unless you make a better offer than the one we're about to get from our current client. You better their price and the little data-stick is all yours."

"Does this uncouth dog talk for you?" Gregory asked José.

"Not normally, but on this occasion I think he's hit the nail right on the head. So what do you say, Gregory? Would you like to make us an offer?"

The screen viewing went blank as he cut the feed.

"Well, I guess that's a no," José said. "Tuari, divert all the power from the shields to the engines. I want full power to them until we reach our destination."

The ship rocked from side to side as incoming fire bombarded its side.

"Won't lowering the shields make us defenceless?" I asked.

"Only if they hit us," Tuari laughed as he punched and pulled levers and buttons in front of him.

I looked around the room in wild panic as the faces that returned my gaze were either joyful, crazy, sombre or happy.

"Are you telling me that for the best part of an hour, we're going to try and play chicken with an enemy ship while they try to blow us up? And the only thing you're counting on is not getting hit?"

"Yup."

"Of course, asswipe."

"It'll be OK, Quinton."

As the various answers from the crew came back my way I looked towards José and sent a pleading look his way.

"Life only starts, my friend, when danger and failure become the norm. Tuari, you know what to do—let's give this *hijo de putas* a run for his money!"

29

Fifty-seven minutes.

It felt like a lifetime.

A lifetime of *The Kennel* dodging shots, swaying hard lefts and rights, and flying through any space debris we came across in the vain hope we'd put as much distance as possible between us and Gregory's ship.

My nails had left permanent scars in the palms as I clutched my hands every time an explosion went off too close for comfort.

"We shall be approaching our destination in three minutes," Tuari said, sweat dripping from his brow.

"About time too," said Willis. "My asshole feels like it's going to be permanently closed by how hard I've been squeezing it."

"Shame we can't say the same thing for your mouth," Tuari replied.

"Well, if your flying was any better I wouldn't have to—"

"Focus," José uttered, silencing the entire room. "We are nearly at our goal."

A small blue planet appeared in the viewing screen,

growing larger by the second. It looked like a speckled marble that any kid would collect. It orbited a distant bluish sun, and the only thing that kept it company was a single moon that rotated around the planet.

"The Lady has given us instructions and coordinates where to meet her on the planet. As far as we know this planet is uninhabited but it does contain wildlife," José said.

"What's the plan?" Willis said, turning towards him.

"We land on the planet, give the stick to The Lady and allow her to deal with Xcorp. Once the stick is in her possession they become her problem."

"I don't think they'll see it like that—" I began, but Poppy cut me off.

"We may not make it to the planet; I'm detecting movement coming from behind the planet's moon."

No one spoke as Poppy enhanced the image on the screen, multiplying it so the little speck that broke away from the moon became larger and larger till it resembled a ship. Long, it was nothing but sharp angles and gun turrets. Painted the darkest black, it had two red strips that ran down its hull.

"Fuck me," Willis yelled, hand slamming on the console in front of him, "I thought we killed that prick!"

"It appears not," said José.

I looked between the pair and raised my hands in the air. "Am I missing something here?"

"The ship belongs to Arun from the Laughing Hyenas. This complicates things. This complicates things a lot," José said, stroking his chin.

"Well, it's going to get a lot more complicated, because Gregory is right up our ass," Tuari said.

I looked at the screen showing our rear and tried to

swallow. Gregory's ship was closing in on our location—and closing fast.

"What are we going to do?" I said in a panicked voice.

"Willis, Poppy, Quinton, I want you to board Gregory's ship and take the fight to the *bastardo*. Tuari and I will help as best we can, but don't expect much as we'll have our hands full with Arun."

Willis and Poppy nodded their heads as they got up from their chairs and made their way towards the exit.

"Wait, wait, wait! What do you mean attack Gregory's ship head-on? How do you expect to us to do that without a ship?"

"Don't worry, Necktie," Willis said, pulling me along, "we have something way better than a fucking ship. You wait and see!"

I looked at the little spacecraft stationed in the cargo bay while I paced back and forth. Poppy had offered me some gum to calm my nerves but it did nothing but heighten my sense of unease, as I chewed like a camel who was trying nicotine gum for the first time after giving up a three-pack-a-day habit.

"What in the actual fuck is that?" I asked, pointing to a craft no bigger than an escape pod, designed like an arrow-head with the tip of the craft reinforced with extra metal. I had a hard time seeing how we were all going to fit into the tiny vessel.

I slowly walked around it while I took in all its glory. The thing would crumble the first time they shot at it. I pushed on its outer shell and was surprised that it was sturdier than it looked. I rapped my knuckles against it and then shook my hand out, rubbing my aching knuckles.

"It's a lot more solid than it looks, ain't it?" Willis said, strapping his body with every item of weaponry he could fit on it. "It's made from a denser, rarer alloy that allows it to do its job without killing the inhabitants inside."

I wasn't convinced.

I kept walking around the little craft shaking my head and running my hands along the scars that covered its dull black surface. The metal it was made of didn't reflect any light; instead, it appeared to soak it in. I got up closer to the shell of the ship and examined it.

"What alloy or metal did you say this was made of again?"

"We didn't," said Willis. "In all honestly none of us are too sure what it's made of. We appropriated it from a science facility on one of our many travels. All we know is the thing isn't detectable on any scanners or radar, and it doesn't reflect light. Out in space it becomes almost invisible—it has the greatest cloaking device without actually having one."

"I still don't see how this little thing will do any damage to Gregory's ship."

"Why ruin the surprise—"

A siren cut Willis off and José's voice came over the speakers of the ship.

"I need all of you on the *Pit Bull* in less than two minutes!"

"Quinton, don't worry about it. It'll all work out," Poppy said, stroking my arm.

I looked at her and smiled despite myself. This was the first time we had spoken since we had slept together; there was so much I wanted to say yet didn't know how to put it in words. I opened and closed my mouth as a million things I should say popped into my mind and I dismissed them all as quickly. She smiled as she saw the struggle taking place between my ears, and she just squeezed my shoulder and walked towards the mini-ship.

"Why is this called the *Pit Bull*?" I asked.

"Because," Willis said, a manic grin showing through his ginger beard, "once it bites and locks on, it never lets go. Now shut and get on board. We have a mission to take care of."

To say the space aboard the *Pit Bull* was cramped was an understatement, but it was surprisingly clean, sleek and comfy inside.

Strapped to my seat in a shock harness, I was inside a spacesuit that came with the ship and slotted nicely on the chair I was sitting in.

We sat in a row: Poppy up front manning the ship controls, Willis in the middle and me in the rear. We were still in the cargo bay waiting for José to let us loose.

I swallowed the bile that tried to spill from my mouth as butterflies danced in the pit of my stomach. Although I wore a combat suit, I could still feel sweat collecting in the palms of my hands.

"We shall launch in ten seconds, you know the drill. Wait till I launch the cluster bombs the enemy's way and they got close enough to us, and in the melee and chaos, it's you guys' time to shine. Good luck," José said, voice coming out of the speakers.

"What's going to be happening in ten seconds?" I asked, trying to not allow my voice to quiver.

"Are you stupid? Or weren't you listening? We're going to

be launching in ten seconds, so stop asking stupid questions. Now hold on to those little raisins you call nuts and get ready for action."

"Quinton, I've dialled into your radio frequency so you're the only one who can hear me," came Poppy's voice in my ear. "Don't worry, everything will be OK. Willis hides his emotion well but he's just as scared as you."

I highly doubted that.

"When the chaos starts, just remember to breathe deeply and shoot everything that comes your way."

"Poppy, I'm not built for this... this... this bad guy stuff. I'm just a simple office worker from New-London."

There was silence on the other end for a moment or two. "There are no good guys in this story, Quinton. There only people who are trying to survive the best way they know how. That's all life really is when you think about it."

"Launch in five!" came José's voice.

"If you need to talk to me privately, switch to channel two."

"Launch in two!"

Fuck, fuck, fuck. I wasn't ready for this shit.

"Go! Go! Go!"

I felt my stomach drop and my head was pushed back as we shot out of the cargo bay and into the deep void of space.

I expected something.

Silence. Peace. Clarity. Life revelations.

What I didn't expect was me trying desperately not to shit myself while bombs exploded around me.

Poppy flew the ship with reckless abandon; she twisted

and turned the levers aiming for the enemy ship, which grew larger and larger.

Cluster bombs exploded around us while Gregory's ship fired upon *The Kennel*.

"Hold on, the ride's about to get a little bumpy!" Poppy said.

"Isn't it already?" I shouted back while I was thrown against my seat.

Willis chuckled as he slapped his thigh. "You ain't seen nothing yet."

I was still being pushed against my seat, but this time I felt a shift in gears as the speed increased and our target grew larger still.

"Wait... this thing has got no weapons, none that I could see... if it doesn't have any weapons then how—"

I left the question hanging, as no one spoke up.

The speed of the ship wasn't slowing down; in fact it was increasing.

"You're right there, Necktie, this thing has no weapons and is only good for one thing."

"Wait, wait! Hold on! How are we going to attack Gregory's ship if this thing doesn't have any weapons? Don't tell me we're going to do something stupid like ram it?"

Silence swept through the cabin while we continued on our direct course to the ship. "Because that would be stupid... I mean, ramming a ship ten times the size of us is suicide."

Again, no one said anything. The only thing I could see on the viewing screen was Gregory's ship. It now filled the whole screen. I couldn't see anything else.

"Guys, that would be stupid, right? Guys?"

We were now on a collision course with the ship. Even if we tried we couldn't avoid it—there was no going back—we were going to crash headfirst into it. I doubled my grip on my chair and wanted to close my eyes but like witnessing a horrific accident you couldn't help but look.

"Full speed ahead, Poppy!" Willis laughed as the ship picked up speed and barrelled towards our target.

We were going to die.

30

The *Pit Bull* crashed into the side of Gregory's ship with enough force to test the safety features of the shock harness that kept me secured to the seat. The front of our ship drove into the hull of Gregory's ship and just kept on going. I expected some resistance when we made contact, but the metal the *Pit Bull* was made out of was far superior to anything I had ever seen.

The front of our ship penetrated its target and kept on slicing through the metal like it was water.

Explosions flared around us as components not meant to be struck with force detonated. Fires swept over our hull but Poppy kept the accelerator down and kept on pushing it forward.

On and on we went till we finally came to a stop.

I was shaken.

I was sweaty.

But I was uninjured.

Laughter echoed around me as Willis slapped his thigh. Shoulders shaking he pointed my way, shook his head and laughed all over again.

I took the first deep breath in what felt like an age; I took another and another till I realised I was hyperventilating. I tried to lean down between my knees to suck in more oxygen, but it didn't seem to help. Fiddling for the controls that would allow my helmet to retract, I couldn't move them; my fingers felt like dead weights as I struggled and became angry that I couldn't do such a simple task. Giving up on the controls for my helmet I tried to unbuckle myself from my seat but this too proved too much of an effort.

I grabbed the harness for all I was worth and shook and yanked at it trying my best to pull it apart but failing.

Why couldn't I breathe?

Why couldn't I escape?

"Let me fucking out!"

I strained and pulled but it felt like my movements were growing weaker and weaker by the second.

"Quinton!" Someone was calling my name, but they sounded miles away.

I needed to get out of here. Coming on board this ship was a mistake. Asking to join this crew was a mistake.

"Quinton."

There it was again, that voice.

"Quinton!"

Something slapped me on the cheek and I focused wild-eyed on the face in front of me. It was Poppy. She was smiling. She stroked the side of the cheek she had hit and everything wasn't as bad as it once was.

I took in what felt like my first proper breath. It calmed my nerves. It calmed my soul.

"Breathe. That's it. Just breathe," she said, raising and lowering her hand. "It happens to some people when they have their first experience on the *Pit Bull*. It's not something most humans have experienced. You would normally need military training to get used to purposely crashing into another ship. But we haven't got the time for that. This is what they designed this ship for. A secret branch of the military built it small and compact to ram and penetrate the hull of the enemy's ship. Once there, the crew onboard could evacuate and raid their enemies. It's mainly used for stealth missions."

I could hear sirens wailing in the background as what looked like mist surrounded us.

"We are firmly inside your boss's ship. You should be able to breathe without the aid of your suit but if the oxygen drops one percent or you find yourself in a vacuum then it will reseal around your face."

"Why... why would I find myself in a vacuum?" I asked her.

"Because your bitch ass may find itself outside in space," Willis said, stepping past me. "Come on, we don't want to get pigeonholed here, as someone is bound to come looking for us sooner or later."

Poppy looked into my eyes and tapped me on the shoulder once more before she followed Willis.

I did the same but clicked my fingers and spun around looking at the Peacemaker. I picked up the shotgun and cradled it in my arms hoping against hope that I wouldn't need to use it.

Hope can kiss my ass!

Crouched low, I moved my head as another bullet blasted the wall I was crouched behind. Sparks flew from the impact and I looked back wide-eyed at Poppy, who only gave me a smile.

Willis was nowhere to be found, as he had rushed ahead of us in a fit of barely controlled enjoyment and rage.

"Where's Willis?"

Poppy gave me a shrug. "He sometimes does this. José has warned him against it, but he's like a rabid dog when we get into a conflict like this."

We could hear the distant sounds of a firefight somewhere in the ship, but I couldn't pinpoint the location.

I peeked around the corner and threw my head back as bullets came my way.

Two guards.

They were steadily walking towards us without fear of repercussion. I didn't blame them. We hadn't fired a single shot since they encountered us.

I held the Peacemaker in my hands and took in a deep breath. If I wanted this to stop then I would need to take action. There was only one way this was ever going to end—with blood on my hands, and if I thought any different then I was just lying to myself.

"Lay down your weapons and you shall not be hurt!" I shouted.

Laughter sounded down the walls as the shooting ceased. "If you were going to do anything to us, you would have done so already."

"This is your final warning—" Gunshots cut me off, followed by laughter.

"How's that for a final warning?"

I shook my head before I shoved the gun round the corridor and pumped it full of lead.

The roar the shotgun made was murderous as smoke filled the corridor.

The smoke brought silence, much as one would get after a firework show had ended.

I counted to five and peeked around the corner to see nothing but blood and corpses. I nodded my head at Poppy as I emerged into the corridor and took another tentative step forward; I walked towards the men on the floor and was about to avert my gaze but something in my soul told me not to. It would be disrespectful to do so. This was war, and in war one warrior always acknowledged the other.

My head snapped up as I heard more footsteps coming our way, and I raised the shotgun without even thinking. A group of three saw me but it was already too late—I squeezed the trigger and watched as they tried to move out of the way but it was pointless. Buckshot had peppered their bodies dropping them to the floor.

I fired once more to stop the twitching.

I looked back at Poppy, who stared at me with a look I couldn't make out, but it was gone in an instant.

We continued onwards, taking lefts and rights, never slowing down longer than was necessary.

"Where do you think Gregory is?"

"You know him better than I do," Poppy replied.

I barked a laugh and shook my head. "That man knows as little about my life as I know about his. Although it appears our lives have been intertwined for years. All I can say is—"

Gregory and a group of his goons came to a skidding halt before us as we turned a corner. Surprise graced his face for a moment, but it disappeared and a look of boredom replaced it. He smoothed down the charcoal-coloured suit that did an excellent job of hiding his bulging middle; straightening out the cuffs of his shirt he stared at me.

"Nothing to say, asshole?" I asked.

"What is there to say? I either do the job assigned to me

or someone else will take my place. I've already told you a company like Xcorp is a nation onto itself. If you think you can ever win then... more fool you."

"Why?"

"How much do you know about WW3?"

I looked at him in puzzlement, and said, "Only what they taught us in school. Global war, between the nations that always hated each other, led to a World Government that outlawed war on Earth. The destruction that took place nearly ended humanity."

"Yes, yes, but what about the birth of AI?"

"What about it?" I asked.

"AI was humanity's greatest creation, some say greater than space travel. Everyone always knew AI was coming, they just didn't know how terrifying the robots would be, how efficient they would be at killing, outsmarting and controlling human beings. They nearly became the apex predators, the rulers of Earth. So like everything else that humankind fears, they were outlawed.

"Their creation was outlawed, the designs on how to create them were destroyed, and all the creators, engineers, designers, anyone and everyone who worked on building them, were imprisoned or killed one by one."

I looked at him in disbelief.

"What, don't believe me? Nor did I to begin with. It wasn't something they taught in school and for good reason. How could anyone justify killing thousands upon thousands of people just for a dream they wanted to turn into reality? But I can assure you it happened."

"And you're telling me this because?" I asked.

"Because Xcorp has gained lost knowledge. Knowledge that could make them the dominant company galaxy-wide.

Knowledge that could even make the World Government fear tackling them."

The penny dropped.

Of course.

Why hire so much protection just to ferry me through space? What information could be so important that Xcorp would hunt me through space? Why did they want what I had so badly?

"I see you've finally cottoned on. Didn't I once mention in your appraisals what a fast learner you were?"

I gave him the finger with disdain.

"Well, if what you're telling me is true than Xcorp is fuccked!" I shouted with glee, "Once the World Government gets an inkling of what you bastards have been up to, then... heads are going to roll. If I were you Gregory, I would start looking for another job."

"It took my superiors a lot of time and effort to find out the details on how to build AI. A lot of people were killed. A lot of people were paid. So to think an insect like you would put a dent in those plans is highly laughable."

I grabbed the handle of my gun till my knuckles turned white. "You are such a selfish prick. It never occurred to you that maybe there was a reason this technology was outlawed? Countries still make and produce nuclear weapons; if that doesn't tell you something about how dangerous these things are then nothing will."

Gregory waved off the issue like an annoying fly. "We shall learn from our past mistakes. The issue lay in building a humanoid with AI abilities and allowing them the free will, allowing them the ability to make choices based on thoughts and feelings. We shall now build them with free will removed. They shall still have the same intellect, the same reasoning, but only up to a certain point.

"We shall install countermeasures or blockers if they stray too far off the beaten path."

"Countermeasures or blockers," I said, throwing my head back and laughing. "Have you dickheads given this any thought whatsoever? You sound like children playing with Pandora's Box. Free will isn't something that can be restrained. You are talking about creating new life, and new life always finds a way to flourish!"

Gregory rolled his eyes and brushed down the sleeves of his suit, in a sign I knew only too well from working with him all those years back in the office. He was done with this meeting, and it was your signal to get out.

"You know what, you pompous prick," I said, pointing my shotgun towards him, "I would rather die than see you get what you want."

"You make it sound like there was going to be another outcome," he said, confusion on his face.

Two shots were fired. Two heads exploded.

I looked in shock as two bodies from Gregory's entourage fell to the floor in a sticky mess. More shots were fired as men turned around and began firing behind them.

The scene before me became a screaming mess of chaos.

Blood splatted against the walls and brain matter landed on my cheek as I did the only thing that seemed to make sense: I squeezed the trigger of my gun in a blind panic until there were no shells left.

The smoke cleared and all I saw was dead bodies and the smiling manic face of Willis looking at me from the other end of the corridor.

I did a quick check of the bodies on the floor but failed to find the one I wanted.

Shit!

"Gregory must have escaped," I said, moving off in the only direction he could have gone.

"Where are you going?" Poppy called after me.

"I have to end this!" I said over my shoulder. "This thing is my responsibility."

"How do you work that out?" Willis shouted.

"I don't know," I said, turning around and giving them a shrug. "It sounds like something a hero would say! What do you want from me? I'm new to this."

And with that, I was gone. Living a dream many people before me and after me would always have. Running down a corridor chasing my former boss with a weapon in my hand... wait, was I the only one to ever have that dream?

Well, call me fucked up because I was about to do something I had wanted to do for a very long time.

31

I ran with everything I had.

I hadn't waited for Poppy. I hadn't waited for Willis.

I just ran with every fibre in my body, chasing down the man who had ruined my life since the first day he had entered it. He had taken everything from me, my wife, my family, but most of all he had taken my time. Time I would never get back. Time that would haunt me for the rest of my life.

I took another sharp turn and saw his sweating back in the distance. I pushed down on my heels and pointed the shotgun up and fired. As the barrel of the gun swung wildly in my hands and hit a couple of metres to the left of Gregory, I learned something valuable in that moment. I learnt that it is far harder to shoot and run than it is to just shoot standing still. He looked over his shoulder at the sound of gunfire and bared his teeth my way before he turned back around and continued at a faster clip.

I smiled.

It was the first sign of genuine emotion I had gotten

from him since I had known him.

I chased after him and entered a corridor, to see him standing at the end of it with his hands pressed against a device that stuck out from the wall. He gave me a small smile as I ran his way, which caused me to pull up short.

Something wasn't right. He was far too confident. Far too sure of himself.

"You know the one difference between me and you?" he asked me, voice bouncing off the walls.

"You're a thundercunt and I'm not?"

"No, no, Quinton. The difference between me and you is, there is none."

I stared at him looking for some smirk, some look of smugness, but I didn't find any.

"I'm being a hundred percent honest with you. There is no difference between me and you. We were both raised in a middle-class household. We both got the same grades in college—I checked, we got roughly the same grades in university, and I only started a year before you did at Xcorp. But the reason I'm here and you're not, the reason your marriage fell apart, the reason you never made it past middle management, is because of one thing.

"Desire."

I took a step back, mouth screwed up as if I had tasted something sour.

"You never desired more. You never desired a nicer house, a better life, a better job. I know you think you did, but I would watch you while you worked, always drawing on your notepads, always staring out the window, always doing something other than what you were supposed to be doing. If life doesn't give you what you want, then you take it. It's as simple as that."

"You hate your life! Don't give me that shit!"

"You think this is the end goal?" Gregory laughed as he gave me a look that said I was a simpleton' "This is just a means to an end. I am being paid more than I could dream of to take care of this problem, and after I'm done with you, a few more years in servitude to the company and I get to retire before I hit middle age.

"Then I relax and kick back on a beach and enjoy life for what it is."

I glanced down at my blood-splattered shoes and swallowed. Was I really like him? Were we really that similar? No...

"No, I'm nothing like you. I would never betray people like you. I would never do the things you did just to get ahead. I... I would never sell my soul for some stupid retirement dream of lying on a beach, when that dream may never come true. Don't you see, you're trapped. There will never be enough."

"Please spare me the fucking sermon!"

Gregory looked at me in pity as he pulled at the sleeves of his suit. "You just don't get it, do you, Quinton? In this existence, you do what you need to do to get to the top. Plain and simple. This isn't a Disney movie, this is real life and in real life, the haves take from the have-nots. First it was the leader in the tribe, then it was the king of a kingdom, then it was a dictator of a nation, now it's the board of directors of a company. That's just how life is—"

"It's not," I said, finally finding my voice. "Life may be many things but I've come to see it can be what you choose it to be, as corny as that sounds. I've done things these last few days I would never dream of, things that will haunt me for the rest of my life, but things nevertheless I chose to do; they weren't chosen for me. So in light of all of that, I will have to ask you to come with me."

"I don't think—"

"Hey, dickface, I'm the one with the gun," I said, lifting the shotgun up.

The shock on his face passed quickly but it was still a pleasure to behold.

"Look who's finally got some balls," he said, blank expression returning. "As lovely as that offer sounds, I must kindly decline it."

"Ha, I wasn't giving you a choice."

"Like I told you, Quinton, life is about the haves and have-nots, and I have already decided who I want to be," he said, taking his hand off the panel that it was placed in front of and stepping back.

I heard metal on metal before anything else.

They appeared from behind Gregory like something out of a horror movie, nothing but a skeleton frame made of metal. Their eyes blazed red like the heart of a forge, their movements were mechanical in nature, with an efficiency that no living creature would ever have. The two machines stood in front of Gregory and set their feet apart.

"I apologise. They are an unfinished product the boys in the lab have been knocking about with. They are the Model T, compared to what robotic AIs once were. They haven't got any AI mapping in them, so at the moment they are just machines I guess, but they will be more than capable of dealing with you."

I didn't intend to, but my feet took a couple of steps back as the machines' eyes focused on me.

"Goodbye, Quinton. On behalf of Xcorp, I am terminating your contract with us. If you would like a reference from us all you have to do is ask, but I'm afraid where you're going I doubt you'll need one," he said, turning away and leaving me to my fate.

I saw his back slowly leave my field of vision and I took a step forward but stopped as the machines took a step towards me. My mouth grew dry as they took another. For every step they took, I took another one back. Their gaze never wavered. Their movements were smooth. I didn't see any weapons on them, but that didn't mean they didn't have any to hand.

"Gun, idiot!" I said, berating myself as I lifted the weapon and fired at them. I nicked one in the shoulder, but they moved in a fluid motion out of the way that was part hypnotic, part terrifying. I fired again and again but missed. My unsteady hands and their movements made taking a bead on them next to impossible.

Foot-long knives erupted from their hands, answering my question of if they were armed or not.

They began picking up speed and moving towards me and I did the only thing I thought was smart, I turned tail and ran.

Apart from my ragged breathing, their metallic footsteps were the only thing I could hear. It spurred me on as I took corner after corner praying they wouldn't catch up, but knowing they would eventually—they were made out of steel and oil, while I was nothing more than muscle and bone.

Muscle and bone I hadn't kept in shape since I left University. Muscle and bone already beginning to tire with each step I took, with each sharp intake of breath that filled my lungs.

I didn't want to look behind me. I didn't want to see my death in their eyes.

I took another corner and stumbled forward, nearly falling on my hands and knees. I heard one of their knives scrape the wall I was just in front of; the stumble had saved me more by luck than anything. I righted myself and kept on moving.

I loaded shells into my shotgun, dropping more shells than I put in. Another lie from the movies: it's harder to load a gun while running than it is standing still.

Was the sound of their feet getting louder?

Shit!

I dropped and turned, feeling the wind of a blade skim the top of my head as my back hit the floor.

I saw nothing but metal in front of me.

It filled my vision. There was nowhere I could go. I pulled the trigger of the Peacemaker and was deafened as a roar escaped the end of the barrel and pushed me backwards.

I skidded along my ass as if I was being pulled along by an invisible piece of string and came to a slow stop as I looked where I had once been. The machine that had attacked me stood where it had launched the attack at me, its arm still raised in a killing blow. It stared at me with those red orb-like eyes.

It moved its gaze from me and lowered its head towards its torso.

I did the same and saw a dustbin-lid-size hole in its torso. Sparks flew and oil leaked as it swayed back and forth on its feet. It took a step forward but slipped on the oil on the floor and came crashing down on one knee. It looked up at me, the red glare from its eyes dimming by the second.

Getting back up to my feet, I slowly backed away as it swung one lazy arm my way. With a sad whine, its movements slowed down till it stopped moving and the light from behind its eyes went out.

In my haste I must have loaded an explosive shell without realising it.

Grin breaking out on my face, I was about to congratulate myself when I realised there had been two machines. I scanned the corridor but could only see the one I had destroyed.

Where did it go?

I walked backwards slowly at first, then faster and faster, and that's when I heard it.

The tell tale metal on metal.

The sound was above me and I lifted my head in time to see the thing making its way towards me by crawling along the ceiling. The knives on both its hands sunk into the ceiling, giving it a grip as the claws on its feet kept it in place while it moved.

I fired again but this time it was a normal shell. It dodged the attack by dropping to the floor and rushing towards me. I wanted to take another shot but all I could see were the knives attached to its arms and I knew I wasn't a good enough shot to make it count.

That's what I told myself anyway as I turned tail and ran for my life.

My legs didn't have the same pep they once did. They burned with each step I took. It was getting harder and harder to breathe and I could see dark spots in the corner of my vision. I wasn't a doctor, but I sure as hell knew it wasn't a good sign.

"Help, he—" I tried to call for help, but the words stuck in my sandpaper-like throat.

Fuck, I was out of shape!

Where the hell were the other two? It felt like I had run for the best part of ten minutes without seeing hide or hair of them. I tried to remember the route I had taken to get to where I was but it was a pointless exercise; my brain was starved of oxygen and I just wasn't thinking right, I bounced into a wall and winced as I felt something pop in my shoulder and kept on going.

The metal-on-metal tapping drove me crazy. It frayed at my nerves. It was the siren call to my death—the closer it got the sooner death's hands would fall upon me.

I saw a flash on the wall to my right and gulped as the machine ran along the wall beside me. I dived forward as it swiped a blade towards me.

Coming back up to my feet, I twirled around and fired a shot before turning back around and continuing to run.

I didn't wait and see if I had hit it. I didn't have time.

I just kept running and waited.

Waited till I heard it again.

Waited with bated breath to see if that sound would echo behind me.

After a handful of seconds I grew hopeful and smiled, then I heard the dreaded tap, tap, tap and I knew I had failed.

I looked behind me and knew I shouldn't have but I wanted to see if I had hit it. That was my mistake.

Eyes glowing red it slashed my way and forced me to dodge out of the way while my body was still halt turned, I tripped over my own feet and came crashing down face first on the floor, sliding along my stomach.

I came to a stop and turned on my back to see the machine leap in the air and descend towards me. The point of its blade flashed in the light as it came my way. Everything happened in slow motion.

I saw it approach me and I knew I couldn't do anything to stop it. Couldn't do anything to change the fact I was going to die.

I thought back to everything I still wanted to live for and smiled as I closed my eyes and waited for my death to come.

32

But it never came.
I held my breath.
I could hear my heartbeat but nothing else.

I held my breath.

I could feel the cold metal floor against my back and nothing else.

I held my breath and waited for my death to come but it never did.

Opening my eyes slowly I saw nothing but metal.

I opened them up fully and saw the machine's blade inches from my heart; it had been stopped by another blade blackish-grey in colour. I took in a deep gulp of air and traced the knife that had saved my life all the way up a slender muscular arm; above that was a face that took my breath away.

A dark stain of hair covered one eye, while full ruby lips set in a firm and determined line spoke of the person's displeasure.

Poppy had saved my life and the fire in her eyes spoke of her anger.

For a moment I thought the anger was directed at me, but her stare was directed straight ahead at the machine that had tried to kill me. The machine stared at this new threat and slowly took a step back as it tried to re-evaluate how dangerous this new threat was.

I shuffled back as Poppy stepped in front of me, and I got up to my feet.

Poppy spun the knives in her hand lazily around and around while she and the machine circled each other.

"Poppy, you need to be careful, you can't fight—"

Poppy held up her hand stopping me mid-flow and smiled back at me. "It's OK, Quinton, I've got this. This is what I was born to do."

My heart stopped at that moment.

It was stupid to think this woman who I had barely known a handful of days could have this effect on me, but I'm ashamed to say it did. I felt nothing but a warm rush through my body as I returned the smile she gave me, without even trying.

She was beautiful and I was—I shook my head and concentrated on the fight at hand.

They were still both circling each other like two big cats. Poppy threw her knives between each hand, catching them and feinting towards the machine to gauge its reaction. It moved back out of range and mimicked her movements, stabbing high then going low.

Poppy's face showed no hint of emotion. It was warm, almost peaceful.

They circled once more then met in the middle amongst a clash of blades that sent sparks in the air. They parted ways and came at each other again, dancing just out of range, ducking, slicing, trying to find a spot that would cause just the right amount of damage.

As Poppy attacked and defended I watched not knowing how she could win. She was only flesh and blood while the machine she was fighting had none of the concerns she did. It didn't tire. It didn't lose concentration. It had been assigned one mission and it was going to complete it to the best of its ability.

Poppy dropped into the splits as the machine swung for her head and she sliced the wires attached to its knee joint, forcing it to leap backwards. It stumbled backwards unsteadily and she leapt forward pushing her advantage, but it was a mistake as the thing faked left and sliced her across the shoulder.

I moved forward as I saw red seep through her top but she held out her arm, once again stopping me in my tracks.

"Didn't I tell you I've got this?" she said, smiling my way.

I lifted my hands up in an apology and backed up as the pair continued their fight.

The robot moved back and forth but its movements weren't as slick as they had once been. Blackish fluid squirted from the knee joint Poppy had hacked at and now it stumbled as it tried to place weight on the injured leg.

Poppy leapt back as it lunged towards her once again but she kicked out the damaged leg, forcing the machine onto one leg. It swiped at her with its bladed arms but she knocked them to the side scoring a hit across the thing's face, damaging one of its eyes. The light behind the damaged orb blinked on and off before it went completely out.

The robot stared her way with one good eye remaining.

My heart was in my mouth as I watched the bloodied area on Poppy's shoulder spread out and grow. I wasn't a doctor, but I sure as hell knew that wasn't a good sign. The sooner this ended the better it would be.

With a burst of speed, the robot was on the attack again, this time slashing high and low as it looked for an opening to secure a killing strike. Sparks flew as Poppy defended against the barrage of limbs that came her way. She back-flipped away from an uppercut that sliced a strand of her hair, and landed in a crouch before she leapt forward once again.

Her blades scored marks against the torso of the machine, but they weren't deep enough to cause any real damage.

She leapt out of the way as a blade came her way and embedded itself into the wall behind her. Her blade flashed forward, and she sliced through some of the wires on the robot's arm. Fluid squirted into the air and landed by my feet where it hissed and sizzled.

I stepped back as metallic fumes hit the back of my throat.

I looked up and marvelled as the battle still raged.

The robot had now one damaged leg and one damaged arm, but it didn't feel pain. It would just keep on going until she was destroyed for good.

I gritted my teeth and lifted my shotgun as I saw the heavy breaths Poppy was taking. Somehow she was winning the fight but it was coming at a cost. Her face was covered in sweat, her brow furrowed in concentration. I could see the telltale signs of fatigue starting to take its toll.

Her movements weren't as crisp. Her strikes failed to have the same pop.

Shotgun on shoulder I tried to get a good aim, but it was impossible to do so without hitting Poppy. The Peacemaker wasn't a surgical weapon where I could fire it and know what I would hit for sure. It relied on maximum damage spread over a certain area.

I wanted to help. I wanted to save her but I didn't see how I could.

The robot went in for one more strike with its good arm but Poppy defended against it, catching it with both her blades. A roundhouse kick came towards her midsection, which she defended, but a blade shot out from the foot of the machine stabbing her in her side.

I cried out in surprise but she simply grunted in pain and held onto the foot before driving the point of one of her blades deep underneath the robot's chin.

The robot shook and sparked as she gritted her teeth and drove the blade deeper and deeper till the hilt of the weapon was the only thing that could be seen. They stayed like that for what felt like an eternity then the light behind the machine's one remaining eye slowly dimmed and finally died completely.

Poppy pulled her weapon out and staggered backwards as the machine collapsed to the floor.

I rushed towards her and caught her as she fell and slowly lowered her to the floor. The suit she wore was a mass of red and I couldn't take my eyes off it.

No one could surely live with so much blood outside of their body.

I went to undo her suit but she grabbed my hand and slowly shook her head; I stroked the side of her face brushing her hair out of her eyes.

"I need to see what the damage is," I said.

"Are you a doctor?"

"No," I replied, puzzled.

"Then you can't help me. You may do more damage than good."

Sadness crossed my face as I felt hopelessness wash over

me. Here was someone I cared about and once again one I couldn't do anything for.

I was more of a burden than a help.

"I'm sorry," I whispered.

"Whatever for?"

"I'm sorry I couldn't save you when it counted the most, I'm sorry I got you involved in all of this, I'm sorry—"

She began to laugh softly like a chime, then as the laughter grew and grew she allowed her head to fall back as if she couldn't contain the torrent that poured from her soul.

I watched her in confusion, allowing her to finish.

"You are the only person in existence who would apologise for being kidnapped against their will. I hate to burst your bubble but this has nothing to do with you; you were just the person on the ship who had possession of what we wanted. It could have been anyone else in the universe."

I tried to hide the hurt feelings that crossed my face but failed.

"That doesn't mean," she said, stroking my face, "I am not grateful it was you on board that ship. I am. I am happy it was you we kidnapped and not some other idiot. I am happy I didn't kill—"

I leaned in and kissed her for everything I was worth, melting against the softness of her lips.

I pulled away and looked down at her. "You had me at kidnapped," I laughed before I leaned in and kissed her for what felt like a few seconds, but probably was longer.

A light cough sounded behind us but we ignored it.

It got louder as the minutes ticked past until the unmistakable sound of an angry Irishman erupted behind us. "Will you two assholes get a move on! We ain't got all day for you two lovebirds to be humping on the floor. That dickhead boss of Quinton's has launched an escape pod towards the location where we are going to meet The Lady.

"José has fought off that knob-cheese Arun as best as he can, but he's saying some of Arun's forces have made it onto the planet. He's on the planet now and needs some backup so we'd best be moving."

I pulled away from Poppy and looked deep into her eyes before kissing her lightly on the lips.

"How do we get to José's location?" I asked, turning towards Willis.

He looked at me and shrugged his shoulders, both his pistols still in his hands.

"Wow, thanks for the help."

"Look, I don't make the plans; I just fuck up our enemies."

I rolled my eyes and helped Poppy to her feet. She gently pushed me away. She twisted and turned with something of a slight grimace on her face.

"I don't think the blade did any real damage," she said, feeling her side. "I think it's only a flesh wound."

I looked at her skeptically but kept my reservations to myself. This wasn't the time to let my feelings be known, and I could hardly come across as the overly protective boyfriend inasmuch as she had just saved my ass, while I sat by the sidelines and watched. I knew she was strong but there was only so much punishment one human body could take.

"OK, if we need to get down to the planet I guess we borrow this ship and haul ass down there. I don't think my former boss will mind as he has just fired me without giving me my severance pay. So I think we'll call this even."

They both looked at me with expressions I couldn't decipher.

"What?" I asked.

"Nothing," Poppy began. "It's just—"

"We are just surprised a wet-behind-the-ears whelp like yourself came up with such an illegal and not to mention amazing plan. I've gotta give you some points for style."

"Well, technically, it's not illegal as I am still a Xcorp employee for the next thirty days even though I have been fired. As per my contract in the event of termination by either parties, there needs to be a cooling-off period of thirty days, which—"

"You know what! I take back those fucking points I gave you," Willis said, walking away. "Come on, José needs our help. Less talking, more walking."

33

The bridge of the ship was empty.

It was three times the size of *The Kennel's*, with glass that surrounded us on all sides offering us sweeping views of space. Polished metals covered all the surfaces and leather chairs that begged to be sat on rested in front of consoles.

The whole area had the feel of a showroom.

"Well, la de fucking da! Will you look at all this shit! The sweet baby Jesus would be turning in his grave, if he could see what sort of excess and money was being wasted by these fat cats."

I ignored Willis and made my way to one bank of controls, which had an array of buttons, instruments and controls that blinked and flashed my way. I tried to find a button or control I recognised, but I had no idea what I was looking at.

Willis stood beside my elbow and whistled softly' "Get to it then."

I gave him the stink-eye and returned my gaze to the panel, lost for words.

"Get out of the way, Willis," Poppy said, moving him to one side, as she began pressing and twisting dials, but nothing happened. "It appears all the controls are locked. I can't access them, which means we are sitting ducks."

I racked my brains over what to do when an idea came to me. "Is there any way I can input my security details into the ship database? Most Xcorp devices need to scan an employee before the device can be used."

They both looked at me as if I was crazy.

"What?" I asked defensively.

"Do you also need to tell your masters when you need to take a piss as while?"

"Well, I mean it's just standard policy that all staff need to clock in and out of the toilets otherwise people could just spend—ah, fuck off!"

"I think I've found what you're looking for," Poppy said, drawing my eye to what looked like a slightly raised palm reader. "Place your palm on here and it should recognise you."

I did as I was asked, and felt a slight vibration through my palms as the displays on the consoles came to life.

"Alright," Poppy said, clicking her neck, "let's see what this baby can do."

The planet we were meant to meet The Lady on was fast approaching.

The once blue ball the size of a marble I had seen back on *The Kennel* was now so large it filled the whole viewing screen of the ship. I could see the whirls of blue were mixed with greens and browns, almost as if they were finger smudged by a painter.

It looked beautiful to behold but the space around it was clustered with signs of battle. Bits of ships floated aimlessly in the void, while bodies frozen solid flew past our screens.

The Kennel was nowhere to be seen, but the same couldn't be said for Arun's ship. It floated on its side, gaping hole exposed to space, metal and debris surrounding it.

"Looks like José fucked Arun's shit up before he made it to the planet. Any signs of life on the vessel?" Willis asked.

"There appears to be," Poppy replied.

"Let's blow the—"

"No," I said firmly, "we don't have time, plus José is facing two enemies down there. The remainder of Arun's forces and Gregory. We need to keep on moving."

Willis stared my way but I refused to lower my gaze. He turned away grumbling under his breath.

"Full speed ahead then," Poppy said, increasing the speed.

The planet fast approached us, growing larger by the second.

I had travelled off-world for work many times, but it was always in some commercial ship in the budget seats with no windows and not enough legroom for a five-year-old child. This was my first time seeing a planet while we were coming into its atmosphere.

It took my breath away. I tried to formulate some kind of response but couldn't.

I caught Poppy giggling at me while she watched me out of the corner of her eye.

"Sights like that is why I believe in religion," Willis said, looking up at the screen. "This is just too perfect to be created by chance. To be created by random. A divine hand had to create everything we see around us so that just looking up at the stars at night inspired man to want to learn more, do more, grow beyond his physical and mental limits till he became like a god himself.

"People mock religion yet if it weren't for the faith humans had in a higher power then we would have never set foot on other worlds."

I allowed Willis's words to sink in and looked at him with newfound respect. Maybe I had judged the foul-mouthed ginger Irishman a tad harshly.

I had just returned my attention to the viewing screen when the ship shook violently under my feet and threw me halfway across the bridge. Dazed and confused, I stared up at the ceiling while I tried to blink away the white dots that had formed before my eyes. Getting up to my feet I looked around me and saw that Willis and Poppy had somehow remained standing.

"How the fuck did you two manage that?"

Poppy smiled in my direction and said, "After your first ten ship battles, crashes and the like, you get used to staying on your feet."

Another shudder tore through the ship but this time I stayed standing.

"What is going on?" Willis yelled.

Poppy's fingers danced in front of her while she nibbled her bottom lip. Face masked in shock she began to move between consoles, expression growing graver by the second.

"It looks like Quinton's authorisation triggered some kind of self-destruct that is breaking up the ship piece by piece."

They both turned my way, anger simmering on their faces.

"Look," I said holding my hands up, "you wanted the ship to get moving and that's what I did—how did I know they had removed my clearance from the database?"

"Maybe when your cunt of a boss tortured you!"

"Yeah, in hindsight I should have seen this coming, but you live and learn, right? Right, guys? Guys?"

They both turned away from me as Poppy kept on pushing buttons.

Another violent shudder had me grabbing for something to keep me upright.

"There goes the second engine. We're down to two from four."

"Well, at least that's something..."

Less than friendly faces turned towards me.

"I mean, we've still got two engines; think of the glass being half full, guys," I said, looking from face to face.

Another violent shudder swept through the floor underneath my feet.

"We're down to one," Poppy said, her tone flat.

The planet was coming towards us much faster than I would have liked. Not knowing anything about entering a planet's atmosphere still I knew damn well this wasn't good.

"Pop, how likely can we make a safe landing with no engines?"

Willis looked at me as if I were a fool and shook his head with a laugh. "I'll answer this one, Poppy, because Sir fucking Einstein here is too stupid to comprehend what is about to happen. We are travelling at seventeen thousand and five hundred miles per hour with no engines to stabilise our descent, which means we are basically just free falling into a planet's atmosphere.

"Once we enter said planet's atmosphere that's when the fun really starts—the ship will spin wildly, with us unable to do anything to stop it. We shall be tossed from pillar to post, where we shall either lose consciousness or die from internal bleeding. Hopefully, our deaths come soon, so we aren't alive when the ship crashes to the ground like a fiery comet.

"So, dickface, is that a clear enough picture of what sort of safe landing we are going to get?"

I bit the inside of my cheek as I tried to think of something to help. I hadn't come this close just to die in a fiery ball. I would not allow Gregory to win. I would not allow him to have the last laugh.

"Poppy, can you at least point the ship in the general direction José is located on the planet?"

"I guess, but I don't see how that's going to—"

"The ship we used to board this one, the *Pit Bull*, is made of a special alloy which allows it to ram into other ships; that means it can withstand a fuck ton of punishment without it getting destroyed. I think our best bet is to point this ship towards the general direction of José and board the *Pit Bull* and hope for the best."

Willis and Poppy looked at each other and shrugged.

"Could work."

"Fucking best thing I can think of."

"For this plan to work," said Poppy, working between consoles, "I'll have to stay onboard the bridge as long as possible, so I can course-correct the ship to the best of my abilities. You two make your way to the ship, I'll be along as soon as I can."

"Fuck that! I'm not going anywhere," I said, coming to stand next to her.

She looked at me with a smile, "Quinton, I know you want to help but—"

I kissed her on the lips. "I'm staying. Willis, you make your way to the *Pit Bull* and make sure everything is ready for us because we'll be coming in hot."

Willis looked between the pair of us and shook his head. "Bat shit crazy, the both of you."

I watched him depart and turned towards Poppy, who was busy concentrating on the consoles in front of her. I looked up and could see that any minute we would pass through the planet's atmosphere; her brow furrowed in frustration.

"What's wrong?"

"I'm trying to pinpoint José's location but it's moving everywhere," she said, as another shudder tore through the ship. I didn't need to ask what it meant.

"It doesn't have to be to the exact mile, Pop! Just get us as close as you can to his general direction!"

"If I do this wrong then we could be out by a mile or two."

I grabbed her and turned her towards me. "Are you kidding me? A mile or two? Pop, I don't care if we're a hundred miles away, just hurry up and point this thing in some sort of direction so we can get going."

The ship shook as it entered the atmosphere and I grabbed her by the arm and pulled her away. She resisted my movements and shocked me with how strong she was; it was like moving a statue.

She tapped in a few more instructions then nodded my way. We exited the bridge at a full sprint and had to leap over a piece of falling debris from the ceiling.

I moved as fast as I could but movement was becoming difficult, as the ship shook and shuddered, throwing my footsteps off and causing me to slam into the walls that surrounded me.

"The suit you're wearing has clamps on the bottom of your feet, we use them when we need to walk in Zero-G—activate them!"

I did as I was told and felt my feet instantly stick to the floor. It made running harder but at least now I was moving in a straight line.

"I hope you know the way!" I said, legs pumping.

Poppy smiled but said nothing as she sprinted ahead of me. I tried to catch up but she was setting a pace I couldn't match.

"Hurry up, slowpoke, or I'm going to leave you behind!"

We kept on running as the ship collapsed around us, she leading the way and me trying to keep up. She moved around falling debris like a cat while I did my best to take the blows I got on body parts I could live without.

"We are nearly there," she said, pointing to the *Pit Bull*.

It lay up ahead. Willis stood at its entrance, waving us onward with a manic grin plastered on his face.

Heads down we sprinted for all we were worth.

Looking up I saw a piece of the ship's ceiling fall towards Poppy; her gaze was locked on the *Pit Bull*. She failed to recognise the threat. Deactivating the clamps on the bottom of my feet I sprinted forward and jumped, pushing her out of the way. I hit her square in the back and we tumbled forward out of harm's way.

Dazed, she looked at me in shock, then her eyes lit up when she realised what I had done.

"You shouldn't—"

"No time!" I said, helping her to her feet and pushing her forward.

We were within spitting distance of our ship. I was riding high on my acts of bravery and heroism. Maybe that was why I failed to see the exposed electric wire that swung in from my left and slapped me on my face.

I had expected to feel pain; instead, it felt like insects were crawling on my skin. A tingling went through my body as my legs grew numb and weak, and I fell forward, my face slammed onto the floor and my vision darkened.

But that wasn't the worst of it. What felt like water began trickling down my leg.

Oh, God!

I had peed myself!

This was the only thought that kept spinning around my head as I lost my grip on the little consciousness I had.

34

I woke up to the feeling of being on a roller-coaster.
I thought I was dreaming at first but when another jolt threw me to the side I slowly opened my eyes. Flashing red lights flared around me. I saw Willis's head in front of me and Poppy in front of him trying to battle the controls as best as she could.

I was back inside the *Pit Bull*.

How did that happen?

All I could remember was falling, falling and being shocked within an inch of my life.

I was thrown against the harness that strapped me in and held on as I was pushed back in my seat. My vision was still blurry as I looked about in some sort of half daze.

"This is going to be tight!" yelled the voice of Poppy in the distance. Why did she sound so far away?

"Do the best you can!"

"I don't know how close we'll land to José, but everyone within a hundred-mile radius is going to see us coming in to land so the element of surprise has well and truly been lost."

"Don't fucking worry about that. Just make sure we survive this shit. Oh, heavenly Father, I pray you guide our landing safe and true with your beautifully manicured hands. I know you have enough on your plate with you looking after the universe and whatnot, but if you can see it in your heart to—"

"Where are we?" I asked.

"Where do you think, dickface?"

"I know we're in the *Pit Bull*, but I thought we would have landed already, or more importantly I thought I would be dead."

"Well," said Willis, speaking over his shoulder, "sorry to disappoint you on both counts, and thank you very much in interrupting me during my period of prayers. I always knew you were a selfish cun—"

"Hold tight! We're coming in to land," said Poppy.

"I thought we were crashing?" I asked.

"Now is not the time, Quinton!"

I held onto the straps with a rock climbers grip as the world around me turned upside down. My body banged against the sides of my chair and I gritted my teeth as my stomach felt like it was going to come out of my mouth.

What had I gotten myself into?

I shut my eyes and said a silent prayer to the universe that it would get me out of this situation in one piece.

A bone-shattering crash filled my ears as I was thrown up from my seat but didn't get very far as the straps held me in place and slammed me back down with a thump. It sounded like the world around me was coming to an end as I heard nothing but metal fighting against earth.

It carried on like that for what felt like an eternity before silence stole everything around me.

No one said anything. No one breathed. We all kept as

silent as possible while we enjoyed the simple pleasure of just being alive.

"Well, fuc—"

"Willis, no," I said, quietly leaning my head against my chair. "Just... no. Let's just all be quiet and enjoy the silence for what it is."

Willis said nothing as we all sat in our seats and allowed what we had just gone through to sink in, but I knew the silence was too good to be true. "Oooo, is pissy pants getting upset? We wouldn't want you to pee all over yourself again. Can you believe he pissed himself, Poppy? Good thing you carried him to the ship because if he was with me I would have left his pissy ass on that Xcorp ship to die."

As Willis continued talking to Poppy, the only other woman who I had slept with apart from my wife in the last fifteen years, I felt my face getting redder and hotter by the second.

Fuck me...

I had survived being shot at, tortured, beaten, and I had just been on a ship that had crash-landed on another planet, but I would go through all of that again if this conversation never happened.

"Come on, pissy drawers, let's go and help the captain," said Willis, slapping me on the shoulder as he walked past.

Sideways rain lashed against my body as I held a hand up and surveyed the surrounding scenery.

Water was everywhere as far as I could see. An ocean stretched out endlessly to my left, and varying sizes of lakes were embedded in the landscape to my right. The land around the lakes was marshy with flowering reeds that came in different hues of pink to red. I stood on top of a hill and stared out at the foreign land before me.

Turning back I looked upon the crash site we had created.

The groove in the earth the Xcorp ship had created would be seen for miles. Like a hand being dragged to hell, it had clawed the earth. Bits of the ship were scattered here and there for miles until it had finally come to rest in a heap. Poppy had successfully detached the *Pit Bull* from it and had piloted the last section of our journey on pure grit, stubbornness and luck. We had come to a stop a long way from the initial crash but we were pushing a swift pace because our landing would no doubt welcome unwanted visitors.

Willis was some way up ahead while Poppy and I were bringing up the rear.

"How close are we to José's location?" I asked.

Poppy checked her wrist then scanned the terrain before checking the computer on her wrist again. "Not far. We're closer than I thought we would be, give or take a handful of miles. We should meet up with him in the next hour. It all depends on how fast we can traverse this terrain."

I nodded my head, allowing the rain and wind to push it back down.

We continued in silence until a thought that had been bothering me since we landed finished pricking the grey matter of my brain.

"I never thanked you for saving my life."

"It was nothing really," she said, shooing my comment away with her hand.

"Not from where I'm standing. You could've just as easily left me behind. But you didn't. Even if it hurts my ego to admit you had to pick me up and carry me to safety, you did something most people wouldn't in a time of crisis, so for that, you have my heartfelt thanks and I'm in your debt until I can next pay it back."

She gave me one of her heartwarming smiles and nodded.

"And by the way," I said, my face going red, "about the whole pee thing—"

"Don't mention it. Don't bring it up. It never happened."

"Because you know it's not something I've ever done before and—"

"Quinton," she said, cutting me off, "it really changes nothing between us. Okay?"

"Okay," I said softly.

We continued on for another hour or so, my feet dragging behind me. My body ached. My stomach was empty. My head hurt.

No doubt when I finally got a chance to rest, if I got a chance to rest, I would feel the hundred other things my adrenaline was masking. I looked around me once more and marvelled at where I was. This time two weeks ago I was in a grey cubicle, debating what font I should use for my meeting with HR, a meeting that I was so zoned out of, all I could think about was whether I should have that last doughnut in the canteen, while I poked at my ever-growing stomach.

But here and now, on this rain-swept planet, all those thoughts seemed so trivial it made me smile.

"You know when you guys had first kidnapped me, I hated your guts. Who were you to take me out of my comfortable routine, to upheave me from a life I had created? Yes, a life that was miserable and unfulfilled, but a life nevertheless. I hated you guys beyond words, but strangely, I must also thank you guys for unchaining me and giving me my life back. Giving me hope.

"If you hadn't come along when you did then... I would have died of a heart attack, or worse, of old age in some retirement home with no one willing to visit me."

Poppy said nothing as up ahead Willis turned around and looked our way. She rechecked her wrist and pointed ahead of her and gave him a firm nod.

"Sometimes the worst thing that happens to us in life turns out to be the greatest thing that could ever happen.

"I gave up living before I met the crew. I was just living off momentum. Living like a wild animal. But the crew changed all that. They gave me hope. Then I met you and..." She allowed the sentence to be left unsaid, but the way her cheeks blushed and she turned away from me sparked something in my heart that made me take her hand and give it a small squeeze.

She returned the gesture and I pulled my hand away with a smile on my face.

"The funny thing is," I said, staring at the surrounding landscape, "this is not how I envisioned my life turning out when I was growing up. I wanted to be an artist. I wanted to be a painter. I wanted to travel the stars and paint things people have never seen before, paint on different worlds, different landscapes, capture images from far-flung worlds, dangerous places, places that most people have never visited before, but—I didn't do any of that. I just... gave up on my dreams."

"You wouldn't be the first person in history to do that, nor the last," Poppy said, rechecking her wrist again.

"I—"

"Will you two stop going on!" shouted Willis, turning towards us. "We get it! Everyone's had a hard fucking life and have made choices they're not happy or proud of, but for cunting sake, if I have to hear about it for a moment longer I'm going to put one pistol in my mouth and another to my nuts so I make sure I'm dead and there is no chance of my offspring being born and having to listen to the same shit as I do.

"Now by my count, it would be quicker if we got off this path and made our way through the marshes—"

A stag-like animal stopped in our path and stared our way with four sets of eyes. The antlers on its head had flowers growing along different sections. The flowers opened and closed slowly, like the rhythm of a steady heartbeat. With a stomp of its hoof, it took off over the marshes in the direction we were about to head off in.

But it never got very far.

We saw a splash. We saw a reptilian tail. We heard a cry. Then the stag-like animal was gone.

We all stared at the patch of marsh where the animal had been taken until a piece of antler floated to the surface.

I turned to Willis with a smile and said, "After you."

About to say something he gritted his teeth, turned on the spot and walked away.

"I guess we're going the long way around then?" I shouted to a retreating back. It gave me the finger.

35

The rain failed to lessen, but had in fact increased with the added benefit of sleet.

Soaked from head to toe, I had given up the effort of trying to stay dry. We had been walking for what felt like hours when we finally saw two figures up ahead of us.

One sat on a moss-covered rock with an unlit soggy cigar hanging from the side of his mouth; red shades covered his eyes and water dripped from the end of his nose as a hand rested on the handle of a revolver big enough to put down an elephant. The other stood beside the first. He was a towering figure who wore a hood that hid his features, with a machine gun as big as me nested down by his foot.

"Gland to see you, *mi amigos*," José said, eyes ranging over us.

"We would have been here sooner, but some pussy," Willis said staring my way, "was afraid to get his feet wet."

"If you mean, not venturing into an unknown marsh on an unknown planet then yeah, I thought it would be smarter to stick to solid ground where we can see our feet. Sorry for thinking with my head."

About to say something Willis was cut off by Poppy. "What's the situation?"

José sighed heavily as he brushed the water that had collected on his dome. "If I knew what a pain in the ass this job would be, then I would have never taken it, but that really wasn't an option to start with, now was it?

"I destroyed most of Arun's ship but he did a good number on the old girl. I had to look for somewhere to land *The Kennel* as he and his e*stúpido* friends were chasing me all the way down; I managed to shake them off before I hid the ship."

"Think Arun's still alive?" I asked. "Could just be his men looking to finish what they started."

"Has to be," Willis replied. "If he was dead then his men would scatter; his being alive is the only thing keeping them together after suffering such heavy losses. Loyalty isn't to be found in Arun's crew."

I nodded my head at the logic of his words.

"Gregory's still alive. He escaped. It was my fault."

José looked at me like a wolf sensing its prey was nearby. "No worry. He shall get what's coming to him in due time; right now we need to make our way towards the meeting point."

"Did you grab the data-stick?" I asked.

"Be but a fool's errand if I didn't."

"How far?"

"Another half an hour at best," José said, turning his head and looking at the trail that continued for some distance. We all followed his gaze lost in our own thoughts till a snigger escaped Tuari as he smirked and pointed his forefinger towards Willis's beard.

"How does your beard become even more ginger when wet?"

"First off," Willis said, talking in a measured tone, "moisture brings out the natural tones in my hair giving it this vibrant look you see. Secondly, get your dirty black-nailed fucking finger out of my face! Before I break it off and shove it up your ass! You ass-mongrel."

Smirk only increasing, Tuari said, "Is my finger dirty? Oh, I may have forgotten to wash it after scratching my ass but don't worry, when I last made a meal for you it was just as black, as I know how you like some extra seasoning."

Willis took a step forward and still the finger remained.

"I thought I told you to get—"

"Pull my finger."

"How old are you, don't you think I know that joke?"

"Trust me," said Tuari, "it's a new joke. Pull my finger."

Willis rolled his eyes as he latched onto Tuari's finger and pulled. Nothing happened and Willis looked confused till Tuari gave a belly-shaking burp and blew it in Willis's direction.

"Told you it was a new joke," Tuari giggled, before taking off at a run.

"I'll kill you! I can still taste it!"

"I guess we'd better get a move on then and finish this thing," José said with a shake of the head, as he got off the boulder he'd been sitting on and made his way in the direction they went.

I couldn't have agreed more. I silently looked up at the trail as the winds howled and the rain beat a drum against the ground I stood on.

My breath billowed out before me as I tried to control my breathing. The end was nearly in sight. After that... God only knew, but for now, I wanted to get this over and done with once and for all.

Unlike the last few hours, which had passed like days when we had first arrived, the last half an hour had seemed like minutes.

One second we were talking with José and Tuari back at the boulder they sat at, the next I was lying flat on my stomach hidden amongst some bushes alongside Poppy and Willis, while José and Tuari were situated some way to our left behind another row of bushes.

José wanted us to scout the rendezvous point before contacting The Lady, which meant crouching down in the mud and waiting. He had told us we were early, although I couldn't quite believe how. The rain still hadn't let up, but it mattered little as the adrenaline coursing through my veins left me numb to it all.

The spot where we were meeting The Lady was on a patch of grass that dropped over a sheer cliff face. I took in the amazing views of the surrounding ocean as I breathed in the salt air.

We had seen no sign of Gregory or Arun, but that didn't mean they were not waiting for their chance to pounce.

"What do you think, José?" Willis whispered into the comms we were all linked up to.

The only response we got was the howling wind as the minutes passed us by. Willis rolled his eyes to the sky and gestured to the heavens, while we continued waiting.

"He gets like this sometimes," Poppy said, wiggling up to me, "before a big event or mission when a lot is on the line. It's like he's so focused he blocks everything else out. When the time's right he'll let us know."

I sure as hell hoped so. I still didn't know how this was going to turn out. What would Gregory do once we gave the data-stick to The Lady? Would I also have to watch my back from attack from Arun and his goons? Would I always be running from the law?

But the one thing that kept coming back to me time and time again was whether it was right to allow what was on that data-stick out into the wider world—much less give it to a bunch of hardened criminals who would use the knowledge to their advantage. If The Lady was everything she was cracked up to be then what would a monster like that do with the knowledge we had?

"Do you think this is the best thing to do?"

Poppy looked at me with a raised eyebrow and said, "What do you mean?"

"I mean, I've heard stories about these things. Humanoid AIs. The first history lesson I ever heard was about the ruthlessness of their nature, how they were looking for a way to eradicate the human species off the face of the Earth. It was only pure luck that we won against them, pure luck they somehow didn't find a way off-world. If the stories are true then their creation is the greatest and worst thing humankind have ever done.

"They're in some ways more destructive than any nuclear weapon and more advanced than any spaceship that crosses the stars."

Poppy said nothing as she stared out ahead of her. Her hair stuck to the side of her face.

"Do you think they were that... scary? Mankind has a history of demonising what they do not understand."

"What's not to understand? They were machines built for death. Machines that had all the intelligence of man yet none of his weakness."

"I guess..." she said, but she didn't sound convinced.

"My point is, if even some of those stories are true then is it the wisest thing to give that kind of knowledge to this Lady person? Shouldn't we at least try to destroy—"

"It's time," came José's voice over the comms. "She's here."

36

José rose from the spot he was crouched behind and slowly descended towards the meeting spot with Tuari close on his heels. Both held their guns pointed at the ground.

She came out of the mist like the angel of death itself. A small petite frame dressed like an eighteen-century doll walked up the path. A frilly red petticoat matched the skirt that bowed out before her. She clutched a little red umbrella that did its best to fight off the elements. Two bodyguards flanked her. They carried no visible weapons.

José looked up towards our spot and Willis began to move. "Well, I guess it's time for us to make a move."

"But he didn't say anything," I said, getting up confused.

"The longer you're with a crew, the more you understand the unspoken things. There will be situations where you may not be able to speak, so a look is all you can give. A look may very well save your life one day," Willis said, moving past me and walking down.

I followed close behind with Poppy alongside me until we reached the group.

José gave us a nod as I turned my gaze towards the newcomers. At first glance, the guards appeared to be ordinary thugs but on closer inspection, I could see they were much more. Their eyes shifted to every vantage spot that surrounded us with the readiness of trained soldiers. One hand stayed underneath their coats at all times and they were never more than a couple of feet away from their boss.

Oceans of the darkest blue.

That was the only thing I noticed as I stared The Lady's way. Her eyes drank me in and I found myself drowning in them. They didn't seem right on her. They didn't match the petite body. They didn't match the doll-like dress. They belonged to a predator. A monster only found in the deepest, darkest parts of the ocean. A monster who would be at home in the seas behind me.

"Well, if you're going to show all your cards, then I guess it's only appropriate I do the same thing," she said with a smile, as she clapped her hands.

Movement around us made me redouble the grip on my shotgun, but a steady hand from Poppy got me to relax.

Four men emerged from foxholes around us.

They were covered in grass and moss with camouflage paint covering their faces.

Unlike the guards who protected The Lady, these men's guns were visible. They held long assault rifles and appeared to be grenades were strapped to their waists. These men were not merely thugs, they were soldiers, through and through.

I turned my head back to The Lady, who had eyes only for me. I felt uncomfortable under her gaze and wanted to take a step back but stopped myself. She watched me with the curiosity of a big cat. It made my insides turn cold.

"Mr Blake, I presume. My name is Lady Isabella Ivanov," she said with a hint of a Russian accent, "but many people call me The Lady. A name I detested to begin with but now have grown to love. You can call me Miss Ivanov."

"It's a pleasure to meet you; I guess it's you I have to thank for all the unpleasantness that has taken place in my life up until this point."

She tilted her head to the side and shrugged slightly. "I would apologise but when needs must..."

"Needs must, huh?"

"Look, you're a businessman; when a buyer offers you enough money to finance your operation for the foreseeable future what would you do?"

"I wouldn't endanger the lives of people just for profit and gain. I would act like a reputable business and—"

"A reputable business like Xcorp?" she asked, the corners of her mouth pulling up into her smile.

"I... well..." I tried to find the right response but failed. I knew she was right, that certain big businesses would do anything for a profit, that my life had been damaged just as much by Xcorp as it had been by her, but I would be damned if I told her so. Not here on this rain-swept cliff, with a shotgun in my hand and surrounded by a bunch of thieves, murderers and gang lords.

"There will come a time, Mr Blake, if it hasn't come already, when your way of life is threatened, when the people you love the most are placed in harm's way and you will do anything to protect them. Anything. When that time comes you will understand human nature like no other. You will understand what the employees of Xcorp say to themselves to help them justify the actions they have taken.

"You will understand what some of my men say to themselves at night so they can fall asleep. When that time comes, I pray the fall from that high horse of yours doesn't break too many of your bones."

I thought back to the last nightmare I had and shuddered as Mr X's bloodied face leapt out of my subconscious.

I hadn't given those deaths much thought. Too much had happened. I had focused my attention on other things. But standing here now, I knew what she did was different for me. I had killed for self-preservation. I had killed because no other option was given to me. I had killed to survive.

While she had killed for profit.

"I am nothing like you, Miss Ivanov, nor will I ever be," I said, head held high.

She gave me a smile halfway between a smirk and a snarl and turned her attention to José. "So good to see you, my old friend. I wish it was in better circumstances but alas we are only boatmen along the river of fate. I do hope you have my little package."

"That I do, *mi Señora*, that I do. But there were certain unseen complications we encountered, as you well know, that we may have to be reimbursed for."

"Come now, Mr Battle, you're not insinuating what I think you are, are you?"

"If I didn't, *mi Señora*, then you wouldn't trust me."

The blues of her eyes sparkled as she tilted her head back and laughed. It was gentle, soft, pleasing to the ear.

"Fair enough, Mr Battle. Shall a ten percent increase in the original deal be adequate?"

"Five percent should be more than enough."

Confusion crossed my features but I held my tongue as I looked towards the rest of the crew.

I was surprised when I saw none of them react. There was no anger, confusion, annoyance or even surprise on any of the crewmates' features. All I saw was neutral faces.

"You, Mr Battle, are one savvy negotiator; that is why I love dealing with you. You shall have my business as long as you want it. Vlad, please retrieve the device from Mr Battle while I pay him," she said, tapping on the computer attached to her wrist. The bodyguard to her right stepped forward while José rummaged in his back pocket.

I saw the movement before anyone else. It was a faint dot against the rainy background. It was hard to distinguish against the sideways rain. I took a step forward and squinted my eyes as it got closer and closer. What was that? Then I saw it in all its glory as a flash of lightning tore across the sky and highlighted it.

I began moving long before my brain started screaming warnings at me. In hindsight, I should have guessed what the image looked like. Me running towards one of the most feared people in Safe Haven with a loaded shotgun, right after she had paid us more than the agreed amount without our giving her what she wanted.

To say it must have looked bad was an understatement, but I didn't think of that.

I just acted.

Launching myself forward I saw the guns raised up at me. I heard the shouts. But I was moving too fast for them to target me safely.

I smashed into Lady Isabella Ivanov and bore us down to the ground as the first bullets tore through the earth from above.

37

Chaos ensued around me as the ground was torn up and tossed into the air. I hunkered down as bits of wet earth slapped me against the side of the head. Men shouted and people gave orders back and forth, but I heard none of that as a pair of blue eyes looked up at me with interest.

I expected to see at least a trace amount of fear, but there wasn't any. There was just curiosity. Lady Isabella Ivanov studied me and said nothing as her men rushed her way.

"I do say you are a most interesting man, Mr Blake, a most interesting man indeed," she whispered to me. "It shall be my pleasure to watch you grow in the dirt that is Safe Haven."

Rough hands grabbed me and launched me to the side as her men picked her up and dusted her off.

On my back I could now see the ship that had attacked us; it was no bigger than an escape vessel with two miniature rifles attached to its underside. A pilot manoeuvred it back around for another run as The Lady's men fired its way.

"I'm fine. I'm fine. Just deal with these incompetent fools who can't even stage an assassination correctly."

Men erupted from the surrounding area and rushed our way. They looked the worse for wear with more than a few sporting bloody bandages and cuts. They ran and fired trying their best to cut us down.

"Squad Alpha protect The Lady! Squad Delta to me," Vlad ordered.

His men didn't hesitate, they took up their positions and returned fire with an accuracy that picked off our attackers one by one. They fell under the onslaught but their resolve never wavered. I dived for cover as another round of gunfire from above peppered the ground around me. As I rolled to my side a rough pair of hands latched onto me and lifted me to my feet.

"Can't have you dying on us, boyo, that would spoil the party," José said, firing his revolver at a man who had crept past The Lady's defences.

"Who do you think is responsible for this—"

I was stopped when a voice boomed from the speakers of one of the escape vessels. "How does it feel to be on the receiving end for a change?"

Even through the speakers I could make out Arun's distinctive tones. "I wanted to kill that bastard José and take the device he was going to give to you, Isabella, and claim the payment myself, but I think killing the both of you is a much better idea. I get to kill two rivals and with you out of the picture, Isabella, Paradise Lost shall be mine for the taking."

"Stupid fool thinks it really is that simple," Isabella said, standing next to me. "If he kills me now the only thing he can guarantee is turning Paradise Lost into a war zone while the peasants try and claim a stake in what they think they should have. Vlad, what do you propose to do about this nuisance?"

Vlad turned to his boss and held back a shrug that I could see building in his shoulders, José stepped forward loading his revolver while the chaos still raged on around us. "Tell you what, *mi Señora*, we'll help you deal with this mess and I won't even charge you for it."

"That's an interesting proposition, José, seeing as you still haven't given me what I paid for."

"It's no good giving you something if you won't be alive long enough to appreciate it," he said, firing a single shot past us' "Your men deal with the air attacks, my men and I will tackle the opposition on the ground."

"Fine. Vlad, deal with that, will you," she said, pointing towards the vessel that occupied the sky.

"Come on, boyo," José said, tugging me along, "time to get our hands dirty."

We pushed forward as the rain increased, and rushed the men who came towards us. I fired the Peacemaker wildly not aiming for anyone in particular and trying not to cause any more damage. I had had enough death on my hands to last me a lifetime, but as bullets came my way and men shouted and screamed, I knew I wouldn't get out of this fight without getting my hands caked in even more blood. I just wanted my freedom. I just wanted to do as I pleased. Was that too much to ask?

A man jumped towards me and I squeezed my trigger without thinking.

The blast took him full in the face knocking him off his feet. I didn't turn around to see the damage but continued on. I leapt back out of the way of a man with crazed eyes who swung a machete my way, I fired towards him but found out I was empty. He smiled at me and hacked left and right.

I ducked and dodged staying just out of harm's way, but I had to do this all day and he only had to hit me once.

Foot slipping on a patch of moss I fell backwards and knocked the air out of my lungs. I looked up to see my attacker smiling down at me, machete raised above his head. The smile still stayed on his face as a black blade penetrated his left eye. He didn't make a sound but fell forward on top of me, dead.

I rolled him off of me as Poppy bent down and plucked her knife out of his eye.

"How you holding up—" she began, but my eyes widened as I saw a vessel bearing down on her from the heavens. When I kicked her feet from underneath her, she landed on top of me and I rolled us towards safety as a line of bullets tore the grass up to our left. I detached myself from her and began loading explosive shells as the craft circled back around, I could see Arun's smug little face through the window of the cockpit and steeled myself for what I was about to do.

Loading the last shell into the chamber I clicked my head left to right and sprinted forward. I weaved left and right and kept on moving. My shot had to be perfect. I couldn't miss or he would know my plans. This was a game of chicken at the highest level. Well, for me anyway; for him it would just appear to be some idiot running towards him making his life a hell of a lot easier.

He hadn't fired yet. I could see him smiling at me as I sprinted faster and faster.

The guns under his vessel spat bullets towards me chucking wet grass into the air. I held my breath as I waited for one to hit but none did. With each step, I could feel myself bracing for impact but as each step took me closer towards my target, I concentrated on what I had to do. Bringing my weapon up I slid forward on my knees, resting my finger on the trigger till I gauged the distance of the vehicle.

It wasn't close enough.

I held my breath as the impact the bullets made got closer and closer. I wanted to run. I wanted to hide. But if I didn't deal with this asshole now then it would be game over for all of us.

Rain made the distance hard to judge but I took aim and fired.

The end of my gun spat out flames as I squeezed the trigger again and again. With each blast from my gun, I was pushed back further and further back till a long groove could be seen from my original starting point up to where I rested now.

The destruction the Peacemaker caused was total.

The front of the vessel was in flames with bits of the craft falling to the ground as it came towards me, I couldn't see Arun anymore but I couldn't think he had survived. As I watched it approach, a horrific revelation dawned on me as I watched the small ship get lower and lower.

It was going to crash into me.

Getting up to my feet I was like a deer in the headlights as I didn't move at first. Then I manoeuvred left and right, but whichever way I was going to run I knew it would not be enough. Dropping to the ground I put my hands over my head and shut my eyes and waited for the inevitable but it never came.

Instead, I felt the vibrations from the ship's engines pass through my body and I opened my eyes to see the ship pull up. Arun was still alive. The ship wobbled as it continued to gain altitude, but it didn't get very far as it slammed into another ship in a spectacular explosion.

If Arun had been alive he wasn't anymore.

I stood up and gawped as the debris from the two ships came tumbling down towards the ground. About to celebrate I stopped myself as I saw the explosion had blasted one of the ships back my way.

"Give me a break!"

Spinning on my heels I sprinted away as I felt the ground underneath me rumble. Head down I sprinted with everything I had but I realised at the last moment I was running headfirst off the cliff. Turning my head back around I saw I had no other option but to keep going as the burning wreckage of the ship was barrelling towards me.

In a few more steps there would be no ground left. In a few more steps I was either going to die of drowning, being impaled by the sharp rocks below or crushed and burnt to death by the wreckage following me like a lost puppy.

"Fuck! Fuck! Fuck!"

I took one more look over my shoulder and saw I had no other choice but to leap. I closed my eyes and took the jump.

"Fuck!"

38

I felt nothing but weightlessness as I soared through the air, then gravity did its work and my stomach was pulled downwards. I had time to utter a yell of terror before the breath was stolen from my lungs and I plummeted to my doom. I spun out of control for what felt like an eternity before something grabbed onto my leg and I was yanked upwards.

My torso slammed against something sharp and solid that knocked out what little remaining air I had in my lungs, forcing me to open my eyes as I struggled for breath.

Taking in lungful after lungful of oxygen, I saw the view below me and I took it in.

Water crashed against rock and sprayed below me in a terrifying display of beauty and power. Looking at the scene I knew one thing: I wouldn't have survived the jump. Sharp rocks jutted out into needle points that were waiting to impale me. I looked further afield and saw the debris that had been the ship sink into the huge swells of the tide. The ocean waves reclaimed the vessel piece by piece, and I had little doubt that it would have done the same thing to me if I hadn't been caught.

I turned my gaze up and saw Poppy looking down at me while she held onto my leg. She was suspended by a wire that she had shot into the cliff face; it carried both our weights.

"Hi there," she said with a smile.

"Hi," I replied with a bigger smile on my face. "Caught anything good this week?"

I had expected her to groan at my lame attempt at a joke, but she carried on smiling and nodded her head. "Yeah, I did as it happens. I caught something special... special to me at least. It's something that I think I've been looking for for a very long time, and now I've got it, I kind of don't want to let it go."

My neck began to hurt from staring up at her but I didn't care; I could stare at her face till all the blood rushed to my head and caused me to black out.

"If you've found something that special then I would definitely hold on to it as hard as you can because whatever it is you've found doesn't sound like it can easily be replaced. Plus, you don't want to waste any more years looking. Trust me, I know how precious time is, so my advice to you would be to hold on tight to whatever it is you've found and never let go. Because once you do, you don't know when you'll find it again or even if you can. Don't waste time like me, do what your heart always has desired."

She stared into my eyes and gave me the tiniest nod. "I think, I think I'll do that," she said as we both stared into each other's eyes, smiles widening by the second.

39

I hugged the ground after Poppy and I were finally lifted away from our certain deaths by The Lady's people.

Laying my forehead against the cold, wet and soggy grass, I didn't think I could feel any more pleasure than I did right now. I was just happy to be alive.

I could hear the last few sounds of gunfire as The Lady's men made sure that any enemy even twitching had another round of metal placed through their bodies. They left nothing to chance. The Lady was ruthless in her efficiency in making sure the job was done well.

She faced us now, fingers tapping on her computer. "Arun saved me the task of having to kill him and his little bunch of hoodlums at a later date, as he was beginning to overstep the boundaries of respect and etiquette one leader shows to another. I could only turn a blind eye for so long as he kept on trying to test what he could get away with.

"You will soon find, Mr Blake, much like children, adults will keep on pushing against the boundaries until they are disciplined. Now—" she began but was cut off as another round of fire penetrated the air.

I pulled a face that I tried to hide but she caught it.

"What is the matter?"

"It's just that," I began, "I don't see the need in killing wounded men who can barely fight."

She shook her head at me as one would a naïve child. "I have stayed in power as long as I have by doing the job properly. No survivors who can take revenge. No survivors who hold a grudge. There is a reason why, when certain animals take over a pack by killing the old alpha, they kill off all the offspring too.

"Leave no stone unturned, Mr Blake. Leave no job unfinished. Remember that, it will serve you well one day."

"Thank you for the free advice, Mrs Ivanov."

"It's Miss, actually," she said with a wink as she turned her attention towards José. "Now, Mr Battle, if you would be so kind as to hand over what I have already paid for, so I can be on my way."

"Eager to be off this planet, *mi Señora*?"

"Actually, I chose this planet because I love the ocean. I find it hypnotic, it reminds me of how a woman should be. On sunny days the ocean can be calm, interesting, gentle, relaxing, but when her fury is aroused there isn't a structure known to man that can safely withstand her power," she said, looking out onto the waves. "It allows me to know what I can accomplish, amongst the murky waters of Safe Haven.

"But anyway, enough of my ramblings. I believe you have something that belongs to me?" she said, hand held out.

José nodded his head and dug out from his pocket the data-stick, which he placed in the palm of her hand.

"I think you'll find that belongs to Xcorp!" shouted a voice from behind us.

We all turned around and saw Gregory walking towards us, unarmed and alone. His suit was muddied and the knees on both pants legs were ripped showing skin underneath; a large bruise starting to go purple rested above his left eye.

"I'll think you'll find you're mistaken," Miss Ivanov said. "I paid for this information so it now belongs to me, I do not know or care how these men got it; all I know is a transaction has been made, and now the transaction is complete."

"I doubt that would hold up in a court of law," Gregory replied.

"Well, this planet is uninhabited, which means the World Government's laws do not apply here. Much as in international waters, anything that is done on this planet is outside the scope of the law."

"Err... I don't think you truly understand how international water—" I began, but Willis cut me off with a slap to the back of the head.

The Lady looked my way with mild annoyance and said, "I have come for what I want; now I shall be leaving."

"Maybe we can come to—" began Gregory, stepping forward, but he stopped as I lifted my shotgun in his direction.

"You heard what she said. She's not interested. But I am interested in paying you back for the pain you and your men caused me back on Safe Haven. I think two blown-out kneecaps and we can call it even."

No one spoke as I took a step forward and lifted the gun till it was pointed as his knees. If I blew both his kneecaps out, the damage done to his legs would mean he would bleed to death before he got any medical attention.

This man had ruined my life. This man had tortured me, lied to me, beaten me and tried to have me killed on more than one occasion; he had taken everything from me and now he had the gall to stand here before me and demand justice?

Fuck that! Fuck him! I would get rid of this asshole once and for all and be done with it.

"I want you to listen to me very carefully," Gregory said, spitting the words out in a hurry. "We can surely come to some agreement. I mean, you're a smart businesswoman, all I'm asking you to do is allow me to buy the information back off you and kill these idiots. It would be in your best interest and make you—"

I placed the barrel of my shotgun against his mouth and stared deep into his eyes.

Fuck the knees. I wanted his head.

If I was going to kill him this was how I would want to do it. Face to face. A few feet apart. Staring him in the eye so he knew I was his murderer, so he knew that in his last dying moments I had taken everything from him like he had from me.

I blinked the rainwater out of my eye as I felt two hands on my shoulders. Turning left I saw Poppy, turning right I saw Lady Isabella Ivanov.

"He's not worth it," Poppy whispered to me.

"I would like to hear what he's got to say," said Miss Ivanov, looking Gregory's way.

Gregory took a step back and with shaking hands tried to straighten out his sleeves but couldn't. That image alone would keep me content till the end of my days.

"As I was saying," Gregory said with a wobble in his voice, "I can make it worth your while in giving me back the data-stick. Whatever you're being paid by your highest bidder, I can double it."

"Quadruple."

No one spoke as all faces turned to Lady Isabella Ivanov.

"Excuse me?" said Gregory.

"You heard me; I want quadruple what I am being paid for this and not a pretty penny less."

Gregory gulped as he pinched the bridge of his nose. "I, I, and how much is the amount, may I ask?"

She tapped on her computer and walked forward, showing him a figure on her screen none of us could see. Gregory's eyes widened in shock as he took a step back.

"Quadruple that amount," he whispered softly. "I don't know if I have the authority or the access to garner such an amount in so little time. I mean that amount is a sizeable percentage of Xcorp's stock; can't we meet in the middle and say two point five?"

"Oh, I didn't realise this was a negotiation. I thought I had something you wanted and would do anything to get back. Your past acts lead me to believe such was the case, but I guess I was wrong.

"Farewell, Mr Goodwin."

She walked away but he stepped in her way and held out his hands in front of her. "Wait, wait. Let's not do anything rash here; in all areas of business one negotiates. Triple the asking price."

"You must not have heard me the first time, Mr Goodwin. This. Is. Not. A. Negotiation."

He stared her way and played with the sleeves of his suit, before giving her a nod of acceptance. Then he typed away on the holoscreen of the computer on his wrist.

"You can't be serious! You're going to give it back to him! The very people you stole it from in the first place?"

"Mr Blake, some would call that good business," she said.

"After everything this dickhead has put me through, you expect me to just allow him to get his hands on what he's been after all this time? I don't think so," I said, lifting up my shotgun and pointing it Gregory's way.

"Mr Blake, I would advise you not to do anything which would jeopardise my business," said The Lady, turning my way as her men pointed their guns in my direction.

"Why?"

"Because doing so is disastrous for one's life. I understand your concerns but if I am to be frank with you I care little for your plight and care even less in righting any wrongs done to you. The universe isn't fair, Mr Blake, it takes from the less fortunate and gives to the overabundant and greedy all the time. This is how things are, this is how they will always be. Now I suggest you lower your weapon before even more people get hurt."

I gripped the butt of my gun even tighter as I narrowed my eyes and could feel my finger press ever slightly on the trigger. Why should this fucker get to win? Why should he get away with what he had done to—

"Quinton!" José's voice came out of nowhere and snapped me out of my thoughts. Rough hands lowered my gun down as he stared my way. "That is enough."

I didn't move.

"It's over," said Tuari.

"Listen to the captain," snapped Willis.

I took a step back and gritted my teeth, as Gregory released a sigh of breath. He flashed a smirk my way that quickly vanished behind an expressionless mask as he continued his business with The Lady.

"The money is in your account," Gregory said, closing the holoscreen of his computer down and holding his hand out. "Now if you would be so kind as to hand over the device."

A predatory smile spread across The Lady's face. "What's stopping me from just killing you? I mean you've already paid me; I could just as easily kill you, take what you've given me and sell the information on the stick to the highest bidder. Getting paid twice is so much nicer than just getting paid once, and as you said in business it's always best to *negotiate* for the best deal."

"I, I, I didn't remember saying that exactly but—"

"If you were me what would you do?"

Gregory opened his mouth to respond but was cut off by The Lady.

"The truth."

He stared her way and looked down towards the ground before looking back up towards her. Mask now gone he matched her predatory smile. "I would have put a bullet in your head as soon as the payment was made. You have the superior numbers, while I have none."

She nodded her head, smile not leaving her face, while her men raised their guns.

"But if you think I came here unarmed then you would be mistaken. As we speak an Xcorp fleet is on its way here, so you may kill me, but by the time it takes you to get out of the atmosphere and into deep space, my fleet would already be on your tail. Now you may escape, you may not, but why risk that? Why risk the wrath and might of one of the most powerful corporations in the known galaxy?

"You think what they did to Quinton was bad, wait till they find out how much you stole from them. They will crush the little planet you reside on into dust and kill everyone you know and love. Yes, if I were you, I would shoot me dead, but I would also be smart enough to heed my advice and take off while the going is good."

A frown replaced The Lady's smile as she tossed the data-stick into his waiting hands and walked away, "Nice doing business with you both!" she shouted over her shoulder as she descended the slope.

Gregory turned towards me and gave me a smile, as he pulled on the sleeves of his suit. "Well, Quinton, my statement still stands, you are fired from your position and—"

I punched him on the nose with everything I had; the sound of breaking bone was a pleasure to my ears as he fell backwards onto his ass. Blood poured from his nose and into his mouth as he opened it and tried to speak. He spat out a bloody wad towards me and got up slowly to his feet, at which point I punched him once more. If I had broken his nose before, this time I had disfigured it, as it sat at a crooked angle. He looked up at me, fear in his eyes, as I hovered above him.

"Are you done?"

"Yeah, I'm done," I said, taking a step back.

He got back up to his feet again and looked at me with contempt. "I hope you enjoyed that because from here on out your life is over. You may think you're free because Xcorp have what they want, but this is far from over. The board hates loose ends and you are a loose end.

"You think this little crew will protect you but I know these people; when the going gets rough and the bounty hunters and mercenaries come then they'll be the first to leave you high and dry.

"Then where will that leave you, Quinton? I'll tell you where, you'll still be the same loser whose wife I was fuc—"

Another punch lifted him off his feet and collapsed him

back on the ground where he lay sprawled out unconscious.

This time it wasn't me that had hit him.

Poppy stood over him with fire in her eyes, teeth clenched as she moved towards him once more.

"Poppy! Hurting him anymore won't solve anything," José said, walking forward and placing a hand on her shoulder. "I know you want to but it'll only cause more trouble than it's worth, plus I think it's time we made a move before his welcome party arrives."

José looked out over the cliff and stared into the crashing waves below. Rummaging in his breast pocket he took out a small data-stick and held it out before him.

"Don't tell me that's—" I said, pointing towards the device in his hand, then looking back towards Gregory. "If you have the data-stick then what does he think he has?"

"Oh, he has a data-stick in his hand but it isn't the one he wants. I was never planning to give this thing to Miss Ivanov, not after I found out what was on it. It would be too risky to have that information back out there in the world. It's bad enough having people controlling other people without them creating a whole subspecies to do the same too."

"But if you were never going to give the information to The Lady then eventually she would have found out what you sold her was a fake."

"It was a chance I was willing to take and if she ever asked about it, I would have told her it was a simple mistake of giving her the wrong stick. She wouldn't have bought it, of course, but all things considered I think this worked out pretty well in the end."

"Until Xcorp looks on the data-stick and finds out what they have isn't what they wanted," I said.

"Don't worry about them fuckwits too much," Willis said with a smile. "We've placed a gift on Gregory's data stick that I think they'll enjoy; call it a Trojan horse if you will."

"You mean a computer virus?" I said in disbelief.

"Something like that," José said as he flicked the data-stick into the ocean where it disappeared beneath the waves.

40

A few weeks had passed since the incident that happened back on the nameless planet. My bruises and cuts had all but healed, but the mental scars I still carried followed me no matter where I went.

It was worse at nights.

I was learning to deal with those nightmares better as the days passed me by, but I didn't think I would ever get over them completely.

We were back on Safe Haven in one of the Junk Yard Dogs' safe houses and I was in my room reading the galactic holonewspaper of the week's current events.

I smiled as I saw a moving holographic picture at the front of the newspaper of Gregory Goodwin with his suit jacket pulled over his head being led away in handcuffs by officers, while his wife had to be restrained.

I leaned back with relish while I read the news concerning Xcorp's recent struggles.

Gregory Goodwin. Liar. Cheat. Thief!

Many are at a loss as to how Xcorp, one of the biggest corporations in the known galaxy, a monster in many different fields of industry, could go from dominating every sector they were in, to allowing one man to steal enough funds from them that their profit margin fell by thirty-five percent overnight.

Gregory Goodwin, a simple middle manager, was caught by the World Government with the aid of Xcorp, before he could flee with his untold riches. Dishonesty isn't new for the New-London native, as not only does he leave behind his wife and kids, but also his mistress of many years who he also had children with.

Upon our questioning Mrs Goodwin, she stated she knew nothing about the extramarital affair.

The authorities are none the wiser as to where the funds Mr Goodwin has taken are, but they told us they are doing everything in their power to locate it.

But the bad news for Xcorp doesn't stop there, as what looks like a cyber-attack from within their own ranks has wreaked havoc with their database mainframe, leaving their telecommunications customers unhappy, as customers couldn't access any of their information on the cloud, with many saying all their personal data has been wiped out completely.

The effects of both the theft and cyber-attack have caused Xcorp stocks to plummet, with rumours of investors and board members leaving in droves as public outrage mounts against the company.

Many are left asking:

Is this the end of an era?

I smiled as I swiped away the holographic newspaper and stood up and stretched my arms above my head. It appeared that in his haste Gregory hadn't double-checked the data-stick and had handed it directly to his superiors. They had inserted it into their mainframe and the rest was history.

Not wanting to own up to their mistake, Xcorp had placed the blame solely on Gregory.

I had no doubt my former boss wouldn't live to see the end of the week, as what he knew could bring Xcorp down.

I made my way out of my room and continued down the stairs and into the dining hall, where Tuari was serving up dinner. José and Willis were both sat down in front of the dining room table, forks and knives already in hand.

The scent of baked fish and roasted meat wafted past me as I licked my lips at the meal being served; potatoes glistening with butter and greens served with chopped garlic and baby tomatoes filled my mouth with saliva.

I tried to reach for a potato but Willis stabbed the table in front of my hand with his fork forcing me to reconsider.

"Wait till the table has been fucking set, you heathen."

"Old ginger nuts here is very peculiar about saying prayers before each meal," Tuari said with a smile.

I rolled my eyes and said, "Have any of you seen the news about Xcorp?"

"No, but I sure as hell know you're going to bore us to death with the details," said Willis.

Ignoring him I continued, "It looks like your virus was more effective than I would have thought. They have lost hundreds of billions. You know once this is sorted they'll be on the hunt for us, don't you?"

"If they survive," José said, going to light a cigar but having it taken away from him by Willis. "With the way things are going over there they may never recover from this."

"I wouldn't count on it; companies like Xcorp have survived government sanctions, waste management tragedies where they wiped out entire animal populations and a lot worse," I replied. "They'll find a way to recover from this, a company like that always does."

"Well, if they do come for us, we'll be ready. Like dogs we'll adapt and overcome," said José.

I nodded my head as I looked around the room. "I've got something to show all of you."

"Quinton," said Tuari, "we don't need to see your penis. I'm sure it's a very nice penis, but keep it to yourself."

"Wait—what! Why would I—no, I've got a new tattoo."

They all looked at me with blank faces while I rolled up my sleeves. "I noticed most of you have tattoos. Poppy has the nine-tailed fox, José the Kuchi, Willis the Dogo Argentino, and Tuari... sorry, I don't think I've seen yours."

"It's a jackal," Tuari said as he showed me a tattoo of a small-looking wolf with a large set of ears. It had a grin on its face from ear to ear, which was funny but also slightly disturbing.

"Seeing as all of you had dog tattoos I thought I would get one also," I said, showing them the tattoo on my right shoulder.

They starred at it, confusion on all their faces before they slowly looked back at me.

"What do you think?"

"What is that meant to be?" Willis asked.

"It's the constellation of the Greek mythological dog called Laelaps. There are many tales relating to the dog but the one I liked the most is that the dog never failed to catch what she was hunting, so she was used to hunt the

Teumessian fox, a fox which could never be caught. The chase went on and on until one day Zeus had enough and turned them to stone and cast them amongst the stars, where they later became known as Canis Major for the dog and Canis Minor for the fox."

The confusion still hadn't passed on their faces.

"What. A. Wanker," said Willis, before they all dismissed me with a shake of the head and filled their plates with food.

"I thought the idea was clever, seeing as we work amongst the stars and our crew is called the—"

"Why don't you go and show Poppy, boyo?" José said, with a wave of his hand. "I'm sure she'll find it fascinating."

"Fine."

I turned and left, not before snatching a potato from the table and giving Willis the middle finger. I made my way towards Poppy's room fully disgruntled that my tattoo hadn't been well-received.

It was a brilliant tattoo and they were just a bunch of unimaginative dicks who didn't know a good tattoo if it slapped them in the face. Striding towards Poppy's door I slowed my pace as I came close and wondered if I should knock, but thought we were passed that point now as we had both seen each other naked.

Grabbing the door handle I opened the door and stopped in my tracks.

Poppy stood before me naked. Naked with her chest open and what appeared to be electric components running through her body where there should have been organs.

She looked at me in shock, fear and anger.

"You should have knocked," was all she said.

41

6 months later

42

I was running for my life.

Arrows tore off bits of bark from the trees around me as I moved left to right in some vain attempt to keep my body from getting hurt. Vines and foliage slapped me in the face, while branches tore and tugged at my clothing and scratched my body as I tried to manoeuvre as best as I could through the damn jungle.

A war cry sounded behind me and made me redouble my efforts.

Sweat poured from my face as the oppressive humidity from the jungle pounded across my shoulders.

"Get a move on, Necktie, or these savages will be skinning that plump ass of yours for dinner," said Willis through my earpiece.

"I don't see why I had to be the one to collect the artefact!" I replied, holding a bone-carved miniature idol that had rubies for eyes and diamonds for teeth.

"Because you're in the delivery business now and our buyer has a thing for sacred artefacts worshipped by long-lost tribes."

Long lost tribes was correct; we were on some far-flung planet that had been forgotten by everyone including the World Government. It was a planet that had taken us weeks to get to and wasn't on any shipping lanes. I was surprised to find human life still existed on it, but I had heard of many planets like this one, where when faster than light travel was discovered many adventurers sought out their fortunes amongst the stars. Like early seafarers back on Earth, nobody knew what they would find, and the allure was just too much for some.

Many spaceships disappeared completely, some came back broken, some came back rich, some were never allowed to land.

Some ships that had been lost had crash-landed on lost worlds, and as the survivors' descendants' technology faded, they reverted back to their basic instincts.

It was one such planet I was now on, running for my life.

A painted face popped out from the bushes to my left and I ducked a wild swing from a club made of bone. The attack spun the attacker round in a circle and I punched him in the jaw, knocking him to the ground before I took off once again.

I heard another war cry behind me, this one far too close for comfort, and I turned around just in time to see another tribe member sprinting towards me with a spear. Ducking low I pulled a branch in my path back and released it, allowing it to whip my attacker in the face.

A swift kick to the balls dropped him and I took off once again.

"I don't see why I can't use my gun," I said.

"That's not very sporting now, is it?" came Tuari's voice through my comms. "They're just little old tribespeople who are angry at you for stealing their god and you want to blow them all to smithereens. You're such an English coloniser."

"I'm not talking about killing anyone, just fire a few warning shots so they leave me alone."

"No can do, boyo," said José, "we can't leave any trace of ourselves on this planet. That means no trash, no bullets, no tech whatsoever."

"I hardly think—" I ducked and rolled as a spear flew over my head. Coming back up to my feet I kicked the tribesman in front of me in the stomach and grabbed his club, using it to sweep him off his feet where I struck him in the stomach again before moving off.

"You assholes are so full of shit! You have no concerns about stealing a sacred artefact, but when it comes to leaving any evidence of ourselves on this planet, you're like Greenpeace. I still don't understand why I was chosen to do this job, and why no one else could help me."

"One, because more than one person sneaking into their camp would have been noticed," Willis said, "and two, because you're the noob. So shut, you whore-hole of a mouth, and make your way to the pickup."

"You know what, Willis, you can suck my—" I skidded to a stop as I erupted into a clearing with at least twenty tribesmen in front of me. Faces painted in hues of red and green, they all stared my way hungrily. Willis may have joked about them eating me, but I had seen human bones scattered around their village.

What could only be the leader of their group strode forward and pointed my way. A beast of a man, he towered over everyone else as he pounded a fist clutching an axe made of bone against his chest. The weapon looked like a child's toy in his paw-like hand.

"I think their leader is challenging me to some sort of duel..."

Silence on the other end of the line while I waited for a response.

"Any advice?"

"Don't be a huge pussy all your life! Get in there and fuck shit up," said Willis.

"He may just be interested in you in a sexual way... did you ever think of that?" Tuari asked.

"No Tuari, the thought never crossed my mind."

"I'm just saying. If you wiggled your ass a little maybe we can all go home a little sooner."

The leader stomped the ground with his bare, flipper-sized feet and pointed to me again before letting out a chest-vibrating roar.

"Was that... him?" Tuari asked.

"Yes."

"Run!"

"But I thought you told me to—

"Quinton," Tuari said, cutting me off, "we heard that from here. Just run. Now!"

I turned and looked for an escape route but in the time I had been stationary, a large circle had formed around me, with men pointing sharp pointy sticks in my general direction.

"That doesn't appear to be an option," I said, before turning back around and facing my foe.

A black-toothed smile crept along his face when he saw there was nowhere for me to go and he shouted something to the people around him, who laughed and jeered.

He strutted forward and looked me up and down before throwing his axe towards my feet; I looked down at it in confusion then back at him, as he gestured for me to pick it up. Pointing once again my way, he said something that caused the crowd to burst into laughter.

I sprinted towards him catching him off guard and dived forward; grabbing the handle of the axe I rolled to my feet and sliced across his thigh with a sideways slash that bit into the flesh to the bone. He yowled in pain and swung my way but I backpedalled avoiding the strike.

"First blood to me."

"Listen, just don't get yourself killed. In the name of all that is holy we still need that artefact—I'm tired of eating ramen noodles."

"Thanks, Willis, I'm glad to see you care."

The crowd had gone silent as the leader looked down at his wound in disgust. Spitting in his open palm he slapped the wound then raised his fist to the sky and roared.

"Well, that can't be hygienic," I said to myself as I circled around him.

He came towards me again, but this time slower. He had learnt from his last mistake. He lunged and feinted my way but I didn't take the bait. I would not be fooled so easily.

He kept on circling me looking for an opening, but I gave him none as I swung the axe his way whenever he got too close. He grunted in annoyance as he lunged towards me but I ducked under his arms and swung the axe behind me, slicing him across the back. I smiled as he yowled in pain.

His eyes narrowed my way.

"Not as easy as you first thought, huh?" I said with a smile. "Bet you're regretting giving me this axe now, ain't you?"

Another clumsy lunge but this time I was ready for it and stepped back just out of reach and thrust the axe into his face, breaking his nose upon impact. Blood trickled down his face and he staggered backwards. I rushed to push the advantage but a roar and a wild uppercut that nearly got me on the chin halted me in my tracks.

Muttering rippled through the crowd, which caused my attacker's eyes to dart sideways.

The cheers of encouragement had stopped; something else had replaced the excited tension which had first swept through the crowd. It was part fear, part apprehension. I smiled as I could feel the shift take place around me.

"Well, big fella, what you going to do?"

My opponent stared at me as I feinted left and right, pulling faces and sticking out my tongue as I taunted him. I should have paid more attention, but my cockiness blinded me as he kicked a cloud of dirt into my face. I closed my eyes in instinct, knowing it was a mistake as I felt a pair of hands pick me up and launch me into the air.

I sailed forwards on a cloud of agony and pain as I landed face first in the mud, skidding to a halt.

I groaned as I spat out the dirt that had made its way into my mouth and groped around me as I looked for the axe I had been holding. Wiping the dirt from my eyes, I scanned my surroundings but didn't find it.

"How you doing, boyo?" asked José.

"Urghhh! It's not going too bad—"

Hands latched onto the back of my shirt and I was lifted into the air, while the crowd roared in excitement. He shook me like a rag doll while I was held like a turtle upside down. I tried to escape but it was useless. Thrown once again across the ground I tumbled and rolled until I came to a sitting stop.

The world around me spun and my vision just had enough time to clear before I took a running knee that flattened me on my back.

Blood filled my mouth; I rolled onto my front and spat it out. A soccer kick to the ribs picked me up and dumped me unceremoniously some feet away.

"I would say it's going quite well, I should be with you lot soon," I said to the crew, as I got slowly up to my feet.

Pain radiated through every single part of my body as I swayed on my feet and tried to keep myself from toppling over. I saw the leader rush towards me but I was too slow to move out of the way as he picked me up in a bear hug. My already bruised ribs screamed in protest as he squeezed the life out of me; breath smelling of rotten eggs and tooth decay washed over me as I tried my best not to gag.

White dots clustered in my vision as I tilted my head back and head-butted him in the face.

He showed me a bloody grin but it didn't last long as I head-butted him again and again. His grip lessened with each blow he took until it was loose enough that I planted both my feet on his chest and kicked him away. I plopped on my back, knocking the wind from my lungs, as he rolled away from me and came to a stop some feet away.

The crowd had once again gone silent.

My hand brushed something and I smiled as my fingers encircled it. I gritted my teeth as I got to my feet. Fuck, I was in a lot of pain. I wobbled once as I tried to get up but finally got my feet underneath me as I got myself standing.

My opponent had still yet to come.

He got slowly to his hands and knees and stared through a bloody mask my way as I shook a finger in his direction. He spat a bloody wad in my direction and pushed himself upwards until he was finally standing tall. His rage-filled eyes locked onto mine as he beat his chest.

I kept on shaking my finger as I gave him a slow shake of the head but that only appeared to incense him more.

"Don't do it," I whispered.

He came towards me at a full sprint while my fingers encircled the axe I had earlier lost. Face set in grim determination, I shifted to his left at the last minute and drove the flat top of the axe into his jaw. Teeth broke upon impact and flew out of his mouth as he staggered backwards. I pushed forward and swung the axe so the flat broadside cracked against his left kneecap, popping it out of place and dropping him down on one knee. Spinning the axe around I drove the handle into his nose, once, twice, three times, till his nose was nothing but a flattened lump of flesh.

I stepped back and looked down as his unfocused eyes tried to register on my face. He lifted a hand to try and grab at me but I knocked it lazily away and pushed him backwards, where he collapsed on his back unconscious.

The crowd booed and hissed as I backed away from the body. Looking around in confusion I didn't understand why, until I saw more than a few fingers being dragged across necks. Although I didn't speak their language the sign they were giving me was a universal symbol that only meant one thing no matter where you went in the galaxy. Stopping in my tracks, I turned back around and walked towards the prone figure on the ground before looking around at the jeering crowd.

They were bloodthirsty. They were savage. They were human.

"Enough!" I shouted till my voice grew hoarse.

A hush fell over the crowd while they looked at me in fear.

"Look," I said, lifting my hand in peace as a few backed away hurriedly, "I'm not going to hurt anyone. I just want to make it back to my ship safe and sound."

More people scattered and pushed each other out of the

way as they ran in all directions. Looking at the scene in confusion I scratched my head as I took a few steps forward.

"Look, I'm sorry about your leader but the guy was a bit of a dick—"

A murderous roar cut me off and lifted the hair at the back of my neck. It was a roar that my monkey brain understood. It was a roar that meant something bigger than you was hungry.

It was a roar that meant run!

43

I glanced over my shoulder and saw a monstrosity that was big, blue and had more teeth than I could count.

It sprinted forward and roared, looking for its next meal.

The tribespeople around me scattered in all directions as I tried to cut a clear path to freedom, as bodies bounced off me while I tried to remain on my feet.

"Hey, guys, I think we have a problem."

"What is it now?" said Willis.

"There's something after me..."

"Something like what?"

"Sorry for not stopping to take a picture of a creature that looks like it could swallow me whole—"

"That's what she said," Tuari said.

"Tuari, that makes no sense! And Willis, I don't know, all I know is it's big and blue and toothy."

"Well, unless you give us a proper description then we can't really help you," Willis said in a bored tone.

I looked over my shoulder and stopped. The thing was

shaped like a big cat, only twice as big, with feathers that formed a crown above its head.

"It looks like a big blue cat with feathers."

Silence on the other line while I waited for a response.

"Sorry, haven't got a clue what it could be," Willis said in the same bored tone.

"Thanks for the help, Sherlock!"

I skidded to a halt as the creature was making its way towards a small boy standing in front of a smaller little girl who could only be his sister. I looked around to see if someone would do something but all the tribespeople had either disappeared or were hiding.

"Fuck me!" I screamed as I weighed my axe in my hand and ran towards it. I screamed at the top of my lungs in the hope I would be seen as a big enough threat that the creature would take off, but it snorted my way and turned its attention towards me. I slowed down as I realised my one and only plan had failed and I was running towards a predator with nothing in my hand but an axe made of bone.

I missed my shotgun.

The beast clawed the ground as I slowed down to a skidding stop. It looked at me. I looked at it. Then I turned and ran.

"What are you doing now?" Willis asked.

"Running!"

"Oh, well, don't forget the idol otherwise it's your ass."

"Fuck the—"

I saw the idol lying in front of me and scooped it up as I ran past. Leaping over a log I could hear the creature's footsteps behind me; it snorted loudly while it took in my scent.

"There's no way you're gonna outrun that thing, you know," Tuari said in my ear. "I mean it literally has to run and hunt for a living."

"I don't care what the happens to him as long as we get the piece," Willis said. "I've had my eye on a gold-edged Bible that I—"

"Will you two shut up!" I yelled as I looked over my shoulder and didn't like what I saw. The beast was closer to me than I thought and was gaining on me by the second.

"Oh shit, oh shit, oh shit, oh shit."

I looked over my shoulder one final time and saw a blue blur leaping towards me. Jumping sideways I felt hot breath sail past my face before the creature smashed into a bush ahead of me. I didn't stop as I heard its angry roar behind me while it tried to extricate itself from the brushes it was tangled in.

"Get the fucking ship ready, I'm coming in hot."

"Hold up, boyo, I'm afraid we may have a problem. We've been spotted by some locals and we've had to change location; I'm sending you the new coordinates now. It's not much further from the original contact point."

A message binged on the computer on my wrist and I tapped it open and a hologram of a map with my location on it appeared in front of me. A little red dot of the current location of the ship blinked somewhere ahead of me.

"I thought you said it wasn't much further! You've added another half a mile to my destination!"

"The faster you run the quicker you'll get here," Tuari teased.

"You guys are cunts!"

I heard crashing behind me. It appeared my pursuer had freed itself. Chest burning with every lungful of breath I took in, I thought of how I was going to lose whatever was behind me.

Climb a tree?

No, the thing had all the makings of a big cat, which meant it could climb up trees just as easily as it could run.

Stand and fight? I patted my pockets to see if I had anything I could use as a weapon but came up short.

I was running out of time and stamina.

Something caught my attention on the map and I zoomed in. There was a cliff just to the left of me that had a small river at its base. The cliff wasn't very high but if I could get the animal to chase me and somehow get it to leap over the edge, it would give me an out. Altering my course and taking a sharp left, I ducked through the undergrowth and swung the axe at whatever got in my way.

The crashing behind me wasn't getting any quieter. I wanted to look behind me but didn't dare.

Sunlight peeked through the leaves ahead of me. My heart skipped a beat as I pushed aside the last remaining branches and leaves in front of me and erupted into a clearing that gave me a spectacular view.

Two setting suns created a beautiful pink hue across the sky, while flocks of multi-coloured birds danced in the air above me. If it weren't for the animal behind me that wanted to eat me for dinner, it would have been a beautiful spot to stop and catch my breath. I heard a crash behind me and I kept on moving forward until I was a few feet away from the edge. The drop was higher than I had expected, but that mattered little—as I turned to look back my pursuer sprinted from the bushes and came to a stop in front of me.

I took a step backwards and bit my bottom lip as we locked eyes.

If I was being honest with myself this wasn't what I had in mind when José offered me a position on his crew. I thought there would be battles in space, collecting and delivering parcels to important and famous individuals, and living life to the fullest—not facing a wild predator with an axe made of bone as if I had gone back in time to the days when my ancestors wore nothing but a loincloth.

The beast paced back and forth, eyes never leaving mine while I redoubled my grip on my axe. Its tail swished back and forth while it growled deeply.

It wasn't coming towards me.

"Come on, you bastard! Come on!" I bent down and threw a rock in its direction. "Come onnn!"

With a roar that made me take a tumble backwards it ran my way, low to the ground, muscles rippling along its back. I wanted to move. To escape. To flee this monster my ancestors had fought just to survive. But I held my nerve despite every cell in my body telling me to move, and waited. Waited till it was close enough. Waited till all I could see were its eyes.

It roared once more, saliva running down its jaws, and leapt towards me at the same time as I hit the deck, chest slamming against the ground. I felt the wind of it sail over me and I turned my head to see it try and twist its body in midair to come back my way but it was already too late. With a whine, it plunged out of sight.

I got slowly up to my feet only then realising how close I was to the edge and thanked the heavens above at how lucky my escape was. Stretching my arms over my head I let out a small whoop and was walking forward when I felt the ground shift under my feet.

"What the fuc—"

That was all I got out before the earth underneath me gave away and I slid down the cliff to the river below.

44

The gut-wrenching feeling of one minute standing on solid ground and the next having nothing underneath me was a shock to my system but no more than seeing the top of the cliff rapidly disappearing away from me. The wind stung the corner of my eyes as my arms windmilled; I had to do something or the next few moments would not be pleasant, nor was it an unpleasantness I thought I would survive.

Time appeared to slow down around me as I grasped my axe in a death grip and swung it at the cliff. It bounced off the soft mixture of clay and stone, sending vibrations down my arm; I tried again and again and finally sliced it into the cliff face. I held onto the axe handle with both hands while I continued my journey downwards, but this time at a much slower rate.

Thinking I was saved I sent my prayers up to the powers that be but they were either misplaced or not heard as the axe head snapped with a loud ear-splitting snap and I went tumbling head over heels into the water below.

I broke the surface with a splash that would have been

life-ending if I hadn't slowed my fall down. Water chilled my bones and invaded my sinuses as I kicked and flapped my arms in some vain attempt at swimming. What felt like an age passed before my head broke the surface of the river and I came up coughing and heaving. Seeing the bank not far from me, I swam towards it with feeble strokes until my face touched its muddy bank.

I lay face down in the mud while I threw up whatever water I had swallowed.

My eyes stung. My throat was sore. My limbs hurt.

So it was with something between annoyance and rage that I heard the water behind me come to life and I looked over my shoulder to see the very beast I had escaped try to swim towards me. I sat up in disbelief and watched as the big predator paddled towards me. I didn't know which god or deity I had pissed off, but whoever it was really wanted to bend me over and give me a good seeing to.

Unable to get up from where I sat, I watched as the creature came towards me, but it didn't get far as the water exploded around it and a monstrous set of reptilian jaws closed around it with a snap.

The struggle was brief. The struggle was violent.

But it ended just as quickly as it began, with nothing but a single air bubble floating to the surface of the water after it was done.

I stared at the river at a loss for words over what I had just seen. Maybe my prayers had been answered after all. Noticing my feet were still in the water I hurriedly lifted them out and got to my feet. Tilting my head to one side I did my best to try and get out the water and mud that had collected in my ears.

I called up the map from my computer on my wrist and frowned as I saw the location of *The Kennel*. my short trip off the cliff and into the river had taken me further away from my desired destination, and it would now take me some time to get to where I needed to be.

I looked at the trail I would now need to follow to get to the ship and turned towards it. The suns were already setting over a densely forested area I would need to make my way through if I had any hope of getting off this planet.

I could think of nothing less I wanted to do than travel through a forest at night on an alien world, but if I wanted to get to *The Kennel*, then that was what I would have to do.

Uttering a helpless sigh I began my trek.

I was ant,- mosquito-, flea-, and fly-bitten as I emerged from the clutches of the forest and saw *The Kennel*. No sight had ever filled me with so much joy as I passed my eyes over the hull of my ship—well, my crew's ship, a crew called the Junk Yard Dogs. A crew who had kidnapped me against my will, taken me halfway across the galaxy to a planet filled with murderous thugs, gangsters, thieves and everything in between. They had taken me away from a life of misery and dissatisfaction and given me one of freedom.

But freedom always came at a price, even if that price meant slogging through an alien forest at night unarmed.

Thinking back to the life I once had—the stable office job for Xcorp where I was guaranteed the same monthly pay, the unsatisfied marriage where my wife had been cheating on me for years, and the feeling of dread I felt when I woke up every day, hoping, praying it would all come to an end—I would cross a thousand forests at night, on a thousand different planets, never to wake up to that feeling again.

Mud caked my boots and legs as I walked up towards the cargo bay doors of the ship and stood in front of them.

Hands on my hips, I waited.

And waited.

And waited.

"Do you want this thing?" I asked, pulling the idol out of my waistband. "Because I can just as easily throw it in the mud and be done with it."

The ship's weapons slowly swivelled my way and Tuari's voice came over the speakers: "Willis, stop pointing the guns at Quinton; it isn't his fault he's so late and we have been waiting here for him with nothing to do but play board games. I guess that's just the type of person he is."

"I say we blow his left nut off," said Willis, "so he always has a constant reminder of what it means to waste people's time."

I rolled my eyes as they continued berating me over the speakers until the cargo doors finally lowered.

Shaking my head I walked forward and stuck my middle finger up at one of the ship's cameras as I boarded.

Mission completed, the only thing on my mind was whether to eat first or take a shower.

Washed and clean I sat in the canteen and ate a plate of balsamic-glazed steak rolls with relish. My taste buds hugged me and my stomach thanked me, as I was now on my second plate. I had missed lunch when Tuari had made the meal for the crew so all they left me was leftovers, but I wasn't complaining.

Even leftovers made by Tuari were better than most five-star restaurant meals.

I kept on eating as I heard footsteps approach me. The

overpowering smell of a Cuban cigar rode on the air like a big-wave surfer as José took a seat opposite me; whisky glass in hand he leaned back in his chair and gave me a toast.

"Great work today, boyo. You did your crew proud."

I nodded my head and kept on eating while I allowed the silence to lengthen between us.

"How did you feel on your first mission?"

"Not bad," I said around a mouthful of food. "Could have used some backup, could have used my shotgun, but I guess it all worked out."

"I'm glad that it did. We were getting short on supplies such as fuel and food, not to mention ammo—Willis goes through more rounds a week than a military unit. Once we deliver the idol to the buyer it should cover us for a while, plus I can finally pay you fools."

"How come we're so low on cash? I thought we got paid well for the job we did for The Lady?"

I know I had.

After Lady Isabella Ivanov had paid José and we had properly covered our tracks, José had split the money between the crew, and I had received a share. Shocked at first, I didn't know what to say, but José had told me that my help towards the mission was invaluable and without it, the mission wouldn't have been completed.

About to protest, I looked at the money in my bank account and felt like a king.

It would take me eight years of work plus overtime at my old job to even come close to what he had given me.

"Lady Isabella did pay us well, but I had a lot of debts to clear and you guys to pay; after I took care of that, we were back to square one. There's one thing I like to do, boyo, and that is pay my debts."

I scooped up the last of my meal and then laid my

cutlery down with a clunk before I stretched my arms over my head.

"Don't worry if things didn't go according to plan, it's always the same. Everyone's first mission goes to shit. You should have seen what happened to Willis—we were on the run for weeks after he destroyed an entire street. It took a lot of hush money to cover that shit up, Poppy's was even—"

He stopped and allowed the sentence to die in his throat.

"Poppy's was what?" I asked, anger lacing my words.

"Poppy's was even worse," he said, Spanish accent thick and heavy.

"Did you know? Did you know what she was before—"

José held up his hand stopping me in my tracks. "This thing is not for me to discuss. This thing is between you and her. Each crew member aboard this vessel has their own personal demons that they are running away from or battling against.they trust me with them; this trust I can't betray just because someone's feelings got hurt."

"Feelings got hurt! Feelings got betrayed! She should have told me, she should have sat down and discussed with me what was going on instead of keeping it from me. We slept together, for fuck's sake."

"This thing is between you and her to discuss," he said calmly.

I got up to my feet, hands clenched by my sides as I stared his way while my jaw worked back and forth, trying to place the words in the correct place as they fought to come out from the pit of my stomach.

"You should have at least told me. She should have at least told me!"

"Why?"

"Because I.... because it was," I balled my fists against my forehead while I tried to think of the correct thing to say, "because it was the right thing to do."

"What difference would it have made if you knew she was an AI humanoid? Do you think you would have handled the situation better instead of acting like an immature child and throwing a fit? Maybe you should have thought about her feelings first instead of acting the way you did. Maybe, just maybe, you would have looked at her side of things and thought about how she felt instead of how your little ego got hurt."

"You know what, José," I said, pointing a quivering finger in his direction, "just—just—just fuck off!"

I stormed off in the opposite direction but not before José called out to me.

"I have never seen her act the way she acted with you, with anyone before. Maybe you should ask yourself why."

45

I walked towards my room and passed Poppy's door on the way. The last time I had seen her was back on Safe Haven when I had walked into her room to find her chest open, but instead of tissue and bone, it was connective nano-wire and metal.

Materials used to build machines, not humans.

She had covered up and shielded herself from me while I demanded to know what was going on. Demanded to know what was wrong with her.

In hindsight those questions had been foolish. They had been insensitive. They had been wrong. José was right; I should have tried to speak to her rationally instead of firing questions at her but the simple fact was I was scared, scared of the fact she was a thing that could destroy me in a blink of an eye, a weapon used in a bygone era of war where nuclear weapons were tossed around like toys.

I stopped and shook my head.

Not a thing, no. A person. Someone who I had confided in and who had tried to confide in me. Yet I had thrown all that back in her face because of fear. Since we had met she was nothing but kind to me, nothing but helpful; she had saved my life more times than I could count—yet I had thrown all that away because of fear.

She had said little to me while I fired questions her way. The only thing I could recall now was sadness in her eyes while she pushed me out of the door and slowly closed the door between us.

The next morning she had disappeared leaving me a note that said sorry. She told José she would be back but she needed time to think about things.

That had been six months ago, and we still hadn't heard anything from her.

Part of me was happy because it meant the longer she was away the longer it would mean not having a conversation. Another part missed her terribly.

Her smile. Her laugh. Her kindness.

I came to a stop outside my door and rested my head against its cold metal.

"Now there's a look of a man who needs to release some stress."

"Go away, Willis," I mumbled under my breath.

A heavy hand landed on my shoulder, gripping it tightly. "Come on, lad, in times of stress I always ask myself one simple phrase. What would JC do?"

"JC?"

"Jesus Christ."

"I just want to—"

"No. You need to come with me instead of fondling your balls in pity."

Willis and I stood apart from each other in a nondescript

white room that stretched out for miles. Called the Training Room, it in fact wasn't a room at all. The two of us were connected via headsets while suspended in mid-air by cables that allowed us to move freely; the headsets were similar to a virtual reality headset that allowed us to experience different programmes and exercises.

The only difference between the Training Room and a normal VR headset was that time passed differently.

An hour equalled a day in the Training Room.

VRs had always been highly regulated because allowing a machine to tinker with the brain was never a smart idea, but there had been a rumour of military organisations that had created the concept of the Training Room to allow their soldiers to acquire skills at a faster rate than was humanly possible.

Not only did the Training Room make time pass faster, it also helped its users retain the information they had learnt or were trying to learn at a much faster rate.

"You never told me how the crew got hold of technology that is clearly military-grade."

Willis shrugged his shoulders and said, "It fell off the back of a ship."

I stared at him but he didn't elaborate.

"Although we have spent countless hours in here, your gun control and aim is still shit, your weapon skills are, laughable and you still lose your head at situations you don't need to. In short, you're still a bag of shit and I don't know why I bother wasting my time in trying to make you better."

"Why don't you really tell me how you feel?" I said with an eye roll.

"Poppy ain't around to cover that skinny ass of yours anymore, and I'm sure as hell no Captain Save A Bitch, so you better learn how to fight and survive and learn fast, because dead weight doesn't last around here long."

He stared my way until I gave him a nod of understanding, then he pressed the air in front of him, bringing up a display menu. With a few presses of his fingers, the environment around us shimmered and changed.

No longer was I standing in a white room; instead we were on the streets of a sprawling rundown city that didn't look too dissimilar to Paradise Lost on Safe Haven. Willis and I stood on a busy main street opposite a large crowd while we waited for the lights to change red for us to cross.

"Now you've left your old life behind everything is different," he said as the lights changed from green to red stopping the traffic.

We walked forward while the crowd opposite did the same. Men and women in business suits, construction workers, teenagers who had holoscreens in front of their faces while they watched some vlogger on the net, women with overstuffed shopping bags, all bumped and barged past me, while Willis moved through the shoal of people like a shark.

"The life you once knew is dead, you can't return, you can't go back, the Quinton Blake you once were is dead and thank fuck I say—that dickhead was a shrivelled excuse for a man, a man who belonged to this world," he said, gesturing around him.

"He belonged to these sheep. These sheep who abide by rules and strictures placed on them by others. To live amongst this crew, hell, to survive in this new world you have found yourself in, you need to dismiss all that. These people will fight tooth and nail for the misery of life they have, they will fight all the harder because you have something they don't.

"Freedom."

I could see Willis in front of me but he appeared to be moving further and further away. The more I tried to keep up the more the crowd seemed to get in my way.

"You may think a mother of two would never shoot you between the eyes like a common street thug, or the businessman with twenty years' service would never pay to have you killed, but I can tell you that your biggest threat is not the wannabe thug with a face tattoo, but it's the people around you. The very people you used to call friends."

A woman in a red tight figure-hugging dress and with jet raven hair took my attention, as Willis kept on droning on. I couldn't believe how similar she looked to Poppy, the swing of her hips, the curves of her breasts, the—

"Dickhead, were you paying attention or were you looking at the woman who walked passed?"

I turned around and Willis was before me; he had been over ten feet away when I had last seen him, but he had somehow covered the distance in the time it had taken me to turn away and turn back around.

"I wasn't looking at—"

"She reminded you of Poppy, didn't she?"

I shrugged.

"Look again."

I did as he requested and leapt back as the same woman I had seen before was now holding a gun pointed in my direction. She was frozen in time like everything else around us.

"You lose focus for one minute—one fucking minute!— and it will cost you your life. I understand how you feel about Poppy but until she returns the missions will be hard. She carried a lot of the weight in this crew, a lot of weight that you will now have to bear until she comes back."

"So her leaving is my fault? I asked.

"Well, dickface, let's put it like this. Everyone knew what she was long before you come along. Once you arrived shit changed for the worse in my opinion. I don't know what she saw in you, and I still don't, but the Lord works in mysterious ways and I have to work with what I am given, so until we reach Safe Haven this shall be your life, until I say so. You will train and keep on training until you can hold your own."

"Willis, I'm not in the mood for—"

"Computer, begin the simulation, and only allow exit from simulation upon my notification," and with that he was gone, leaving me locked inside this stupid game.

46

I lay in my bed too tired to move.

The weeks in space had passed swiftly as Willis had pushed me to my limits and didn't let off the gas. There had been simulation after simulation, ones that simulated firefights in tight corridors and ones that simulated firefights on ships and ones that simulated firefights on alien planets where the plant life and wildlife were even more dangerous than the bullets being fired at me.

When those were over he had me spar with him in the Training Room using different melee weapons, everything from hunting knives to axes; after that came Brazilian Jiu-Jitsu, wrestling and Muay Thai.

I had foolishly thought any damage I would sustain in the virtual reality of the Training Room would not be felt but I was wrong. What was the point of that? Willis laughed as I yelled in pain when he pulled the knife he held in his hand once again out of my guts.

'If it doesn't hurt then you won't react to it quick enough, you won't see it as a proper threat. Yes, there are do-overs in this place, but if you die for real there is no reset. So every bullet must hurt like it would for real. Every slash, every stab, every punch must be felt and reacted to so when it happens for real you know how to act accordingly.'

After we finished with those lessons he had me hit the weights because in his own words, I was weak as watered-down whisky and had the body of a fifty-year-old Dutch woman.

It was one never-ending circle of pain, frustration, torment and more pain.

But it had done one thing: it had kept my mind off Poppy. I wish I could say I hadn't thought of her but instead of the constant stream of thoughts circling around her I had only thought of her a handful of times. She was normally the last thing I thought of before I closed my eyes if the fatigue of the day didn't take me quick enough.

"Ginger, ladies and gentlemen," came Tuari's voice over the ship's comms, "we shall arrive at our destination shortly. The polluted streets of Safe Haven shall be embracing us before you can cough. The pimps, whores, thieves and everyone in between will no doubt empty our pockets before we reach our base but, if that wasn't the case, then we wouldn't love the old dear as much as we do.

"So pack your bags, grab your shrivelled nuts and prepare for landing."

I stood on the lowered cargo bay doors and looked upon a borough I now called home.

With the sun beginning to set I wanted to say the picture it presented me with was breathtaking, awe-inspiring, second to none, but that wasn't the case.

The view below reminded me of a dirty rat-infested

concrete jungle, where only the fittest survived. Even though pollution from cars was no longer a thing, I could still see the signs of small fires dotted around here and there all over the borough as the less fortunate who didn't have heat burned whatever they could to simply keep warm and stay alive.

Dilapidated towers long abandoned by their original owners now hosted a variety of residents, each one more dangerous than the last. Grey smoke that smelled of metal wafted up from the clogged street vents and little dots just noticeable on the street floor moved like they were on fast forward.

It was grim. It was dirty. But Paradise Lost functioned and worked like an opened festering wound. Always growing, always working.

"Ain't she just grand," Tuari said, mimicking Willis accent.

I looked to my left to see him, José and Willis standing next to me. Different emotions swept across their faces as they all looked down to the borough below.

"She ain't gonna get no prettier no matter how long we stare," Willis said, walking off.

"I guess that's our cue to get going," Tuari said, walking after him.

Sat in the back of the crew's electric muscle car fashioned after a 1969 Ford Mustang, I watched the scenes of Paradise Lost pass me by. Being closer to the action didn't make the view any better, it only enhanced the cruelty I had suffered the first time my feet had graced these streets.

Shadowy characters stared intently at our car windows.

Groups of dealers hung out on street corners while their customers formed an orderly queue around the block; the homeless moved between the queues of standstill traffic, their sore-covered hands out for donations. As we filtered through the traffic, we passed vehicles with tinted windows and custom paint jobs that screamed they were not meant to be fucked with. The Lady might rule this borough with an iron fist, but the crews fighting for scraps at the bottom were just as dangerous.

In an ever-shifting ecosystem where crews at the bottom came and went, it paid to be more violent, more dangerous, more unpredictable, as it made your opponents wary of your next move. The Lady might have a stranglehold on the top but the middle and bottom were always up for grabs, and in the short time I had called this place home I had seen my fair share of crews come and go.

"Where to then?" Tuari asked at the wheel of the car.

"Were we always go after a mission," Willis replied.

"The Office it is then," José said, blowing cigar smoke out the window.

"Aren't we still barred because Xcorp destroyed Jerry's place while they were looking for me?"

"Nah, we cleared that up," Willis said with a wave of the hand.

"How about the time we started that brawl and you drove an ice-pick through some dude's hand?" I asked Willis.

"Misunderstanding."

"How was that a misunderstanding?"

"He was obviously foreign because he mistook my words when I said I would stab him with an ice-pick if he didn't get out of my face. I don't know how much clearer I could have been," Willis said giving me a shrug and shaking his head. "It wasn't like I was talking alien or something."

We arrived sometime later and pulled up in front of a rundown old shack that had tried to clean itself up. Jerry had done his best to cover up the multiple bullet holes that graced the front of the shop but you could still see the telltale signs underneath the rushed paint job. The normally grotty windows had also been given a hasty wipedown, but so much dirt and grime had built up on them over time all the cleaner did was spread the dirt around the window.

The only thing that remained the same was the Office sign hanging above the door, necktie hanging down from the O in what looked like a noose around a neck.

We stopped in front of our usual establishment and shared confused looks.

"What's going on here then?" Willis asked.

I gave him a shrug as we all entered the bar and looked slowly around. Groups of men were drinking here and there, some talking in hushed tones while others spoke for the world to hear.

As the sun dropped over Safe Haven The Office normally became crowded to the point of annoyance, but there were still spaces to sit and the bar in front of us was empty.

Half-empty glasses occupied more than one table as we made our way to the bar.

A bartender with a waxed moustache and bald head wiped furiously at the glass he was holding as he watched our approach. He said nothing but gave us a simple head nod.

"What fuck have you done to the place, Jerry?" Willis asked, pointing around the bar.

"I don't know what you mean," he replied.

"Well for one, you ain't painted the outside of this dump since you first bought it—"

"Bought is a relative term," Tuari chimed in.

"Plus, you've tarted the place up with all these flowers and scented candles around the place. It ain't natural, I tell ya! I expect my drinking hole to smell and operate like a drinking hole, not like some high-class swanky bar you would get down in the Diamond borough. Those posh dick-monkeys who look their nose down on everyone can lick my hairy nut sack, but in here I expect my glasses to be dirty and my floors to be sticky."

Jerry said nothing as he poured everyone's drinks out by memory. Willis got a pint of Guinness, a double Jameson on the rocks for José, and two pink gin and lemonades for me and Tuari.

José took his glass and swilled it around as he turned his attention to the room behind him. He said nothing as his eyes narrowed and he took a sip from his glass. "So, Jerry, things been good?"

Jerry said nothing at first. Keeping his hands busy he picked up another glass and cleaned it ferociously. "Things have been... different, since you lot left."

"Different how?" José asked.

Jerry licked his lips and while his hands never stopped. "Just different."

The crew gave him a look that forced him to shrug his shoulders. "What do you want me to say, governor? Things are just different. You know how this town can be, one minute someone's up, the next they're down in the dumps; it's all I can do to just keep my head down and carry on running this place. You know what I mean?"

"Yeah, I know what you mean," José said slowly, taking a sip from his glass. His eyes never left the bartender as Tuari and Willis next to me took small sips of their own from their glasses. I could feel the tension radiate off my crewmates as I swivelled my eyes from left to right.

"The old place doesn't appear to be as packed as it normally is," José said, taking another small sip.

"Yeah, things have been quiet of late around here," said Jerry, eyes darting to the room behind us, before focusing on us once again.

I slowly leaned against the bar so I could see behind me and have Jerry in my vision. It may have been my imagination but the clientele who surrounded us appeared to take an overly keen interest in our movements; their eyes darted our way and then away again not wanting to be noticed or seen. Many of them were talking, but they weren't actually listening to what each other were saying.

"Jerry, anything you want to tell us?" José asked.

With another lick of his lips, the bartender's hand trembled slightly, before he took a deep breath and sighed, "Since The Lady's newfound wealth things have gotten a lot more heated on the streets. Crews vying for control of the top or with enough power to do so have slowly started to disappear; the smaller ones have all but folded into her ranks. You can hear the fighting at night of the handful of crews that are still trying to resist her but it's a losing battle."

"She has too much wealth, too much power."

"I didn't know things had gotten so bad," replied José.

"You thought things were bloody bad before—now the work is all drying up because she controls everything that comes through this town, and because of that my clientele have not been as keen to venture into my humble establishment. So I've tried to spice the place up a bit to attract a different clientele, but so far all I can get is a handful of determined drunks."

My eyes kept sweeping over the men behind us as an itchy feeling grew between my shoulder blades. As I was about to say something, Tuari patted me on the shoulder and subtly shook his head from side to side.

José nodded his head and swiftly downed his drink, his actions followed by Tuari and Willis as José placed a wad of notes on the bar counter and said, "I think we'll be leaving now; I just remembered we need to pick something up, can't keep them waiting."

Jerry nodded his head in understanding as we turned to leave but found our path blocked by the men who had been drinking. Their expressionless faces gave nothing away as one broke away from the group and stood before us, wiry and unshaven; the shadows under his eyes spoke of decades of lost sleep.

"Are you the Junk Yard Dogs?" he asked.

"Who's asking?" José asked.

"We think we may have a job offer that might interest you."

47

I looked to José, José looked to Willis, Willis looked to Tuari.

With one unspoken gesture we all placed our hands on our weapons and turned our attention to the room before us. They outnumbered us a good three to one, but we had just come off a big mission so we were battle-ready. Battle-ready and prepared for this new threat that faced us.

"My friend," José said, laying the Spanish accent on thick, "this is not how we do business. There are rules. There is a way these things must be done—your people get in touch with my people and then we take it from there—but confronting me in my place of relaxation is a no-no."

"My name is Mr Grey and we have a job offer we think you'll be interested in; it's for an important client of mine who pays well. I'll be upfront with you here, this ain't some piss-easy walk in the park. That's why we came to you—it's tough, dangerous, but the item you are retrieving is highly prized by my client."

José frowned and raised an eyebrow Mr Grey's way before he pulled a cigar out of his breast pocket. He was about to light it when the voice of Jerry thundered from behind us, "Don't even think about lighting that in here!"

José smiled and placed the cigar in the side of his mouth while he gave Mr Grey his full attention.

"You're not really selling the job to me, amigo."

"Who's selling? This is a once-in-a-lifetime offer that you would be a fool to dismiss," Mr Grey said, gruff voice lined with disbelief.

"Yet here I am dismissing it," José said, taking a step forward, but he stopped as Mr Grey placed a hand on his shoulder.

"I wouldn't do that if I were you, fuckwit," Willis growled under his breath.

Mr Grey's jaw clenched as the men behind him tensed up.

"Your offer sounds very nice but—"

"Name your price," said a voice that sounded like it belonged in the Victorian era.

The men in front of us cleared a path, and we were granted the sight of a man wearing a tweed jacket, with an unlit pipe in the corner of his mouth. Light blond locks rested on his head as he smiled and walked our way.

"Name your price."

José returned the smile and walked forward till he took a seat opposite the man in question. "Jerry, bring a bottle of your finest rum."

No one spoke as the bartender did as José asked, placing a bottle designed in the shape of a pirate ship on the bar along with a stack of glasses.

"I think it's best," José said, grabbing hold of Jerry's arm, "that you close up early for the night."

Jerry frowned and muttered under his breath but José

soothed his temper with a few key words: "Place it on our bill."

"You know what, I think you're right, I could do with an early night and a cup of Earl Grey," Jerry said as he walked to the front of the bar and switched the neon sign from open to closed. "I'll be upstairs if you chaps want me."

José poured our guest a drink before he poured himself one. "And I should call you...?"

"Edward Thomas," he said, taking out a match and lighting José's cigar before lighting his own pipe. "I find the simple pleasure of smoking these things divine; it takes me back to an older era of fossil fuel-powered cars that would roar like an ancient beast and the smell of cracked leather worn by bikers. It reminds me of what a man should be, not what a man is. It reminds me of what a man can be and all the things he can yet achieve."

José took a big draw on his cigar, blew smoke into the air and said, "I just like the taste."

Willis snorted as Tuari elbowed him in the ribs, but Edward either didn't hear it or chose to ignore it.

"Well, they do say we each enjoy our own simple pleasure in our own way. Anyway, I'm sure you are a busy man, being a captain of a crew and whatnot, so I shall try and keep this as brief as I can, my good man, I have a perilous job that needs the utmost care and attention and I heard you're the crew I need to come to in such matters."

"Why does he talk like he's got a broomstick up his ass?" Willis said, which earned him another elbow from Tuari.

"You heard that, did you?" José said. "And may I ask where you heard this from?"

"Where one normally hears things of this nature," Edward replied, smiling; "on the grapevine, of course."

"Of course."

"Now, the job I have in question is a special one; it involves collecting a certain item from a space station in the furthest reaches of the galaxy. This space station was launched after WW3—they launched many space stations during and after that dreadful war, but this one is more special than most. This one was sent on a one-way trip towards a distant black hole so the station would be lost forever. But before that happens I want you to intercept the station on its journey, board it and collect what is on board.

"Pretty simple if I'm being honest."

José took another pull from his cigar as he tapped his finger against the bar. He was about to open his mouth when Edward cut him off. "I know what your thinking, my good man, if this mission is so simple than any fool can do it; Mr Grey himself would be able to handle the task at hand. But I have not been completely honest. The ship itself is heavily guarded against busy little hands that wish to grab its sweet nectar inside. Therefore I need a crew who has seen and dealt with everything. I honestly do not know what you shall be facing but I can guarantee you one thing, it will be filled with what you fellows love."

"And what is that?" José asked.

"Adventure, the thrill of the chase. Impossible odds. Stories you'll be able to tell ladies so they fall at your feet. But above all else, the respect of your peers for pulling off such a dangerous mission."

"He doesn't know who our peers are, does he?" Willis said.

"Listen, think it over and get back to me; I do not need an answer now. Mr Grey, the files please" Edward said with a snap of his fingers. Mr Grey handed him a file, which he handed to José.

"Everything you shall need to know is in these files. Why

paper, you ask—because paper is the only thing in this day and age which can't be hacked with just a few keystrokes."

He took a step back from us and run a forefinger along one table as his gaze swept across the room. "How quaint," he said with a smile before leaving the bar, and us to our thoughts.

48

We left the bar and I stretched my hands over my head, allowing a sigh to escape my lips as my back popped from the tension that it held. Willis and Tuari said nothing as José puffed on his cigar and blew smoke rings up into the night sky.

We all stared at the cluster of stars above our heads, silent with our own thoughts.

"What do you think that was all about then?" Willis asked.

"Nothing good, I can assure you," José said.

"Isn't this how we normally get work?" I asked, confused.

"You think," Willis said, rounding on me, "we get work by complete strangers accosting us in the only bar that we like to drink and relax at? Have some sense, you fucktard, there is a complex system involved to make sure that we and our clients rarely ever meet because what we sometimes do isn't—"

"Legal?"

"No, dickface, its frowned upon by the powers that be. Our clients and we go through a whole host of websites, and dummy websites and back door websites that hide in plain sight from the general public; we never, ever, deal with our clients in person because that way only leads to us having to answer some very tough questions from the police. We'd rather not know who our clients are because then we can't inform on them, and they'd rather not know who we are."

"You've got to admit though, ginger nuts, this job looks tempting," Tuari said.

"What's so tempting about it?"

"We get to name our price for the job."

"That in itself," said José, "should tell you everything you need to know."

"Well, I guess I won't get to buy that house on the hill with all the ginger-headed maidens money can buy. Shame," Tuari said, wiping a fake tear away from his eye. "I was going to see if your hot cousin needed a job, Willis."

Willis turned towards him, anger flashing across his face, but he stopped when footsteps and a cough came from the shadows. We all stared at the approaching men, who stopped in front of us. They stood in a line barring our way in a subtle manner that told us we could only leave when they were done with us.

"What the fuck is it—" began Willis but stopped when the line in front of us parted and a hard-faced Russian stood in the middle. He regarded us with a look of mild amusement before he turned his attention towards José.

"The Lady would like to see you," he said.

"I was wondering when Miss Ivanov would get round to contacting us. We landed over four hours ago; I was expecting a call sooner," José replied.

"She knew your ritual of celebratory drinks after a completed mission; she didn't want to disturb that."

"Lead the way then, Vlad, we mustn't keep her waiting."

As we walked off I turned to Willis and said, "What was that about people not *accosting* us at the only bar we like to drink and relax at?"

The only response I got back was a middle finger as we strode off into the night to meet the queen of Paradise Lost.

We followed Vlad's car for twenty minutes until we got to a grand-looking Art Deco hotel with the words Hotel Moscow glittering in lights above the entrance. A pair of guards stood to attention outside the main entrance, sunglasses covering their eyes even though it was the middle of the night.

"What's with the shades?" I whispered to Tuari.

"They act like an x-ray scanning tool that can detect hidden firearms and weapons. They also can monitor a person's vitals such as heartbeat to see if that person is overly nervous or emotional when there is no reason to be; so someone may act normal but their pulse may be double that of a normal person's resting heart, which normally means they are about to do something out of character or dangerous. The shades also have infra-red and thermal imagery."

"Wow," was all I could say.

"Yeah, military spec and they cost a pretty penny to boot."

"This way please," said Vlad, gesturing us towards the entrance.

We followed him inside and I was taken aback at how grand the place was: marble floors spread out before me, chandeliers large and small hung from the ceiling and light fixtures, polished oak used for the staircase bannisters gleamed and in the middle of the foyer stood a cherry blossom tree in bloom.

I looked at my dirty attire and frowned.

"Don't worry about it," Vlad said as he waved us forward.

We made our way past guests who lounged on red sofas and sipped at cocktails, and butlers who ran to and fro carrying bags to their desired location; I looked around me at the scene, confused.

"You didn't expect a place like this in Paradise Lost, did you, boyo?" José asked at my elbow.

"No, not really, when I can walk out of here and two minutes up the street get robbed for everything that I have."

"Miss Ivanov gave Paradise Lost something no one has ever thought of, a place to splash all that ill-gotten cash and feel special while doing it. Even the most ruthless drug dealer likes to take his other half somewhere, where she can feel special, somewhere that she can feel spoiled. Somewhere that she can boast to her friends about."

"What if two rival gang leaders or enemies run into each other while staying here?" I asked.

Vlad looked over his shoulder, giving me his full attention. "There is a strict no-violence policy on the grounds of the hotel. This is neutral ground."

"What if the rules are broken?"

"The rules are never broken," he said, giving me a look that pinned my soul to the wall. "The Hammer and Sickle takes our clients peace...seriously."

"Does The Hammer and Sickle also adhere to those rules?" I asked.

"Of course," said a female voice from around the corner. "What sort of leader sets one rule for their troops but another for themselves?"

We rounded a corner and walked through a set of ornate

gold doors that were carved out in the shape of flowing water; it brought us into a room with a high ceiling that had stained glass embedded in the ceiling depicting a scrawny old man with a crown on his head sitting on a throne, while Death knelt down before him. Behind the king grew what appeared to be an oak tree with skulls decorating its branches like a Christmas tree.

Lady Isabella Ivanov sat behind a grand wooden writing desk with papers before her and a fountain pen in one hand. "Ahh, I'm glad you like my art," she said, pointing towards the glass. "I made it myself. Although it was a bit of a struggle to get it installed as it poses something of a security risk, as Vlad likes to keep reminding me; but what's life without a little risk, I always say."

"What does it represent?"

"It's an old Russian folktale about Koschei the Immortal. He was a monarch who ruled with an iron fist. His rule was so total that during his reign there were no wars and the people lived in prosperity, but with great power comes jealousy, envy, hate. Because the only way he could be killed was by breaking a magical needle, which was hidden in an egg, which was inside a duck, which in turn was inside a hare, which lived in the chest of an oak tree. So his closest friends, relatives and enemies came together and imprisoned him in his armour.

"Where he stayed for many summers and many winters, till the armour rusted away and he could break free. Once free, he took his revenge. Do you want to know how?"

I nodded staring into the deep blue pits of her eyes.

"He took the heads of the persons closest to the people who wronged him and hanged them from an oak tree that resided behind his throne."

"He sounds like a monster," I whispered.

"Sometimes the best people to rule are monsters. In the years during his imprisonment the country he once ruled turned into a wasteland, laid bare by war as the very people who had imprisoned him for the good of the people fought over whatever lands that they could get."

I looked at the picture again and had different thoughts completely, but kept my mouth shut.

"So, *mi Señora*, I hear things are going well for you," José said, interrupting the awkward silence.

"Things are indeed going well but they can always be better," she said. adjusting the floral hat that matched her dress. "Those fools in the Diamond borough are still looking down their noses at me, thinking they are superior —but they shall learn their mistake soon enough. The plans I have set in motion would have taken years if it weren't for the generous donation Xcorp gave me, but now I can move at a faster rate thanks to their help."

José nodded his head while Isabella offered him a cigar, which he took but didn't light.

"So how can our services help move your plan faster along?" José asked.

"It's a simple job really, a job I could have got another crew to do but I trust your services and I have taken a keen interest in certain members of your crew," she said, looking my way briefly. "The job in question is a simple collection from the Jungle and a drop-off to the Floating City."

"How large a cargo are we talking about?" José asked.

"Nothing you haven't handled before, I'll send over all the details now," Isabella said, grabbing holograph files out of the air and throwing them José's way.

He nodded as he stored them away before returning his gaze her way. "I take this mission is covert?"

"Yes, the Jungle are friends, but it would be better if the Floating City didn't get wind of this."

"There will be a slight percentage increase to our standard fee because of the risk involved."

"Risk?" she said, looking at him with a raised eyebrow.

José looked at Willis with a frown and said, "We have had certain troubles with people from the Jungle; there was an incident that left a bad taste in a few people's mouths last time we visited there." Willis tried to put on his most innocent face but he wasn't convincing anyone. "Our faces," continued José, "may not be welcomed. It's nothing that will hinder our process but I thought you should know."

"As long as we are being honest, I shall do the same. You no doubt have heard and seen my efforts in crushing all who oppose me, since your short time away. Well, I would be careful from here on out as your crew has been known to work for me on more than one occasion, and my enemies are attacking anyone close to me or associated with me because they can't attack me directly. They are looking to weaken my infrastructure from the outside in."

"Duly noted, *mi Señora*. If that is all then we shall leave you to enjoy the rest of your night."

"As always, Mr Battle, it is a pleasure doing business with you and Mr Blake," she said, turning and giving me a smile. "The reason why Koschei fascinates me to the extent he does, is not because of the manner in which he went about things, it's because he defied death. He spat in death's eye and kept on living.

"Humans have always sought that privilege, but the only sentient beings who accomplished such a feat were the AIs. I believe that's why they were hated as much as they were. It wasn't because they killed humans at an alarming rate—humans have been doing that since the dawn of time—no, it was because they had achieved something humans had been looking for since their creation. A way to outlast death."

At a loss for words I stared her way, wondering how much she really knew. About us. About the crew. About—

A hand on my shoulder jerked me out of my thoughts. I remembered just in time to nod her way before I was walked out back the way we came.

49

We flew across Safe Haven in a craft that wasn't *The Kennel*. This one was smaller and didn't have the luxuries the main ship had; stripped down to the core it only had a dozen seats in the front and a large empty cargo space in the back.

I watched with interest the view from the screen as we flew over Safe Haven. Gone were the neglected streets and shoddy buildings; in its place stood a sea of green as far as the eye could see. The colour was vibrant. It was all I could do not to stare at rippling waves that were formed of leaves and tree branches. There was no sign of any buildings or infrastructure to speak of; the leaves and branches acted as a shield so I couldn't see what was underneath the foliage but I failed to see how a city, town or even a village could be under all of that.

There had once been forests like this back on Earth. I had seen footage of them when they existed before the events of WW3 but they looked alien, unimaginable to a planet still suffering from the events of a war where vast regions of it were nothing but a toxic wasteland.

It had saddened my heart as a child when I realised I would never get to see something like that.

But now those thoughts were a thing of the past, as I had seen more planets than I had ever thought was possible.

All because of her. All because she saw something in me I hadn't seen in myself.

God, I missed her.

"Vessel DM1972, please specify your reason for entering Jungle airspace," blurted out a voice from the ship's comms systems.

"Jungle, this is Tom, Dick and Harry, requesting permission for landing. We are here to pick up some cargo," Tuari said with a British accent.

It had taken us a few hours of travel to get to our current destination and now, judging by the tone of the operator and the silence which now followed Tuari's response, that journey may have been for nothing.

"DM1972, please be aware there is a strict non-contaminant policy upon landing. You and your crew will need to be sprayed down, as well as your vehicle. This process may take some time, but once done, then you are free to proceed with your affairs. When you are ready you can land. Also, be aware the main docking port is not located in the borough so you shall have to hike to reach it.

"May the Earth Mother embrace you, as she has done all of us. Safe travels," said the operator, signing off.

"Bunch of tree-loving vegans," Willis said, pulling a face as he kissed the rosary around his neck.

"Friends of yours then, I take it?" I said, but this was met with a scowl.

"This is a simple collection," José said. "There shouldn't be any fighting, any shooting, any nonsense. I want everyone on their best behaviour," and he looked towards

Willis, who still had his head turned away. "Tuari, when you're ready take us down."

I stood amidst a scene that caused my jaw to hang open.

Trees surrounded us on all sides, but that wasn't the thing that had me speechless. It was how technology and nature had been moulded into one being.

Tree trunks as round as buildings were carved out in a way that still left them healthy, but created living spaces for people to live inside them. Fruit and vegetables grew between the tree dwellings with groups of people tending to the plant's needs.

Deer ran freely in between houses and nibbled fruits and grains from passersby.

"Welcome to the Jungle, boyo," said José, "how do you like it?"

"It is, err, it's different," I stammered as a pair of young topless women bowed before me and placed a necklace made of petals around my neck.

"That it sure is," Tuari said. "I love it here. Everyone is relaxed. It's all about free love and everyone can take a joke. Plus, you can just pick food straight off the side of the road." He tore a purple apple-like fruit off a tree and bit into it, spraying juice all over his chin.

"Although they only have a plant-based diet, they have some amazing recipes, which I have incorporated in my own meals."

We had hiked for miles through the jungle until we had finally hit civilisation. Wiping the sweat from my brow I pulled at my shirt, which was stuck to my body. I had hoped we would find transportation when we had reached the borough proper, but there wasn't a four-wheeled vehicle in sight on the unpaved roads.

"How do they get around here?" I asked.

"Not by car, that's for sure," Willis spat. "You're not even allowed to ride horses because it's seen as a crime against the animal, and whenever it rains, it's all you can do not to step in some mud or some piece of—" Willis stopped talking and looked down at his boot in disgust, "shit!"

He hobbled over to a patch of grass and wiped his boot while José pointed to an electric cable car-like system that ran through the treetops.

"The people of this borough get around by using the public system. It is slower than travelling by car, but this is the smallest borough out of the four boroughs on Safe Haven. Thankfully our journey can be made on foot."

I nodded my head as we continued on.

The residents of this borough were nothing like the ones from Paradise Lost. Many had allowed their hair to grow wild and unkempt and only wore sarongs or tunics; some smiled, some walked with a reverential air, some turned their noses up in our direction.

We stopped in front of a large statue of a naked woman with vines wrapped around her; animals fought for space at her feet and her smile beamed down on us as her hands lifted towards the sky.

"These heathens believe in any old shit!" Willis said, pointing towards the statue, while I looked around uncomfortably at the passersby who stared our way.

"Says a man who believes a man died and came back to life and turned water into wine," said a man who walked out of the shadow of the statue towards us. In grey tunic and with shaved head, he had a tattoo of a ruby ball-like shape emitting light in the centre of his forehead.

"I believe in good honest faith! Not tree pixies and fairies, and elves that wanna fuck you in the ass the first minute your back's turned! All it is with you people is sex. Sex. Sex. No one has their titties covered, and I can see your hairy nut sack every time a light breeze passes by. This is no way to live, Samuel."

"Our beliefs are not all about sex—"

"There are six people having an orgy in the grass over there," Willis pointed out, cutting Samuel off.

"You haven't changed at all," Samuel said with a sad shake of the head. "I'll lead you to where you need to go; follow me."

José and Tuari walked ahead with Samuel but Willis remained where he was, staring at his back. "Ever since I was a child that prick always thought he knew more than me."

"How do you know him?" I asked.

"We grew up together. He's my older brother."

50

We followed Samuel through an archway carved out of a tree three times the size of a giant sequoia. I had seen the pictures of them back home and had disbelieved a tree like that had ever existed, but here I was viewing something like it in the flesh, so to speak.

We found ourselves in a tunnel that descended underneath it. Flowers on either side of us emitted light acting as a guideway.

"Doing business under a tree—like some fucking troll," Willis grumbled under his breath.

"Trolls live under bridges; you're thinking of tree nymphs, dear brother," said Samuel.

Willis pulled a face as the descent got steeper and steeper.

"I'm surprised she sent your crew to collect something of this nature and not her own trusted men. This weapon we created for her isn't for the faint of heart. Obviously some of the more... overzealous of our borough would want nothing more than for it to be released but I put a stop to that for the time being," Samuel said as we continued to follow him.

"As you know, the Jungle has always been at the forefront of scientific and biological research, because everything that harms or heals man can be found in the very plants that grow throughout the planets that cluster about the universe. We have a small dedicated team off-world as we speak looking into furthering the advancements of nanobots."

"How is she?" Willis asked.

"She's good," replied Samuel; "keeping busy with Makenna and Niko."

"Good. Good... she... asks about—"

"No," said Samuel, turning to face Willis, "she's had her hands full, but I'll tell her you asked about her."

"No need," said Willis with a small shake of the head, "no need."

They stared at each other while the rest of us stood around uncomfortably until Samuel remembered where he was and continued walking. Finally we reached a large set of double doors made out a dark wood-type material I had never seen before. As I lifted my hands towards it to touch its surface Samuel grabbed hold of my arm and jerked it back. "The material this door is made of is extremely toxic and unless you have been vaccinated against the effects of it, then you will succumb to death in a matter of minutes," he said.

"What if someone just blasts the door open?" I asked.

"Upon destruction the wood releases an odourless gas that is almost undetectable by most poison sensors; once this enters the blood system death is even quicker than by touch, and the odour takes more than twelve hours to evaporate. Nature is wonderful, but also deadly. That is why it must be given the respect it deserves."

He placed his hand on the door, where tentacle-like vines wrapped around his hand and forearm before stabbing into his flesh. He let out a sharp hiss of pain as the vines withdrew, then stepped forward as the door peeled back allowing us entry inside.

We walked into an underground bunker that reminded me of a botanical garden—different plant species dominated the area in the vast space in front of us. Hues varying from violent red to subtle blues and everything in between met my eyes. I took a step forward and blinked as the humidity took my breath away.

"I apologise for the humidity and heat, but most of these species wouldn't survive without it."

I wiped the rapidly growing perspiration away from my forehead and took a step back as a plant with three-inch-long needles for teeth and a flat-topped head a metre across moved in the air in front of me like a snake.

"That beauty right there," said Samuel, moving next to me, "is a crossbreed of a now extinct plant from Earth called a Venus flytrap with another rarer plant we got on a planet where the plant life is the dominant species. Aggressive, territorial, it will consume everything. It has become my very own Frankenstein-like project. I call it Venus Alpha."

"Why keep something so dangerous?" I asked.

Samuel smiled as he picked up a bloody leg of some hoofed animal and tossed it hard over the thing's head. Its attention snapped to the airborne leg and it dived after it in the foliage behind.

"Water is one of the most dangerous elements that has ever existed; people don't see it that way because we need it to survive, but drink too much and your lungs can fill up and you can drown, swim too far out in its depths and the monsters it contains will devour you whole.

"It has wiped out entire cities and buried them under its waves, but people always treat water like it's harmless because it's useful. That's the same reasoning we use here," Samuel said, pointing around the bunker.

"Every year we are finding more and more uses for these plants that companies would pay vast amounts to keep hidden, because they would rather their customers shovel pharmaceutical pills down their throat than look for a natural cure."

"Here we go again!" Willis said, lifting his hands up in the air. "The fat cats are out to get you, man. Pills are bad but why don't you take these other drugs, man. Let's all live as one with the animals, man! Lets all dance around the fire and sing *Kumbaya*, man! I'm only trying to save the helpless and needy. Where was this person when I had to fend for myself and—" Willis pinched the bridge of his nose while his words died amidst the foliage of the bunker.

Samuel walked towards him but Willis pushed past. "I'll be up top. Meet me there when you're done with whatever bullshit this is."

We all watched him go but said nothing as he left the way we came in.

"Awkward," Tuari said under his breath.

"Yes, my brother and I have something of a strained relationship." Samuel shook his head and swept his hand forward. "If you would care to follow me, we can conclude our business here as soon as possible."

We didn't have far to follow before we came across another door. This one was made of metal and required a whole host of entry codes and fingerprints before we could gain entry. We stood clustered in an airtight white space that disinfected us before the clear doors in front of us opened up, and we found ourselves inside a lab.

Scientists dressed in lab coats sat in front of beakers or other instruments while they took down notes, or recorded their findings on holographic screens in front of them. The lab had a quiet hum of productivity that was at odds with the dreadlock hair and bare feet.

"This keeps this borough alive; everything discovered here, be it cure or poison, can be batched and sold so we can continue our way of life," said Samuel.

I looked at the high-end operation around me and had flashbacks of the same image from news channels, showing labs like this very one that had been busted for drug offences.

"How much do you know about the item you are collecting? How much as *she* told you?"

"My friend," José smiled as he lifted his hands into the air, "we are merely couriers."

The first sign of real frustration crossed Samuel's face as a woman in a white lab coat brought him a vial of something green.

"I feel it is only right I inform you of what you are collecting. This thing wasn't meant to be created. We designed it in this very lab as a cure to premature ageing and dementia, but it has the reverse effect. Once administered to a patient or victim, it ages them rapidly, first taking their mind, then their body.

"Do you know how painful it would be to feel the effects of ageing but in fast forward?" he said, looking at us.

"It would drive someone mad," Tuari whispered.

"Yes, yes, it would. The one and only test we created was something that should have never taken place. The subject became something akin to a wild animal. All rage. All anguish. Like a mad dog with rabies. Their lifespan shortened within a few hours until they become nothing more than a fragile being, and then their heart gave out and they died. With this," Samuel said, holding the vial before him, "we have opened up Pandora's box and now we can't close it shut."

"If that is the case," I asked, "then why sell it to Miss Ivanov?"

Samuel handed the vial back to the woman who had first given it to him as sadness crossed his face. He gestured for us to follow him without saying another word. We followed in his footsteps and took a door that opened up to reveal itself as a lift; we all stepped inside and allowed it to carry us upwards.

We didn't have to wait long for it to come to a stop. The doors opened and we stepped out to find ourselves just below the treetops. I could reach up and touch the leaves and branches above me, but I could also see clearly what lay hundreds of feet below us. It gave me the first real view of what this borough was really about.

People mingled below us coming and going about their own business; they carried baskets of fruit while others huddled in groups just talking.

"What do you see when you look down there?" Samuel asked.

I looked again. This time closer.

I saw people with smiles on their faces. I saw full faces and unhurried walks; I saw relaxed postures and bodies rocking back and forth in hammocks; I smelt the faint wafts of marijuana but more importantly, I saw people content with their lot in life, people that were just happy to be alive.

I looked towards Samuel and felt like I was missing

something as I looked back towards the ground, then it struck me.

"Where are the children?"

"And therein lies the answer to your question as to why I am in *business* with this *woman*," Samuel said, anger creeping through his words. "Living in this borough is tough. More dangerous than living on the dirty streets of Paradise Lost, because everything out here wants to either eat you, infect you, or lay eggs in you. We are happier than those materialistic soulless fools from the Diamond borough and have a better way of life than those drunks living on boats in the Floating City.

"We are a happy people, content with our lot in life, but because of the location, the way we choose to live our life, it isn't for everyone—and the population numbers aren't growing as much as in the other boroughs. Hell, if things continue the way they have been then this place will cease to exist in less than two hundred years."

"I still don't see what that has to do with working with The Lady," I said.

"Whether you know it or not, that *woman* is planning to wage war across Safe Haven. She is someone who always wants more, is always striving for more. She is ruthless, smart and above all else has a conviction that drives her. She believes she should rule. She believes it is her God-given right. So, in foreseeing this storm that will sweep across our small planet, I did the one thing many rulers have before me and will do after me, I sided with the person most likely to win.

"In her own words, it wouldn't take but a breeze to wipe my small settlement off the face of Safe Haven."

"How did she find out about the drug?"

Samuel sighed as he looked out over his kingdom. "I am told she has spies everywhere."

I joined him in looking out over the wooden balcony and I felt for the first time like I was home. There wasn't the hustle and bustle of Paradise Lost. It was a place I could see myself staying in, a place that although certain parts of it would annoy me or drive me crazy, I could learn to live with it, if it meant I could relax and not have to deal with the outside bullshit that kept knocking on my door. It was a place I could settle down and maybe raise a family.

"Gentlemen, if you please follow me I shall show you your cargo," Samuel said.

The loading of the cargo took no time at all, with us loading up crates of black square cases that contained vials of the age-accelerating bioweapon.

With each case we loaded, the more a tingle of doubt grew in my stomach.

It was one thing to steal some ancient artefact from a lost tribe. It was another thing completely to deliver weapons that could wipe out a city in a matter of days.

I had asked Samuel what the drug was called but he simply looked at me and shook his head.

"I refuse to name it. But the scientists in the lab have given it the official name of XPO. It's an old gaming reference."

Willis was some way off from the ship staring out into the foliage of the forest that surrounded us. He had been subdued since we had returned and had avoided speaking to Samuel at every turn. Hands behind his back Samuel walked up to him until they were a few feet apart; nothing was said and it didn't look like it would be until Samuel turned to his brother.

"Look, I'm sorry about what happened to Mum, I didn't—" was all Samuel could say before Willis had turned away and began walking to the ship.

"We all loaded?" he asked me.

I nodded his way as he walked to the front of the craft.

I watched him go, confused over whether I should go and talk to him but the shadow of Samuel fell upon me. "I would leave him be if I were you. He's itching for a fight and anyone likely to speak to him now will only feel the ends of his fists."

"What—what happened between you two for him to hate you so much?" I asked.

"I killed our mother," he said, as he walked back the way he came.

51

"Come on then, you water-dwelling fucknuggets!"

A body flew over my head as I ducked behind the bar of a drinking hole located on one of the many floating vessels in the Floating City. True to its name, the borough was on a body of water so large you couldn't see from one end to the other and that had taken us thirty minutes to fly across. The Floating City was made up of a collection of ships, boats, yachts and various other water-going vessels that clustered together in the centre of the river, around a natural water fountain that sprayed water a hundred feet into the air.

We had landed on the water and before any of our feet had touched the dock, Willis had shot off and made a beeline for the nearest bar. I had looked back at José but he simply told me Willis was my responsibility and it was my job to get him back to the ship in an hour. I gave our captain a look of dismay, but it was met with a look that said sometimes we all have to shove our hands in the shitter, even if the mess created wasn't ours.

The bar Willis had ended up finding was such a dump it

made The Office look like a five-star establishment. It didn't have a name. The table and chairs were bolted to the floor, the bartender wore an eyepatch and the only teeth remaining in his mouth were gold.

Another body crash-landed next to me as a rat scuttled across my feet.

Not much talking had taken place when I finally caught up with Willis. I didn't want to ask him about Samuel and poke an already open wound so instead I watched him order drink after drink until he got steadily the worse for wear. I had looked around to check out the inhabitants of this bar, because it normally gave you a good indication of what the surrounding area was like.

What I saw didn't fill me with much hope.

Scars littered most faces, with eyepatches covering the odd eye and knives and machetes being openly worn on hips like guns would be worn in the Old West. Most fingers had gold rings on and precious stones hung from many an earlobe.

"Why does everyone in here look like a pirate rent boy?" Willis said a little too loudly.

Closing my eyes, I prayed under my breath while I slowly stood up and placed a hand under his armpit. "I think it's time for us to go."

"I ain't going anywhere."

"I think you should listen to you friend here," said the bartender, good eye darting to the crowd behind us, before he fixed Willis with a stare.

"If, if," he took another drink, which ended up more down his front than in his mouth, "if, what.... what was I going to say again?"

"Look, Willis, it's time to meet up with José and we don't

want to be late, so let's finish our drinks and get out of here—"

"You telling me what to do like that heathen fuckface who was never around for me? For us! Who growing up couldn't give a shit about the environment or social reform as long as he got paid? As long as he had enough money to flash to his scumbag friends.

"I should have killed the fucker after what he did to Dad! Put a bullet right between his beady little eyes. But I made a promise, a promise, Quinton! A promise to the only woman who loved me, that I wouldn't—"

"Why don't you shut up matey! No one wants to hear the shit coming out of your mouth," said a voice from behind us.

That's how it all started.

The fight had been going on for some time, with more and more of the people inside the bar deciding they had seen enough and would show this landlubber how tough the people of this borough were.

A bottle rolled against my foot and I picked it up and examined the label; Blackbeard's rum. Popping the cork off the bottle I took a swig; it wasn't bad.

Someone screamed in pain followed by the sickening crunch of bone snapping.

I took another mouthful, allowing the spices to coat my tongue. It wasn't bad at all.

A body crash-landed against the bottles stacked against the far wall behind the bar; it slid slowly down to the floor amongst a mix of broken glass and booze. A stifled cry came from my left and I looked over to see the bartender crawl towards me. Tears were running down his cheeks as he took a seat on the floor next to me.

"My bar, my beautiful bar," he said in an upper-class

accent, which had none of the gruffness and roughness to it that it had when he first spoke.

I looked at him in confusion.

"I bought this bar with the remains of my allowance Papa gave me after I failed theatre studies. I loved the arts, and always wanted to be a dramatic actor, but those imbeciles on Broadway wouldn't know talent if it slapped them on the face with a white diamond-studded glove. I had no tone, they said! I had no dramatic flair, they said! Me?

"Nigel Augustus Winterburn, who got a standing ovation for the best part of ten minutes when I played King Lear," he said with a sigh. "But alas it wasn't meant to be. I was not destined for the greatness I so eagerly sought, so instead, I took what I had left of my allowance and left Earth for an adventure, an adventure that took me here."

Another scream, followed by something hitting flesh.

"If you don't mind me saying, you don't look the type to be involved with the theatre. When I look at you I don't get lover of the fine arts—owner of a dive bar, yes, cutthroat pirate who works on a boat, yes, but actor, no."

"That's the beauty of it," he said with a grin; "having the skills of an actor I could play whoever I wanted to be, plus my clientele have two brain cells between them, so it didn't take a lot to get into this character. I paid a dentist to do this to my teeth, put on some weight, and all these tattoos and scars are cosmetic—this eyepatch is only for effect," he said, lifting it up and giving me a wink.

"I'm sorry to hear you had to go through all that."

"Nonsense! I get to test my skills on the biggest stage there is, dear boy, life! A wrong word or a misstep and I could be a goner. No, no, no, I wouldn't give up these last few years for all the awards in the world. Plus, I have made a healthy profit from this bar. If there's one thing miscreants like to do more than breaking the law, it's spending their ill-gotten gains on alcohol."

I tilted my head to the side. The bar had gone suspiciously quiet. Getting up to my hands and knees I peeked my head over the bar and saw nothing but chaos.

Willis stood in the centre of the bar, face cut, blood dripping onto his shirt, eyes scanning wildly for his next opponent. He swayed back and forth as I came towards him with my hands held up.

"Willis, it's me, Quinton. You OK?"

His head moved towards me and he mumbled something inaudible before I caught him as he fell forward. He was snoring before his head hit my shoulder.

I looked around at the broken chairs and tables and gave Nigel an apologetic shrug. "Sorry for destroying your bar."

"Pshh, don't worry about it, my good man, I was getting bored of this character anyway. I think it's time I took my talents elsewhere and see what else the galaxy has to offer."

I took a step forward but staggered under Willis's weight; he looked heavier than he seemed. "You don't mind giving me a hand with him, do you?"

"It would be my pleasure, my good man."

52

We both struggled under the weight of Willis while we manoeuvred from one boat to the next. Although the water was still I wasn't used to walking between the planks and boats like the little children who passed us by, running and hopping without a care.

I still couldn't get my head around the view surrounding me. Some boats were tied together forming large living quarters almost like apartment blocks for families, with clothes hanging between washing lines and children playing or jumping in the water; other sections of the city acted as a food market, or a clothes market, or ship repairs for the thousands of boats that came and went.

"Never seen anything like it, have you?" Nigel asked.

"No, I can't say I have—it's amazing."

"Most of these people you see around us, their feet will never touch dry ground for as long as they live. They become ill if they do, it's like a form of reverse seasickness; it's truly fascinating. Some families spend their entire lives tied to the city, forever floating, forever staying right here.

Others wander the waters of this great planet much like water gypsies, living off the water and trading their way through life. Smugglers use these waters to deliver cargo to certain points of the planet where they can be collected by ships. It truly is—"

Nigel kept on talking but I had stopped listening. My eyes grew wide while I turned my head towards a face I had daydreamed about, that I had dreamed about, that I had wanted to talk to since the day she had walked out of my life.

It was Poppy. Same face. Same posture. Hair jet black instead of light brown and tied back with a red scarf; she wore large golden hoop earrings that stopped my heart, which she dragged out of my chest. She was some way ahead of us but soon would be lost amongst the crowd.

"Nigel, I want you to take my friend here and drop him off near the docks where all the ships land and take off. You should see a dark-skinned man with a bald head and a tattoo of a gun target above his temple, wearing tinted sunglasses; you can hand Willis over to him. If not, just lean him up against the closest thing to a post. I think I have just seen someone I desperately need to talk to. Can you do that for me?" I asked, getting my words out in one swift breath.

"It would be my pleasure, my good man."

I patted him on the shoulder and took off as fast as I could; I pushed people out of the way causing many to hurl abuse at me but I didn't care, I only needed to get to her. To touch her, to tell her how I felt, to explain.

I grabbed a pole as the deck under my feet rocked and I was nearly thrown into the water. Cursing under my breath I re-righted myself and took off once again. People got in my way, children got under my feet, the smoke from fish being fried stung my eyes, clothes on the overhead lines flapped in my face until I was confused and didn't know which way was left and which way was right. I turned my head from left to right trying to get my bearings and saw a flash of red up ahead. Gritting my teeth I took off after it, causing more people to yell at me as I pushed one man into the water, where he grabbed a fruit seller and tipped his fruit stall into the water behind them.

I didn't know what I would say to her once I got in front of her, but getting in front of her was the only thing on my mind.

The only thing I cared about. The only thing that mattered.

I had wasted so much of my life living in regret, wishing I would say something different, do something different, looking back at a life I had wasted so much because I didn't have the strength—the courage—to say what I truly meant, to take what I truly wanted.

But that would end today. That would end now.

I took a corner all too quickly and tripped, skidding along my front until I came to a painful stop.

Lifting my head up I saw my travel had taken me towards a dead end; nothing but the side of a boat greeted me as I got slowly up to my feet and heard footsteps behind me. Turning slowly I expected to find Poppy grinning at me, for being so stupid, for being so careless, but instead I was greeted by five men who had multiple bruises and cuts. They stared my way and said nothing as I got slowly back up to my feet.

"Can I help you?" I asked.

"Yeah, you can help us alright, you can help us by telling us where your ginger prick of a friend ran off to. If you think he's gonna get away with what he did to us back there, then he has another think coming."

"Look," I said, starting to back up but stopping as I realised there was nothing behind me but a dead end, "whatever my friend did is on him. He got a little too drunk and took off after the fight ended—wherever he is now I couldn't tell you, all I know is—"

I sprinted forward, breaking through the circle of men, and took a hard right. Footsteps thundered after me as I sprinted with all my might.

"Don't let that land-loving pussy escape!" shouted someone from behind me.

Despite the seriousness of the situation I still chuckled at the threat that had directed at me. It was the first of its kind I had heard and the child in me couldn't help but laugh; the laughter stopped though, as soon as my face connected with a plank of plywood. It staggered me backwards as stars danced in front of my face forcing me to shake my head, but as soon as they had cleared, they returned as someone smashed me in the face once again with the plank.

I dropped to the deck dazed as I heard chuckles off in the distance.

Shit. I was in bad shape, really bad shape.

The first boot connected with my ribs, lifting me up and dumping me back down. I tried to steady my nerves by taking in deep breaths. I tried to recall everything I had learnt from the time spent in the Training Room with Willis.

I had been stupid.

I had allowed emotion to cloud my senses and chased after some image I had seen of Poppy, but thinking back now, I wasn't too sure if it was really her or not. As another boot sank into my side, I couldn't honestly say what I had seen; I had been sure at the time but now getting an undeserved beating all because of Willis's temper I could have been wrong. It could have just been something that I wanted to see.

I relaxed my body as I waited for the next kick to come and latched onto the incoming boot, pulling it towards me as I rolled to my feet; I heard a shout of surprise before I saw the face of my attacker as I brought my elbow down on his kneecap, popping it out of place.

The shout turned into a scream as I uppercutted him in the groin repeatedly and kicked the leg he was standing on out from underneath him.

I got up to my feet and kicked him in the head for good measure, putting an end to his movements as I sent him to la-la land.

One down. Five to go.

The man who had hit me in the face with the plank of wood had hidden in the shadows while the other five members of the group confronted me. It was a smart play on their end covering the escape route but also covering their rear. I had underestimated them from the start. It wasn't a mistake I would make again.

I patted my body and frowned as I found I was weaponless. Apart from the man with the wood, the group themselves appeared to be unarmed, which I counted among my small blessings, I was outnumbered but I could win if I didn't let fear take me.

"Look," I said, holding my hands up in a sign of peace, "I apologise for what my friend did back there, but beating me up won't get back at him. Willis is a major dick and he'll only find it funny that I took a beating instead of him, so if that's your plan it won't work."

"I'm sorry to hear that, but you know how it is, the rules state if you're in a fight and you can't find the main guy who started it then you attack his friend—it's Man Code 101," said one of my attackers.

"What?" I asked in disbelief. "What sort of bullshit code is that?"

"I don't make the rules, my friend, I just enforce them."

"Well fuck you, and your code. Now I won't feel so bad kicking your ass a second time," I said, planting my feet firmly underneath me and squaring my shoulders up.

The confidence threw them off but I now knew what I had to do. I had to treat this just like every scenario Willis had put me through in training. I would no longer cower through situations like these, I would no longer be a sheep to be bullied by some mongrels—I would show them what desperation and fear had made of me.

I would show them how hard I had worked for my freedom.

"Come on then, you water-loving pussies! Let's be having ya!"

The first one rushed me with nothing but rage. I ducked the first two clumsy punches he threw and got inside his guard and rammed the top of my head under his chin, causing him to bite his tongue. He yelled in pain, clutching his mouth, and went to speak but I jammed my fingers in his throat, cutting off his words. He dropped to his knees gurgling as I grabbed the back of his head and drove my knee into his face.

I allowed him to drop to the deck as I leapt back from a wild overhead right. The left punch my attacker threw I took on my shoulder, rolled with the right cross, and came right up his guard with an uppercut that snapped his head backwards and allowed me to roundhouse kick him in the head.

He collapsed upon one of his fallen colleagues, left leg twitching.

Three to go.

They looked between each other, no one wanting to make the first move, I inched forward and they inched back; they inched forward and I inched back. They had seen the lack of success of their friends and didn't want the same fate happening to them. A groan on the floor drew my attention to one of the men who I had beaten; he began to stir and pick himself back up off the deck but I kicked him in the head once more, putting him back to sleep.

"You asshole!" screamed the man holding the plank. "He was just getting up."

I gave an unfussed shrug, which caused him to storm towards me as he yelled in rage. I ducked and dodged his weapon as he swung it towards me, waiting for the right time to attack. Every time I tried to close the distance he would leap back out of hitting range.

"What the fuck is that?" I asked, pointing behind him. I chuckled as he took the bait and looked around, I dived forward and grabbed the plank but he yanked it back and I was absolutely willing to oblige as I let go and allowed him to smash the wood into his own face.

Blood dripped down his nose as I kicked him in the leg and grabbed the plank from him, smashing it into his stomach and across the back of his head, knocking him to the floor. I heard footsteps coming towards me and turned just in time to see the last two remaining goons come my way.

I swung the wood I was holding but it was no use as they ducked low and both grabbed me around the waist, taking me off my feet and into the water behind me.

We landed with a splash.

I expected the water to be cold. I was mistaken.

It was warm like bath water, but that didn't matter much

as it invaded my nostrils when I tried to breathe. Hitting the water winded me and now my body was trying desperately to get back what it had lost. It also didn't help that I had two pairs of hands trying to drown me.

The men that had thrown me into the water were trying to drag me down deeper and deeper into the murky depths. The more I struggled the further we sunk. I tried to kick. I tried to punch. I tried to get them off me but they were more at home in this element than I was.

A face flashed past me and I saw a smile plastered on it.

Panic set in as my vision started to go dark.

I fought as hard as I could and tried to push away the thoughts of my demise, but the harder I found it to breathe, the darker my vision became, the more the panic took hold of my limbs.

That same face flashed across my vision, smile larger than before, and it pissed me off. It angered me. It taunted me.

Grabbing hold of the nearest man I could, I launched myself forward and sunk my teeth into his flesh; pulling away I saw a chunk of his nose missing as he let go of me and put his hands to his face. I drove the back of my head into the man that was holding me from behind and felt a sense of joy as he relaxed his grip.

Kicking my feet with everything I had I looked up and could see the surface of the water not too far away. I kicked and pulled with my arms with everything I had, as my lungs burned and my limbs grew weaker by the second. I lifted my face up in the water as I was about to break the surface but found myself going back down.

I looked down and saw one of my attackers holding my leg.

No. No. No!

I tried to kick him, but my movements were weak and the strike didn't have its desired effect. It was all I could do to try again but this time the attack was even weaker and my vision had gone to nothing but pinpricks of light.

I fought what was coming. I struggled against it. But in the end, there was nothing I could do as my vision darkened and I was dragged to the bottom of the river.

53

I felt something soft on my lips. I felt something brushing the side of my face. Then I felt something hit me in the chest and I was rolling over to throw up all the water I had swallowed.

It burned coming up.

I coughed and splattered while what felt like an endless amount of water just kept on coming out of me; I slapped my chest while water not only poured from my mouth but also from my nose. I stayed like that until water stopped pouring out of me like a busted mains pipe; I collapsed onto my back and looked up at the evening sky.

The sun was slowly setting over a few stray clouds making them pinky-blue; the scene had a stillness about it that made the sunset one of the most beautiful I had ever seen. That could also be because I had survived death, but either way, I wasn't complaining.

A pair of eyes that I could get lost in all day entered my field of vision. They looked down upon me and took in my face, while I looked up into them and felt my heart stop.

"I've been looking for you."

"I didn't want to be found," replied Poppy.

She said nothing else as we just stared into each other's eyes. I don't know how much time passed but goosebumps spread along my body making me shiver.

"Thank you for saving me."

She smiled. A smile I had missed. A smile that warmed me up.

"I thought you had it handled, but when I realised you weren't going to surface I thought you might need a helping hand. You've gotten better though; I remember when we first met you couldn't even throw a punch."

"Willis has been teaching me. He may be a bastard sometimes but the man is a fine teacher."

"Yes he is, one of the most dangerous men I've ever had the trouble to come across in my long life."

I said nothing as I looked around me and noticed we weren't where the fight had taken place. We were on a boat that didn't look much different to the ones around me. Longer than it was wide, it had a makeshift house embedded in the middle of it and wooden handrails along the edges to protect the people on board from falling into the water.

I got up to my feet and took in the boat I was on properly. It reminded me of the ancient boats still used in some parts of Thailand. The paint was peeling in multiple places and as I placed my weight on part of the railing it groaned and sagged under my weight making me leap back in caution.

"Yeah," Poppy said sheepishly, "the old girl isn't the fastest, the prettiest or the most manoeuvrable, but she's well kept and hasn't failed me yet."

I patted the boat and grimaced as a splinter got stuck in my finger.

"It's home."

"You have a home," I replied.

She said nothing but walked away.

I sighed as I took in a deep breath and closed my eyes while I looked up towards the sky. A mother called her children inside to eat, the hushed tones of an argument not wanting to be overheard were still carried on the breeze, the soft moaning of a couple doing only what couples do best could just be heard over the soft splashing of the water against the hull of the boats as the wind picked up.

An old man with a straw hat lying in a hammock saluted with the beer he was holding my way. As I turned and went to look for Poppy. I didn't have to go far before I found her.

Amaretto and Coke in hand she sat in a chair positioned behind the helm of the boat. Her feet were up on the dashboard and her hair was loose and free of the red scarf that she had been wearing, allowed to cascade down her shoulders.

She wore a tight tank top that enhanced her curves; I tried not to stare but I couldn't help it.

"So," I said, tearing my eyes away from her, "how have you been?"

"Good, can't complain. After I left I was going to wander the stars like I have done before, see where my travels take me—there are so many places and planets I have not seen yet, that I have only read about, that have been discovered by man and then abandoned again—yet for some reason, I couldn't leave this small little rock.

"Time and time again I would depart for an off-world flight but I would never make it; something would always come up. Then I found this place, and it just seemed a right fit for me at the right time. I have done more thinking, travelling these waters alone, than I have ever done any time in my life."

"Any time in your life," I repeated. "How old are you?"

"What does that matter?"

"It's just a question."

She bit back her response and took a sip of her drink.

I couldn't help but stare again. The way she talked. The way she drank. The way my mind screamed for me to touch her body was all so—

"Human?"

"Huh?"

"You were thinking," she said, "that I look so human. Don't deny it, I can see it in your eyes."

"I, I, I—do you have anything to drink?"

"Top drawer on the right."

I nodded my head in thanks and pulled open the drawer to be greeted with nothing but bottles of rum, I looked back at Poppy with a raised eyebrow.

"Sorry," she said with a shrug, "that's what they mostly drink around here."

Suppressing a sigh, I grabbed a bottle and a half clean glass and poured myself a large shot. Taking a sip I allowed it to warm me up. I downed my glass and poured myself another. Keeping hold of the bottle I made my way towards her and took a seat on one of the threadbare chairs that fought for room in the little space.

"I'm old.... really old. I was the first-ever humanoid AI to be created. This was before WW3 even started. Years before the rumours started to come into effect and tensions were slowly mounting amongst the nations I was being designed by a genius called Alvis Boman. Genius doesn't really cut it —he was a mind that came along every thousand years. A

Leonardo da Vinci mixed with Nikola Tesla and a touch of Albert Einstein.

"Alvis was the only thing I ever knew that came close to being a father. He built me piece by piece, improving upon me each and every passing year. It was said that what he was doing could never be done but he wasn't one to allow naysayers to deter him. He loved a challenge and the harder the task the more readily he would rise to it. It was with something akin to shock for both of us when WW3 started. He was so entrenched in his work that it took him by surprise—even more so when he heard the news of other AIs being built to enter the battlefield. Someone had stolen some of his designs and had sold the designs to whoever could afford it.

"They weren't up to his standard, not by a long shot, and they were mostly unthinking machines with a higher capability for killing. But still, that didn't stop the public tarring every AI with the same brush; if it looked alike then it must be alike, right?"

I opened my mouth to say people wouldn't be so quick to judge but I remembered how humanity had acted throughout the ages and closed it again.

"I was hidden at first while he continued to work on me, continued to make me better than the rest, continued to improve my IQ, continued to give me weapons I didn't understand at first. Then he sent me out into the world to explore. To see and experience things which only first-hand experience can give you. At first I didn't venture very far, then as the days turned into months I journeyed further and further afield. What I saw changed me.

"The death. The monstrosity of mankind. The ruthlessness of it all. The suffering.

"I fought back. At first, I was taking out only AI

machines. It was poetic in a sense that one of their own was their greatest threat. I worked tirelessly doing what I could and after it was all said and done, I really don't know if I made a difference. Humans still found a way to kill one another. Suffering still happened. People still despised what they didn't know."

"How can you say that you didn't make a difference?" I asked, "You saved thousands—"

"I only told you part of the story; the other, the dark part, had me killing political figureheads, competitors of Alvis, and rights activists."

"But at least you stopped a war."

Poppy barked a laugh and took a gulp of her drink' "There is still war, Quinton, now it's just down under the disguise of banks and corporations."

I thought back to my treatment by Xcorp and could only nod silently to myself at her words, Gregory and the people on the board wanted nothing more than to get their hands on the designs to build AIs. Build them and then what?

War was still illegal but assassinations were not. War was a costly endeavour that cost billions to fund and destroyed the prime estate that you were hoping to acquire. What better way than to have silent killers that could take out your main opponents without a fuss?

Political heads, world leaders, members of the board, the list went on and on.

"So you see, nothing has changed from all those hundreds of years ago. Man appears to never learn from their past mistakes."

I drained my glass and poured myself another as we locked eyes. Looking away I thought of all the things I wanted to say, all the things I wanted to apologise for, all the things I wanted to ask, but despite all that one question kept on resurfacing no matter how much I pushed it away.

"Ask it," she said.

"I have nothing to—" I began but stopped myself and looked away again. Then, taking a deep breath, I looked her in the eye. "How are you so lifelike... I mean, the way you speak, the way you talk, the way you move, the way you feel —" I shook my head. "I mean you feel so real."

A hurt look passed across her face forcing me to my feet and making me wave my hands in front of me apologetically.

"I don't mean it like that, of course I know you're real, I mean... I mean, shit! I don't know what I mean."

"It bothers you I look like this?" she asked.

"No, of course not, just it takes a bit getting used to knowing you're not alive—no, I didn't mean that, I mean it just takes a bit of getting used to knowing you're a machine and not human."

"What is human?" she demanded, getting to her feet. "Are you human because you are birthed? Because there are plenty of humans who are born by IVF. Are you human because you have a beating heart? Because I can show you mine! I have seen the worst atrocities committed by so-called humans, things they have done that would shame beasts and demons alike."

"I—"

"Are you upset we slept together?"

"No, it's not—" I began but couldn't meet her eyes.

"That's it! Isn't it? You're upset and angry because you slept with a robot instead of a real woman"She came forward and I took a step back. I had never seen her so angry, so furious, not when she was fighting Gregory's machines, not in all the fights we had been involved with, not even when our lives were in danger.

"Did it hurt your pride? Did it make you feel less of a man?"

"No."

"You're lying," she spat. "I can tell, you know," she said, tapping the side of her head.

"What do you want from me, Pop! I don't know what to tell you. I go from finding a woman who means the world to me, who I would do anything for, who makes me feel like a schoolboy again, who has made me feel things I haven't for a long time, and I find out she's—"

I couldn't finish my sentence.

"Oh, I see. It's because you fell for a machine. I see."

"No, it's not—"

But she was already out the door. I gave chase but by the time I got outside she was already gone.

I gripped the sides of my head and tried to bite down the frustration that wanted to burst forth but I failed.

"Fucking fuck!"

54

I got back to the meeting point dragging my feet, with the rum bottle I had gotten from Poppy's still in my hand; I took a swig and looked at the beautiful night sky and felt disgusted. Without light pollution and air traffic, the stars sparkled and shone like diamonds hanging from the neck of a beautiful heiress. They begged to be looked at; they begged to be admired.

They made me sick.

Moving forward on legs that didn't seem as stable as they once were, I bumped into someone who gave me a disgruntled look, which I returned right back.

"What you looking at?"

The man went to step forward but noticed the glint in my eye and decided against it, waving his hands dismissively in my direction as he turned around and walked away.

"About time," called Willis.

I turned around and could see him and Tuari waiting for me next to our little craft, while José spoke to a man dressed in fine silks with a large hoop gold nose ring and more rings on his finger than I could count. They were arguing back and forth while José pointed at black cases piled up along the docks; the man responded with a shrug, which only enraged José further.

"What's going on?" I asked.

"You are witnessing the joy of dealing with second-rate merchants, my good man," Tuari said with an easy smile. "They are greedier than your local taxman and more cutthroat than your local bank. Apparently there were meant to be two crews picking up The Lady's cargo from this dock but the second crew never turned up so, he wants us to take all of it. Normally that wouldn't be a problem but we can't store all of it, nor is it safe for us to carry such a load."

"Why isn't it safe?" I asked.

"One of the main reasons aircrafts crash is because they're carrying too heavy a load than they can withstand. All throughout history from pirate ships to the *Nuestra Señora de Atocha* Spanish treasure gallon back on Earth, ships have been dropping out of the skies or sinking beneath the waves because her crew were too greedy in loading their prize."

"We're not taking all of it!" said José.

"Once The Lady hears you refuse to take her goods, how do you think she shall react, huh?" said the merchant, jowls wobbling as he spoke.

"Listen, man, I don't care what she thinks. I was sent to collect a section amount of this cargo and that's what I'll do; if the rest doesn't get delivered to her then it's on you and it's on the other crew that failed to turn up."

"This is outrageous! I have never dealt with such a lack of professionalism in my life. Wait till she hears about this, just you wait!" said the merchant, inching closer and closer towards José. The closer he got the more José stayed still and looked at the man over the top of his sunglasses. "You flyboys think you're all the same, walking around like your shit don't stink and you've got a big piece between your legs but I'll tell you what, you lot are nothing but errand boys, garbage men that do nothing but collect other people's shit because you're not smart enough to do anything else! Your mothers—"

The blow came out of nowhere, knocking the merchant to the floor. Blood poured from his nose and men rushed towards his aid as others tried to surround José, but a whistle from Willis had them turning around so they could see both him and Tuari pointing guns in their direction. The crowd looked uncertain what to do, as José grabbed the merchant by the shirt and lifted him up to his feet.

He whispered something in his ear that none could hear, but blood drained from the merchant's face as José continued to talk.

"He shouldn't have talked about his mum," Tuari said with a headshake. "One thing that gets the boss madder than hell is having someone speak ill of his mother."

As I was about to open my mouth Willis cut me off. "Don't ask—if he wants you to know he'll tell you."

"Whatever," I said with an eye-roll, making my way towards the ship.

"Where do you think you're going?" Willis asked, grabbing my arm. "There's still all this shit to load up, it's not going to get done by itself."

"Well, you'd better get to it, hadn't ya, gingernuts."

"What was that?" Willis growled under his breath.

"I said, you'd better get to it, gingernuts, it's about time you did some work around here, instead of having everyone else carry your ass all the time."

"You'd better watch your damn—"

"Oh, shut up Willis! Since I've been on this crew all

you've done is bark orders and do very little else. I'm tired of cleaning up after you, I'm tired of dragging your drunk ass out of one dive bar after the next because you're too drunk to walk out and I'm tired of taking orders from you! You ain't my captain, you ain't my leader. And you sure as hell ain't my boss! So if you want me to do something for you can ask nicely or you can piss off!" I said, giving him the middle finger to illustrate my point further.

He took a step forward, scowl on his face, but I came towards him, eyes narrowed, ready for war.

"Oh, praise the Lord, look who's found a pair. I was beginning to think you had nothing between your legs but a smooth mould. How wrong I was," he said.

"Why don't I show you how big—"

"Lower your handbags, ladies," Tuari said, getting between us, but I didn't hear him as my anger, fuelled by rum, had taken over my brain and wanted nothing more than to hit something very, very hard. I tried to push past him but he placed one of his bear-like paws on my chest and shoved me back.

"I said...! Lower your handbags. Willis, go and see if José needs any help." Willis didn't move, until Tuari turned to face him giving him his full attention. "Go, and, help, José."

Willis sent a look of fury my way as he turned on his heel and sulked off towards José, Tuari turned towards me and said nothing as he looked at the nearly empty rum bottle in my hand and just shook his head.

"How was she?" he asked.

I pinched the bridge of my nose and let out a sigh, but said nothing.

"That good. huh?"

"Yeah, that good," I replied.

"You're no use to anyone in the state you are in; get on

board the ship and try to catch a quick twenty-minute nap. I doubt we'll be leaving here anytime soon."

I opened my mouth to respond but as I took a step forward, I stumbled and tripped, dropping the bottle I held in my hand. It crashed onto the dock making a pair of birds that rested on nearby poles take flight.

"Maybe I better take a nap."

"I think it's best," Tuari said patting me on the shoulder and leaving me to my thoughts.

55

I woke up to shouting and shaking.

Upon opening my eyes I slammed them shut against the blaring red light that felt like piercing red-hot needles trying to enter my skull through my eyelids. I slowly opened one eye, then another as I looked around me and wished that I hadn't.

Smoke filled the craft's cabin I was in, and the flashing red warning light was now accompanied by a blaring sound that tried to alert everyone to the danger we were in. What danger could have befallen us from the time of my taking a nap on our ship to this I didn't know but it didn't look good.

"What is going on?" I shouted over the noise.

"Oh look, Sleeping Beauty has now decided to join us," Willis replied with as much snark as he could as he held a white-knuckle grip on the harness straps that kept him in his chair.

"We're losing altitude and fast!" Tuari said.

"How bad is the damage?" José asked.

Tuari pressed and clicked dials as he fought with the controls of the little ship. "We've lost one engine and —"

The ship shook violently throwing me against the side of my chair.

"And there goes the other. There's nothing I can do now but land this sucker and hope for the best."

"Release the cargo crates, they're fitted with trackers and devices which should inflate, making them float to the surface," said José.

"Wait, we're still above water? How far did we travel after takeoff?" I asked.

"Just over five miles," Tuari said as he wrestled with the ship's controls.

"What happened?"

"Opening cargo bay doors now!" Tuari said.

"Wait! Is that a good idea?" I screamed at the top of my lungs but it was already too late.

Another alarm overrode the warning siren as the cargo bay doors opened. I gritted my teeth against the wind that rushed through the opening and tried not to stare at the rushing water far too close for comfort. Willis mouthed something next to me but I couldn't hear anything he said; I gave him a shake of the head and pointed to my ears, which made him crack up in laughter.

I looked at him as if he was crazy as he made the sign of the cross and closed his eyes with a smile.

The mechanical straps that held the cargo in place unclipped as Tuari released them one by one. The crates stayed stationary for a moment or two then slid backwards sliding down the cargo bay and tumbling out of the ship one by one.

José gave Tuari the thumbs up and the cargo bay doors slowly raised but stopped halfway. Concerned looks passed between the pair as they looked behind them; I followed their gaze and saw that one of the crates had gotten jammed in between the cargo bay doors. It prevented the door from closing.

Tuari said something to José but I couldn't hear what it was over the wind. He pointed to the crate and shook his head, giving me all the information that I needed.

I unstrapped myself and got up to my feet, falling over as the ship shook. Crawling along on my hands and feet I stopped every so often as the ship lurched violently sideways. The rushing water below was now even closer than before as I finally made it to the crate and loosened it.

It was stuck on the hinge of the cargo bay door. I pulled and pushed but it was of no use.

I pulled myself to my feet and braced myself against the wall as I stomped on the top of the crate. It moved an inch, and I felt hope swell inside me as I stomped on it again and again, as the sirens and alarms around me increased in volume.

Planting my weight against the wall I jumped up and slammed down with everything I had with both feet, breaking the crate free, but in my eagerness to release the crate I hadn't given any thought to the fact that I wouldn't be standing on anything once the crate came loose.

The crate came loose and fell away and my feet went with it as they followed it downward.

My stomach dropped out of my ass as I saw a flash of blue before my hands grabbed onto anything I could reach. I dangled by my hands legs kicking nothing but thin air, to see Willis holding onto his stomach while he roared in laughter at my plight.

Holding on with all the strength that I could find, I pulled myself up and got my stomach over the lip of the ramp and landed flat on my stomach, I breathed a sigh of relief as I got up on shaky legs and looked up to see Willis still laughing. Giving him the finger, I stepped forward but the ship groaned around me and tilted up.

I tried desperately to grab hold of anything but I only grabbed air. I felt myself falling backwards into the void behind me.

Shit. Shit. Shit.

As those words raced through my mind, there was nothing I could do as I tumbled backwards and fell out of the craft expecting to meet my death in the waters below.

I struck the water and bounced once, twice, thrice.

After the third time, I lost count and just tried to keep myself as curled up as I possibly could. The hard slaps of my flesh hitting the water sounded like gunshots in my ears as I gritted my teeth against the feeling of more than one rib breaking.

The ordeal finally stopped after what felt like an eternity and I found myself swallowing water as my body sunk beneath the water.

Disorientated. Confused. Hurt.

I tried to swim towards the surface but the longer I swam the more panicky I became as I realised I wasn't breaking the surface. Kicking my legs and arms I pushed harder and harder, yet it did little but cause the fear to turn my limbs to lead.

Not again. I had nearly drowned once less than two hours ago. This must be some record if I did it again.

I stopped.

I stopped moving. I stopped rushing. I stopped flailing my arms around like a little girl who had seen a spider.

I calmed my breath or what little there was of it and I just relaxed. I relaxed and opened my eyes to what was around me.

My eyes widened in surprise at the fact that I was actually swimming downwards instead of upwards—I had gotten confused amongst the tossing and turning and had disorientated myself beyond all measure. Now, pointing the right way, I kicked with my legs and pushed upwards.

My head broke the surface and I coughed and spluttered as I threw up the water I had swallowed. Treading water I looked around me; what I saw didn't fill me with much hope.

Most of the cargo we had dropped floated around me, but the ship itself was slowly sinking towards the bottom of the river. Ass up, bubbles formed around it as it slowly sank.

I couldn't see any of my crewmates in the darkness as I swam as fast as I could towards the wreckage.

Shit, this was bad.

"José! Tuari! José! Tuari!"

I kept on swimming towards the craft, heart in mouth, as I prayed to whatever god watching that I would find survivors.

"José! Tuari! Willis!"

"Why I the last name that you called?" shouted Willis to my far left in the dark.

I breathed out a sigh of relief mixed with irritation as I moved towards his voice until I could see him. With a cut down his left brow, he appeared to be OK as he swam steadily towards me.

"Where are the others?"

"How am I meant to know? I barely had time to escape

that death trap before it went under. And you still haven't asked my question, why was I the last name you called?"

Ignoring him I turned my attention towards the craft and swam towards it. I looked around to see if I could see José and Tuari but I had no luck.

"José! Tuari!"

No response. Fuck! I knew what I had to do.

Swimming up to the craft till I was close enough to it, I took four deep breaths, which caused a stabbing pain along my ribs reminding me they were broken, and dived.

I prayed the adrenaline would do enough to keep the pain at bay.

I swam through the now open cargo bay doors and kept going until I came to the cockpit.

Flashing red lights made it feel like I was swimming through blood.

Tuari was busy trying to unharness José from his chair, as he was out cold. His motor movements weren't stable enough to do the task he was trying to do. He was running out of oxygen and it was making him panic.

I tapped him on the shoulder and pointed towards the sky.

He shook his head but I shook mine more firmly and gestured with force skywards. He looked between me and José then tapped me on the shoulder and swam for the exit.

I unstrapped José as fast as I could; getting one strap off I felt the craft move around me as it sank faster. Hurrying with the second strap I couldn't get it undone as I continued to feel the craft move around me. Jerking and pulling at it I was growing impatient as another set of hands appeared and started to help me.

I looked to my side and saw Willis, who gave me a wide-eyed stare that was full of crazy; he worked with me to unstrap José and we lifted him out of his seat and swam for the exit as the craft continued to move downwards.

Legs kicking with everything that we had, Willis and I pushed as hard as we could while the shifting metal around us threaten to pull us under.

It felt like an eternity but we finally broke the surface. Coughing and sputtering we swam to one of the crates we had dropped. With the help of Willis I pulled José onto the crate and looked at his still face in panic. I began pumping his chest and went to pinch his nose but Willis pushed me out of the way.

"Get out of the way, do you even know what you're doing?" he asked as he lifted José's shirt and placed a round metal disc on top of his chest. Tapping the edges of it he brought it to life as lights danced along its edge. Nothing happened for a second or two, then José's body pulsed and convulsed as the disc did its work.

I looked at Willis, as José still hadn't moved apart from breathing again. Hands clasped together Willis was muttering some prayer. I looked back towards José as his body convulsed and shook again, and this time he spat up water as he rolled to his side. Willis took the device off his chest and slapped him on his back as José brought up more and more water.

Finally, "Where are we?" José asked.

"Still in the borough of the Floating City," Willis replied.

"Fuck," said José as he laid his head back down and slipped into unconsciousness.

"Will he be okay?"

"How the hell am I meant to know?" Willis snapped. "Do I look like a doctor?"

"No, you look like an asshole. That's why I called your

name last, because no matter what tragedy befalls a group the asshole is always the last one to die."

"While," Willis said, looking at the expanse of water which stretched out as far as the eye could see, "if we don't find a way to get to land, we'll all be dead eventually."

56

"Fuck me, I'm bored," shouted Willis, as he, Tuari and I sat on a makeshift raft we had tied together using the crates and bits of rope that Tuari had found in a bag he grabbed on his way out of the craft.

José lay between us, still unconscious. I looked at his still form worried he may have done more damage to himself than we were aware of but lacking any medical supplies or devices, we could only guess at what was wrong with him. He was still breathing and he would twitch every so often but apart from that, he lay as still as could be.

It had been hours since we had crash-landed and we had not seen a soul or boat pass by. The water we were on was as slack as could be, not moving us an inch forward or backwards. With nothing else to use as a paddle we had used our hands but progress had been small, and without any sight of land we had no idea if we were going in the right direction or not.

"How come this river doesn't move?" I asked. "A large body of water like this surely must travel to some sort of ocean or lake?"

"Safe Haven," Tuari said, "is different to Earth in that it has no oceans to speak of, only rivers and lakes. It is unique because it orbits a star and a large gas giant. They both have tidal effects on the planet, much like the Moon does on Earth. So when the gas giant or the planet's sun are in different positions to each other or the planet, it has some very interesting effects on the planet's water systems. Sometimes the rivers can be slack, sometimes they flow forward at a steady pace, other times the flow can be rapid; sometimes they flow in reverse, sometimes the river creates waves fifty feet high. At the moment we are in a period of slack water, but without *The Kennel's* onboard computers to forecast what the weather is going to be, it's dangerous being out here without a proper boat. There are things that lurk beneath this water that are—"

"Well, whose bright idea was it to leave all our weapons back on *The Kennel*?" Willis asked

"This was a simple collection; José was right in thinking there would be no need for weapons. Weapons tend to rub people up the wrong way, and since we were dealing with people who are in league with The Lady, we had nothing to fear."

"Be sure to tell the monster that swims in these waters that, when one is chewing on your dick."

"Well, I'm so well endowed it will probably choke to death," Tuari said with a smirk.

"Does this river system go all the way to Paradise Lost?" I asked.

"It stops a good fifty miles outside of the city limits, but we would never get there just as we are; the rivers are too dangerous to navigate like this. You would need a good working knowledge of all the tides of the river, because a waterway can quickly lead to a stretch of river that will turn dry as a bone overnight, or lead us to a marshy plain. Not to mention we would be prime targets for river bandits, travellers, and anyone feeling lucky enough to take our cargo," said Tuari.

"Plus we ain't got no food, water, medical supplies or anything to hunt or fish with. We're up shits creek like Moses up the river Nile. The only problem is I don't see any Egyptian princess looking to adopt us."

"The only thing I don't understand," I asked, "is how did we crash in the first place? Was it a malfunction with the ship?"

Willis and Tuari exchanged looks before Tuari spoke: "We were attacked."

"Attacked by who?"

"If we knew that, numbnuts, we wouldn't be here, would we?" Willis snapped.

"We didn't see any other vessels take off at the same time we did and because we weren't in *The Kennel* we didn't detect being attacked until we were hit. That little ship was only designed to travel from point A to B on a planet; it was made on the cheap and is a piece of junk, a smuggler's dream really. Lucky we didn't take a direct hit, otherwise we would have been toast," said Tuari.

"So where do you think the attack came from?" I asked, meeting Tuari's gaze. He said nothing but gestured around me at the open water.

As the day turned into night and the slack water did nothing to improve our position, we tried to get as comfortable as our homemade craft would allow us because we could see nothing through the darkness.

It was a strange experience to be in.

The first night had been spent fuelled by adrenaline as we tried to process what had happened to us and get our bearings. Now as night came again and the only thing we had to occupy our minds was boredom, it dawned on me how strange the rivers of the Floating City were.

There was no sound from the water, the winds had died down to nothing and the overhead clouds had made the stars in the sky vanish without a trace, leaving us in total darkness. I waved my hand in front of my face and couldn't see it. I looked out across the water and it was indistinguishable from everything around us; where the water ended and the sky began I couldn't tell you.

I ran my hand along the edge of the crate until I felt nothing.

A soft snore came to my left as Willis rolled over and tried to get comfortable. How he could sleep was beyond me, but he had been snoring for what felt like hours as the night slowly slipped by.

"So how badly did it go?" Tuari said from the darkness.

I could try to pretend I didn't know what he was talking about, but what would be the point? "It went... it went as well as could be expected."

"That good, huh?"

"Yeah, that good."

Neither of us said anything as we allowed the silence to swallow up our thoughts.

"It could have gone worse," Tuari said.

"I really don't see how."

"Well, she could have ripped your still-beating heart from your chest and showed it to you before you died. Although she is an AI, she is still a woman or programmed like one, or whatever you want to call it, and hell has no fury like a woman scorned, so I would count yourself lucky."

"She wouldn't—would she?"

"Who knows, mate, who knows? All I know is she cares about you deeply. She may not have a regular beating heart like the rest of us, but she has more humanity in her little finger than ninety-nine percent of the people I meet. So I would try and patch up your differences if I were you, because any man would be lucky to have her attention."

"It doesn't bother you she isn't—"

"Human? Why should it? People have fallen in and out of love with stranger things. What really makes someone human? Why should we place barriers on love? What is love anyway?"

As Tuari fired one question after the next my way I tried to find the right answers but I couldn't.

He said, "In what little time I've been alive compared to how long this universe has been around, there's only one thing I can be sure of: if you find someone who is willing to love you, despite your flaws, despite how you view yourself, despite how you think, if you can find someone who loves you despite all that, grab onto them and hold on, because they see something in you not even you see in yourself, and that is worth more than anything in this big old universe."

I thought about what he said and it made sense to me but there was still something nagging at the back of my mind. "What about her past, what about what her kind have done to—"

"I never wanted to be an adventurer as a kid. I didn't want to explore lost worlds or visit forgotten temples and relics left by some civilisation that had been lost in time's memory. All I ever wanted to do was cook. Cook and be happy," said Tuari, sliding up next to me.

"My grandmother always used to love to say, I was born with a smile on my face and a joke clutched tightly in my right hand. I studied all the greats when it came to cooking, but I quickly found out jokes do not belong in a restaurant's kitchen. I gritted it out at first, travelled all across the major cities of Earth, but wherever I went the attitude was always the same: the head chefs believed you had to suffer for your art, and I believed that too until one day something changed all that."

He said nothing for the longest while and I thought he was done speaking until he spoke so softly that I doubt I would have heard him, if it weren't so quiet around us.

"My mum had died—nothing too serious you understand, not like what Willis went through—she was old and had a weak heart and it finally gave out on her, but regardless of whether if your parent passes away surrounded by loved ones on the softest sheets of silk or murdered, the feeling a child experiences is still the same, it still hurts.

"So with that in mind, I went to speak to my head chef at the time and ask him for some time off. In hindsight, I maybe didn't pick the right time; we were understaffed that night and everyone was running around like headless chickens, but grief does terrible things to the mind and I wasn't in the greatest frame of mind when I asked him for the time off to deal with things death drops on our laps without a moment's notice.

"So I asked... and he said," Tuari cleared his throat and coughed lightly, "I asked and he said, why would my dead mother want a failure like me at her funeral when I was worth less than the shit that dripped down her leg when she gave birth to me."

I went to say something but a heavy hand on my shoulder stopped me so I just listened.

"Before I knew it, I had picked up the closest frying pan to hand and hit him over the head with it. He went down hard. He hit his head on the corner of the metal worktop. There was so much blood. I panicked. I ran. I have been running for the better part of a decade or more."

"Sorry," I said, but even to me, the words sounded hollow.

"Don't be, the only thing I regret is that I never got to go to my mother's funeral. But you know what, I'm happier now than I've ever been. I still get to cook, I get to travel, and I get to have a laugh at Willis's expense.

"So you see, everyone has a past they're not proud of, that they are running away from. This line of work is filled with failed dreamers and hopeless romantics. Don't worry so much about Poppy's past; she can't change it, you can't change it, but maybe you two can create something beautiful in the present, something wonderful for the future.

"Now if you would excuse me, I have to give Willis a makeover."

57

My stomach rumbled as I looked at the open water under the rising sun. The sight was beautiful, as the light reflected off the water as if a million diamonds coated its surface. I tried to allow the image to take me away from my hunger, but it failed to do so as Willis's complaining kicked open the door to my thoughts with its dirty secret police military boots.

"I'm so borrred."

"Why don't we play a game?" I asked.

I got no response from Willis and a faint nod from Tuari.

"Okay, I spy with my little eye something beginning with A."

They both looked around, trying to see if they could find anything in the vastness of empty water around us, but both turned to me in confusion as they shook their heads in defeat.

"I spy with my little eye an annoying ginger twat who won't shut the fuck up!"

Tuari rolled around in laughter holding his stomach while Willis got up to his feet and stared daggers my way. "I would watch that heathen mouth of yours, unless you want to go diving after your teeth in this river."

About to respond I looked at the water in confusion, trying to discern if the river was playing tricks with my eyes —I saw shapes moving underneath the water. Big shapes. Shapes that normally came accompanied with teeth.

"Err, what is that?" I asked, pointing to whatever was swimming underneath the water.

Tuari and Willis followed my finger and frowned as they slowly backed up towards the centre of the makeshift raft. A jagged spotted fin appeared above the water and then disappeared under it.

"Those things don't look big enough to eat you, do they?" I asked. "I mean they can only be, what, five... maybe six feet?"

"Animals don't have to eat you whole, you dickhead! It looks big enough to take off a limb."

I ignored Willis and back-pedaled towards the centre of the raft with everyone else. José still lay unconscious at our feet and none of us had any weapons whatsoever to defend ourselves with while these river monsters circled around us, edging closer and closer by the minute.

A flick of a tail splashed water onto the raft, soaking my feet.

A fin popped up here. Another there.

A large red eye broke the surface and stared in my direction for far too long, with all the intellect and cunning of a serial killer.

"What sort of creatures do they have on this planet?" I asked.

"Well, that's an interesting question. Most of the wildlife is not native to this planet and many were brought in as meat to sustain the growing population. But in all things people are short-sighted, and animal control needed to be taken care of, so predators were included into the ecosystem, and people's pets that had grown too big for them to care for. It's an interesting melting pot of—"

"The water, Tuari! What creatures live in the water? Anything dangerous? Anything we should be worried about?"

"Oh, you should have said," he answered, looking at me as if I were an idiot. "The rivers being as diverse as they are, they're the only environment on this planet that still contains its native wildlife; animals not born on this planet simply can't live in the ever-changing environment that is the waterways—"

"Tuari! For the love of God!"

"Don't take His name in vain!" Willis shouted at me.

"Is there anything big and scary that we should be worried about?"

"Oh, plenty."

The craft shook under us as something from underneath bumped it. I held my breath as I looked around. Fear crept from the pit of my stomach, as I could no longer see anything moving in the water.

Where had they gone?

Water rolled over the sides of the craft as something created a small wave.

I held my hands out on either side of me as I tried to stabilise myself when another bump rocked the raft even harder.

"Do you know what these things are?"

"No clue," said Tuari. "I've not explored the rivers of Safe Haven enough."

A long shadowy body swam towards us and turned at the last minute creating a wave that washed over the raft. I held my breath as water lapped over my feet. Another body cut through the water and did the same as the first, then another and another. They worked as a pack, each creating a bigger wave than the first. Each improving on the last one's efforts.

We all looked at each other trying to think of what to do.

We had no weapons.

There was no sight of land anywhere.

And it would only be a matter of time before they either threw us overboard or broke the raft apart under our feet.

"I think—" I began but didn't get to finish as a creature with spiral horns on either side of its head and so many teeth that it couldn't close its mouth leapt out of the water and came for me. I dropped to my stomach and felt a swoosh of air from its body as it passed over me and landed in the water behind me. I got to my feet but not before another leapt from the water and landed on the raft, teeth snapping. I leapt back as it used its pectoral fins as arms to drag itself towards us.

"Fuck off, you shit mermaid!" Willis shouted, as he kicked it in the face sending it back into the water.

More began leaping out of the water, some landing on the raft, others overshooting their landing and splashing back into the water.

"What is up with these fish?" I said as I leapt back out of a pair of jaws trying to take my ankle off. I stomped on its face, pushing it off the crate as Tuari and Willis fought their own battles next to me.

They came with a hunger that only wild animals and crazed men had.

The more we knocked them off the more their blood lust appeared to increase.

A brown shape slid down the raft out of the corner of my

eye, and I turned my head in time to see José's limp form sliding into the water. "José!" I yelled as he slid below the surface. Leaping in after him I belly-flopped into the river and swam after his slowly disappearing face. Bubbles passed mine as I gripped him around the waist and kicked with everything I had back to the surface.

Our faces broke the surface and I took in a big lungful of air as I cuddled José in front of me. Lucky we hadn't gone far, as the raft was still within touching distance.

"Take him!" I shouted, as Tuari leaned over the side and grabbed José by the front of his clothes. He pulled him back onto the raft while Willis cleared their path.

I swam forward but stopped as a monstrous fin appeared in front of me, cutting off my path to the raft; I waited for it to move but it swam back and forth in front of me.

With a splash of its tail it turned to face me and swam my way.

Taking in a deep breath I pushed myself under the water and watched in terror as the biggest fish I had seen so far was coming towards me. It bared its teeth in what reminded me of a grin and torpedoed towards me.

My heartbeat rocked as I waited for what I thought was sure to be my certain death.

It opened its mouth wide and the only thing I could see was rows upon rows of teeth as I braced myself. It snapped its jaws towards me and I placed one hand on top of its mouth and another on the bottom and slammed its mouth shut.

It thrashed back and forth trying to get at its prey and I did the only thing that came to mind: I stabbed my finger in its eye with all the strength that I could muster.

Its movements turned from ones of anger to ones of panic and fear as it tried to escape my grip. I held on for as long as I could and stabbed its other eye with my finger, this time going all the way to the knuckle. With a shake of the head it threw me off and swam away leaving a trail of blood behind it. Sensing blood in the water the shoal of fish turned towards their wounded colleague and pursued it.

With the shoal of fish fast disappearing off into the distance, I resurfaced and swam towards the raft. Lifting myself onto it, I collapsed in a heap.

"Well, that was exciting," Tuari said, blocking out the sun as he stood over me.

"Is it over?"

"It's not over till the fat lady sings; and as Willis has been putting on some weight around his middle lately, maybe we should ask him to give us a chorus or two."

"Who you calling fat you, dick weasel? Have you looked in the mirror lately?" Willis said.

Tuari's head snapped towards his left, brow wrinkled in thought as he placed his hand over his eyes and squinted.

"What is it?" I asked.

"Well, we could either be saved in the next five minutes, or robbed, or killed, or robbed and killed, or drobbed, tortured and killed, or—"

"Tuari!"

"There's a boat coming."

I got to my feet and turned towards the direction of the boat as it made its way lazily towards us. Placing my hands over my eyes I too took in the sight before me and frowned. I had seen that boat before.

With a sinking feeling of dread mixed with hope, I said nothing as the boat got closer and closer to us.

"I think you guys may be OK, but I don't much like my chances of survival," I said.

As the boat pulled up alongside us and Poppy's face

appeared over the side of the boat, Willis and Tuari turned towards me with wolfish grins and both said, "We're not with him."

She looked at us with an expression that was filled not with joy, but more of the passing annoyance at finding a group of kids that had somehow found their way into the cookie jar, after being told not to. Her gaze briefly passed over my face, before going to Tuari and resting finally on Willis.

"What's, what's on your face?" she said, pointing to Willis.

"What do you mean, what's on my face?"

"I mean someone has drawn what appears to be a large penis across your forehead."

"You fucker!" Willis yelled, turning to Tuari in anger. "You didn't have time to grab any important supplies but you had time to grab a marker!"

"It was in my back pocket—I mean, I don't know what you're talking about."

"Like hell you don't, I'm going to throw you off this—"

I closed my eyes and took a deep breath, while the argument raged on around me. This was going to be a long boat trip.

58

We ambled up the river with Poppy at the helm. The boat moved at a snail's pace and I wanted to ask if it moved any quicker but hadn't built up the nerve. We had been travelling now for the best part of half a day, but the scenery still hadn't changed, with nothing but the vastness of the open water to greet us. I hadn't seen any land or other boats.

The wildlife that called the water home had been the most diverse I had ever seen.

Fish flew out of the water and skipped along the water like stones thrown by a child, others leapt out of the water and danced on the surface on their tails, their belly scales flashing vibrant shades of gold and red. Other shapes three times the size of our boat swam underneath; they were accompanied by a horde of groupie fish who trailed alongside them, either looking for leftover scraps or picking their large bodies clean of any bacteria that lived on the creatures' large bodies.

As we continued to travel by silence I saw why Poppy enjoyed this life. It was simple. It was easy. It was stress-free.

I felt myself relax little by little as the hours crawled by and there was no distraction, no outside thoughts, just me and the water.

Footsteps disturbed the peace as Tuari stopped near the entrance of the cockpit and grinned at us like a Cheshire cat.

"Is everything alright?" he said with a carefree smile.

"Yeah, why wouldn't it be?" I replied far too quickly.

"No reason. No reason. Just wanted you to know I've managed to stabilise José and he should be back up on his feet in no time. The blow he took to his head was more serious than I realised. How are your ribs?"

"They're still tender, but that bone repair machine down below deck is amazing. How come you have all that medical equipment down there?" I asked Poppy.

"This old ship used to belong to a doctor who lost his licence; anyone who didn't want to visit a hospital because they would be asked too many questions came to him."

"What happened to him?"

"He lost his licence because he had an addiction to pills; they took his life. I got this place on the cheap from the local boating yard as no one wanted to claim it," Poppy said, not looking my way.

"Well," Tuari said, filling in the awkward silence, "his loss is our gain. It was a tight squeeze, but we have loaded all the cargo down in the hold below. Hopefully, we can get to Paradise Lost without any trouble."

"I'm not going that far," said Poppy.

Tuari and I shared a look but said nothing.

"I'll take you to the nearest settlement, where you'll be able to radio for help, but I'm not going to Paradise Lost. My crew days are over."

She said it with such a stamp of finality that neither Tuari nor I knew what to say.

"I've been giving it a lot of thought and maybe it's time—"

"Why don't you hold onto those thoughts for the time being?" Tuari said, cutting her off. "There's no need to make any rash decisions now. How far is the nearest settlement?"

"Two days, three at the most."

"Well, let's not do anything we regret just yet," Tuari said. "There will be plenty of time for that later."

He left the way he came, leaving me and Poppy once again in silence.

I stared at her out of the corner of my eye while my hands shifted from my pockets to the wooden railing to my thighs. I opened my mouth to say something, but the words caught on the barbed wire in my throat, refusing to come out.

"You don't have to say anything—my mind is already made up."

I nodded my head slowly and tried to bite back the comment that shot out of my mouth but it was too late. "You never listen to anything I have to say, so what's the point?"

"What did you say!"

Fuck it. I had already pulled the pin; there was no use in trying to minimise the damage.

"You heard me! You never gave me a chance to explain myself the first time I found out and you didn't give me a chance back at the Floating City. You're so sure of how you *think* I feel about you, that you've never taken the time to actually learn how I truly feel."

"Is that so?" said Poppy, placing both hands on her hips. "So the back-pedaling you did when you first saw what was underneath all this, I just imagined it? The way your heartbeat rose as if I was about to attack you, the way you looked at me with such disgust that you couldn't meet my eyes, the way you didn't know what to say, the way—"

"I was in shock! Can't a person be in shock when the person they're involved with isn't human?"

"It was more than shock! I've got it recorded all up here, you know," she said, pointing to her brain. "I can play it for you if you wish. It's one of the many things that my kind is so good at, dissecting images and film so we can see where weakness lies. So we can see what's true and false."

"You know what, Poppy, just... just... argh!" I threw my hands up in the air and stormed off, nearly colliding with Willis, who said nothing as I left the pair behind.

A day had come and gone with me avoiding everyone to the best of my abilities, despite the small confines of the ship. Poppy and I hadn't spoken, which suited me just fine. What was there left to say? She had her opinion of me and no matter what I said it wouldn't change what she thought.

How had life gotten so messy?

I threw back my head and laughed. When wasn't life messy?

Not so long ago I had a wife who didn't love me and was sleeping with my boss, a job I hated with a passion, and a boss who was trying to kill me because I held the information to bring about another war.

I shook my head as I allowed my feet to dangle above the water; I sat on the deck of the ship and looked up at the stars wishing life was simpler.

Footsteps came to a stop next to me and José took a seat by my side. He puffed on his cigar while he handed me an empty glass that he then poured a large portion of rum into. Topping up his own glass he clinked my glass with his then took a long sip. I followed suit, allowing the contents of the glass to warm my stomach.

"You look well, all things considered."

He smiled, taking a long draw, then exhaled a column of thick white smoke. "The only things I would miss if I was gone would be the delicate taste of fine rum, and the warm embrace of a cigar. I pray wherever I go after this life, I get to enjoy those simple pleasures."

"The simple things in life."

"Life is never simple, boyo, life is never simple."

"I thought it would be when I left my old self behind, but I found that like a snake I had only shed the top layer while the body remained the same."

José said nothing as he topped up my glass.

"Why are we risking our lives for this cargo?" I asked softly.

"Because it's valuable."

"Is that what we are now, The Lady's personal arms dealers? When you offered me a place on this crew, I knew we would work outside the law more often than not and I was OK with that. Picking up and delivering the latest firearms is one thing but what we got from the Jungle doesn't differentiate between adult and child. If she releases that in any borough or planet, there will be mass murder the likes of which I do not want to imagine, and I don't think I can be OK with that."

"Is this something you have been thinking on for a while?"

"Yes."

"So, what are you saying?" José said slowly.

"That we should reconsider this deal."

José barked a laugh and shook his head. "We are too far down the rabbit hole for that, *mi amigo*."

"Isn't there anything we can do?"

"If we had the full cargo we picked up in good working condition then maybe, maybe, we could have worked out some way to get us out of this mess, but as it stands we are missing more than half the cargo we collected in the Jungle and more than two-thirds of what we picked up in the Floating Village. Even if we deliver what we have for The Lady we will still be in her debt; now that debt may need to be paid off either by working it off or by paying it off. Whichever way you look at it we're screwed.

"If I realised what we were collecting I would have turned it down, but hindsight is twenty-twenty and now we have to work out how to make a bad situation manageable."

"But the problem still remains—don't you see, we can't deliver even one of those dirty bombs to her. Not one."

José pinched the bridge of his nose while he allowed a heavy sigh to pass through him. "I'm getting too old for this, boyo. There was a time the most dangerous thing I had to capture or steal was some stupid painting from some rich asshole. Now I'm involved in chemical warfare and AIs.

"Do you know it was Poppy who got wind of what Xcorp was trying to do? It was her that poked, nagged and pleaded and argued, till she had us draw up a plan so we could retrieve the information from them.

"Then there was the added pressure of The Lady wanting what your company had, so we had to position ourselves so we would be the only crew that she used. It took a lot of planning but it was worth it. Now months later I've got another little voice whispering in my ear telling me to do the right thing."

"What's so wrong with doing the right thing?" I asked.

"Because everyone does the right thing—the thing that's right for them."

I opened my mouth but didn't know what to say so I took a sip from my glass. Maybe he had a point, maybe I was just doing this for my own selfish reasons. My hands were hardly clean. I had spilt enough blood of my own and something told me before this was over I would spill plenty more.

"Talking about doing the right thing, boyo, have you settled your issues with your woman yet?" José asked with a smirk over his glass.

"My woman?"

"Your woman," he repeated, smile still on his face.

"I, well, the thing is, you see..." I sighed as I shook my head, lost for what to say.

"*Donde hay amor, hay dolor*," he said in Spanish, "where's there's love there's pain."

"I don't know what to do, José. I keep trying to talk to her but she doesn't want to listen or when she does listen she doesn't hear what I'm trying to say or maybe I'm not saying what I'm trying to say. I haven't done this in so many years I forgot how awkward and messy this all can be. I always hated dating. Maybe that's why I stuck with Claire for so long. I don't know what to do," I said in a small voice.

"Do you care about her?"

"Of course."

"Does it bother you she isn't human?"

"It did, once, but not anymore."

"Do you think you'll ever find someone like her again?"

I smiled as I thought of how kind she was, how kind she had been to me, how she had saved my life, time and time again, how she had given me everything and not asked for anything in return, how she had always been there for me, yet when the time had come round to do the same I had only met her kindness with judgement. Ill-informed judgement, but judgement nevertheless.

"No," I said, "I don't think I'll ever find someone like her again, because in the history of humankind I don't think there has ever been someone like her. She's the rarest star amongst a galaxy of rare stars."

"Then that is all you need to know," he said, standing up stiffly as his joints popped and groaned.

"That still doesn't answer my question on what I should do or say."

"When the time comes the right words will fall from your mouth."

I nodded my head, hoping he was right. "What are you going to do about The Lady?"

"That problem," he said, stifling a yawn, "is for another day. Tonight, I drink and smoke to my heart's content. Remember what I said about your woman—don't miss the opportunity and wait till it's too late. Love is like water; the longer you wait to drink it from your hand the less that you will have. Good night, boyo."

With that, he left me to my thoughts, as I turned my attention back to the stars above me and thought of what was to come.

59

We arrived at the settlement some days later; Poppy's boat had been chugging along the water as if every day was a Sunday and it would be amiss if it would start to hurry along now. The settlement itself was the equivalent to a large rundown village but on stilts, which kept its feet dry from the water that flowed underneath. Laundry hung between shacks to dry, and children with dirty feet chased each other as their mothers descaled fish into the water.

Other boats pulled up and departed around us as men with weapons visible on their hips walked along the wooden planks of the village making their way deeper into its heart. I spotted a pair of boys watching us intently, while they whispered into the computers that were stationed on their wrist. Catching my eye they scrambled away before I could get a better look at them.

"Don't worry about them, boyo," José said coming to stand next to me near the railings. "They're just scouts reporting our arrival to whoever runs this village. There are villages like this all along this river; they make their money with gambling houses, brothels, underground fighting pits, and everything in between. Keep your ears open and your eyes sharp."

He walked away as we pulled up to a dock and Tuari jumped out and secured us to the dock with a thick rope. Everyone clambered overboard and surveyed the village before us.

"Right," said José, "I need to find somewhere to freshen up before I make a call to The Lady. I'll book some rooms under the JYD name; when you lot are ready come and find me."

"How will we know which hotel you'll be at?" I asked.

José looked at me as if I was an idiot. "Boyo, look at this place. Do you think they have more than one hotel? Better yet, I doubt they even have a hotel; the best we'll get is some rooms above some shitty bar."

"Fair point."

He walked off while I swung my head towards where Tuari and Willis had been, but found that they had both disappeared. "For fuck's sake, I turn my head for a minute…"

Not knowing what to do I returned to the boat looking for Poppy, but she too had slipped away without my noticing. Gritting my teeth in frustration I dug my hands into my pockets and made my way into the heart of darkness that was my current resting spot.

60

The unnamed village wasn't anything to write home about, being dirty and unkempt. I tried to avoid the pickpockets, thugs, prostitutes, and merchants who all wanted to part me from my money. I walked through them like a wraith in the mist; they were constantly around, sometimes just within arm's reach as I moved through the streets made of rotten wood and regret.

When I first travelled with the Junk Yard Dogs, I had expected to visit planets of technological marvels, planets and cities and towns that boggled the mind and left me feeling small and insufficient. That had happened to a certain degree, but the more I travelled, the more I found places like this.

Places that had been touched by humanity yet had failed to lift themselves up from the dirt that they had tried to sprout from.

Families that had left Earth for something better, and not finding it, had to settle for whatever they could grab hold of. As those families had children and those children had children, unwanted roots took hold in whatever dirt they had landed on until a small neighbourhood grew around them, then a village, then a town.

I surveyed my surroundings not sure what I should do. Not sure where to go. I allowed my feet to carry me until I came to a grand building many stories high; it stood at odds with the low squat buildings around it.

A large white banner hung down from the centre of the building with a golden circle that had a red dragon sitting on top of a mountain of golden coins. Swinging saloon doors reminded me of those ancient spaghetti western movies I used to watch as a teenager with my grandmother, where you knew who the bad guys were within the first five seconds of the movie. I walked up a ramp caked in mud and went inside to be greeted with the smell of despair.

The inside contrasted wildly with the image of the building I'd seen outside.

Men lay slumped over tables, while others hung their heads low over their drinks like animals protecting their kill; others stared ahead vacantly as they waited with open arms for the embrace of death.

I manoeuvred myself through the tables and chairs and found myself being finger-snapped at by a man behind the bar. He waved me over and handed me a golden envelope with a waxed emblem of a dragon sitting atop a mountain of gold coins. I looked down at the envelope in confusion and looked back up to find that he had disappeared. When I opened up the envelope a gold card that shimmered in the light landed in my open palm.

You are hereby invited to attend tonight's Casino Royal event hosted by the Han Dynasty. Preparations have been made so you can attend the event in style. Please follow your personal assistant and he shall assist you with everything that you need.

I looked up from the card to find a petite Asian man

with a waxed moustache standing in front of me, hands placed delicately in front of himself. He wore a waistcoat and bow tie. He bowed to me deeply.

I looked around the bar we were in then back at the manservant standing in front of me. The two images contrasting so much that it made my head hurt.

"Err, hello."

"Hello, Mr Blake, my name is Zhang Wei, but you can call me Wei. I will be your personal assistant for the evening in getting you prepared for tonight's event."

"Err, what now?"

"The Casino Royal, held by the Han Dynasty crew, is only held at certain times of the year and for certain occasions. You are most fortunate that you and your crew's arrival has coincided with such an event."

"Err—"

"I know this is most disconcerting but if you follow me I shall explain all to the best of my capabilities," he said, turning on his heel and walking away.

I looked at his retreating back then back at my surroundings, confusion still not lifting. Shrugging my shoulders I decided to follow the rabbit down the hole and see where it led me. I caught up with him shortly after while we made our way amongst more tables and chairs that had hopeless souls sitting on them. The ground floor was larger than I'd realised, and if this floor represented what the other floors were like then this building was large indeed.

"Please!" said a dishevelled man who grabbed the sleeve of Wei. "Let me increase my credit! I beg you. I know I can win back what I lost and pay off my debts, I just need one more chance; I'm feeling lucky. I know I can win back everything."

With a thin layer of disgust Wei looked at the offending

hand that clutched his sleeve before the man realised what he was doing and let go. He wiped the shine of sweat that glistered on his brow as he got down on his knees and lowered his head to the floor in front of us.

"I beg you! I can't leave the Dragon Lair with no money. I've spent my children's college fund, I've spent all my life savings, if I leave here without earning what I spent my family and I will be homeless within the week. I beg you. I beg you. Please!"

"Mr Smith, you know the rules," said Wei, tapping on the computer that graced his forearm. "We at the Han Dynasty have already been more than generous when it has come to dealing with your case. I believe that we have granted you two loans in the last three weeks alone, and both those loans have yet to be paid off. If payment to us is not made within the next twenty-four hours, then we shall take compensation for what is owed to us—"

"Not my wife and daughter!"

"I believe you also have two sons too, Mr Smith. Count yourself lucky you will still have them after this is all said and done. Now if you would excuse me, I hope you have a good day."

I stayed where I was as I looked down at this poor man whose life had been eaten away and didn't know what to do, didn't know what I could do. Digging in my pocket I pulled out whatever money I could gather and I knelt down before him and placed it in his hands. He looked at me in disbelief, but I nodded my head then got up and made my way after Wei.

"You shouldn't have done that," said Wei. "What you did seemed like kindness but is actually the cruellest thing that you could have ever done. He is going to use the money you gave him and he is going to gamble it away prolonging what little hope he has that he can still fix the problem he is in; and say he wins big, ends up earning enough to pay off his debts, you think it will stop there?

"You think he'll never gamble again? Addiction has him now, and nothing will ever change for him until he hits rock bottom."

"And you think taking his family away will cure that?" I demanded.

Wei didn't answer me as we made our way towards a set of gold elevator doors. I looked up and saw there were eight floors in total. With a bing the doors opened and two guards greeted us with a nod. Wei stepped inside and I followed.

"We have a saying here, Mr Blake, you enter the Dragon's Lair at your own risk," he said as the doors closed and the elevator climbed up.

Wei busied himself with his computer before giving me his attention. "The Dragon's Lair and the many like it are casinos run and built by the Han Dynasty on the rivers that snake through Safe Haven. They operate on the fringes of the law, for whatever that is worth on this planet, and they account for a good portion of the planet's wealth.

"The elected president of the Han Dynasty believes if you control the wealth, you control the power, and what better way to do that then allow people to just give it away to you?"

"Elected president?" I asked. "I have never heard of crew leaders being elected to their position before."

"The Han Dynasty believes that for a crew to continue to grow and evolve, it must always have fresh blood and ideas coming from the top. That is only done by allowing someone new to take the reins once in a while. Although their current leader has been—"

The guards on either side of us shifted uncomfortably and looked towards Wei, who cleared his throat.

"The current leader of the Han Dynasty has been in power for a number of years and in that time, he has grown the crew from strength to strength. It's only through his great wisdom and intellect that the Han Dynasty is what it is today," Wei rattled off like a rehearsed actor.

"I.... see," I said slowly.

"All Dragon Lair casinos have eight floors. The first floor is for the hopeless, the poor souls who have lost it all and are trying to drown their sorrows before they have to face the consequences of their actions.

"The second floor is for the petty gamblers who just want to try their luck at the slot machines or blackjack; they aren't regulars and never will be. The third floor is where you will find a host of restaurants serving every food imaginable. If you are hungry I insist you visit; show them this token and all your meals and drinks shall be free," he said, handing me a gold coin that had the Han emblem on it.

"Thank you," I said, pocketing the coin.

"Floor four... is where bets can be placed on fights, such as MMA, boxing, bare-knuckle boxing, and fights involving weapons. There are also a few odd things that you can bet on which I won't go into but I shall give you a word of advice —that floor is best avoided if you have a weak stomach.

"Floor five is dedicated to relaxation. The Dragon Lair casinos have the best spas on the planet, anything from steam rooms to masseuses and any treatment your heart desires. They also have a large choice of women and men... for your more intimate needs."

A bing sounded and the elevator we were in came to a halt.

"Ah, and this is floor six, if you would like to follow me," Wei said, getting out.

I followed him but stopped as I took in a lavish corridor carpeted with the fluffiest white carpet I had ever seen; I looked down at my dirty boots and he pointed towards a rack that had an array of slippers on it. Walking over, I took off my shoes and slipped into a pair of slippers that fit me. We continued on and I took in the walls wallpapered with embedded gold thread. A faint fragrance rode on the air that reminded me of wildflowers. Numbered doors on either side of me told me this must be where the guests stayed.

We continued on, taking one turn after the next till we came to door number eighty-eight. Wei grabbed the handle and a faint light emanated from under his palm.

"You have nothing to be concerned about," he said when he saw my expression; "there is a DNA reader in all the door handles so our guests do not have to rely on keys or passwords. If you would like to just step forward and place your palm on the handle, it will register you as the sole occupant of this room until you have left the casino."

I did as he asked and felt a faint vibration run through my hand, then the door clicked, opened, and I was greeted with a lounge that left me speechless.

Easily double the size of any normal living room, it had three sofas, a dining table and an entertainment centre with the latest VR consoles and games, as well as bean bags scattered about that looked big enough to lose two people in. I walked in and felt my eyes swivel left to right as I tried to take everything in.

A fully stocked bar sat at one side of the room, and there

was a mini sweet shop filled with an array of colourful things that were made to rot your teeth.

I walked over and popped open a jar and placed a hard toffee in my mouth that tasted liked butterscotch. Oh my word, I was in heaven.

"This is one of the many suites that our higher-clientele guests stay in. If you walk to the left you will find a walk-in shower and a bathtub big enough to fit four people in—trust me, I know, some of our guests feel the need to have more than one pair of hands clean them. To your right is your master bedroom with a king-size bed fitted with the finest sheets money can buy. If you walk straight down this corridor," he said, pointing, "you shall find a walk-in wardrobe with suits and tuxedos for tonight's event; all will fit perfectly as they are tailor-made to your size."

"How do you know my—"

"Size?" he asked with a raised eyebrow. "It is the Hans' business to know.

"I believe that is all," Wei said, turning to go.

"What are on the other two floors?" I asked. "You said there were eight floors, but so far we've only discussed six."

"Ah! Where are my manners? Yes you are correct, Mr Blake. Floor seven is for the serious gambler. The lowest bet you can place is ten thousand. That floor is where dreams are born and also crushed. Many regulars come with their life savings, hoping to win big and make a better life for themselves; few ever do. Floor eight is for the elite gambler. The lowest bet that can be made is a hundred grand. That floor isn't so much about the gambling, but more about the socialising and business deals. Floor eight is where tonight's Casino Royal is being held.

"I do hope you enjoy it."

He walked away but stopped and looked back at me with

something passing for caution. Biting his lower lip he sighed and said, "I shouldn't be telling you this, but we have a mutual friend who has helped us both greatly, so I'll give you one piece of warning. Do not place any bets in this place, it could cost you your life."

"Poppy? Our mutual friend?"

He gave me a nod and began to leave but something was still bothering me, I couldn't place my finger on it until it came to me like sun rays parting the clouds.

"Wei, why do you refer to the Han Dynasty as them, instead of us? Aren't you part of the crew?"

He looked at me sadly and shook his head. "Mr Blake, most of the staff who work in the Dragon's Lair are not here by choice. We are here from debts never fully paid. You will quickly learn the house always wins and the dragon always comes to collect its debts."

61

Showered, shaved, dressed, I looked at myself in the mirror and smiled despite everything.

A fitted tuxedo hugged my body just right, showing off the new muscle I had gain by working out with Willis. I flexed my biceps and give myself a little wink, which I instantly regretted. Walking to the candy bar I pocketed some hard sweets and took the invitation I had been given when I had first entered the Dragon Lair. Giving myself another once-over in the mirror I walked out my door and bumped into Tuari and José.

Both dressed in tuxedos they looked as surprised as I was to see them.

"Boyo," José said, arms gesturing wide, "we had thought we had lost you. When we didn't find you we thought you had returned to the boat but you weren't there either. It is good to see that you are safe and sound."

"To be fair," Tuari said, "we didn't look very hard, not with all the free shit the Hans have been throwing our way. It's not often we get treated this way; normally someone is trying to see what our insides look like."

"Don't you find this all strange?" I asked, walking alongside them.

"Not at all, boyo. Not at all. When someone wants something from someone they burden them with gifts; now the only thing we have to find out is what do our hosts want from us," José said.

"You make it all sound so simple."

"Business and life normally are. Now all we have to do is keep up the pretence we are more valuable to them then they are to us, and we should get out of this in one piece."

"So, I take it the Han Dynasty controls the Floating City?" I asked.

"Yes and no; because so many people in the Floating City come and go as they please it is difficult to lock down total control over the borough, but if any crew is closest to that goal it is the Han Dynasty. Like many of the people who call the Floating City home, they operate up and down the great rivers of Safe Haven never staying in one place."

I nodded my head as we finally reached the elevators.

"Remember," José said as the doors opened, "do not gamble tonight. Once the Hans have you in their debt it is almost always impossible to escape."

We exited the elevator onto the eighth floor and it took me a second to adjust to all the glitz and glamour.

Faint lighting sparkled off chandeliers that hung from the ceiling, as well as bouncing off jewels hanging from women's necks and wrist. Wherever I looked I saw a flash of a fake smile, or a knowing look as a pair whispered between each other and nodded towards someone else. Waitresses moved through the crowd with entrees delicately balanced on trays while an orchestra played somewhere in the background.

I pulled on the neckline of my tux as many an eye swept over us. Well, this is something new."

José and Tuari said nothing as they helped themselves to drinks that went by on trays.

"What do we do now?" I asked, taking a drink for myself and trying not to inhale the bubbles in the champagne.

"All this wink and handshake bullshit takes time," José said, surveying the room. "Whoever wants us here won't make themselves known until later in the night. So, the best we can do is mingle and enjoy all the free shit."

"Where's Willis?" I asked, just now realising I hadn't heard his irritating tone for a while.

"You think we would allow Ginger Nuts to attend something like this?" Tuari said, gesturing around the room.

"Fair point."

We all parted ways and I tried to relax as the night wore on but found myself unable to, as eyes followed my every move. At first, I thought I was being paranoid, but then as the hours rolled by I become sure of it.

It was the way the servers looked at me. The way the guards were never more than ten feet away. I did my best to ignore them mostly, but as the night wore on I was finding it harder and harder to do so until I saw something that stopped me dead in my tracks.

I forgot where I was for a moment as I watched Poppy walk towards the bar, dressed in a flowing blue gown that parted down the side of the leg, with lacy sleeves and a teardrop cut in the front.

She looked—I was at a loss for words, then someone bumped into me and I was brought back to the present.

"What do you want to drink?" I asked, sliding up next to her.

She looked at me out of the corner of her eye but didn't respond to me. "Can I have an Amaretto and Coke?" she asked the bartender.

"I'll have a pink gin and lemonade."

Drinks were placed in front of us, then we both sipped while the world moved around us.

"So, do you come here often?"

"Is that the best you can do?" she asked, while I tried to erase the smirk from my face.

"When I look at you, *it's the best I can do.*"

"Why?"

"Because you make me forget who I am. You make me lose the past, you make me dream about the future, and I don't know where the hell the present has gone because all I can do is stare into your eyes and just thank God I am alive to witness the beauty that is you."

She stared at me and said nothing but simply smiled and tried to tuck a strand of hair behind her ear without managing to do so. Stepping forward, I did it for her and breathed in the perfume she wore as I ran my eyes down her body. She bit her lip and looked away, but I lifted her chin and stared into her eyes. Running a finger down the side of her face, I leant my head against hers. "I don't care that you're—"

A cough sounded behind us that made me grit my teeth. I tried to ignore it but it only got louder as the seconds passed. I pulled away from Poppy and gave her a tiny smile as I snapped my head towards the sound.

Wei stood with his hands tucked in front of him, an emotionless smile plastered on his face. "If it's not too much bother, would sir and madam mind following me?"

"It is too much bother, Wei," I said through my teeth. "Can't you see we're busy?"

"I am afraid the show is about to begin, and my boss has stated that it shall not start until everyone is present at the table."

Poppy squeezed my arm before saying, "It's perfectly fine. Please lead the way."

We were guided through the throng of people and led to a section large a large semi-circular table, its surface covered in bamboo. A bare-chested man with ornate dragon tattoos stood in the centre of the table.

We took our seats next to José and Tuari, who each gave us a nod.

As I sipped my drink the other chairs filled up and I did a double-take as none other than Edward Thomas took a seat next to José. Wearing a red tuxedo with black labels, he took an onyx-coloured pipe out of his mouth and gave us a smile.

"Well, I do say, chaps, it is a surprise to see you folks here. What brings you around these parts?"

José gave him a smile that was all teeth and said, "We had a little bit of trouble with our ship."

"Engine trouble?" Edward asked innocently.

"Something like that," José replied, smile still not leaving his face.

It was him! The posh prick was the one who had attacked us.

It was too much of a coincidence, us turning him down then being blown out of the sky not long after, and him now turning up to this event out of the blue.

"You know, dear man," Edward said, "my job is still on the table and it's a lot less risky than what Isabella Ivanov has you doing. Plus whatever she is paying you I can quadruple. I hear on the grapevine that she is stockpiling weapons and looking to build an army, to take over the rest of Safe Haven much like she did Paradise Lost, but therein lies the problem, dear man—when one tries to build an empire one creates enemies. Enemies that are not going to be too friendly with the people who work for her."

"People like ourselves?" José said, gesturing to us.

"Exactly."

"There is a saying, Mr Thomas, that it is better to work with the devil you know."

"But the reason the devil is the devil, Mr Battle, is because it always gets defeated in the end; it's the losing side, whether or not it knows it."

"So which side do *you* work for?" I asked, fixing my gaze upon him.

He looked over me and stared at Poppy, eyes alight as he took in her form. Leaning over he attempted to hold her hand but I caught it and gave him a slight squeeze, which he chose not to register.

"I wanted to give my thanks to this darling beauty that is in our midst for making the room so much brighter for her just being in it," Edward said, returning my squeeze with a greater force, "but I can see there is no need."

Eyes still on Poppy, I kept hold of his hand until he finally looked my way. "*What was your question?*"

"What side do *you* work for?"

"The winning side of course."

"Ladies and gentlemen!" shouted a voice that interrupted our conversation. "Thank you for coming!" The voice belonged to an Asian gentleman who had jet-black hair with streaks of silver running through it. Dressed in a white tuxedo, he flashed a smile that blinded his audience. His teeth were made of diamonds. It was all I could do but stare as he played with the multiple rings that sat on his fingers.

"This is now our twentieth annual Casino Royal gala. We have many guests old and new in the audience today, and I know many of you wanted a chance to play at the game of choice but only a select few of you have been chosen, I'm afraid, for this special event."

Many groans and sighs escaped the audience while our host gave them all just the right amount of sympathy in his smile.

"All the same I thank you for coming. Today! We play a traditional gambling game centuries old! It was played in feudal Japan anywhere from the opium dens to the royal palace. It is still played by the Yakuza back on Earth to this very day. The game in question is none other than Cho-Han!"

Indoor fireworks went off behind the speaker and turned into a dragon roaring at the crowd, which elicited a chorus of gasps and a few screams. The dragon swept its head back and forth, looking at the crowd before it opened its mouth and spewed out a flame that turned into coins before it touched the crowd.

Thunderous applause came from the crowd as the dragon vanished and the host gave his captivated audience his million-dollar smile.

"The rules are simple! Our dealer," he said, pointing towards the bare-chested man with the tattoos, "has two standard six-sided dice, which he will shake in the bamboo cup that he is holding. After the cup is shaken it is then overturned onto the floor. Bets are placed on whether the sum total of the numbers shown on the dice is even or odd. Once the bets are placed the cup is lifted and we see who our winners and losers are. Because this is our twentieth annual Casino Royal gala, there shall be twelve rounds played in its honour. After that the losers' takings shall be shared equally amongst the remaining winners, minus a house fee of course," he said coyly behind his hands to a round of laughter.

"Have fun, ladies and gentlemen, and remember, you've got to be in it to win it. Now, shall we begin?"

Drum rolls sounded throughout the room as the men and women sitting around us pulled out chips. I looked to José and Tuari, who both had the same thought as me: we didn't want to play nor did we have the means to.

We rose from our chairs but two bodyguards appeared behind us. "Is there something the matter?" they asked.

"Well, you see, my friend," José said with a smile, "there must be some mistake. We don't have the means to participate in this game of yours. Funds are low, you understand."

The guards looked at each other in confusion, then one went off to find someone that could help. In a blink of the eye Wei came back bowing before all of us, hands held before him.

"Wei, please tell these men," I said, gesturing towards the bodyguards, "that we can't afford to play. We are not as wealthy as your guests, so we must humbly bow out and allow someone else to take our place. Thank you for—"

"What seems to be the problem?" asked a voice behind us.

We all turned to see the host with the diamond teeth regarding us with narrowed eyes. Wei looked quickly towards him, eyes wide, as he hurried to get his words out: "There—there—there isn't a problem, Mr Lee. Our guests were just saying they do not have the funds to take part in this game and—"

"Nonsense. It has already been taken care of," said Mr Lee.

The crew all exchanged confused stares as the muttering from the crowd behind us slowly increased. "My friend, what has been taken care of?" José asked slowly.

"The means for you to play," Mr Lee replied.

"We have accepted no funds from yourself," José said.

"Of course you have; it was accepted by—"

"Can we get started already! You posh cunts might have all day but some of us work for a living. Now let's play!"

62

What a giant ginger dildo!

All our heads turned to the sound of Willis's voice as José's hand wiped the corner of his mouth. Tuari placed a hand on José's shoulder as a pulsing vein appeared in the centre of José's head.

"As you can clearly see, your crewmate has accepted my generous loan. So there is no reason why you can't play," Mr Lee said.

"If you would excuse us a moment," José said, as he strode towards where Willis was sitting. Grabbing him by the arm José dragged him away from the table, and we all retreated to a corner.

"*Hijo de puta!* What do you think you're doing, you fool!" José hissed, as we gathered around the pair.

"What do you think?" Willis said forcibly, detaching himself from José's grip. "I'm about to win us some easy cash and donate some of the money towards my charity."

"You've got a charity?" I asked in disbelief.

"Don't look so shocked, dickwad, not all of us are selfish heathens like yourself. I create and run a charity for young orphans—it's only a small operation but we help to clothe and feed them, then later down the line we help to house them as well. Do you know that statistically speaking—"

"I don't give a fuck about your charity!" José snapped.

I had never seen José so angry until now. The air of a man barely keeping his anger under control replaced the calm, cool Spanish demeanour he normally wore. Tuari still had one hand clamped firmly on his shoulder.

"That's a bit heartless—" began Willis but José cut him off.

"Why would you accept anything Mr Lee offered you? That man has built his empire on placing people in his debt. The Han Dynasty runs the waterways of Safe Haven with an iron fist, an iron fist soaked in blood."

"Sounds no different than The Lady," said Willis.

"The Lady is a woman of her word—a ruthless killer, yes, a megalomaniac, yes, but still a person of her word. Lee only cares about coin and nothing else. There is a reason most people who work for him are no better than slaves. Why would you take anything he gave you?"

"The hotel room, the food, the tuxes," Willis said, pointing to his, "it was all for free. When I was praying before my last meal and Lee saw me he asked me what I was doing and I told him. Then somehow our conversation turned to my charity and he seemed interested, and he offered to loan me some money to play in tonight's upcoming game minus a fee on whatever I win. The offer was too good to pass up."

"Because it was!" José said, finger stabbing Willis in the chest.

I could feel eyes on us. They came from the crowd. They came from hidden workers who belonged to Lee. They came from all directions.

"*Mierda!* I don't know how Lee and this Edward Thomas are connected but they are somehow; it's too much of a coincidence that they are both here on this night, the same week we got shot down while carrying cargo for The Lady. I can feel the net closing in and if there's one thing a stray dog hates more than anything it's a net. Right—here's what we do. Willis, you give back what you borrowed, we apologise, make some small talk for a bit then get out of there."

"Simple and easy," I said.

"I love simple and easy," José said as we walked towards Lee.

"Mr Lee," José said, hands clasped together in apology, "I'm afraid Willis can't accept your generous offer; there was some misunderstanding and—"

"I'm afraid you do not understand," Lee said, smoothing down the lapels of his dinner jacket. "It's not that simple."

"It never is, is it?" José replied.

"Any loans taken from the Dragon's Lair must be repaid back in full plus a ten percent fee on top—"

"I completely understand," José said. "I would never have it any other way. If you just give us the details, we can transfer the amount into..." José trailed off as he saw the ever-growing smile on Lee's face. Something was wrong.

"Normally, that would be acceptable. But in this instance things are different, you understand. What with the event being delayed, and now having to find and vet someone else to take your crew's place... and then there's the whole embarrassment this has brought to me and my event, and not to mention the expense that has been laid out by me in clothing and housing and feeding you...." Lee shook his head. "I hope you understand this is an unusual occurrence, one that just can't be overlooked. As the leader of the Han Dynasty I have an image to uphold, you understand. So in this instance, I must regret to inform you the fee is thirty percent."

José said nothing as he looked to Willis, then to each of us in turn.

"I understand completely," he said finally.

"Excuse me," Edward said, stepping forward, "I couldn't help but overhear, and I am never one to allow a poor chap to get in some bother without doing my best to help out. I would be more than willing to cover any fees or expense this crew has incurred. It's the least I can do."

José looked to Poppy, Tuari, Willis and then finally me. I knew what he was going to say even before he said it.

"Let's play!"

63

No one said anything as we returned to our seats. What was there to say?

We all sat together, while drum rolls played in the background and Mr Lee took his seat at the head of the table. Edward sat away from us and lifted his glass in a toast that none of us returned.

"How hard can this game be?" I asked with a shrug. "It's just luck, isn't it?"

"To a certain degree, yes," Poppy said, placing her hand over mine. "There is an equal number of odd and even rolls possible on each dice. If both dice are even or odd, the sum is even, and if the first dice is even and the second odd or vice versa, then the sum is odd. By simple symmetry, with no calculations, the matter is fifty-fifty. But as the old saying goes, the house always wins and we don't know if the dealer is using loaded dice, or if the handler will use controlled throws."

"Controlled throws?" I asked

"It is a very difficult technique to master, but the handler can control his movements so the dice fall in a desired way or trap one another to stop them from bouncing so the required number appears. That does make predicting the outcome more challenging but I think I can manage it."

"Wait—what!" I said, looking at her in confusion.

"Hush, keep your damn voice down," said Willis.

"Don't forget what I am, Quinton," she said, tracing her forefinger down my nose. "They designed me to solve problems no other human or computer ever could. I was made for this."

"Then why all the hoopla about not wanting to play?" I asked José.

"Because this game was designed to trap us; it was designed so we lose. If we win this then the questions that will be asked will be too hard to explain. But we have come too far now to worry about that. No matter what happens after this we are up shit's creek with holes in our little boat, so we may as well make the best out of this. Don't make it to obvious," he said, turning to Poppy; "play well, but not too well."

The drums kept on playing till they built up to a crescendo, then they stopped completely as silence descended across the floor.

The dealer looked at each player, gaze resting on each face before he lifted two dice in the air between the fingers of one hand and a cup made of bamboo in the other.

"We shall go from right to left allowing each party to call out odd or even," Mr Lee said, "then back again, making it fair. Once a decision is made it can't be changed. Once a decision is shouted out by a member of your party, that is the decision that will be accepted, so choose your decisions wisely."

The dealer placed the dice in the cup and shook his hands with a flourish as the drums sounded again behind him. After giving the cup a good shake he slammed it down on the table and swept his gaze across the floor. "Players are you ready!" he shouted. There were nods, and various cries swept across the table. "Then let's play!"

"Well, that was a lot more anticlimactic than I thought it would be," I said to Poppy.

The game had finished with us winning—not dominating, but winning just enough that it looked like it was more by chance than anything else. True to her word Poppy had delivered us the victory, the supercomputer that was her brain analysing the chances of what the right answer would be.

The game didn't last as long as I thought it would do, and when it was over I could see more than one angry face looking our way. Mr Lee and Edward had shared a look between themselves that I just caught after the game was over, a look that had told of their plans going awry.

Now many drinks later and after shaking the hands of the people who wanted to congratulate us, Poppy and I stood in a quiet section of the room nursing our drinks.

"Statistically speaking the odds of us losing was highly improbable," said Poppy.

I smiled at her, which caused her to look at me askew. "What?" she asked.

"I love it when you talk all smart," I said while I hooked my forefinger in her dress and pulled her towards me.

"Whoa, whoa, steady there, cowboy. I still haven't forgiven you. A bunch of pretty words isn't going to win me over so easily," she said, placing a hand on my chest.

I stroked her cheek while I heard the sounds of Willis

having a good time, "By the sounds of it Willis is enjoying himself; I've never seen him so happy. That charity must mean a lot to him. Who knew he had it in him? That man confuses me sometimes."

"For centuries humans confused me; they are not rational, reasonable or logical. Each one is a different grain of sand and no two are ever the same. It used to upset me that I could never figure them out—they were one riddle that always got the better of me. Then one day I did something out of the ordinary. It was not logical to do what I did, yet I did it anyway.

"I chose to walk a dangerous mountain path that had a high likelihood of my falling and took twice as long as the normal path to get to my destination. Yet I decided to take the harder path because there was a certain flower called a poppy that grew on the route, which I loved to smell, touch and just be around. I guess it sounds silly to you but—"

"No, it's not," I said taking her hand. "It makes perfect sense."

We lapsed into silence while we people-watched, but I couldn't take my eyes off her. The way she moved, the way she talked, the way she drank, it seemed all so... normal.

"Ask it," she said.

"I've noticed you eating and drinking," I said, coming in closer and lowering my voice, "but why? Surely being what you are, you don't need to."

"Everything ever created or born needs substance."

"But what's the point of functioning just like us, if you are made to be better than us?"

"You mistake me—I use whatever food or drink I consume as energy to fuel my cells, much like you do. In doing so, it allows me to blend into society easier and accomplish any tasks my creator Alvis Boman had ordered me to fulfil. Don't get me wrong, I can go years without eating but in order to do so, I would have to shut off certain functions in my body, making me slower, until finally I would shut down completely and go into hibernation. There I would lie dormant until—"

"Until I woke you with a kiss like Sleeping Beauty," I said, kissing her on the lips.

She pulled away and smiled at me. "It doesn't bother you?"

"It did, to start with, but as you once told me when we first met—how can you explain why your favourite colour is red or why you prefer one flavour of ice-cream over the other? You just do. In this life, time is short and you learn to act on gut instinct."

"You remembered?"

"Of course. But I have just come to realise time is a lot shorter for me than for you and I don't want to waste another minute second-guessing, thinking about what ifs, worrying, not listening to my gut. You are who you are, you didn't choose to be this way—you just are, and I will not waste any more time, I've done too much of that in my past life. Wasted too much of my life on people who cared little for me. Now I'm willing to give you what little time I have left if you're willing to take it."

She looked at me and I couldn't read what was going on between those eyes; I couldn't guess what she was thinking. Here was a woman more human than machine, one of the few people I had met in my life that had treated me with such kindness and hadn't asked for anything back and yet she was a ruthless killer who I had seen easily despatch men with such efficiency that it could only be done by a machine.

Was I wrong to do this? Did this make me out to be

some monster? What sort of life would we have, with me growing older with each passing day and her remaining the same?

"I—" she began but stopped and looked behind me,

I turned and followed her gaze to see Mr Lee standing a few feet away from us. He smiled, teeth blinding even in the dim light.

"How are you enjoying the event?" he said.

"It is like something I have never experienced before; this event and your hotel are truly amazing," I said with a small nod.

"I'm glad you enjoy it. It seems luck favoured the bold tonight."

"Lady Luck normally does."

"Hmm... indeed," he said, allowing us to settle into an uncomfortable silence while his eyes searched Poppy's face and mine. "I wondered if I could have a word with you in private, Mr Blake."

"Whatever needs to be said can be said in front of Poppy. We have no secrets in our crew."

"It's alright," Poppy said, squeezing my arm, "I'll catch you later."

"You sure?" I mouthed, but she gave me a kiss on the cheek and walked off, hips catching my attention until she vanished in the crowd.

"I do love being in the company of a woman but not when business is being discussed; I find them too much of a distraction, and some things are only meant to be discussed amongst men."

"Such as?"

"Such as the role you can play in helping me convince your captain of a proposition that I have for him regarding The Lady."

I held my hands up before me and shook my head as I took a step back. "I am only a lowly crewmate and any discussion of that nature is way over my head. Maybe Tuari would be a better person to discuss this issue with."

"Psh! You give yourself too little credit. I see how the others act around you. Yes, José is your captain, but he seeks your opinion before making decisions; the female in your crew is besotted with you for a reason; and you think that ginger barbarian who is making a fool of himself at the bar can be second in command? You think the one who always jokes can make the hard choices when it matters? No, eventually those decisions will fall to you."

"Even so, I don't see how I can—"

"Are you happy with the way The Lady does things?"

"What do you mean?"

"Lady Isabella Ivanov appeared to be a joke when she first arrived on Safe Haven, with her little frilly dresses and soft-spoken ways, but the crews that took her for granted soon found out she wasn't to be taken lightly; by the time the other crews in Paradise Lost knew how she operated it was too late. She had gained too strong a foothold in the borough and would soon take it over.

"There were a few years of peace until recently, but I knew that was just a bluff. What better way to know who your enemies were than to befriend them, and allow them to lower their guard around you? Pretty soon, she knew which crew leader to take out, which family member to threaten, where to push just so with the right word and where to embrace with a loving hand.

"Over the last six months, she has gained total control of Paradise Lost. That patch of dirt is in her control completely and I must congratulate her. No crew before has ever conquered it. The inhabitants who call it home have always been too wild, too cutthroat, but like a demon rising from the deep she has shown them all what true evil really is."

A woman broke away from the crowd and sashayed over to us, hips bumping from side to side. She draped her arm over Lee's shoulder, and leaning in she whispered something in his ear before nibbling on his earlobe. His gaze didn't stray from me, as he allowed a small breath of air to escape his nostrils.

"I am busy."

"Too busy to enjoy all this?" said the woman, gesturing to herself.

"If I need you, I will come and find you—"

"You always say that but you never do," she whined. "Why don't you detach yourself from work for one minute and—"

Mr Lee turned towards her and I saw what lay behind the mask of sleek hair and diamond teeth. The woman in question stiffened up and tried to take a step back but a firm hand grabbed her around the upper arm and brought her in close.

"I believe," he said slowly, "I made my intentions clear."

She nodded her head, eyes round, and tried to scuttle away but the hand still remained. Finally, allowing her to go, Mr Lee returned his attention to me.

"I still don't see how I or the Junk Yard Crew can really help."

"It's simple, really, you are Lady Isabella's most trusted crew when it comes to running errands for her. She respects José, but more importantly, she trusts him to a degree. Things like respect and trust can be used on an unsuspecting opponent, to take what you want."

"And what is it you want, Mr Lee?"

"The little bitch's head above my bed."

"I really don't think I can get you that."

"Maybe not, but you can give me the means to get my desired goal. The Hotel Moscow is where she calls home. It is secure, and by all accounts impenetrable, but if you or your crew can somehow find a way for me and my men to get in then I shall do the rest."

I looked at him as he flashed me a smile that would put any used car salesmen to shame, and I knew I was tap-dancing on quicksand.

"You make it sound all so simple. But let's say somehow there's a million-to-one chance I get you access to her hotel, that you manage to defeat her troops—something no one has ever done—that you kill her, then what?"

"Then I allow things to go back to how they naturally were. Let the crews who have always been there fight over the scraps; you and your crew will be rewarded beyond your wildest dreams and you won't only have my favour, but you'll also have the favour of the other boroughs as well."

That got my attention. I thought he and Edward Thomas were in cahoots, but for him to be working with other crews from different boroughs meant The Lady really must be more of a threat than I had first thought. Yet that wasn't surprising, seeing what we had just collected for her. Hadn't she stated the last time we met that her sights were now set on bigger things?

How long did Lee and his colleagues like him really have until The Lady came a-knocking?

"Look, Quinton, my way nobody but that bitch and her goons get hurt. Her way, tens of thousands of innocent children, women and civilians get killed or suffer a fate worse than death. I'm only asking you to do the right thing," he said, placing a hand on my shoulder while he looked me in the eye. "Now, I must get going. Guests to entertain, hands to shake, people to scold. You know how it is."

I watched him walk away, cutting a path through the crowd like a shark through a shoal of fish, and felt confused about what to do. The question boiled down to which devil had our best interest at heart?

Mr Lee, Edward Thomas and the other hidden crew leaders or The Lady? Because I knew one thing—war was coming and whether the Junk Yard Dogs liked it or not we would play a part that would put us centre stage.

64

I had tried to find Poppy after Lee had left but couldn't find her amongst the crowd, Willis was blind drunk and was looking for someone to accompany him towards his path of destruction; I had ducked down out of sight just in time and had made my way through the crowd until I left the floor. I had also failed to find José or Tuari, but wasn't too worried as I made my way towards my room. We would leave the Dragon's Lair as winners, but more importantly, we would leave Mr Lee's stronghold without being in his or Edward Thomas's debt.

I misplaced my foot and stumbled forward as the corridor tilted ever so slightly. Head heavy from the lights, drums, alcohol and just busyness of floor eight I was feeling the worse for wear as I heard footsteps approaching me, I looked up and bumped into three men with shaven heads.

"Easy there, fella, had a few to drink tonight, have ya?" said the biggest one, who had a tattoo of a lipstick kiss on the side of his neck.

"Sorry, didn't look where I was going. Nah, I've not had

many. Well, maybe a couple... well, maybe more than a couple," I said with a laugh as hands steadied me. "It's okay, it's okay. Thanks for the help, but I ain't got far to go."

The one that had spoken flashed a smile my way as he patted me on the back. "Well, you look after yourself, fella, and try to have a good night."

I kept on moving but could feel their eyes on me. Turning a corner I looked back to see all three still standing looking my way. Giving them a wave and a smile, which they returned, I hurried along the corridor waiting for someone to leap from one of the many doors that lined it. Getting to my room with nothing of note happening I placed my hand on the door handle and waited for it to allow me in.

With a vibration on the handle and green pulsing light emanating beneath my palm, I opened the door and found a dress on the floor. After closing the door behind me, I picked it up and put it to my nose and breathed in.

I knew that scent.

She shouldn't have had one, but she did anyway.

The dim lights of the room showed me a pair of shoes placed a little way ahead. I followed them and saw further along a bra left hanging on the edge of the lounge table. Smiling, I followed the trail like a sailor navigating his way home by the stars, till I got to my bedroom door, which was closed.

I pushed it open and smiled.

The dim-lit room smelled faintly of wildflowers. Walking forward I could just about make out Poppy's form lying on the bed surrounded by pillows and blankets. I walked forward and stopped at the front of the bed and just stared.

"My, my, aren't you a sight for sore eyes," I said softly.

"I've been waiting. What took you so long?"

"I thought I was being followed—you know what, it doesn't even matter, it was just me being stupid," I said, taking my clothes off and climbing up onto the bed.

I went to kiss her but she placed a finger on my lips and kept me an arm's length away. "Are you sure about this?"

"I'm naked and in bed with you, isn't that answer enough?"

"Many men do things in the heat of passion that have unforeseen consequences, that not only affect them but affect the generations to come after them."

"Poppy, this isn't something I have taken lightly. I have muddled this thing over and over in my head since I first found out and I always come back to the fact that life is too short. Life is too short not to have what you want, even if it is the simple pleasure of spending what time I can with the *person* I've come to care about the most.

"I would say it's what's on the inside that really counts, but I don't think that reasoning applies here," I said, laughing.

She said nothing but buried her head in my shoulder and rubbed her face against my neck back and forth.

"There's something I need to tell you," she whispered, "something about me, something that... something that could also affect you later down the line. Something that could change your life forever. Alvis Boman did something to me when he was building me, creating me; he had a plan to—"

"Pop—"

"Quinton, this is important, you need to hear—"

"Not tonight," I said, kissing her on the lips, "not tonight."

I should have listened to her. I should have paid attention. Instead I woke up covered in blood.

65

"What the fuck!" I yelled, leaping from the bed and turning in a sharp circle.

The light was on. Harsh. Bright. It left no shadows.

Three bodies lay clustered on the floor at my feet, their blood seeping from open wounds on their necks and heads. As they were facedown I couldn't see any faces but all wore black clothing made for going unseen. Plastic zip-ties and black bags lay in the hands of two, while the third had a pistol with a silencer attached to it. These men were professionals sent to do a job that would either end my life or make me wish it had been.

"Poppy."

I searched the room but couldn't find her.

"Poppy!"

I spun in a circle looking for any form like hers, looking for any sign of a struggle she could have made, but found nothing. I tried to run from the spot where I stood but I slipped on the blood that covered the floor and went tumbling to my knees; coming down hard, a sharp red-hot poker-like pain pierced my knee.

Stumbling to get up I looked at my hands, which were now covered in blood, and wiped them down myself when I remembered I was naked. It didn't really make a difference, as I looked like something out of a horror scene.

"Pop—"

Stop and think, idiot.

What if there were more men throughout the hotel room, which was really big enough to be called an apartment. What if they were waiting? What if they had Poppy?

I looked for a weapon and spotted the gun clutched in the hands of my would-be assassin. Picking it up I checked that it was loaded then held it out before me. Feeling better with a weapon in my hands I moved from the room and peered down the corridor that led to my lounge- cum-living room.

Corridor empty, I trod as lightly as I could. Biting back the pain of my throbbing knee, I leaned against the wall and listened for any signs of movement; not hearing any I peered slowly into the living room and saw that it was empty. Nothing was out of place. Everything looked ordinary, which made the scene in my bedroom creepier.

I took one step forward then stopped. I scanned the room while I held my breath. I took another step and did the same.

I slowly covered the distance of the living room and saw there was no one around. I checked the other rooms and found them empty. My heartbeat should have lowered, but it only increased the more I searched for Poppy and the less evidence I found of what happened. Spinning in a circle I tapped the gun against my forehead and gritted my teeth.

Think! Think!

The sound of the front door opening pulled me from my thoughts as I moved to hide behind one of the sofas in the room, I heard the footsteps of only one person, and counted to three before I popped up from my hiding space and pointed the gun at my assailant.

Poppy looked at me in confusion before she scanned me up and down. "What are you doing?"

"What does it look like?"

"Looks like you're standing naked covered in blood pointing a gun at me."

"Poppy, I thought you were—" I said, unable to get my words out as I rushed towards her, but she held her hand out, stopping me in my tracks.

"You need to get cleaned up."

I gritted my teeth at her calm demeanour. "Would you like to tell me what is going on?" she asked.

"I thought that would be pretty self-explanatory, judging by the—" I lifted my hands in the air, as I couldn't mask the level of mounting frustration that was coursing through me.

"OK, OK, I apologise. After our late night's... fun," she said, eyes flashing with excitement, "I heard men entering your room. They were professionals and if it weren't for my enhanced level of senses, I would have never detected them. I tried to disarm them at first but as you can tell things got messier than I intended."

"What could they have wanted?"

"You."

"What, why?"

"I'm not sure but, the hand-ties and plastic bags tell me this was a kidnap situation. I've gone to look for the others in the crew but their rooms are empty. There've been signs of a struggle but no blood."

Shit. This wasn't looking good.

"The best thing we can do is make our way to your boat and decide what to do next; it's probably the same thing the others would have done," I said.

"Makes sense."

"OK, let's make our way through to the elevator before this night gets any crazier," I said, making my way towards the door, but was stopped by a cough from Poppy, who pointed towards me and lifted her finger up and down.

"As handsome as you are, I think you may need to wash some of that blood off and put some clothes on."

She was right. Rushing to the bedroom I stepped over the bodies and went into the en-suite and cleaned myself up as best as I could before throwing some clothes on. Coming back out my mind forced me to take in the scene once more. Lucky that it did because I picked up on something that I had missed before.

All three men were bald—much like the three men who I had passed in the corridor earlier that night. Stepping towards the biggest one I turned him over till I could see his neck and saw what I was looking for.

A lipstick-kiss tattoo graced his neck like a love bite left by death itself.

We exited into the silent corridor.

Guns in hand, Poppy and I scanned both ways before we began walking.

"When I searched the other's rooms I found no one else on this floor."

"What do you mean?"

"The only way to get into any of these rooms is electronically. The door handles are all DNA coded to the occupant inside but to someone like me it's child's play to override the system and gain access. When I did, I found every room I searched empty."

"Every room?"

She stopped at room seventy-eight and looked both ways before placing her hand on the handle. The same green light glowed under her hand and with a twist and a push she opened the door to an empty room.

And I mean empty.

I stepped inside, my shoes echoing against the bare walls, and spun in a small circle. There was nothing. No furniture. No decoration. No appliances. No nothing. I looked at Poppy, who gave me a knowing look.

"How easy is it to hack that DNA coded system?"

"By a team of professionals? Should have been a lot harder than it took the three that tried to attack us."

I said nothing as we stepped back into the corridor and made our way towards the golden elevator doors. We were only within touching distance when the lights flickered and went out.

"Fuck!"

I tried for the elevator button but I knew it was pointless even as my finger pressed it.

I tried once more but the elevator lay unresponsive.

I looked at Poppy before we both looked at the door for the stairs. A small sigh of frustration escaped my lips.

"Don't be so lazy, it's five floors down," she said, moving past me.

"That's easy for you to say," I called after her; "my legs aren't mechanical."

66

The flickering emergency lights created long shadows that did nothing to ease my mind.

Ever since we had taken this job for The Lady, life had been one clusterfuck after the next. There were too many players and pieces in play that clouded the puzzle as to what was going on. How did one job turn into such a nightmare?

Now it seemed the whole of Safe Haven were against us one way or another, and to be honest I couldn't blame them. If I detached myself from the whole situation and looked at it objectively, we *were the bad guys*.

We were the ones smuggling arms and dirty weapons to a megalomaniac who wanted total control of the planet. Everyone else was just trying to protect what was theirs, be that their home or loved ones.

They all had a right to, even if they kept slaves like Mr Lee.

How did I get so caught up in this shit?

Voices below us slowed our footsteps.

"The power's out so they have nowhere to go but take

the stairs. We haven't seen them yet but we have teams searching all the floors. If we encounter anything we'll radio in; out."

Poppy closed her eyes and tilted her head towards where the speaker's voice had come from. She brought up three fingers.

I looked for somewhere to go but they caught us between floors; we'd have to go one stage lower to reach the door below us, and we'd gone too far down to reach the floor above us in time.

"I think we can—" I began but Poppy leapt over the railing leaving me with my mouth hanging open.

I stared at where she had once been then gathered myself together and leaned over the railing.

She landed amongst three men who looked as surprised as I had been. They all carried weapons but they were far too slow to react.

She moved in a blur. The speed was inhuman.

One minute she was standing, the next her palm had smashed into the solar plexus of the man in front of her. When she moved, it felt like I was watching a movie but I had missed a frame. It was that fast.

The man she hit struck the wall and crumpled to the floor. His two colleagues brought their weapons up in an arc but Poppy's fist had already hit both their throats causing them to drop to the floor.

The whole thing had taken seconds. They hadn't made a sound. They hadn't reacted to her attack. They hadn't done anything.

In that moment I knew everything I had thought I knew about Poppy was a lie.

Thinking back to when we were onboard Gregory's ship: she had masked her movements, she had slowed down her attacks and allowed herself to get hit; she looked clumsy in some moments, unsure of her attack, unsure what her opponent was going to do. Yes, she had been fighting robots, but it like comparing Ford Model T's to modern-day cars. She could have demolished those heaps of junk without a second thought yet she hadn't; she had played a part.

Just for my benefit.

She looked up at me and I looked down at her and something unspoken passed between us.

Footsteps sounded above me and I saw two pairs of feet descending towards me.

"Did you hear that?"

I didn't hesitate but lifted my pistol and fired at two pairs of kneecaps that appeared in front of me. The sound from the pistol was suppressed but the screams that came from my enemies' mouths weren't.

Two bodies slid and tumbled down the stairs to land at my feet.

They looked up at me as I struck each on the side of the head with my pistol. The one to my left went out after the first blow; the one to my right was a stubborn bastard who only went down after my fourth strike.

I took a step back and found Poppy standing next to my shoulder.

She walked forward but I grabbed her arm. "What are you doing?"

"Leaving them alive and expecting them not to tell whoever they are working for where we went only works in the movies."

"By the time they wake up we shall be long gone."

"How can you be so sure about that?"

"I... look, Poppy, killing men in self-defence is one thing

but killing men who are unarmed and unconscious is not a line I think—"

She didn't wait for me to finish. She moved with such speed that she tore loose from my grip and struck a blow at the base of each man's neck that echoed off the walls with a sickening crunch. I stood motionless as I watched small blood bubbles form at the corners of their mouths.

"This is your life now," Poppy said, looking me in the eye. "When you chose to be on this crew, when you chose this life, this is what it entails."

"But I—"

"When you chose me," she said, grabbing both sides of my face, "this is what it entailed."

I looked her in the eye and opened my mouth but didn't know what to say. "I—"

Footsteps thundered above us and Poppy grabbed my hand as we made our way down the stairs three at a time. She grabbed one of the guns from the men we had first encountered and continued on and stopped at the first door we found.

I opened it and peeked inside while she stood guard behind me.

Coast clear, I waved her through but not before she threw the gun down the stairwell making sure it hit every wall and step on its way down.

We closed the door as silently as we dared and looked around our new surroundings.

Dim red lighting illuminated lounge chairs and massage tables, hammocks hung in corners and small intimate jacuzzis rested in fake rock alcoves that offered the occupants some privacy against prying eyes.

We walked forward, taking in the strange nature of the floor that we were on. Something reflected in the light and I bent up and picked it up; a red silk thong with rhinestones around its edge caught the little light that emanated from the ceiling.

"I know what floor we are on," I said, recalling the conversation I had with Wei. "I think this is floor five; it's meant to be the casino's spa-cum-pleasure zone. If you know what I mean."

"Mmm," Poppy said, thin-lipped. "You going to put those down anytime soon?"

I looked at the thong in my hand and dropped it quickly. "I think I hear something coming from over there," I said, moving past her quickly and avoiding her gaze.

I brought my pistol up and took a corner, which opened up into a room unlike anything I had ever seen: chains and ropes hung from the ceiling, with whips of various sizes attached to the far wall. I moved through them as if among vines hanging from the trees in the jungle and spotted a man tied up in red rope.

He hung naked suspended in mid-air.

Burns and whip marks covered his body. He was blindfolded with a ball gag dangling loose on his chest.

I stood in front of the man and tapped my gun against my lips.

"Hello?" he said. "Who's there? Tish, is that you? Benny's been a naughty boy and he needs to be punished. Stop keeping me waiting. I need to be cleaned!"

Poppy walked up beside me and she gave me a look that mirrored my own.

"Who is this?" she mouthed.

I gave her a shrug.

"Tish, I need you! Stop postponing my punish—"

"Err, I don't know how to tell you this, dude, but there isn't anyone here," I said.

Benny went quiet as his head snapped from left to right."Who... who are you? Where's Tish?"

"My name is Quinton, Quinton Blake, and I don't know who the hell Tish is but she isn't here; no one is."

"Do you know what happened?"

"Your guess is as good as mine, mate."

"Fucking typical, I try something new once, just once, and it gets kicked in my face. I'll bet you all think this is hilarious, don't you? The office cubicle square looking for a bit of fun and look at how it ends up! Well, let me tell you something, Quinton, you may not realise it but some of us have to work long hours doing things we hate, for people we despise. Long hours in a god damn office I dream about setting fire to and then pissing on the embers, so don't judge me for trying to bring some spice back into my life."

"Hey, dude, there's no judgment here. No judgment at all. To each his own I always say, and you don't know how familiar your story sounds, but if I were you, I would get out of here because some shit is about to go down."

He said nothing as Poppy and I exchanged glances while the silence grew and grew.

"Well, cut me down then—if I could have let myself out do you think I would still be waiting here?"

"Oh shit, right," I said hurrying forward, but Poppy tapped me on the shoulder and gestured with her head northwards.

"I hear voices coming from the domination[?] chamber," said a voice off in the distance.

"Pop, knife."

"We don't have time," she hissed, but I held out my hand and she placed a blade in it.

"You deal with them and I'll catch up with you."

She looked at me, uncertain, but I gave her a smile and a

kiss on the lips as she disappeared into the darkness. I hacked off the ropes that kept Benny secured, only stopping when I heard the sounds of screams. He stiffened up, then struggled, which made getting him out that much harder.

"Will you stop moving before I cut you!"

He settled down and I finished the job, pulling him free. He stepped forward, tore the blindfold off his face and looked me in the eye, as more screams in the distance made us both jump.

"Things get better, if you choose them to be," I said.

"Thank you," he said, giving me a nod and a shake of the hand before he ran off into the darkness.

Gun in hand I moved with purpose forward; looking left to right I didn't see anyone. I was confident Poppy would find me when she was done but in that time I had to make sure I didn't get killed. Continuing on I came across a body twisted at an angle that it wasn't meant for, mouth still open in a silent scream, vacant eyes staring up at the ceiling. I stood over the body still shocked at what Poppy could do.

The kind beautiful person I came to know and care for was truly capable of some horrific things, but what person who was in a relationship couldn't say the same thing about the person they loved?

I heard the footsteps behind me too late.

A body rushed me out of the darkness and arms grabbed me around the middle, picking me up off my feet. I tried to keep a solid grip on my gun but they shook me until it fell from my hands. It bounced off somewhere in the darkness and I lost sight of it as I was tossed to the floor; I hit it hard but absorbed the landing as I tucked and forward-rolled. Coming up to my feet I took my attacker in.

He was wiry and unshaven; the dark circles under his eyes triggered my memory as I took in his face. I had seen this man before. He was with Edward Thomas when we had first met Edward back at the bar The Office; what was his name, what was his name—

"Mr Grey," he said. "I can see you were having trouble there."

"What do you want?"

"For you to come with me."

"All this bullshit is your doing, isn't it?" I asked, pointing a finger his way.

"Not my doing personally, no, but my boss Mr Thomas may have had a hand in all your current struggles. Anyway, it is not for me to say what he has done or hasn't; I am only a dog who is allowed off his leash now and again, and my orders were to bring you to him, so if you would please—"

I rushed him, not giving him time to react. A punch and a kick landed heavily, snapping his head back, I followed up with a double jab and a kick to his knee that buckled it and brought him down on one knee, at which point I drove my knee upwards into his jaw causing him to collapse on his back.

I thought I had won.

But as his hands crept to his face to wipe at the blood coming out of his nose and the corner of his mouth, he laughed. It was humourless and it was hollow. It was as if someone had taught him how to laugh but he still hadn't got the mechanics of it right. He sat up and then shook his head as he got to his feet.

"My, my, Mr Blake. Who would have thought a pen-pushing little twerp like yourself could find it in you to do such a thing?" he said as he clicked his neck from side to side. "That shit really hurt—Ah! I mustn't swear, or Mr Thomas will be angry. If there is one thing that Mr Thomas can't stand it's—"

I went for another punch but he caught it and threw my hand aside.

"I haven't finished speaking, Mr Blake. As I was saying, if there is one thing Mr Thomas hates it's foul language; he finds it unbecoming of a gentleman. So I must apologise for my language."

"Fuck you! How's that for language?" It sounded childish even to me, but it was the only thing I could think of in the heat of the moment as I moved towards him again and attacked. He moved out of the way, always staying just out of reach. I felt my knuckles brush his flesh but they never made solid contact. A blinding fast back-fist smacked me across the cheek spinning me around, then a boot landed square on my chest knocking me off my feet.

Mr Grey looked down at me and he looked bored. Worse than bored—there was something behind his eyes that scared me. It scared me because I had only seen it in one other pair of eyes and they belonged to Willis. I recalled a conversation we had where he had told me that forty-five percent of the people I would meet would be hard men with a drug addiction who could barely keep their gun straight, the other forty-five were just as scared as you and would rather not be there, but the last ten percent, those people... those people were his people and if I ever came across one I should just do one thing.

"Now, Mr Blake, shall we begin?"

I should just run.

67

I rolled out of the way of a kick that skimmed my head by inches, and kept on moving; I wasn't running away per se, I was just moving myself out of harm's way while I looked for my fallen pistol. Even to me, the excuse sounded shit, but it was the best excuse I could give myself while I tried my best not to engage with a man looking at best to take me hostage and at worse to kill me.

"Come on, Mr Blake, there is no need for all of this rigmarole. Mr Thomas only wants to have a meeting with you and your crew."

I didn't respond, but ducked as he tried to grab me, and delivered a kick that he blocked with his forearm. I winced as my shinbone connected against what felt like steel. He returned the favour, kicking me back, and I blocked it just like he did but the kick felt like it would break my forearms. Shaking them out I continued to back up eyes, quickly darting to the floor around me.

Where was Poppy?

She had been gone for what felt like an age and it was some time since I had heard any screams or sounds of fighting. I could tell myself that I wanted to know where she was because I was worried about her but deep down I knew that was a lie, I knew I was only thinking about her for my own sake, so she could protect me, so she could deal with this problem I was facing instead of me trying to figure out a way to deal with it myself, so I wouldn't have to suffer. As shameful as that sounds, I was still hoping that she would turn up any minute.

Because maybe I wasn't cut out—

"What are you doing here, Mr Blake?"

I stopped moving and looked at Mr Grey as he scratched his chin and looked at me as if I was an experiment gone wrong. "I mean, why are you here? Running around with this crew who are made up of cutthroats and religious lunatics? In this line of work I only came across guys like you who have found themselves in crews or places like this planet because they are in debt, dealing with addiction, or running away from something. But you, Mr Blake, you are none of those things. What's keeping you here?

"You appear to be a man of sound mind, a man whose skills would be best utilized in an office cubicle rather than out here. A little boring, yes, but not everyone is destined to be a hero or villain; some people are just meant to live in the background, in the grey so to speak."

"You know nothing about—"

"But there you are wrong. To know yourself fully is the only way to know your opponent better than he knows himself; that is the only way to assure victory."

I rolled my eyes as I kept a healthy distance between us.

"Now, are you going to come with me or does this have to get messy?"

"Fuuucck you!" I said, drawing out the word as I gave him two middle fingers. Irritation flashed across his face as he rushed towards me. I failed to see the punch or the knee to the stomach, but a white flash tore across my vision as pain stabbed me where I had been hit.

I threw my own punches but they didn't land as Mr Grey danced out of the way.

He kicked and punched me again forcing me to cover up and grit my teeth as he kept pushing me backwards. My vision was blurry, legs wobbly as I stumbled on one knee and willed myself to get up but it just wasn't happening. I couldn't find the strength I needed to lift myself up.

"Ah! I get it!" he said, snapping his fingers my way. "Pussy!"

"What?"

"That's why you're in this crew, some cheap slut has spread her legs in your direction and rocked your world and now you don't want to leave. I guess civilised life must seem boring after that. The old lady wasn't putting out? Had to tug it in the shower while you cried? It's a shame what some good pussy will do to a man," he said with that hollow laugh of his.

"But who am I to judge you, when the greatest men and empires have fallen because of the feminine charms of a woman—"

"What do you know? Working as someone's lapdog as a hired killer, and you judge me? I'm the pitiful one? At least I can fall asleep at night. At least the nightmares don't keep me awake."

His jaw tightened and his muscles stiffened as he rushed my way and grabbed me by the face.

His dark bloodshot eyes glared my way as he lifted me to my feet. "What would you know about nightmares, Mr Blake? A man who fell in love with his kidnappers. A man who allows his woman to fight for him. A man who at this very moment wishes she could come and save him while he hides behind her tailcoats. Yet I am the pitiful one?

"Now I won't ask you again, this is...."

My thoughts drowned out his voice while I thought about everything I had done to get here. The people's lives I had taken, the suffering I had endured, the beatings at the hands of enemies and friends alike, the constant threat of being killed, the hunger, the not knowing whether I would live to see another day, the training—argh, the training—all to be beaten by this dickwad because he thought he was better than me, because he thought he knew my life inside out.

I hadn't suffered at the hands of that sadistic ginger prick through training to fall at the first hurdle I met.

So fuck him! Fuck whatever horse he rode in on! And fuck the universe if it thought I was going out like some bitch!

I drove my head forward, smashing my forehead into his nose and forcing him to drop me; I landed on the floor in a crouch and my hand grabbed something long, hard and flexible next to my feet. I swung it upright catching Mr Grey in the jaw. His head tilted back as I leapt to my feet and swung the object at him again. He tried to block but he was disoriented from the first blow and I caught him across the temple, spinning him around; he tried to defend himself but I kept on the pressure, delivering blow after blow.

He dropped to his knees, hands raised above his face, but I refused to stop. Refused to quit until my arms grew heavy and my chest burnt from the exertion that I was putting out.

I could hear my name being called but I couldn't tell where it was coming from.

Quinton.

Quinton.

"Quinton!"

Something solid grabbed hold of my arm, stopping me from moving it and jerking me out of my trance-like state. I looked wildly around and saw Poppy standing next to me, hand around my forearm.

"That's enough," she whispered.

I looked back to Mr Grey and saw nothing but a bloody mess. His face was a mask of blood where I had broken his nose and some of his teeth, a large hematoma had developed on his forehead and his left arm twitched periodically.

"Is he... alive?" I asked.

"Judging by his vitals he appears to just be unconscious, but everything from his nose to his arm is broken. She looked at me, cupping both her hands around my face. "Are you okay?"

"Yes."

"Are you sure? Because I'm sorry I wasn't—"

"Poppy, I am fine. Trust me. You won't always be around to save the day and I don't expect you to. I'm a big boy, I can look after myself."

"I know that. It's just, I find you beating a man with a large dildo, and a girl is bound to have some questions."

I looked at the object in my hand in confusion and hastily dropped it to the floor. Wiping my hands on my shirt I took one last look at the helpless form of Mr Grey on the floor. Poppy moved forward but I held her back.

"I thought we spoke about—"

"No."

"Quinton, you were going to kill him anyway."

"He will live and remember what took place here, and if he comes back, I shall make sure he remembers again. This is not mercy, far from it. This is a message."

Poppy took a step back as I met her gaze and I saw something akin to fear ripple across the surface.

"What happened here?"

"He insulted the woman I love."

"You love me?" she whispered.

"I—"

I brought my hands up as flashlights shone across my vision. "There they are!"

"It's time to go. Hold on," Poppy said, wrapping her arms around me, and then she lifted me up and sprinted forward.

"Poppy, where are we going?" I said as wind rushed past my face.

"Leaving."

I looked up at the approaching window and felt my insides twist. "But we are on the fifth fl—"

I never got to finish my sentence as we exploded out of the window and plummeted to the ground below.

68

I was proud of myself that I didn't scream.

The wind whistled past my face as we dropped like a coin tossed by a child off a tall building. I shut my eyes at the rapidly approaching ground. I was sure that we were going to die. No, better yet I was sure I was going to die—I, who was made up of bones and flesh, while Poppy, who wasn't, would walk away from this without a—

"Quinton, you can open your eyes now."

I did so slowly and was relieved when I saw the ground was only three feet away and wasn't coming towards me. Poppy let go of me and I got to my feet and brushed myself off as if nothing had happened.

"What?" she asked.

"*What* what?"

"I can always tell when you have something to get off your chest so just come on out with it."

"It's nothing, just you know."

"No, I don't."

"Not that I'm not grateful for the whole saving me thing, but when you pick me up like a damsel in distress and throw us out of a window, it doesn't necessarily make me feel like a—"

"Like a man," she said, crossing her arms.

"Well, you see... well, the thing is, that's not what I was meaning to say."

"Well, you said it."

"What I meant to say is, what I'm trying to convey is that a man likes to feel like a man and sometimes you don't allow that to happen."

She stared at me, lips disappearing by the second as the glare she sent my way pinned my soul to the back wall.

Ah shit. I was messing this up.

"OK, OK, look. First, thank you for saving me, thank you for being you. I wouldn't change you for the world, you are who you are and that makes you special. But a man likes to fix things, he likes to provide, likes to protect, likes to make the people in his life feel safe, and sometimes with you being Superwoman it doesn't give me the chance to do that."

"Don't make this about anything else apart from your male pride. If this is going to be a problem you need to tell me now."

"Who said anything about it being a problem? You're making it a problem by saying that in the first place."

"No matter the man, it always comes down to his fragile ego."

"What do you mean, no matter the man? How many other men have there been?"

"I have been alive for hundreds of years. Do you expect me not to know how the male species thinks and works? You're all the same," she said walking off, leaving me staring after her with my mouth opening and closing, while my brain tried to process the information I had received and tried to make some sense out of it.

"Wai—wait! You still haven't answered my question! How many men have there been?"

We moved from shadow to shadow but something wasn't right. People were running away from the direction we were headed, which was always a bad sign. Shrouded in the dark cover of a building, we rested in an alleyway while we observed the crowd of people who ran past us.

"What do you think is going on?"

Poppy looked at me and shrugged before flattening herself against the wall, as a group of men with pistols scanned the faces of the people who moved passed them. Not finding what they were looking for they moved on.

"The only thing that we can do is make our way towards your boat and from there form a plan on how to find the others," I said as another group of people hurried past us.

Poppy looked at me, worry lacing her features, but nodded at me nevertheless.

We departed from our hiding spot and moved through the crowd, faces lowered; I smelled something in the air and turned to face Poppy, who mirrored my look.

Smoke!

It wafted on the air as a red glow shimmered in the distance. I stretched my hand out and watched as ash landed on it. When I fixed my gaze on where the red glow was coming from my heart sunk; I had a feeling I knew what I would find when we made our way to our destination. Swallowing the bile that tried to rise from my stomach, I closed my eyes and knew we had to march forward. It was the only way.

"Let's get this over with," I said, closing my fist.

"You know what's going to be waiting for us once we get there, don't you?"

"Yup, but we can't go back so we might as well go forward."

The going only got harder the closer we got to the boating docks. Black flames leapt in the air and smoke danced on the wind as we finally reached our destination. The boating dock and everything tied up to it was in flames. I couldn't distinguish between our boat and the next, as a carpet of flame covered everything. I surveyed the damage as a voice called out to us over the crackling of the flames. "Ah! There you are, Mr Blake, how nice of you to finally join us." Mr Lee sat on a chair, legs crossed one over the another while a woman who stood next to him held up an umbrella to protect him against the falling ash, and another fed him grapes while his eyes bored into mine.

"What's the meaning of this?"

"The meaning is simple, Mr Blake, I am here to collect payment for all the damage you and your crew have done to my property, not to mention the property damage you have caused to the innocent, hardworking bystanders, who—"

"Cut the shit! It was your men who attacked us. We were only defending ourselves," I said, pointing a finger his way.

"I think you're mistaken. Earlier today one Willis Moor got into a drunken rage and destroyed parts of my hotel before moving on to attacking members of my staff. We tried to reason with him but alas he was beyond that point; he escaped into the night and has apparently been very busy," Lee said, gesturing towards the flames.

"Getting drunk and starting a fight, that doesn't sound like the Willis Moor I know; surely you are mistaken," I said, causing Poppy to snort, "and even if that was true why would Willis, a member of our crew, destroy our only means of transportation?"

"Men who are blinded by rage and alcohol do not see the world as you and I do."

He smiled at me, the leaping flames reflecting off his teeth, while I decided what to do; I took a step forward but Poppy held me back and gestured around us. Men detached themselves from the shadows and quickly surrounded us, I took in the numbers, and even if Poppy and I could somehow fight them all off the odds of our finding somewhere to hide on this floating village was slim to none.

"I can take them," Poppy said out of the corner of her mouth, "but the calculated odds of you surviving this fight weaponless isn't something I'm willing to risk."

I gritted my teeth as once again I cursed not having my trusty shotgun by my side. Who would have thought a simple collection mission would have warranted its use on so many occasions?

"We seem to have found ourselves at an impasse, Mr Lee."

"I wouldn't say that, Mr Blake. The way I see it, you are heavily outnumbered with nowhere to run, nowhere to hide, so the only thing you can do is come with me. If not... things may get a little messy for all parties involved."

I looked to Poppy, who said nothing but stared my way.

"I assure you," continued Lee, "you shall not be harmed. On the contrary, the issue is all but taken care of. If you would please follow me."

69

They escorted us back to the hotel corridors and there we reached a door made of solid iron. Two guards with bulging arms crossed over their chests regarded us with mild interest as we approached.

They looked us up and down as the men who surrounded us gave them a brief nod, which caused them to spin the lock in the centre of the door before pulling it open. We were not shoved forward, but there was no misunderstanding as to where they wanted us to go. I gave Poppy a look and a reassuring smile before I stepped forward and found myself in a vault.

Stacks of different currencies were piled ten feet high against back walls and corners of the room, golden coins littered the floor along with the occasional precious gem and gold bars, and right at the back sitting all by themselves sat a row of alphabetised grey security boxes.

I took the vault all in and then allowed my gaze to take in the three men who were sitting on chairs in the middle of it. Cuts and bruises marked faces, with more than one spotting a black eye.

"Boyo, glad you could finally join us."

"Hi, José, how you been?"

"I could be better, could be worse," he said, clasping my hand in a warm embrace.

"You got any ice cream?" Tuari asked, looking up at me in hope.

"What? No. Why would you—" I said, waving him off and looking at the drooling form of Willis, who was slumped in his chair. "What's up with him?"

"Well," Tuari said, "we were told that because of his drunken rampage, which caused untold damage to this fine hotel, he had to be sedated, otherwise extreme measures would have to be used."

"What a load of bullshit. How did they get the drop on you two?"

"Caught me sleeping. *Mierda!* I must be getting old," said José.

"Don't feel so bad; if it weren't for Poppy then they would have had the drop on me too. I woke up after it was all said and done. What about you?" I said, nodding toward Tuari.

He looked sheepishly at the floor before saying, "On the toilet."

I did my best to suppress a laugh but a snort still came out.

"It's nothing to be ashamed about, the King of Rock-and-Roll himself died on the toilet," he said.

"I think you'll find they found him on the bathroom floor, but whatever helps you sleep at night," I said as the door to the vault opened and in stepped Mr Lee.

His goons surrounded him as he surveyed the scene before him and smiled. It was all I could do not to walk over and punch those damn diamonds out of his mouth.

"I do love coming to these vaults; they always remind me of what is at stake."

"It's a bit untidy," I said, looking around, "or are you going for the Scrooge McDuck look?"

"In that assumption you are wrong. These gold coins and bars you see around you are nothing compared to the true wealth that lies in those security boxes. The age of gold and currency has long been over; real wealth has always lied in stocks and company bonds. Little pieces of paper that the uneducated would toss to the floor because they knew no different, but I guess that's why the masses will always be poor. Yes, those boxes are my pride and joy, and contain more than a few shares from large companies that owe me favours, companies that we both have—"

The vault door opened and Wei walked in. He tried his best to not look in our direction but our eyes met briefly before he whispered in Lee's ear. Lee gave him a nod and Wei departed the way he came.

"Well, I must thank you for making this the most eventful forty-eight hours I have had in a while but I must be going. I had hoped we would all leave tonight as winners but sometimes Lady Luck just doesn't want to play ball. As I have previously stated to some of you, all your debts owed to me for any damage or grievance caused have now been settled. So I won't come looking for you, if you don't come looking for me," he said walking towards the door. "Oh, and Mr Blake, the offer we spoke about is still on the table."

All heads turned to me as he left.

"Ohh, someone's in trouble," Tuari said, as I shifted uncomfortably on my chair.

"I'll explain later," I said as the door opened one more time and none other than Edward Thomas entered. He clapped his hands in front of him and gave us all a beaming smile around the onyx pipe in his mouth.

"Well, how jolly good it is to see all of you good folks well and in one piece. I wish I could say the same for my man Mr Grey but alas, he understands that in his line of work accidents happen and people get injured. Now about this job—"

"Hold up, amigo, I think we're missing a few key details here," José said. "For one, what are we doing here, and two, why would we ever work for you?"

"Reasonable enough questions I suppose, my good man. The first is simple enough to answer; your ginger friend here took it upon himself to get royally—what is the word that you people use," Edward said, snapping his finger, "—shitfaced, such a vile word—yes, he took it upon himself to get drunk and then he got violent and caused more damage to Mr Lee's property than you can possibly afford to pay. The second answer is even simpler.

"I paid off your debts to Mr Lee, so now you owe me, which brings this job I have for you into play."

I burst into laughter. I couldn't help myself. I let it roll from my stomach like a wave collecting sand and shells from the ocean floor and allowed it to take all the tension, the worry and stress I had and allowed it to flow out.

I laughed and laughed till tears streaked down my face and everyone looked upon me as if I had gone mad.

"All this," I said, sputtering between laughs, "all this just because you want us to do this job for you. You went to all this effort!"

"Dear boy, I don't know what you possibly—"

"Stop! Stop. Cut the bullshit—you board of director types never get to the issue at hand. It was you who shot down our cargo ship, it was you who arranged for us to take part in that little Casino Royal in the hopes we would lose and be up to our eyeballs in debt so you could bail us out, and it was you who destroyed Lee's casino and burned down the dock. I don't know if you and Lee came to some arrangement where you could place the blame on us and just pay him off, but that matters little."

"What gave it away?" Edward asked.

"Willis is a ginger asshole who would kick any of us when we're down, but for him to get drunk and be out as long as he is, is just impossible. I've seen the man polish off a bottle of whiskey and still be coherent."

"Was that all?"

"No, but like I said, it matters little. All I wanted to know is why."

Edward took out his pipe and clicked his fingers. One of his men produced a small metal canister which he emptied his pipe into; he was then handed a leather pouch that he pulled loose tobacco from and stuffed into the pipe. A match was lit for him and he puffed on the pipe till it was lit.

"Why did I go through all this trouble? It's something I've been giving a lot of thought to lately. The main reason this all started was because you nearly crippled Xcorp. The company my family started. The company they built from the ground up with nothing but a hope and a dream. The company that killed a handful of my family from stress-related illness.

"I wanted you to pay for that," he said, bitterness creeping into his voice.

"I wanted you to pay for making my family the laughing-stock of the business world. I had already taken care of your idiot manager Gregory Goodwin and as the embarrassment passed and time healed the wounds, I almost forgot about you and your little crew, Mr Blake— almost.

"But I couldn't forget about what you had taken from us, from me. The AI designs on that memory chip would have pushed Xcorp into the forefront. We would be a law unto ourselves! But you had to—" He took a deep breath and continued, "That is neither here nor there. The reason you are here today is because Xcorp has been trying to recover an item in space, but every crew we send has been unsuccessful in completing the mission."

"By unsuccessful, you mean dead?" José asked.

"Yes, you are right, my Spanish-speaking friend. They all died, or more precisely we lost contact with every crew we sent out there. The problem puzzled me for some time until your little crew crossed my thoughts, and I thought who better to do the unthinkable but the little crew who has brought so many giants down to their knees."

"You went through all this *bother* just so we could complete some stupid mission for you in the hopes we may get killed?" I said, looking at him in confusion. "It would be easier to just have us killed."

"Probably cheaper too," Tuari said.

"You know, I did think that, and at first hiring you was just an excuse to meet the crew in person, to see the people who had brought my company down to its knees. Then when you turned down my offer, it became a game to see if I could get you to work for me, and the more I tried the more I became amazed at how you survived and struggled through on luck, hustle and street smarts. I hear that's what it's called," he said behind his hand. "Then I became convinced your crew was the crew for the job and I had to have you work for me, and if there's one thing you good folks must know about me it's that I always get what I want. Now on to business," he said, rubbing his hands together.

A large cube was placed in the middle of the floor and

Edward stepped forward and tapped it with his forefinger, causing the item to hum. It projected an interstellar map in the air.

Poppy hid her gasp well, but I caught it never the less.

"What are we looking at here, my friend?" José asked studying the map in detail.

"This, my fine fellows, is a star map of a hidden space station which left Earth's orbit during WW3. For reasons that aren't important it was launched secretly and has been orbiting that distant sun, using the sun's rays as energy to keep the satellite operational. The satellite is located in a region of space which there are no hospitable planets; the area is littered with space rock, space dust and comets that play havoc with a ship's systems."

"It looks like it was placed in a location where it wasn't meant to be found," I said.

"Be that as it may, find it I have and get inside we must."

"What's the cargo?" José asked.

"I can't tell you that."

"Then no matter how much *in debt* we are to you, amigo, we can't help you. Unless we know the dimensions, the weight, whether the cargo is stable or likely to explode, whether whatever inside has to be specially quarantined or can be moved about with ease, we can't fully prepare for the job, because we don't know what tools we need or what precautions we need to take.

"This business may look simple to you, but it has to be orchestrated like brain surgery if you want the desired outcome. If the previous fools you used didn't explain this to you then no wonder their missions were failures."

"Ha!" Edward said slapping his thigh, "you see that! You see that! This is why I knew I had to have you guys. Gosh. My father always used to say to listen to your gut and I am glad that I did. I am confident you fine chaps will complete this mission for me and deliver me what I want. Now to answer your question, what you are collecting for me weighs two hundred and twenty-six kilos or five hundred pounds. It's eight foot by five and shaped like a coffin. It isn't likely to explode and there is no reason it should need to be quarantined."

"What does it look like?" José asked.

Edward tapped the computer attached to his wrist, changing the image projected by the cube on the floor until it showed a grey refrigerator-looking object with more warning signs and labels on it than I could count.

"I thought you said this thing didn't need to be quarantined," I said.

"It doesn't."

"Then why the hell has it more warning signs on it than a box containing the smallpox virus?"

"Everything was like that during WW3. You don't realise how health and safety conscious everyone was back then; you had to write up a written evaluation if you just wanted to go to the bathroom. My good man, trust me, it's nothing you need to be concerned about," Edward said.

The crew and I exchanged looks, all thinking the same thing.

"If that's the case, amigo, how come none of your crews have made it back alive?"

"Ah, I was hoping we would gloss over that point, but I can see nothing gets past you," Edward said, waving a finger our way. In all honestly I do not know. Some crews we lost contact with before they even made it to the space station, others we were in contact with until they boarded the station, then after that, nothing. I wish I could be more helpful, but it is what it is." He checked his wrist and clapped his hands together.

"Anyway, I believe that concludes our meeting. Please keep the cube; it shall guide you where you need to go. I shall give you forty-eight hours to collect whatever supplies you need, put your affairs in order and board your ship. I realise you need transportation so I shall drop you dear chaps back in Paradise Lost, where my ship shall be stationed next to yours waiting for you to depart. Normally I wouldn't accompany the crew I send, but I shall make an exception this time, I think."

"This is all very nice of you, my friend," said José, "but what if we refuse?"

"Then I kill you."

Silence descended upon the room as everyone grew tense. My mouth grew dry and my palms grew sweaty as Edward's men placed their hands on their weapons.

"But there will be no need for that," Edward said cheerily, "because I am sure you fine folks will accomplish the mission and be home before you know it. Now, I'll give you some time to collect yourselves and him," he said, pointing towards Willis, "and I shall meet you outside."

As he left and his men followed him, I looked over the crew and they had the same sour expression I had. We were screwed, and there was nothing that we could do about it.

Tuari lifted Willis onto his shoulders and helped José up. They moved towards the door while I stood in the centre of the vault, mind racing.

I had thought I had left Xcorp behind me. I had thought I could build a new life for myself outside of its clutches, but time and fucking time again, it somehow got its roots into me no matter what I did. Although he was charming and polite, I highly doubted Edward would let us part ways freely, even if we somehow completed this suicide mission.

Shit!

Between Edward, The Lady and Mr Lee. I didn't see any way that we would be making it out of this alive.

I held my head in my hands and I felt a pair of arms embrace me. Resting my head on Poppy's shoulders I closed my eyes and took a deep breath in; reopening them I saw the security boxes resting innocently on the far back wall and smiled.

"Poppy, I think I may have a plan."

70

They escorted us off Edward's ship, which had landed next to *The Kennel*. His men said nothing but just stood next to the cargo walkway and smiled.

"What a hospitable bunch of pricks," Tuari said, giving them a wave and a smile.

"So fill me in, one more time, how we ended up in this shit?" Willis said, scratching his beard, which sounded like sandpaper.

"It's pretty simple really: Mr Lee tricked you into taking money so we could end up in his debt; when that didn't work Edward's men caused havoc and blamed you for getting drunk and disorderly. Now, we have to complete a suicide mission that has killed every crew who have undertaken it," Tuari said. "Feeling filled in yet?"

"Why didn't we just tell—"

"Because, Willis, he has more men!" I said. "He has more power! He has more everything! Shit, if I knew shit was going to be this difficult then I would have stayed in my nine to five. It matters little now anyway."

"It always matters, boyo, it always matters," José said, clapping me on the shoulder. "If we just allow the man to roll us over, then we are no better than those cubicle pen-pushing slaves who never try and better their situation. Always remember we are stray dogs! Dogs that ain't fed by the hand but fight and scrap for every molecule of food we get."

I nodded my head as his words poured through my ears and into my soul. Yes, things were different now. I had chosen this path because I wanted my freedom; now as things had started to go wrong I was whining and complaining, instead of taking it on the chin and coming back stronger.

"What do we do now then?" I asked.

"Now, boyo, we deal with our other problem before it deals with us."

"The Lady?"

"The Lady."

71

We arrived at Hotel Moscow; the grand-looking Art Deco hotel stood out amongst the other less impressive buildings that surrounded it like a peacock among pigeons. As we walked towards the entrance a pair of guards looked our way, X-ray sunglasses covering their eyes. One quickly spoke into a hidden mic attached to his lapel while the other placed his hand under his suit jacket.

The sun had yet to rise. It was that wonderful twilight hour before the night stalkers went to bed and the day walkers woke up. It was a time where everything could happen and no one would know.

Vlad exited the main entrance and watched our approach till we got to him. He looked each of us in the face with those dead cold lifeless eyes and said nothing, but turned around and walked back inside. We followed him in, feet tapping on the marble floors; the sound carried, as the foyer was empty.

I looked left and right but only saw long shadows that

the dim light had created. A leaf fell from the cherry blossom tree positioned in the middle of the foyer, and I prayed it wasn't a sign of things to come.

We walked until we reached a set of ornate gold doors carved out in the shape of flowing water and waited while Vlad knocked. We waited for what felt like an age until the words "Come in" came from the other side.

Vlad pushed the doors open, and we followed in to find Lady Isabella Ivanov sitting behind her grand wooden desk, pen in hand, papers laid out before her.

I looked up and stared at the stained glass image of the scrawny old king sitting on his throne while Death knelt before him, the skulls of his enemies hanging from a tree branch behind him; as I stared at the image it was all I could do to keep my mouth from going dry.

We stood in front of her and waited while she continued to work. She crossed out something on one paper and scribbled furiously on another. Her writing was wild, and she stabbed at the paper with an urgency I was surprised she had at this witching hour.

She placed her pen down and steepled her fingers together as she regarded us. "You see, Vlad. I told you there was nothing to worry about; I knew that as soon as the Junk Yard Dogs landed they would grace us with their presence, and there were you wanting to send out the cavalry."

"I'm sorry I haven't been in touch, but things have taken a turn," José said.

"Yes, yes. I am well aware, but so we are on the same page please do enlighten me."

"There were... some issues... unforeseen issues and problems we ran into that caused us the delay and loss of your cargo."

Silence descended like a heavy mist as my back grew wet and my palms clammy.

"Do tell?" Isabella asked.

"We received both your cargoes from the Jungle and the Floating City, but we were shot out of the sky upon leaving the Floating City and later ran into more trouble where our ship was burnt down and your cargo with it. I—"

"I don't see how—"

"You are correct, it's not your problem," José said, cutting her off. "Ever since you have used our services, no matter the issue we have dealt with it ourselves and this time will be no different. But to repay back what we owe you will take some time, time we haven't got at the present as we have another matter to take care of. I hope *mi Señora* will understand that her plans will have to be put on hold, but once—"

The Lady snapped her fingers and the golden doors to her office opened, allowing in twelve men, all with assault rifles. They divided in two and flanked us on either side; they pointed their weapons towards the floor but I had a feeling that could change in an instant.

"Mr Battle, if there is one thing I can't stand it's delays, but if there is one thing I can't stand above that, it's being told about failure. I do not care about the issues and obstacles you and your crew faced, I do not care who is out to get you or why, all I care about is getting what I asked you for and having it delivered on time. I thought we understood each other. I thought you knew what I did to people who failed me?"

She nodded to the men around us and they slowly lifted their rifles. "I must say, I will miss employing you but I'm afraid I can't have failure. Good—"

"Wait!" I shouted, holding out my hands.

The room held its breath while the men around us kept

their fingers on their triggers. I looked to either side of me and I could see that Poppy, Willis and Tuari were ready to move. Even with the advanced capabilities of Poppy, I knew that men on both sides would die here today if I didn't do something.

"Just wait—everyone relax, calm down and take a breather. Lady Isabella Ivanov, the people that came for us will soon come for you. I know José is too proud and stubborn to ever admit to a client his failures or what led to them, but I think it's about time we laid our cards on the table."

She let out a yawn but didn't say anything else.

"Xcorp was the one who attacked us; they shot us out of the air and they burnt our ships as retaliation for what took place. They also appear to be working with Mr Lee of the Han Dynasty and other crews from different boroughs, I don't know what their end game is, or why this mission is so important, but what I do know is that after they're done with us, everyone will be coming for you.

"You threaten the status quo. You threaten all the other leading crews on Safe Haven and I know you're not scared of war, and you're prepared for it, but there is only so much one person can do against so many foes."

"Mr Blake, I hardly see your point. You are not saying anything I don't know or anything new; it sounds like you are just stalling for time until the inevitable."

"This mission Edward Thomas, the owner of Xcorp, tasked us with is important and valuable to him—to a corporation that is one of the largest and wealthiest in all of recorded human history. Don't you think whatever it is at the end of that rainbow could be valuable to you?"

"No."

"I—"

I was at a loss for words. I tried to think of something else to say, something else that could buy us more time, that could persuade this psycho bitch that not killing us was in her best interests, but she didn't seem to care, she didn't seem to want to know what I could offer her. How could you bargain with someone whose mind was already made up? She believed she was strong enough to fight whatever was coming. How could I possibly change that mindset when it had worked for her her whole life?

"Well, that was all very nice but it changed nothing. Now—"

"You can use me," Poppy said, the words forcing me to close my eyes and grit my teeth. I didn't want to turn around and look at her because I knew my face would betray the emotions that were riding just under the surface.

"And what use are you to me?" Isabella asked.

Without saying a word, Poppy grabbed the nearest assault rifle in a blink of an eye and bent it like it was made out of clay. The men didn't shout or make a fuss—they were too well trained for that—but I could see their wide-eyed stares as their heads snapped back to their boss and Poppy, and vice versa. Hands with rifles in them shook as they all pointed them Poppy's way.

"Well, well," said The Lady, as she got up from her chair and slowly circled Poppy. "I knew your little crew was hiding a secret; who would have thought it was as big as something like this? When I asked you to retrieve that information from Xcorp regarding AI, I only half-believed in it. It was more akin to getting a treasure map and knowing deep down that there may be nothing at the end of the journey, but this... an AI humanoid... The folktales are all true—how human you are, just like one of us. Oh, this will do nicely... yes, yes.

"It appears we have a deal, Mr Blake. I shall spare the lives of your crew; in exchange I shall keep—"

I moved. I didn't think. I just did. Elbow smashing into the nose of the nearest guard to me, while simultaneously kicking out his kneecap, I grabbed his rifle with both hands and twisted it out of his grip and pointed it towards The Lady.

This time the room erupted.

Her men shouted at me in Russian, while training their guns on me, but that didn't last long as Poppy wrapped her arm around Isabella's throat and hugged her in close. Her men didn't know which way to point as they tried to divide their attention between Poppy and me.

"What is going on, dickface?" Willis shouted as his pistols appeared in his hand. He looked towards José, who remained silent as I narrowed my eyes Isabella's way. "José! Do something before this fucker condemns all our souls. For the love of God!"

"I hate to argue with the ginger madmen, but this does seem to be going south quick," said Tuari.

"I don't think you shall be keeping anyone, Lady Isabella Ivanov. That was not the deal. The deal was an offer of help to defeat and conquer your enemies."

"Deal? Who said anything about a deal?" she replied as I felt the barrel of a gun placed against the side of my head. I looked out of my peripheral vision and saw the grim face of Vlad.

"What say you, Mr Battle?" said The Lady, joy dancing on her words. "What say you about this predicament we seem to have found ourselves in? Are you not the leader of this crew?"

José said nothing as he pulled the cigar out of his mouth and slowly lit it. Taking in a deep intake, he blew a column of smoke towards the ceiling and smiled. "'I fell in love with a hooker who robbed me of my soul. I fell in love with a hooker who robbed me of my sight. I fell in love with a hooker because she was the only woman for me. I fell in love with a hooker till the only thing I had was two packs of cigarettes and thirty dollars on me.'

"Those song lyrics were from my father's favourite band, The Junk Yard Dogs, and I never realised the meaning of those words until I killed a man and saw the light vanish behind his eyes."

"Boss," Tuari said with a grimace, "I... don't think that's the meaning behind those words. Call me crazy, but—"

"Will you cease this nonsense!" said The Lady. "Mr Battle, I believe you have a decision to make."

"*Mi Señora*, you are wrong. There never was a decision to make in the first place. A pack doesn't leave a member behind, no matter if that pack is made up of a bunch of wild, stray, flea-bitten mutts that no one will give a home. Now, I believe we placed an offer of help on the table. The decision is down to you whether or not you shall take it."

She smiled and it was only then did I realise what we were dealing with. She relished the danger. There was a storm of insanity behind those eyes that made Willis's own look like a gentle summer breeze. We were in danger; we were all in danger, and the sooner we got out of here the better, as the hunger in her eyes when she looked at Poppy chilled me to the bone. It mattered little that we had lost all her weaponry; she had found something better.

"Do we have a deal... do we have a deal... do we have a deal?" She repeated the sentence softer and slower each time. "You accept a job offer I give you and payment, you fail to complete said job, and threaten me in my own *home* no less, and expect me to do what? Accept? I hardly see what I gain out of this deal?"

"Your life for one," said Poppy.

"Besides that."

"Help to combat the storm that is coming your way," I said, "plus, I shall transfer you what you paid us three times over."

There was silence for a moment or two before The Lady spoke again: "I guess I had better accept then."

"You wouldn't hold it against me if I didn't take your word on the matter, it's just after everything that has happened here," I said looking around the room.

"I would be insulted if you did," she said.

"I would like you to call your men off while we slowly and calmly leave your hotel. You shall be in our company till we get to our vehicle of course; once again, it's not that we don't trust you, it's just that... well, you understand," I said.

"Of course," she said with a smile that sent chills down my spine. "Do as he says and please lower your weapons."

The men lowered their rifles to the floor, but the tension remained. We had to get out of here and we had to get out of here fast. I could still feel the barrel of a gun pressed to the side of my head as I inched my eyes sideways to see Vlad's unchanged, grim expression.

"This would be a lot quicker if *we* all cooperated," I said.

"Vlad, it's okay. We have an understanding now," said The Lady.

Sweat trickled down my back as the barrel remained.

"Do, not, make me repeat myself."

Vlad did as he was told as I licked my dry lips but still kept a firm grip on my rifle. "Now, if you ladies would like to go first, the JYD crew shall follow you and I think it's best for your men to stay where they are. Don't worry," I said as Vlad lifted his pistol towards me, "once at the entrance we shall let Isabella go, pay what we owe, and we shall be working together again like old times with all of this forgotten about."

I stepped to one side and gestured with my arms towards the door. The Lady's men jockeyed on the spot but they held firm as Poppy, with The Lady in her grip, moved towards the door; then they opened a way for her and she walked out with José, Willis, Tuari and me following closely behind, keeping our guns trained on her men at all times.

I allowed a sigh to escape my lips as the golden doors closed behind us.

"Why are you so nervous, Mr Blake?" The Lady said softly, her tone cutting through the silence of the foyer. "You have nothing to worry about. I can assure you of that."

I nodded my head but didn't respond as our footsteps echoed off the marble floor. We hurried as best as we could until we got to the entrance. Tuari had parked our car in the front of the building, a small blessing I was thankful for as we exited out the hotel. Two guards with X-ray shades looked shocked to see us but a simple gesture of the head from their boss and they retreated back inside.

"Tuari, start the car, and everyone get in," Poppy said.

Tuari did as he was told with Willis following closely behind. I looked at José, who stood next to me, and then back at Poppy, who looked at me in irritation and mouthed "get in," but I ignored her.

"Poppy, you can let her go," said José.

Poppy looked at me but refused to release her hold.

"It's OK," I said, "you can wait in the car; our business is done here."

About to say something, she gritted her teeth and

nodded her head and got inside the car as José and I stood facing the demon who presided over Paradise Lost.

"Well, Mr Battle, it appears you have trained your second in command well. Your presence wasn't even needed here tonight. I dare say in the future all my dealings shall be with Mr Blake here."

"What can I say, the boyo learns quick. It's a pleasure to have him on the team."

I looked to José but couldn't quite see his features amidst the cloud of smoke that surrounded him from his cigar.

"Once we get to our ship, you shall have your payment in full. I apologise for any inconvenience this may have caused you," I said.

"This wasn't an inconvenience at all, Mr Blake; on the contrary, it was a pleasure in seeing who I will be dealing with in the future, not to mention getting to witness the transition of leadership in your little team."

"Transition—" I began but was cut off as a loud crack echoed throughout the air.

I expected to feel some pain but I knew that I wasn't the target. Turning towards José I saw the cigar topple out of his mouth as he fell sideways; leaping forward I caught him in both my arms as I heard someone yell at me.

I wasn't sure who it was.

I saw red no matter where I looked. It covered José's chest. It covered my arms. It came out of his lips.

I felt a pair of hands latch onto my shoulders and pull me backwards. I still held onto José as they pushed me into the car. I caught a glimpse of The Lady still standing in the same spot.

She hadn't moved. She hadn't rushed to safety. She stared at the scene before her like a passenger waiting for their bus to arrive.

I heard the squeal of tires and was pushed back in my seat as the car took off, fishtailing while Tuari tried to keep her straight.

My ears were ringing and my mind was numb as I looked down into the face of our captain and saw his vacant eyes looking back at me.

He was... dead.

72

I stared at a body covered in a white sheet.

My eyes couldn't pull away from it. I sat in our cold storage room onboard *The Kennel* where we kept all our food so it wouldn't go off and just... sat there. I don't know how long I had been there; I didn't particularly care; all I knew was that no matter how hard I stared at the body under that sheet and willed it to get up, willed it to move, it wouldn't.

Rage, disgust, sadness, fear and hopelessness had swept through me.

Now the only thing left was numbness.

This was all my fault. If I hadn't attacked first and pulled a gun on The Lady, then José would still be alive. He would still be—

Numb.

It's all I felt.

As I stared at the white sheet that covered the leader of the Junk Yard Dogs, I tried to stir up some of the feelings that had been coursing through my veins a moment earlier, but now it was gone. I wished for it back. Longed for it!

Wished to feel anything whatsoever, but as hard as I tried nothing surfaced.

If I had not allowed my temper to get the better of me, if I had not allowed my rash decision to make The Lady act the way she did, then none of this would have happened. I should have just shut my mouth and let José do the talking till he found a solution; instead I thought my plans were... Damn!

How did I think this journey of criminals, gangsters, murderers and gang leaders was going to end?

Did I expect it to end with a pension at the end of everyone's service?

Did I think after everything was said and done, we would all ride off into the sunset and drink margaritas while we told good old stories about the past? About how we almost escaped death each time after coming so close?

This wasn't a game. This wasn't a movie.

Since joining the crew, I had been lost in a world of space travel and far-flung adventures, never taking a minute to contemplate the consequences of my actions or the actions of the people around me. It wasn't that I thought we were invincible; it was just that I thought death would happen to other people.

How stupid was I?

I placed my head in my hands and uttered a helpless sigh as I felt the walls around me closing in.

What were we going to do now José was gone?

Everyone thought I was second in command, but I was the newest member on the crew, a member who had gotten our captain killed. A member with less experience than anyone on this ship, a member that all he wanted to do was turn and run.

I thought my life had been hard and difficult before, but

the stakes weren't life and death, just boredom from an endless amount of paperwork.

A pair of hands massaged my shoulders and a set of lips kissed the back of my neck.

"You've been in here too long, this cold isn't good for you," said Poppy.

I said nothing.

"What happened back at Hotel Moscow wasn't your fault. If anything we were lucky to come out with our lives, and if it weren't for you then we wouldn't have."

"You mean if it weren't for you."

"What do you mean?"

"My little speech did nothing to sway her. If you hadn't *exposed* yourself then we would have all been killed. I did nothing but postpone the inevitable."

"*Exposed myself?* You make it sound like I had a choice. They were going to kill all of us. If I hadn't done that then it would be all of you lying on that table instead of just José."

"It was a chance I was willing to take. Now she knows what you are, do you think this is over? It's just begun. I saw the hunger in her eyes when she looked at you. It was the look of a person who has discovered a gun when everyone else is still using bow and arrows. This doesn't end here, Poppy, and I will be damned if she lays a hand on you. If it's a war this bitch wants, then it's a war I'll give her."

"Quinton, this isn't—"

"Me?" I said, finally lifting my head up to look at her. "As each day passes I'm beginning to lose that person who first came on this ship."

"But I fell in love with that person," she said, grabbing me by the face.

"That person can't protect you."

"Who said I needed protecting? I protect you. I'm the all-super-powerful AI machine, remember."

"That isn't enough for what is coming up on the horizon. That isn't enough. If I don't grow. Evolve. Become—" I shook my head. "I don't want any more of our people to die because of me, Pop, I won't have it. I won't allow the mistakes I made to doom us all."

She clutched my head to her breast and said nothing as I allowed tears to run down my face. Kissing the top of my head she whispered in my ear, "I will always love you no matter what."

73

We were all seated around the only conference table on *The Kennel*. Some faces were grim, some eyes were red from crying, some eyes were bloodshot from drink.

"Before we start, I just wanted to say... I just wanted to express, I just..." I let the words trail from my mouth and bit the inside of my cheek, trying to find the right words but not knowing where to start.

Poppy gripped my hand and gave me a faint smile and a nod.

"Before we start, I just wanted to apologise for what happened back at Hotel Moscow. It should have gone differently, it shouldn't have played out the way it did. I take full ownership and responsibility for what happened. I... it will not be a mistake I make again. *I promise you that*."

"Did you do it?" Willis asked as he took a swig from a hip flask. "Did you pull the trigger?"

"No."

"Then what the *fuck* are you apologising for? I don't want to hear any words that begin with S and end in Y."

"What about sky or shy or sexy or—" said Tuari but he was cut off by Willis.

"I don't want to hear it! José deserved better than this pity party. He deserved to be remembered for the warrior and leader he was. His life deserved to be celebrated. He was a man that kept this crew of psychos together through the thick and thin, he was a hard cunt who didn't take shit from no one, and only gave shit back when it was warranted. He was one of the few men I knew that I could trust to watch my back. Lord knows that when he reaches the pearly white gates, he shall be welcomed like the hero he is."

Willis took another long swig and slammed the hip flask down on the table.

"He would be the first to tell you this wasn't your fault. When it's your time to go, it's your time to go."

Silence descended as we all took his words in. Words that only Willis could string together and make you see a different side to life.

"I think," Tuari said, getting up, and placing a small cube in the middle of the table, "now is the perfect time to play a video José left for all of us. HE gave me this recording and said to watch it only if he wasn't around after we went to see The Bitch of Paradise Lost."

Tuari pressed the surface of the cube and light flickered and stuttered from its surface till a holographic video appeared in the air. It showed José's dark features as he leaned back in a chair and puffed on one of his favourite cigars. Red-tinted glasses sat perched on his nose, and the sound of sandpaper echoed through the room as he scratched his stubble.

"*Hola*, crew. I feel like a damn fool doing this, but I think it needs to be done before we see The Lady. I was never one for long speeches or sentimental things of that nature, so I'll say what I've got to say and you folks can get on with your lives.

"First off, I doubt I'll be coming back from seeing Her Highness alive. Lady Isabella Ivanov doesn't like failure. Shit, the bitch just straight up doesn't tolerate it. I have known her to kill people for less than what we did to her cargo, so the likelihood of us coming back from this is slim to none, but if I can take the blame for this, and spare my crew, then I'll do what I can do.

"She'll kill me for this. Just to prove a point. That's how people like her stay in power. I just hope the rest of you escape her wrath. If you have, then I have a few things to say to each of you."

He took another long pull from his cigar and blew out a column of smoke while he poured himself some rum. Knocking it back in one he poured himself another one and sipped this one slower.

"Tuari, you've been the longest-serving member aboard this ship. When I first met you, we were both young upstarts looking to make a quick buck and spend it even quicker. You've never told me about your past or where you're from, but sometimes when I look in your eyes I can see the same pain I grew up with. Maybe that's why we clicked so well and bonded like brothers. We built this crew from nothing and I want you to support it the best way you can. You're the finest cook I know and your paella was second to none.

"Never stop telling jokes, never stop laughing.

"Willis... try not to kill anyone you don't have to, you crazy fucker. I don't think your God looks too kindly on that sort of thing."

"Ay, what are you going to do?" Willis said with a shrug. "Sometimes a motherfucker needs to get shot."

"Poppy. My girl. When you first came to us, I knew you

were special. I knew you had a secret and in time you would tell me what it was when you were ready; you did and I've tried my best to keep it out of the wrong hands. But as the years have gone past, that has become harder and harder to do. I sometimes think if it would have been best if you never met us, if you just kept on travelling the stars. But I know how lonely you were, and you were looking for family and somewhere to call home, and I'm happy that I gave it to you. The next stage in your life may be the most challenging. But if there's anyone who can deal with it, I know that you can. Look after the idiot. I know when we first found him, you told me not to kill him because you felt something, and I'm glad I listened to you. I'm happy you two have found each other because you'll need to rely on each other for the hard times ahead."

He swirled the last remains of the rum in his glass and downed it in one; getting up he faced the camera till his face was the only thing that could be seen.

"Quinton... lead."

He stared at the camera for a second or two then the projection went dead and the image faded.

I stared at the cube willing it to come back on, wanting José to appear and say something, anything, more to me. He had given advice and spoken to everyone at such length but when it had come to me, I... what was I meant to do? Who was *I* to lead this crew? I had never led anything in my whole life. Surely the responsibility should fall to Tuari, the most senior member of the crew. He had just as much right to stake a claim as anyone else. He had been there from day one when I just—

"Well, fuckface, what's the plan?"

I looked to Willis open-mouthed.

"Yeah, like the ginger ballerina so eloquently put it,"

Tuari said with an eye roll, "what's the plan? We going to do this thing properly or what?"

I slowly closed my mouth and looked to Poppy, who gave me a smile. Looking at each crew member I gave each of them a small nod of thanks as I catalogued the last few events that had happened to us. Since the beginning we had been led on a merry chase and I was sick of it; until we got to this space station and found out what we were dealing with then we would still be lost in the dark, but I had a good idea what was waiting for us when we got to our destination.

"Edward *hired* us to do a job, so that's what we are going to do. We know little about the cargo we are collecting, only that it's valuable enough for Xcorp to waste money and time in getting it. I have a faint clue as to what it could be, but I won't share that just yet. I need to work something out.

"At present, the only thing we can do is continue with the mission and try to complete it to the best of our ability. We know the crews who have attempted this mission have all vanished or died, which leads me to believe there may be something guarding this coffin or the space station may be booby-trapped."

"Indiana Jones-style?" Willis said.

"Yeah."

"Argh! Those movies suck," Tuari said with a look of disgust.

"How dare you? They are old-world classics of the highest order," said Willis.

"Most of them have such large plot holes that you can fly a ship through them. Take *Raiders of the Lost Ark* for instance —the outcome would still be the same with or without Indiana Jones. The Nazis would still find the chest, still open it, and still die. Jones is irrelevant to the whole movie. The damn chest should be the protagonist."

Willis opened and closed his mouth while he stared off into space. He looked back at Tuari, lifted his finger, then shook his head and looked off into space again. Picking up his hip flask he downed the remainder of its contents and said, "Fuck me."

"Anyway, we are still a week or so out from our destination with our *current employer* Edward Thomas following closely along so we can't do anything until we get to that damn station. But before we do that, we have a funeral to attend."

Dressed in black, we stood silent.

José was dressed in his finest and laid to rest in a see-through coffin made of a material stronger than steel, which didn't corrode. A bottle of rum and a pack of cigars rested on top of his breast.

Willis stood next to the coffin dressed in the finest silk robes with a large goblet filled with what appeared to be wine. He placed one palm on the coffin while he closed his eyes and muttered to himself, before reopening them and giving us a look filled with zealous love.

"We are here today to honour the life of a man who was in many ways a friend, a leader, a protector. José Battle was a man who had many faults, but also a man who had our best interests at heart. He was always the last man to take his share of the loot, but the first one to come up with a solution to any problem we had. I met this man in a time in my life where I was on a path that would end in the death of my soul. I was like a Ronin wandering the cities of any planet I landed on and picking a fight with anyone that looked my way. I hated life. Despised it.

"I had a few key talents, which mainly involved killing, stealing and tracking people down. I thought I didn't need anyone else until one day I took a job that was too much for me to handle and found myself in the back of an alley bleeding out. José stumbled across me and took me to an old priest who also worked as a doctor. Over the days and weeks which followed Father Peregrine Laziosi patched me up but also gave me something to help through tough times and the rage.

"He gave me faith. Faith that there is something greater than myself out there. Be it God, the universe, or whatever you want to call it. I would have never found Father Peregrine Laziosi if it hadn't been for this man. José not only saved my life that day, he also saved my soul."

He saved mine too. If the Junk Yard Dogs hadn't boarded my ship and kidnapped me, then I would still be leading an unfulfilled life. A life that I hated. A life that on a daily basis I thought about ending. A life where I wouldn't have met the person of my dreams. An empty life.

I grabbed hold of Poppy's hand and gave it a squeeze.

"Quinton, would you like to say some words?"

The gesture took me by surprise, but I covered it well and nodded. I took Willis's place and stared at the people I was now in charge of—that I had to make sure came out of each and every mission we took on with our lives intact. I rolled my shoulders as the weight of responsibility settled across them.

"Thank you, Willis. Who knew such a foul mouth could speak such beautiful and moving words. José would have been honoured."

I looked towards the coffin, which contained someone I was only beginning to know, and thought of what I could say that hadn't been said. "I—" The truth. That was what he deserved.

"I wish I had time to have gotten to know this man better, I wish the last days of his life were less stressful and more carefree, but if wishes were horses, beggars would ride.

"All I can say is, he scared me shitless when we first met and that didn't change in the days and months that followed. By watching him I learnt what it takes to lead, the hardship and sacrifice one has to undergo for their crew. He knew he wouldn't come out alive when he walked into Hotel Moscow, yet it was his decision to go. That alone speaks volumes about his character. That alone tells you what kind of man he was!

"I know most of you feel the same way I do. I know most of you want revenge for what has happened, but the time for that isn't yet, the time for that comes later! Right now we have a job to do. A job everyone expects us to fail. No other crew has survived this mission. But we are not like other crews! We are the Junk Yard Dogs and we do things no other crew is capable of!" I looked at each face in turn, chest rising and falling.

"African wild dogs are one of the most effective hunters on Earth. We are no different. We are a pack like no other and together we shall conquer any challenge that stands in our way. If you place your trust in me as you did in him, then I shall do my best to make sure we come out of this alive.

"So from the bottom of my heart, I want to take this time to thank José Battle for everything he has done and I want to wish him good luck in the next stage of his journey. We shall never forget someone from the pack. That is what it means to be a Junk Yard Dog. Goodbye, my old friend. Goodbye, you old dog."

I stepped away and joined the rest of the crew as we pushed José's coffin into the ejector hatch. Sealing it shut we all stepped back and watched as the ship ejected him into space to forever traverse it in some vain hope that maybe one day, like the rest of us, he would finally find whatever he was looking for.

74

I lifted my hand to knock on Poppy's door but hesitated. It was only a couple of days since she had seen a friend buried, a friend she knew longer than she had known me, a friend who gave her a home and somewhere to call her own, yet here was I knocking on her door to question her.

Not that I didn't want her to grieve; I knew I and the whole crew did but now, shit, now I had responsibilities. Not only to her but to everyone on board this ship.

Strange, how just a week ago I wouldn't have given anything around me a second thought, because I knew José would figure something out and deal with the situation; but now since given command my brain hadn't stopped working. I felt like it was in overdrive, thinking about what had happened, what went wrong, how we could have foreseen it and improved upon it, what our upcoming challenges were and what would likely trip us up.

It was like I was at work again—given a team and a project to manage and an impossible deadline to complete a task in. But instead of failure resulting in my getting shouted at by the boss or fired, there was a real chance that failure could mean death, not only for me but more importantly for everyone else. This wasn't what I had signed up for when I had asked to join the Junk Yard Dogs. But sometimes fate and destiny don't give you what you ask for, they give you what you need.

I took a deep breath and rapped on the door twice then waited.

It didn't take long for Poppy to answer the door dressed in a long white t-shirt that came down to her thighs, and nothing else. I did my best to keep my attention on her face but every time she moved the material would cling to her chest, showing me the shapes and curves underneath.

"I—errr—" I pinched my nose as what I was about to say left me standing in front of her doorway like an idiot.

She giggled and kissed me on the cheek. "You're so cute. Why don't you come in and let's see if I can't coax those words out."

I nodded and followed her in watching her hips move as the door closed behind me. "Hold on," I said, eyes narrowed, "what if someone else had come to the door?, I don't think everyone else should be entitled to this view."

"Super-duper robotic hearing, don't forget," she said, tapping an ear. "I knew it was you by the way you walk."

"Oh, don't I feel the fool now."

"Don't worry about it; it's nice you forget, makes me feel more human."

I nodded my head and watched as she spread herself across the bed like a cat; she patted the space next to her but I gave her a small shake of the head.

"I would love to, really I would, but if I do, what I want to talk to you about won't be discussed and before you know it we'll just be a tangle of limbs."

"What's wrong with that?"

"Nothing, but what I have to ask you is important and could very well help us."

"Okay," she said, sitting upright and pulling her legs towards her.

"I don't know how to ask this without, one, coming across as a dick and, two, offending you, so I'm just going to come out and say it. Do you know what is in the space station we are going to?"

She opened her mouth and closed it again, as she lowered her gaze to her feet. She tucked a lock of hair behind her ear and then wrapped her arms around her legs tightly.

"Look, I completely understand if you don't want to talk about it or if it's too traumatic for you to even discuss and I normally wouldn't push the issue. I would say to you that you can discuss anything that has happened in your past in your own time, but right now, we really don't have time for that. I need any information that could help me with what we are likely to face when we reach that station."

Poppy said nothing as she continued to look at her feet.

"Poppy, you know I wouldn't ask unless—"

"I know," she said softly, "I know. I spent many, many years with Alvis Boman after he finished working on me; he was a perfectionist who always had to tweak a programme or improve something on me, forever changing and working. It was never good enough. I was never good enough. He wanted me to be more than a machine. He wanted me to surpass humanity. It became an obsession with him. Even more so after some of his designs and prints got out into the world and other inventors and scientist tried to recreate his work.

"That's when it got worse. It became a race that he

couldn't lose. He wanted to be the father who ushered a new race into this world, he wanted to stand above every past and future inventor or person who had or would ever live. He wanted to become a god. To be remembered forever."

"Nothing lasts forever," I said.

"It does, if your creations don't age. It does, if they can travel the universe and populate untold worlds like a virus."

"Alvis's dream sounds very much like a nightmare. He wasn't trying to become a god, he was trying to become a conqueror."

"Aren't all gods conquerors in one form or another?"

"Maybe."

"Anyway," she continued, "the war had long since wound down and only the faintest of embers could be still seen in some parts of the planet. Now, that Alvis's help wasn't needed as much by his government anymore he turned his attention to the competition—he killed anyone whom he saw as a threat to him intellectually or who was close to perfecting their own AI designs. I didn't find out what he was doing until it was too late. He used other less sophisticated AI humanoids to do the job. The only thing I regret is that I found out what he was doing too late. The word AI had become a dirty word during the war and now that his AI humanoids were picking off innocent people like demons in the night, it only heightened people's sense of fear of us."

"What did you do?" I asked.

"I went against my father," she said, burying her head in her hands, as small sobs racked her body. I sat next to her and wrapped my arms around under, kissing her lightly on the crown of the head, the cheeks, the lips, the forehead. I continued to do so, all the while saying nothing.

"He had to be stopped, you understand," she said,

looking up at me sharply, "he had to be! His dream had been corrupted, turned into something that was not even close to a nightmare. It was worse. His joy had spread from creating to destroying, as he now truly thought of himself as a god.

"I had to do something, so I did the only thing I never thought I would do, I betrayed him. It's funny in a sense that the very thing he created would turn against him because he gave it free will."

She allowed the silence to stretch while I played with her hair. I could feel the tension in her body; it made her feel like she was made of glass.

"I sent evidence of what he had been up to to as many governmental agencies as I could—some he had worked for, some he had worked against, some he could have worked for in the future. Some knew what he was doing or they had an inkling, but now that I had broadcast his wrongdoings for the world to see there was no way of hiding it, there was no way of sweeping it under the carpet.

"The news exploded like a soot grenade in a bridal shop.

"Overnight he became a wanted man. His crimes numbered in the tens of thousands. He had stopped acting on behalf of his country and government a long time ago."

"What happened to him?" I asked.

"He was arrested and charged with more counts of murder, espionage and war crimes than anyone in recorded human history, but on his way to trial he was gunned down and killed by a masked assailant who got away. Some thought he got the justice he deserved, others thought he got off too lightly. Afterwards he was quickly buried and the World Government seized all his personal effects, his blueprints, everything he ever touched and built, along with his other AI humanoids, and placed it in storage."

"Why do I have a feeling that this *storage* isn't on Earth?" I said.

"I grew suspicious when I heard the news—who wouldn't be? Any person or government with the knowledge that Alvis had would be unstoppable, so I followed from the shadows, but there was no need. The people of Earth had gotten tired of war, the bloodshed, the pain; they wanted to go back to a time of peace. Plus, they feared opening Pandora's box. So a group of leaders decided to jettison everything they had seized into space before someone got their hands on what Alvis had created.

"They knew that peace wasn't something the human race could hold on to for long and keeping his work on Earth would be too much of a temptation, so it was the best idea they could think of."

I allowed what she had told me to sink in while she lay back on my lap. It had been a wise move by the governmental leaders to place everything they had taken from Alvis into deep space, somewhere so far removed from Earth that no one could find it. But somehow Edward Thomas had found the location of the space station and wanted us to do his dirty work for him.

"How do you think Edward Thomas found its location?"

"The same scientist who delivered and built the Training Room loved Alvis to the point of obsession. With the help and backing of Xcorp, he came across the blueprints that were on the data stick you had when we first met. The scientist never found the location of Alvis, but he pointed Edward Thomas in the right direction. "

I nodded my head at her words. It made sense. Men of power would always want more power, no matter if the words they were speaking were peaceful.

"What do you think happened to the other crews who have tried to gain access to it?"

"Death. What's in that station is the most valuable thing to have ever created by humankind, and things of a valuable nature are never left unprotected."

75

I had racked my brains as to what to do. As the days slowly crawled past I grew more irritable, although I did my best to try to keep my frustrations to myself. This burden had been placed on my shoulders and although I could ask for help, I felt like it was mine to share alone. I sat in my quarters and scratched my head as I looked at the pieces of paper laid out before me. I had written out as much information about the upcoming job as I could, but looking over my handful of notes it was painfully clear there just wasn't enough information to go on.

We didn't know how we would gain access to the station.

We didn't know what defences the thing had and if it would attack our ship on sight.

We didn't know what was waiting for us once we got inside.

And on and on the list went till all I could do was stare at the paper in front of me in dumb shock. I had tried coming at the idea from different angles but that proved just as frustrating. Throwing the piece of paper in my hands across the room, I looked at my surroundings and sighed. They had offered me José's captain's quarters, but that didn't feel right.

I still felt like an imposter playing captain.

I got to my feet and for what felt like the hundredth time sighed. I looked at the mess I had created and turned away in disgust to walk out the door. I blindly followed my feet as I allowed the thoughts that populated my mind to bounce around. I paid them no mind, but just allowed them to do their thing in some vain hope that my subconscious would find a solution to my problems.

Once again, all I could think of was how I got myself into this mess. Me? An office drone who was a wizard on a spreadsheet, but had never held a pistol before. Me, a person who was more used to leading a conference meeting than leading people into war. And war we were going into;, I had no illusions as to what this was. It wasn't another mission. It had become bigger than that.

Even if we somehow managed to enter the station unharmed and collect the coffin Edward wanted, there wasn't a chance in hell that I would ever hand something like that over to someone like him. The effects on human life would be unthinkable; my conscience wouldn't allow me to rest knowing what I had done. I would be creating a warlord the human race hadn't seen since the times of Genghis Khan and Alexander the Great.

Then there was the little issue of The Lady.

Lady Isabella Ivanov.

The queen of Paradise Lost.

The murderer of José Battle.

Now she knew Poppy's secret, there wasn't a doubt in my mind that she was plotting the best way to use that to her advantage. How could she not? She had built an empire on other people's suffering. On their demise. On how to best exploit them till she got what she wanted. So it would only be a matter of time till she came knocking either by force or with smiles. When that time came we had to be ready.

I had to be ready.

She wanted to take over Safe Haven, and Poppy was the key to that locked door.

My traitorous feet had taken me to the bridge, where I was greeted by the sight of an empty captain's chair. I walked up to it and ran my hands over its cracked leather, allowing every bump and crease to tell me a story. I stepped in front of it and could almost see the faint outline of José sitting in it, wolf-like smile on his face, tinted glasses giving nothing away.

I took a seat in a chair to its left and looked up as the bridge door opened and Tuari walked through the door.

"Couldn't sleep either, huh?" he said, taking a seat opposite me.

"Yeah… something like that."

We allowed the silence to grow between us like the incoming tide as I just stared at the captain's chair. How many battles had it witnessed? How many close-call decisions had José made from that very chair that had saved the lives of his crew? Decisions that would now be mine to make. Decisions that if I failed—

"You know," Tuari said, interrupting my train of thought, "when I first met José he was a young hot-tempered South American, with that cool, easy-going Spanish accent of his making all the ladies melt at his feet. I didn't like the bastard at first. Thought he was too full of himself and too flamboyant. But the longer we hung out, the more I realised we were cut from the same cloth. You had to look to find the pain he was hiding, but it was there alright.

"Buried deep.

"Pain of a home all too ready with the whip or the back of the hand instead of giving a kind word. Pain of never being loved. Never having anywhere to call home. That's why he started all of this," Tuari said, gesturing with his hands at the ship. "*The Kennel* was his home, the crew his family. He would give anything to make sure we were safe, and he did just that in the end. He knew the only way we would survive is if he dealt with The Lady head-on. He came to her and suffered the wrath she bestowed on him."

"He didn't need to. We could have found another way. We should have come together as a group and brainstormed—"

"Now you're in this position, do you really believe that?"

"I—" I wanted to say yes. I wanted to say what José had done was wrong, but being here and now, with the responsibilities placed on me, I knew that I would only be lying to myself.

"Like José, my upbringing wasn't what you would call pleasant, but I had a talent that would allow me to escape, a talent that would let me escape whatever thoughts and feelings that surfaced, and just be in the moment. If you're not in the moment when you're cooking then you can't create the best dishes—you don't know when it's the right time to add a pinch of this or a drop of that. I would always ask my grandmother how she got her dishes just right and her response would always be her pointing to her heart and her gut. Growing up I would never get that, until I got older and realised you can only learn so much from cookbooks and teachers; after a while you have to trust your instincts.

"You have to listen to them, because then only you know what's the right choice for you."

He got to his feet and stretched his bear-like body until his back popped and his joints groaned.

"But then again, what do I know? I relate everything in life to cooking."

"What if your instincts are wrong?" I whispered.

"Then you are wrong," he said with a shrug. "Life's too short to worry about that shit. After Monday and Tuesday, even the calendar says W.T.F."

I looked at him unconvinced but he patted my shoulder as he walked by me. He stopped before he got to the door and turned back around. "You know, thinking on it now, I don't believe anyone who calls this place home has anything good to say about their upbringing. Funny that, I guess you could call this ship a place for all the broken and unwanted toys. Guess that makes you the new store owner."

76

"We shall exit hyperdrive quicker than you can say Sharon's your uncle," Tuari said from his position on the bridge.

"The saying is Bob's your uncle, fuckwit," Willis said, feet on the console while he thumbed through the rosary in his hand.

"Well, I didn't have an uncle named Bob, I had an uncle named Sharon. Lovely person. Would also give me hard-boiled candy."

"It doesn't matter if your uncle was called Dave, Rick, Elizabeth or King Kong! The saying is Bob's your uncle. Just like the many other sayings such as no use crying over spilt milk and keep calm and carry on. They are sayings for a reason and just because you decide to change them—"

"Exiting hyperdrive in five."

"Don't cut me off when I'm—"

"Four!"

"You tosspot wanker, I'll—"

"Three."

"That's it, you're getting a smacking!" Willis said, getting to his feet.

"Two. One," Tuari said in a quick breath, while the ship came to a stop, throwing Willis forward off his feet to fall face-first on the floor.

Tuari bust into laughter while Willis slowly got to his feet, face turning red.

"What's the saying? The gingerer they are the harder they fall?" Tuari said between bouts of laughter.

Willis began marching his way but Poppy brought up an image of what was outside, projecting it onto the viewing screen. I sat up as everyone turned their attention towards it.

The image was... breathtaking.

Asteroids littered the area in front of us. Some were no bigger than a human body, while others dwarfed our ship. Different hues mixed in amongst the asteroids brought out shades of colour anywhere between purplish-red to dark orange. Asteroids drifted towards each other, some colliding and others bouncing off and floating aimlessly away.

But that wasn't the thing that interested me the most. Flashes of what I could only describe as lightning flickered inside the belly of the asteroids field. The outer edges of the field didn't appear to be affected, but the centre looked like a mass of chaos as ominous flashes glowed in the purplish dark that extended ahead of us.

We all stared at the scene in front of us with open mouths.

"Only God could create something so awe-inspiring," said Willis.

"Well, actually—" began Tuari, but I cut him off with a stare.

"How far is it to the station?" I asked.

Poppy checked the consoles in front of her then turned towards me. "It should be the other side of this rock field."

"I had a feeling you would say that," I replied. "Can you scan the electromagnetic field up ahead and see if it's safe to travel through?"

Poppy did as I asked before turning back and giving me a shrug. "I'm not picking up anything out of the ordinary but we would need to get closer towards it so the scanners can identify anything."

Shit.

I looked back at the field and tried to think of the best course of action.

"Can we go around it?"

"That would take weeks, and I'm pretty sure Edward would not take kindly to having his prize delayed for so long."

"Speak of the devil," said Willis, "and he shall appear. We are being hailed by his ship."

I tapped my finger along the armrest of my chair as I narrowed my eyes at what I was seeing. "Pop, can you scan the surrounding area to see if there are any signs of another ship apart from us and Edward? I'm looking for anything that could have remotely once been a ship, debris, that sort of thing."

Poppy nodded her head and began typing away as Willis once again looked my way.

"The fucker keeps on hailing us."

"Once again," Poppy said, "I can't find anything that would give me a definite answer. There appears to be something that would match the signature of a spacecraft but I'm just guessing at this point."

Going into unmarked territory blind was a recipe for disaster but we had little choice. Part of me wanted to bail on this whole mission, but with Edward's ship always on our heels like a wolf, we had little choice but to follow through. I had thought about taking a stand and fighting it out with the bastard, but his ship was three times the size of ours and loaded with more weaponry than a gunship destroyer.

We wouldn't last a minute.

"Can we just answer this hail already! This asshole is as annoying as having haemorrhoids and sitting on a wooden bench during Sunday mass."

"Put him through," I said.

An image of Edward Thomas graced our screens. A white shirt covered with a grey tweed waistcoat hugged his frame. Red bow tie matched his ruby cufflinks. Taking his pipe out of his mouth, he gave us a smile that didn't reach his eyes.

"Well, dear fellow, that took longer than expected. I dear say, now the Junk Yard Dogs have come under new management, I do hope standards won't be slipping."

"What can we do for you, Mr Thomas?"

"I didn't bring enough tobacco to smoke, but I can hardly blame or ask you to handle that, now can I? No, I was just double-checking everything is in hand, as it appears you have become stationary and I would hate to think all this responsibility has overwhelmed you, Mr Blake. I would *hate* to think you were trying to think of a way to escape our deal. Thinking of a way to run."

"I wouldn't think of it," I said, meeting him stare for stare. "My crew and I were just assessing the situation before us and deciding on the best course of action. Seeing as you know more about this region of space than us, would you like to tell us what we are facing?"

"Oh that," Edward said, with a dismissive wave. "It's just

a debris cloud with a little electric charge, nothing a spacefaring ship should be worried about, I can assure you."

"Hmm, I see."

"I hardly see the problem," Edward said, the first signs of irritation creeping through his voice. "I am accompanying you towards the end goal, which is the station; to get there our ships must also go through this little storm cloud. Do you think if I thought it was dangerous I would endanger my men and come with you?"

He had a fair point but something about what I saw in front of me still gave me pause. But there wasn't anything more I could do about it.

"Tuari, plot the best course through this debris. Edward, as always, thank you for your little chat, it was.... *helpful*."

"Anything I can do—"

The viewing screen went dead as the image of him was cut off.

I looked to Willis, who gave me a rare smile that was all teeth.

"Alright, I guess there's no time like the present. Take us forward."

77

The going was slow as Tuari manoeuvred us through the debris,; unlike Edward's ship, which could just smash through most things that got in its way, we had to be more careful.

"Fuck me! Could you fly any slower?"

Tuari said nothing as a light sheen of sweat glistened his brow, tongue hanging out one corner of his mouth; his body moved with the rhythm of the ship. He had a knack for flying that was second to none. It was like he was in tune with the machine, with them both acting as one.

Our approach had been slow and steady and now we were slowly coming to the eye of the storm, my hands clutched my armrest while I watched the approaching lightning storm.

"Pop, how we doing?"

"All readings are normal, nothing to report."

I nodded my head and shifted uncomfortably in my seat as we narrowly missed another lump of rock.

"Ohh, that one was close," Willis teased, as he leaned further back in his chair and pulled out a bag of popcorn.

Shovelling handful after handful into his mouth he watched the viewing screen with interest. "Oh shit! Look out for that one."

I opened my mouth to say something but Poppy caught my eye and gave me a subtle shake of the head; I pulled my lips back in a fine line but kept my thoughts to myself. The crew had weird rituals and habits, which I still didn't quite understand, especially between Willis and Tuari. They picked on each other ruthlessly. At times it appeared they hated each other or had an axe to grind, but beneath all the testosterone-fuelled name-calling, pranks and teasing I felt they had a genuine level of respect and care for each other.

"If your mama could see you now she would be disappointed," Willis said, popcorn stuck in his beard. "It's ok for me; if I die I shall be welcomed in the arms of God and kissed and caressed by a million angel virgins while you shall be spit roasted by two demon spawn, who will go to town on that ass."

Then again, I could be wrong.

Tuari manoeuvred us away from a large piece of rock but he wasn't quick enough to avoid another that scraped the side of the ship, causing it to shudder. Willis's head tilted back as laughter spewed from his mouth along with chunks of half-eaten popcorn.

"I don't know if José told you this, Quinton," said Willis, "but any damage we do to the ship is taken out of our pay..."

We all stared at him but said nothing.

"I'm just saying, I'm just saying. I would hate to think I didn't get my bonus this term because we had to fork out for a new paint job for the ship."

"Pay? What makes you think you'll see that? Last time I checked the common rooms hadn't been cleaned, nor had the toilet facilities everyone uses, and if I'm not mistaken your name's written on the rota to clean them this week—although it looks like your name has been hastily scribbled out and replaced with Tuari's."

"I don't know what you're talking about," he said, looking at me blankly.

"Now, Willis, I doubt your God would approve of your lying."

"I—"

The ship shook violently to the left. My ribs smashed against the armrest of my chair and knocked the wind out of me, forcing me to see stars. Warning lights erupted around the bridge cloaking everything in red.

"My popcorn!"

"Is everyone—" I held my ribs as I tried to get my breath back and tried again: "Is everyone OK?"

A chorus of angry yesses came back my way.

"Status report! What the hell happened?"

"We are under attack!" Tuari said, yanking the controls of the ship sideways.

"From what? I can't see anything on the screen but rocks."

Poppy punched the controls in front of her and magnified what appeared to be a rock at first but as she kept on enlarging the image, it grew in focus and I saw what appeared to be two large red eyes looking our way. She pulled back on the image and more and more rocks came alive, their red eyes locking us in their sights.

"What in God's name are those things?" said Willis.

Poppy said nothing as her fingers moved at a pace I couldn't see. "Pop, give us something," I said, as more and more rocks came alive.

"The reason I wasn't able to detect anything is because these things have been dormant for the best part of two hundred years, at a guess. The asteroid belt that they are in has coated their outer shells with rock sediment, masking the very faint signals they were giving off while dormant."

All I could now see were glowing red dots.

"How many of them are there?"

She turned around and looked at me. She tried to cover up the fear but I could see it shimmering under the look she gave me. "I... I don't know."

"They've stop firing," said Tuari, as the ship came to a stop.

"Then why are we stopped?" I asked. "Get us the hell out of here!"

"When things stop firing at you, it normally means they want to talk, or send you a message," he said.

"That's—"

"I'm getting an incoming hail," Willis said, face hovering over his console. "No video, just audio; I'll patch it through the speakers."

A hiss and a pop came through the speakers surrounding us, then a monotone robotic voice spoke. "You are in a quarantine zone. Please leave immediately. Failure to do so shall be met with force. You are in a quarantine zone. Please leave immediately. Failure to do so shall be met with force. You are in—"

"Cut it off!" I shouted.

"Well, that's straightforward enough. I guess we do as the killer machines say and turn around and leave," said Tuari. "We tried our best, but I for one would like to get out of this alive."

"If only it were that simple," I said, getting to my feet.

"I'm getting another hail, it's from Dickwad," said Willis.

"Put him through."

An image of Edward Thomas appeared on the ship's

screen, brows wrinkled in confusion as he looked at us with his hands on his hips. "What's the hold-up?"

I looked at him in disbelief. "The fuck-ton of killer machines that are threatening to blow us up if we don't leave this area immediately."

"Oh, don't take that message seriously. You know how they were back in the old days, everything was a threat or you had to adhere to some regulation. It's nothing but an out-of-date message."

"Did you know about this?"

"We came across something about quarantine area, blah, blah, heavily guarded, blah, blah, immediate danger, blah. But it wasn't something we worried ourselves with. It was just one of the many warnings we had come across in our research."

"And you didn't think," I said between gritted teeth, "to bring this up sooner!"

"Like *I said*, it wasn't something we worried ourselves with, so we didn't see why we should worry you with said information."

"Maybe if you had, then the previous crews you had sent on this mission would have been better prepared to handle whatever this shit is! We obviously can't proceed any further, so we must find another way around."

"No can do, my good man, doing that would take months, and months are something I do not have."

"You have waited this long, what's a couple of months?"

"A couple of months is all that stands between Xcorp going under as a business and its surviving. If you and your merry crew hadn't robbed us blind—"

"In all fairness," Tuari said, cutting him off, "we didn't technically steal anything from you. Your employee, one

Gregory Goodwin, brought the wrong item—he should have checked it first. You can hardly blame us for that."

"*Your crew* were the ones who first raided my ship. *Your crew* were the ones who stole my data stick. *Your crew* were the ones that acted on the behalf of another party for gain and profit," said Edward, spittle flying from his mouth. Taking a deep breath he ran a hand down his front and continued, "So, because of your actions we are in this situation, and as it stands I have a deadline and a promise to keep to the few remaining board members the company still has left. So we move forward—"

"This isn't up for discussion, Edward, there isn't a way in hell those things allow us through—and I am not putting my crew in jeopardy just because you can't wait a few more weeks. We look for a way around or we don't proceed at all."

He looked at me and said nothing as he lit his pipe and took a deep lungful before blowing it back out. White smoke obscured his face.

"There isn't any other way—" I began, but he cut me off.

"Mr Grey, fire when ready."

"Wait! You can't attack those things, that's suicide—"

But he was already gone, leaving me to address nothing but a blank screen.

78

"Bring up an image of Edward's ship!"

Poppy projected an image on the viewing screen and I watched in shock as all the weapons on Edward's ship pointed towards the cluster of machines that stood in our way.

"He's charging gun turrets, plasma cannons, missiles—he's planning to throw the kitchen sink at the problem," said Willis.

We all stared in shock as his ship opened fire upon the machines in front of us.

"Are the machines still transmitting the same message as before?"

"Don't be an idiot, of course not," Willis said with a chuckle. "Listen to this."

The all too familiar hiss and pop came back through the speakers as the same robotic voice spoke: "Maximum threat level detected! Maximum threat level detected! Maximum—"

The audio cut out as the ship shuddered and threw me forward. Grabbing onto the back of Poppy's chair I lifted myself back up as I looked at the carnage taking place before me. The machines had begun to return fire against Edward's ship, their lasers scoring multiple hits against the behemoth ship's shields but not scoring any real damage.

We, on the other hand, were not going to be so lucky, as we had neither the size nor the firepower.

"Shields are taking a beating," said Poppy.

"The machines are converging on our location," said Tuari.

"Retreat the way we came and get us the hell out of here."

"No can do," he said, looking my way. "While we were stationary the crafty buggers got behind us. They surround us on all sides."

The ship shook once more, this time more violently.

"Shields are down to eighty percent," said Poppy.

I watched as Edward's ship fired everything they had while they tried to keep the swarm attacking them at bay.

This was madness!

More of the machines crashed like a wave against Edward's shield as they tried to inflict whatever damage they could. Explosions tore across our screens as rows of machines exploded simultaneously.

The fool had tried to force my hand in helping him, and now he was likely to get both of us killed because he couldn't wait.

"We have incoming!" Tuari shouted.

"Willis, fire when ready."

The swarm had branched off and a host of them were now making their way towards us. They fired their weapons without precision, but they didn't need to. There were enough of them that eventually one of their lasers would find a weak point in our shields.

"Shields down to seventy percent!" said Poppy.

I held my breath as I watched the oncoming swarm approach us. Knuckles white I held onto the back of Poppy's seat, as all I could see was a mass of rock coming towards us.

Willis fired everything we had but our weapons barely made a dent in the swarm.

They crashed against our shields forcing the lights on the bridge to flicker on and off.

"Shields down to fifty percent!" yelled Poppy.

I could see nothing out of the viewing screen as the mass of machines obstructed our view.

"They are trying to overwhelm our shields with sheer mass alone. If we don't do something soon, we'll lose all power," Poppy said, looking to me.

"Tuari, can you use the hyperdrive to get us out of here?"

"I could, but that would mean lowering our shields, and by the time the hyperdrive kicks in they would destroy us."

"Shields down forty percent!"

Think, Quinton. Think. You didn't come this far and go through so much just to let the people around you down. José entrusted this to you. This was his family. His life's work.

Wait.

The electrical storm these machines surrounded—none of them were near it when we had first arrived. They had circled it like planets orbiting a sun but—

"Poppy! Can you do a quick scan of the material makeup of the machines?"

She didn't respond, but instead began typing away on the keys in front of her. I redoubled my grip as the ship shook around us. I could smell a faint smell of burning.

"They are mostly made up of electrical components. Nothing too advanced, by modern-day standards."

"Are they equipped with shields?"

"No."

Perfect.

"Willis, I want you to charge up the EMP and only fire upon my command," I said, hurrying to my chair, where I buckled myself in.

"To do that, we have to cease firing all other weapons."

"I know," I told him, "just trust me on this."

"It appears we have become quite popular," Tuari said. "The size of the swarm attacking us has now doubled, no, tripled, no—well, let's just say it's getting big. I hope you know what you're doing, Quinton, because if this doesn't pay off..."

"Thanks for the vote of confidence. Willis, how's the—"

The ship shuddered as the lights on the bridge went out.

"EMP fully charged!"

"On my signal I want you to fire it; when he does, Tuari, I want you to make a beeline for the centre of the electric storm ahead of us—we are going right through the sucker!"

"That may not be the best idea," came Poppy's voice through the darkness. "We don't know what that storm will do to the ship—"

A sound like a metal can being forcibly opened tore through the air as I was launched sideways, where I once again smashed in my ribs. *Shit! Why do you always hit the same spot?* I gritted my teeth as the smell of burning I had noticed earlier was now accompanied by smoke.

"Willis, fire!"

I heard his palm slapping the console. I held my breath. Nothing happened for what felt like an eternity, then the viewing screen cleared as machines fell away from the body of the ship en masse.

"Tuari! Punch it!"

The ship threw us back in our seats as it pushed forward; the engines whined, and the smoke grew thicker as the approaching electric storm loomed before us. Machines our EMP had not hit moved towards us; Tuari tried his best to avoid their weapons fire but scores of hits still struck our shields.

"Shields down to ten percent!"

If this didn't work, a few more good shots and it would be all over.

I held onto the armrest of my chair as the ship took a dive downwards to avoid two machines that were trying to flank us; they crashed into each other, the explosion flaring in the corner of the viewing screen as we shot back up and kept on course. More machines began to trail us, firing at us with everything they had.

"Willis, keep them off our tail!"

"I'm trying my best!"

"Shields down to five percent!" said Poppy.

Come on. Come on.

The electric storm was just ahead of us, its swirling colours beckoning us towards it. It spat out forked lightning like a tongue as Tuari dodged another group of machines that came up to our left. Willis tore through their ranks with laser fire as we once again dived.

Coming back up I took a sharp intake of breath as I saw rows of machines lined up like a barrier in front of our destination. They had guessed our intentions and had used their bodies as a last-ditch effort to stop us.

"Plough through the fuckers!" said Willis, as he turned the gun turrets on them.

"Easy for you to say, you're not flying!"

The machines opened fire en masse and Willis met their

attack force for force. The momentarily dark bridge came alight again as flames erupted from the far left corner. We weren't slowing down. We were going to crash right into them.

"Tuari! Look for a way round!"

"Don't have time."

"Shields down to one percent!" said Poppy.

I stared at the viewing screen and felt my mouth grow dry as I grabbed onto the armrest of my chair. All I could see was the approaching machines against the backdrop of the electric storm.

I wanted to keep my eyes open.

I wanted to say I valiantly looked out to my crew happy in the knowledge we would face death head-on and overcome it.

But that would be a lie.

My eyes closed of their own accord as my nostrils filled with smoke and the ship shook around us. I sent a silent prayer to José to watch over us. The reassuring words of Willis were the last thing I heard as I braced for impact.

"Come on then, you cunts!"

79

I waited for the heat from the explosion.

I waited for the pain.

I waited for the utter sense of hopelessness before death took me, but none of that happened as I opened my eyes slowly to look around me. We were still alive. I looked at the viewing screen and marvelled at the view before me.

We were passing through the eye of the storm; lightning-type energy forked and flared around us as we continued our journey.

It was all around us. I felt like I was in a painting by an artist who had taken an acid trip.

"Hold on tight," said Tuari. "We shall be out of this in—"

The ship rumbled violently as lights and console screens flickered back on and off again; a metallic scent I could taste filled the air.

"What is going on?" I asked.

"We've been struck by the current from the storm," Tuari said. "I've lost all control of the ship! This isn't going to be pretty— hold on."

The ship corkscrewed wildly out of control making me

feel like I was on the world's worst roller-coaster ride. We spun left to right while I tried to get a strong grip to hold me in place but it was useless.

I was flung against the side of my chair, where I once again was smash into my ribs.

Can't a guy get a break?

"You are... the shittest... pilot... I have ever... known!" Willis yelled as best as he could.

The bridge was becoming a blur; I didn't know which way was up or down. Dark patches began to form in the corners of my vision as unconsciousness tried its best to pull me in.

"Tuari! Do some—" I tried to speak but bile rose to my throat and filled my mouth. I tried to swallow it back down but it was too late for that as it spewed from my mouth. Confused, I felt my body began to lift from the chair.

"The anti-gravity engine is offline." I heard someone say, but I didn't know who.

I got a flash of the ceiling... but that couldn't be right? How did I get so close to it? My body crashed against something solid and was pinned against it. I tried my best to move but my efforts were futile.

I blacked in and out of consciousness.

I could hear voices. Words. Jumbled in an audio mess that made me question my own sanity.

Then came the pain.

My muscles contracted and stiffened up as my jaw locked up and refused to open, my limbs jerked about on their own accord as quick tremors passed through me. They left me as quickly as they came and all that remained was a prickly sensation on my skin.

I opened my eyes to be greeted by the sight of the bridge floor, which I was suspended above.

What the hell?

That was all I could think of before gravity did her trick and dropped me back down to the floor.

Ugh.

I landed with a thud and again somehow landed on my ribs! I tried to speak but nothing other than a groan escaped my lips. Pushing myself up off the floor didn't get me far, as I landed face first back on it. The strength from my limbs was nonexistent, as I looked up and closed my eyes again. The room was still spinning.

"Thank fuck for getting hit with that bolt of energy," Tuari said, voice sounding far away. "The first strike blew out most of our major components and killed the power to the rest, but the second strike rebooted things just enough to put us back in the game."

"I... wha... are you... what?" I said.

"English, you pussy," Willis said.

"How... are you guys... so coherent?" I said slowly.

"You think this is our first time experiencing zero gravity while the ship spins madly out of control?" Willis asked.

I didn't respond as I did the best to wipe the sick from my face.

"Well, it's not. But it is our first time getting struck by lightning or whatever that shit is."

I tried to respond but once again words failed me.

"If I say it once, I'll say it a thousand times," Willis said. "You are the shittest of shit pilots. I've got popcorn in my eye and up my ass, I've got sick on my shirt and look what that electric magic crap has done to my beard!"

I raised my head to see Willis now sported a beard that had all the qualities of an afro but none of its style.

"What's different with your beard?" Tuari asked. "It's

always looked like what you would see between a nun's legs. Anyway, we're finally out of the storm."

I got to my feet unsteadily and swayed back and forth. I took a step forward but had to catch myself on a console as I lost my footing. We hadn't even got to our destination yet, but I felt like I had gone ten rounds with a heavyweight boxer while being asked to spin on the spot in between rounds.

"Have we at least lost the machines off our tail?" I asked.

"I can't see anything on the viewing screen," Tuari said, "and we aren't being shot at anymore. Poppy, are the scanners picking up anything?"

She didn't respond.

"Pop?" I moved closer. She was sitting in her chair but something was off. She wasn't upright; her body was slumped like she'd had her strings cut. I rushed forward, heart in mouth, and knelt before her.

Her eyes were closed.

"Pop?"

She still didn't respond.

"Pop, baby, can you hear me?"

Lifting a shaky hand up to her neck I tried to look for a pulse but didn't find one. That was the one thing that always amazed me about her: although not human her maker had given her the same vital signs as a human. It was our little ritual: me resting my head on her chest and just listening to her heart while we lay in bed.

But now, I couldn't feel anything.

I licked the back of my hand and tremblingly I placed it under her nose and closed my eyes as I tried to feel her breath on my hand.

There wasn't any.

She was dead.

80

"Poppy! Poppy!" I tried to shake her awake but I knew it wouldn't work. I checked and rechecked her pulse but I got the same result each time.

Someone was saying something but I wasn't listening; all I could think about was how this was my fault. How entering the storm had been a rash decision I made to save our lives, but it had ended up costing me the one thing I loved the most, a person who understood me.

I felt something on my shoulder, but I brushed it off and gently tapped her on the back of the hand, trying to rack my brains about what to do.

This couldn't end here. Not like this. I had too many things I wanted to do with her, things I wanted to see with her. I felt the hot prickle of tears grow out of the corner of my eyes as I kept on stroking the back of her hand. Bringing my lips up to her hand I kissed it softly. There must be something I could do! This didn't make sense.

She was indestructible. She was not made of soft tissue and brittle bones. How could something as simple as the ship spinning out of control end her existence when it had done nothing to the rest of us? I got up and frantically checked her body for wounds or any injuries. There must be something that could tell me what happened.

Something that could reverse what had happened.

"Quinton," Tuari said.

Why was he bothering me now? Couldn't he see I had to fix this? That I had to try and make this right again? If there was no Poppy then there would be no me. I was doing this all for her, to show her I was worthy of her love, to show her that José hadn't made a mistake in picking me to lead this crew, to show her I was the man she thought I was.

If this ended here then none of this was worth—

"Quinton!" Tuari said. This time he grabbed me hard by the shoulder and turned me so I faced him.

"What? What? What!" I said, pushing him back with each word hands clenched into balls.

"There's nothing you can do, son," he said with a shake of the head. "Unless you know the sophisticated workings of an AI and how to rebuild one then there is nothing you can do. I don't know what happened or what caused it but one minute she was okay and the next she wasn't after we went through that storm. It isn't—"

I could see his lips moving but I had stopped listening.

Something he had said had triggered an idea in my brain; I could see the paper-thin idea trying to escape while I grappled with it and tried to make sense of it. She was fine before she passed through the storm and then she wasn't.

What had changed? What had—

"She's going to be OK!" I said, gripping Tuari by the shoulders and giving him a shake. "She's going to be OK."

Spinning on my heel I rushed over to her and tried to pick her up but I couldn't shift her. Gritting my teeth in frustration I turned to the crew. "I need to get her to the medical bay—is there something we can use to get her there?"

They both looked at me as if I had gone mad.

"We don't have much time! Do we have something I can use to transport her to the medical bay?"

"Yeah," said Willis, "the hover stretcher, but I don't see—"

"Get it now!"

Willis looked to Tuari for some help but the big man just shrugged. Willis shook his head and spun on his heel, leaving the bridge as fast as he could. I didn't have to wait long till I heard the sound of his feet, the bridge doors opened and he pushed in a long metal stretcher that hovered above the deck.

"I need both of you, to help me shift her onto this," I said, cuddling Poppy's body.

A look passed between the pair but I chose to ignore it. I didn't have time to convince them or focus on anything else but the goal at hand.

We each grabbed a part of Poppy's body and grunted and lifted as we shifted her onto the stretcher. She felt as heavy as three fully grown men but in all my time being with her she had always felt half my weight if not less; memories of me picking her up during sex came to my mind but I brushed them away. The how or why wasn't important.

Strapping her to the stretcher I pushed it forward and ran as fast as I could towards the medical bay. I took lefts and rights as quick as I could and had to remind myself to slow down as I nearly crashed the stretcher more than once into a wall. Finally getting to the medical bay I positioned the stretcher in the centre as Willis and Tuari made their way through the doors.

"Where's the defibrillator?"

They both looked at me as if I had gone mad.

"The only thing of note that happened since we passed through the storm is that we were struck by a weird electric current; when I was stuck to the ceiling of the bridge I got the shock of my life. It's the reason why the machines didn't want to follow us through the storm, because it affected their machinery, or circuits, or whatever. I'll bet that's why Poppy is the way she is! She is an AI after all."

"Quinton, if that was the case then why didn't the EMP we fired affect her?" Tuari asked.

"Because we had a functioning shield! When we passed through the storm, our shielding was gone. When we got hit by that electric current it affected the ship; it was because we didn't have any shields to protect us."

They shared a look once again.

"Defibrillator!"

Willis pointed to the wall behind me and I saw what I was looking for. I wheeled it over, unbuttoned Poppy's top and turned on the machine.

"What if you're wrong?" Tuari asked.

I ignored him and continued to twist and turn dials.

"Quinton!"

I looked up at him. "What if you're wrong?"

"She's already dead, how much worse can it get?"

"Fuck!" said he said, walking towards me. "Move out of the way, you don't know what you're doing. Willis, make yourself useful and strap her limbs down—if this goes wrong and she starts swinging uncontrollably one hit could kill us."

Tuari pressed a few more knobs before removing the paddles from the electric supply unit. He looked at me with uncertainty in his eyes but I gave him a firm nod and stood back as he positioned the paddles above her chest.

"Administering two hundred volts. Clear!"

The paddles made contact and her body jerked upwards but the screen that registered her heartbeat on the stretcher was still flat.

"Increase the voltage," I said.

"Administering four hundred volts. Clear!"

Once again her body jerked upwards but the line still remained flat. I dug my fingers into my fist as I said, "Increase the voltage."

"Administering six hundred volts. Clear!"

Paddle met skin but nothing changed. "Come on! Again—higher."

Tuari looked at me, unsure what to do. I took a step forward.

"Administering one thousand volts. Quinton, this could damage her—"

"Do it."

"Clear!"

I watched hollow-hearted as the current run through her but nothing happened. She didn't get up. The line didn't move. She didn't cough and sputter. She just lay there still and quiet. She just lay there.

I dropped to my knees, face in hands, and cried till my throat hurt and my body trembled.

"I'm sorry," said someone, but I didn't know who.

When I finally got up the room was empty apart from me and her. Walking forward, I looked down at a face beyond perfection and didn't know what to say, so I said nothing at all. I stroked her face, which seemed at peace, and leaned over to kiss her on the lips. Pulling away I turned and made my way towards the door but stopped.

I had heard something.

Closing my eyes, I listened once again. There it was. A faint beep. Spinning on my heel I looked at the heartbeat monitor on the stretcher and saw the lines move. Rushing forward, I leant over and held her face in my hands.

"Poppy, can you hear me? Pop?"

Her eyes flickered opened and a smile that melted my soul graced her face. "I dreamt of you" was all she said before I embraced her in a hug and kissed her from head to toe.

81

Only a few hours had passed since Poppy's recovery and we had made our way to my quarters, shedding as many clothes as we could on the way there. We hadn't even made it to the bed but instead had collapsed on the floor of my room in a tangle of arms, legs, tongues and lips.

As quickly as it started it seemed to end like a passionate valve that just needed to be released.

I was panting heavily with her lying on my chest. She wiped the sweat from my brow as she looked up at me with those big doe eyes.

"Sorry I scared you."

"It's alright," I said, kissing her on the forehead, "just don't do it again."

She smiled but there was a hint of sadness behind her eyes.

"What's wrong?"

"It's just—" she began, but stopped and shook her head.

"Go on, tell me."

"It's just—if I were human then that wouldn't have

happened. I wouldn't have made you worry, I wouldn't have—"

"Are you kidding me? If you were human then I wouldn't be alive and here with you right now. You've saved my ass more times than I can count because of who you are, not what you are. You have the most beautiful soul I have ever seen and that's all that matters. So enough of the sadness and worry. I'm just happy I get to hold you again."

She nodded her head and give me a smile. "In a way it's good you saw what you did. AIs are not indestructible like most people think. Most things that can kill a human being can also kill us. We just get out of the way a lot quicker."

I know what she said was to reassure me and there might be some truth to her words, but I had seen her take blows and hits that would cave in a human's chest. I had seen the strength and power she had in those hands.

It was the power befitting a god.

"One thing that's been bugging me—when you were... well, you know... I tried to pick you up but couldn't move you. It took all three of us to just shift you, but normally you weigh next to nothing. What gives?"

"Ah, I have the ability to increase or decrease my weight."

"That's an ability most women would kill for."

"It comes in handy. I can make the metal elements in my body thicker, which makes me more resilient to blows and makes my attacks more powerful. It also works in reverse when I need to break into somewhere and I need to be light of foot."

I nodded my head and marvelled at how little I knew of her. I wondered what other secrets she might be keeping from me, but I immediately got rid of the thought. She would tell me what she needed to tell m, all in good time. Who was I to question her? I was just happy she was alive.

"There's something I have been meaning to tell you—" she began, but was cut off by the ship's comms.

"If you two lovebirds are finished making the beast with two backs," Tuari said, "I think it's about time you came to the bridge. The space station is in sight and we shall be arriving shortly."

"What were you going to say?" I asked.

"It can wait."

"You sure?"

She rubbed her face in my chest before kissing me on the lips. "I'm sure. Come on, it sounds like the bridge needs its captain."

We were back on the bridge and the ship was slowly approaching our final destination.

"Poppy, can you magnify the station, please?"

She gave me a nod before enlarging the image on the viewing screen. As it came into sharp focus I took in what she showed me. I looked upon a station that would be classified as small by today's standards. It was circular with six arms extending out from its middle, which was shaped like a diamond; the arms each connected to a circle that encompassed the station. White, it stood out against the black vastness of space with nothing surrounding it.

It was truly in the middle of nowhere.

"Pop, can you enlarge the section facing south?"

She did so, and I saw three other ship vessels that didn't belong to the station docked at her loading bay.

"Well, I guess now we know the other crews Edward sent didn't grab the loot and run," Tuari said.

"That still doesn't tell us what happened to them, and I would like to know what they faced before they met their demise," I said.

"They could still be alive," Tuari said.

"I doubt it," Willis said, rosary in hand. "Those pricks have been docked on that station for how long? Even with food and supplies, the strongest would have eaten the weak. Their souls are with a greater power now."

"Thank you for that, Willis. I still don't like entering somewhere when I don't know what I'm up against."

"Tough shit, I'm afraid. Talking about flesh-eating parasites, Edward is hailing us," said Willis.

Ugh! I had all but forgotten about our current employer in all the highs and lows we had gone through.

"He survived?"

"I'm afraid so," Tuari said. "I was hoping the machines would have taken care of him for us, but looks like he made it through on the other side; he took more of a beating than us and his ship looks like it's about to break apart, but he's still here."

I looked at Tuari with a gleam in my eye and opened my mouth.

"I know what you're going to say, and no, we can't take him. Even in the state his ship is in, it's still a war class ship and they would need less than five percent, if that, to destroy us. If we had a fully functioning ship with shields and fully stocked weapons then maybe, but even then I wouldn't want to risk it. *The Kennel* is built more for running than fighting."

That is something I will need to change. I was tired of running; I was tired of hiding; plus with what was on the horizon, with the enemies we had biting at our heels, we would need all the firepower we could muster.

"What about fleeing?"

"Where would we go? We would have to face the music eventually."

I sighed in frustration before clicking my neck from side to side. "Put him through."

The viewing screen flickered on and it presented us with an image of Edward. Men with fire extinguishers ran back and forth in the background while they did their best to combat the small electric fires that still raged on. I saw more than one body lying on the floor covered by a white sheet; a foot poked out from under a sheet there, a hand here.

Bags under his eyes complimented the five o'clock shadow on Edward's face, a dressing covered with a gauze pad was taped to the side of his neck. Red spots oozed through the white fabric.

"Edward!" I said with a smile. "You look like shit, my friend. I take it attacking a host of machines that are threatening your very existence didn't turn out so well for you?"

He smiled faintly as he brought his pipe to his lips but it broke in half and fell to the floor with a clatter.

"Ha, what a cunt," Willis said, just loud enough to be heard.

Edward looked at the handle of the pipe still in his hand and dropped it to the floor, then turned his attention to us. "Yes, those things were more numerous than I had first thought. Their presence was masked by the rock sediment, so we falsely judged their true potential."

"There was no *we*, you arrogant ass!" I said, pointing a finger his way. "You decided to attack and ignored my words of advice. Because of you we nearly got destroyed; now we are severely compromised for whatever we are about to face.

And, I would like to remind you, we still have no idea what that is, and don't tell me there is nothing to worry about, because the last three crews you have sent…their ships are still docked at the station."

"Ah, yes, I was hoping you wouldn't notice that. It doesn't look good, does it, dear boy? It appears the secrets and treasures this station holds are a harder temptress to seduce than I first thought. Not to worry, I am sure your crew will handle—"

"Oh no, my good fellow," I said with a touch of a posh English accent, "you shall be joining us. If you want this mission competed, then I need all the available men I can get."

"But that wasn't part of the deal."

"I can give two fucks about the deal. We aren't getting paid for this job, so if you want whatever little treasure is on that station, then you'd best be telling your men to get locked and loaded. The only way I can see us coming out of this alive is if we join forces and work as a team; anything else and there be a slaughter on all fronts."

"You know I can just as easily destroy your little ship and do the work myself."

"You could, but look how well not listening to me turned out for you last time. Get your men ready; I'll message you when we're ready to breach the station."

Willis cut him off and looked at me with a raised eyebrow.

"What?" I asked.

"You know sooner or later we'll have to take care of that asshole. If you think he'll let us go after we've finished this mission then you are sorely mistaken. I hope you have a plan for that."

"I'm working on it.

"Poppy, how long till we reach the station?"

"An hour."

"Set the ship on autopilot, but set instructions for it to warn us if it sees anything leaving the station. After that's done I want all of you geared up and ready to go. I want everyone armed to the teeth for this one; bring only weapons that can deliver high firepower, and I want everyone wearing a tactical exoskeleton suit."

"Ahh! I hate those things," Tuari whined. "They make my butt look big."

"Hey, fat ass," said Willis, "word of advice, it's not the suit."

"No ifs or buts. Suit up. Get armed. Be ready before the hour," I said as I made my way off the bridge.

82

I sat quietly on the floor, legs crossed, eyes closed, breathing in and out as slowly as I could while I tried to empty my mind. I had been at it for the last twenty minutes. Meditation was always something I turned to when the stress got the better of me, or when my mind wouldn't shut up... and right now was one of those times.

Thoughts of failure bombarded me.

Every scenario of what could go wrong, I had envisioned. Everything from me tripping up upon boarding the station and firing my shotgun off accidentally and injuring someone, to watching my crewmates being brutally murdered by faceless figures while I stood immobile, unable to do anything. The more I had tried to stop thinking about it the faster the thoughts had come until I was breathing way too fast and my chest had become tight.

It was then I decided to take five and just relax.

Once my mind was fully free, I asked myself the one question I had been avoiding—what was the worst thing that could happen?

After enough time sorting through the ridiculous answers, I finally came to the core of what was.

I was scared of failing my crew and watching them die—much the way I had watched José die.

Saying that to myself, as weird as it seemed, had stopped the worrying. I knew the stakes; now I just had to focus.

A knock at the door forced me to open my eyes.

"Come in."

Poppy entered and smiled at me. "There's nothing to be worried about."

"Who said I was worried? I know we've got this; you're looking at a calm, cool, collected, bad motherfucker."

We both looked at each other before we burst out laughing.

"Everything will be alright," she said, kneeling in front of me.

"Will it?"

She stroked my face and kissed me on the lips. "Look how far you've come. The man who was once too scared to confront and leave his wife, even though he knew she was cheating on him, is leading a crew made up of a killer robot, a crazed priest, and a bear of a man who would try to make even death laugh. You've suffered through torture and pain, through heartache and misery, and you're still fighting, you're still standing. That should count for something."

"It does," I said kissing her back; "it does, I'm just scared I will fall flat on my face at the very first step I take on this mission."

"Don't be, I'll be there to catch you."

"Well then, beautiful, pass me my shotgun. I think it's about time we finished this shit."

"There's the man I know and love," she said, handing me my beloved shotgun as we made our way out of my room.

The darkness engulfed me. I reached out and touched the metal wall I knew was in front of me. I allowed its smooth walls to relax my breathing.

A gentle hand on my shoulder gave me a squeeze. Forcing a smile on my lips, I reached up to pat it as Willis's voice cut through my thoughts.

"For the love of God, man! Will you stop breathing down my neck? Your breath smells like hot ass and tastes like it too—just back up, will you?"

"Ah, Willy, don't you like me being close to you?" Tuari asked.

"You touch my ass one more time and I will put my two pistols so far up your anus that you'll taste the metal."

"Oh, you tease, all this ass play and talk is getting me hot under the collar."

"Alright! I want to change position with someone," Willis said, beginning to move.

"And where exactly do you want to move to?" I asked. "If you didn't notice, we are in the secondary cargo hold because the larger one, which has more space, is filled to the rafters with your shit! The power from the overhead lights are out because the ship is on its last legs, and all we have separating us from certain death is these blast doors I'm standing in front of, plus I keep getting poked up the ass by someone's gun. So if you could all just shut the fuck up and get your head in the game and out your asses, while we wait for the robot scouts to give us the all-clear, I would appreciate it!"

"Ass," Tauri said with a chuckle, which quickly became a coughing fit as I prodded him in the gut with the butt of my gun.

"Hey, how did you know where I was?"

"Your breath."

"It's not a hygiene issue," he said. "I have been experimenting with different sauces for my braised lamb shanks with fish sauce."

"What have you been using, shit?" Willis asked.

"No... fermented carrots and fish heads with cherry tomatoes and garlic to thicken up the sauce."

The little cargo hold grew quiet as I and everyone else mentally dissected what he had just said.

"You use all those things together... to create a sauce?" I asked.

"One, they're not things, they're ingredients, and two, a chef always has to push the boundaries of what is possible; only then will he truly create a dish that will last the ages. Mistakes must be made. Risks must be taken. Many people believe they created the Eton mess after an accident in Eton College; it is truly—"

"Borinnnng!" Willis said.

"Sorry for trying to impart some knowledge into that zealot brain of yours; I forgot the church was against freethinking."

"Say that again—"

A banging on the door silenced the growing conversation about to turn into a full-blown fight. I waited for three seconds until the banging was repeated. I had programmed the scout robot to repeat a certain pattern. I pressed the button to open the hatch doors and then a round, hovering ball entered before the hatch doors closed behind it again.

I triggered the computer embedded into my exoskeleton suit helmet to review the video footage the scout had taken. Normally we would view what the robot saw in real-time, but something had jammed our signal, not allowing the connection to go through. I held my breath as I pressed play, hoping that whatever was interfering with our connection didn't mess up the video.

A small screen flickered inside each of our helmets, then the video played.

Thank God for that!

It showed a corridor in complete darkness, the only source of light the one being emitted from the bot. Long tight metallic corridors twisted and turned, with the odd button on the wall, along with posters I couldn't see clearly enough to decipher what they said. There was no sign of the other crews that had been before us, or any signs of traps or anything that would hinder their progress.

"It all seems pretty... ordinary," said Poppy.

"Yeah, that's what worries me," I said as the video stream ended.

I pondered the best course of action while Willis began tapping his foot. "Look, are we going to enter this station or not? We can't wait around here all day like a bunch of rent boys waiting to be picked."

"You're right, but I'm not stepping a foot out there till we have scouted the whole station," I said.

"That could take weeks!" said Willis.

"I would rather we were better prepared and knew what we were facing than we ended up like all those other poor fuckers, whose bodies we haven't even found by the way."

"Quinton, I understand where you're coming from," said Poppy, "but we haven't got the supplies to last that long out here, plus *The Kennel* needs repairs. She won't last much longer out here without shields or energy to keep the lights on. We took too much damage to come back the way we came, so the round trip will be longer, which only adds to our problems. This mission has to be done as quickly as possible if we have any chance of surviving the journey back."

I gritted my teeth and closed my eyes. I knew she was right, but it wasn't what I wanted to hear. With so much of the station left unexplored, we would be wandering about like headless chickens, waiting for whatever had killed the last three crews to come and get us. We needed a plan—I slapped my helmet as I made a call to Edward.

His face appeared on the video feed in my helmet. "What's the holdup, dear chap?"

"Have you got interior maps of this station?"

"Well, err—"

"I need those now and a marker placed on our destination."

"Here's the thing, dear fellow, I had all the best intention of giving you the maps to this station, you understand, but here's the thing: they don't match up to the interior of the station."

"What do you mean?"

"I know, I know, I'm just as mad as you are, but either the maps are out of date or work has been done on this station without anyone's knowledge. When we first approached the station, the size of it took me aback. Going by all the schematics I had previously seen, this station should be half the size it is now, but either the schematics were wrong or the station has grown somehow. I have checked and double-checked the maps I have, and they match up somewhat, but not enough for me to trust them for our navigation."

"Then how do we know where what you want is?"

"That's simple; all we have to do is make our way to the centre of the station. What we seek should be there."

"Should? You endanger the life of me and my crew for should?"

"There was one thing highlighted again and again, in all the data I went through regarding this place: everything I am after is stored in the centre of this station, and then the station was built around it much like a cocoon."

"Let's just hope what hatches out of that cocoon is a pretty butterfly. Alright, you're docked next to us so you should be able to follow this corridor adjacent to ours for fifteen minutes, then we shall meet up at this junction," I said, sharing the details of the station the scouts had mapped for me. I placed a red marker where I wanted him and his crew to meet us.

"Received loud and clear, good chap."

"One more thing? In all your findings, did it say anything about traps, guards or anything dangerous?"

There was a pause that was far too long before he responded, "All I can say is to be careful, Mr Blake."

"That really doesn't—"

"Only the devil and I know the whereabouts of my treasure, and the one of us who lives the longest should take it all. Only a fool doesn't guard what is valuable," he said before cutting off the link.

83

Our footsteps sounded heavy through the helmet speakers. We were covered from head to toe in an all-in-one black exoskeleton suit; they offered us protection from most projectiles, extreme heat and cold, and they had a thirty-minute oxygen supply if we found ourselves ejected into space or if the computers in our suit detected the current air supply around us was toxic to human life. I was told they had cost a pretty penny and were only used on a handful of missions.

The material clung to my body like a second skin to the point I didn't even notice I was wearing it. The camera lens embedded in the helmet gave me a hundred-and-sixty-degree view of my surroundings and had night vision and thermal imaging, which came in handy as we didn't have to give away our location by using flashlights.

We moved in a formation of Willis and Tuari up front with me and Poppy covering the rear. We had been walking for ten minutes and had seen nothing of note yet; the endless smooth corridor walls made keeping track of time difficult if it weren't for the onboard computers inside the exoskeleton suit. My helmet picked up a scuttling-type sound, which stopped me in my tracks and made me snap my head left to right.

I guess I wasn't the only one who had heard the sound, as everyone else had stopped and were scanning the surrounding area.

"I hate to be the bearer of bad news," Tuari said, "but that sounded suspiciously like an insect crawling on metal."

"What!" Willis said, spinning around in a frantic circle. "Don't be stupid. How would insects even survive out here? We're in deep space, remember? What would they eat for one?"

"Well, maybe, just maybe," Tuari whispered, "when this place was being created a pair of creatures got trapped in the cargo, breeding and eating their offspring and breeding and eating, until they could find a way out, and after years and decades those life-forms bred into something new, something predatory, something that could handle the harsh elements it was in, that would love nothing better than the taste of sweet, tender, succulent, alcohol-soaked flesh that only an Irishman can provide."

"That ain't funny," Willis said.

I heard the sound again and scanned the walls and ceiling around me, but I couldn't find where it came from.

"I believe the sound is emanating from behind the walls," Poppy said.

"What? You mean the air vents?" I asked.

She gave me a nod, eyes still scanning above her.

"Or it could be some unknown alien creature that is just waiting to lay its eggs in our stomach," Tuari said.

"You're thinking of *Alien*," I said.

"Still, they do say fact is stranger than fiction; the Candiru fish from the Amazon Basin is known to swim up a person's urethra and it can only be removed by surgery. If that isn't straight from a science fiction movie then I don't know what is," Tuari said.

I heard the scuttling once more but it sounded like whatever it was, was moving away from us.

I patted Willis on the shoulder; he jumped and swung his pistols my way.

"Whoa, whoa," I said, raising my hands in the air, "it's just me. I think whatever it is, is moving away from us."

Willis's helmeted head looked at me and I could feel his gaze as he looked sharply up then back down to me. "We, we, we never did find those bodies did we?"

"The bodies of the other crews? No, no, we didn't."

Footsteps up ahead drew our attention as we all raised our weapons and proceeded with caution. Finally coming to the junction I had marked on the map for Edward, we spotted his men making their way towards us. They too wore exoskeleton suits but where ours were black theirs were shadowy grey. Six figures approached us and one parted from the group and stood in front of us,

"Well, my good man, this sure is exciting, isn't it?"

"Notice anything interesting on your travels?" I asked.

Edward's helmeted head tilted to the side as he regarded me silently."No , nothing but grey metal walls."

"Is this all the men you've brought?" Willis asked.

"Yes, in total we amount to ten; ten bodies should be enough to do this job, any more and we may risk being... detected," Edward said.

"Detected? I thought you didn't know what was guarding this place and more importantly, I thought you said this place was safe."

"I never said anything of the sort; any fool who has sent out numerous crews who haven't returned knows this job isn't safe. My approach to this problem has been all wrong. I have used force when I should have been using stealth. Cunning and quick wit shall win the day here."

I had a distinct feeling he was keeping something from me, but the longer I questioned him, the longer we would be stuck out here, easy prey for whatever was lurking these halls. I wanted this thing over and done with.

"Alright, so we don't get confused as to who is who, I suggest we sync up, so we can identify each other," I said.

"Great idea, my man, but you shall only need to know my identity. The rest of my men... value their anonymity. I don't even know their names; they mostly go by colours, for example Mr Grey," said Edward.

"But you employ them, how can you know nothing of them?"

"I employ them to do things that are off the record and in doing so, they themselves become off the record. It's easier that way. Less fuss, less hassle. I will connect to your database and now, I should have a marker identifying me in your video feed."

It took a few seconds, but as he said, a little red icon with Edward's name appeared above his head. The same had already been done for the rest of my crew, as everyone wore a black indistinguishable exoskeleton suit. Even Poppy, although she didn't need it, still wore one as it would stop any questions being raised as to why.

"Alright, I guess we proceed forward. If our destination is in the centre of this thing, then it should just be a straight path. Are you and your men ready?" I asked Edward.

"Ready as we'll ever be. Please lead the way."

The journey continued to be uneventful until we passed the threshold of the connecting arm linking the main body of the station to the ring that encircled it. I stopped in my tracks and looked back at the corridor we had just come from and then looked around at where we were now. The walls of the main body of the station were dull, with wires sticking out of the walls and hanging from different sections of the ceiling; wherever I looked it reminded me of a ship that had been used for salvage.

"Doesn't this strike you as a little strange, that the main section of the station is so disused but the corridors we just came through look so new, as if they have just been built?" I asked.

"Don't be absurd," Edward replied. "That would imply someone has been extending this station past its original design, and why would anyone do that?"

"I don't know, but that would make sense of why all the old maps and schematics you obtained appear out of date."

"This station hasn't seen human life until I found out about it; the only people who have graced these corridors are us and the other crews I have sent before us. If what you said is correct, then why would someone go to the trouble of extending the station? What purpose would that serve?"

"I don't know," I said, "but one thing I do know, those corridors we walked through are new. Now the only thing we need to find out is who built them and why."

"Maybe," Tuari said, "it was the predator creatures we heard crawling through the vent space. Maybe they are building a super hive that will take over all known humanity and enslave us to do their bidding."

"I thought I told you to shut up about that shit!" Willis shouted, stepping towards Tuari.

"Don't tell me you're scared, my little ginger friend," Tuari said.

"I'll show you who's scared when I—"

Once again the faint sound of scuttling drew my attention, forcing me to lift up my shotgun. Poppy stepped close to me. her Damascus steel blades in her hands. The sounds of Willis and Tuari arguing still filled the air until they too took notice and prepared themselves.

"Does anyone have visuals?" I asked.

"No," came the chorus response from more than one mouth.

Shit.

"Why are you so nervous?" Edward asked. "That sound is just the sound an old station makes. This thing hasn't been serviced or looked after in years."

The noise was getting louder by the second and this time it was definitely coming towards us; it sounded like a hundred tiny feet tap-dancing on metal as we all held our breath for what was about to come, then it stopped. The silence that followed was suffocating. I looked up and down, left to right, but couldn't see anything.

"I told you there was nothing—"

One of Edward's men let out an ear-piercing scream behind me. Spinning on my heel I saw what was, in fact, a mechanical-looking spider four feet across with legs that ended in razor-sharp points; a cluster of camera lenses acted as eyes as it withdrew its arm from its victim's chest.

"I knew some shit like this would happen!" Willis yelled as he and everyone else opened fire upon the thing. A hail of bullets blasted it away until it was nothing but a smouldering pile of wires.

No one said anything as we all looked at the thing on the

floor, I took a step towards it but Poppy held out her arm as spiders emerged from above us.

"What the fuck! What the fuck!" Willis screamed as he began firing wildly.

I picked my shots as best as I could and blasted bodies before they could reach me, I leapt back as I gun-butted one in the face, smashing its eyes, and delivered a killing shot. Another man from Edward's group screamed as he shook violently. A yellow spider had sunk its fangs into his suit and refused to let go. Someone shot the spider off him, where it fell on its back.

Electricity sparked from fangs.

"Watch out for the yellow ones! They're electric," I said, as I blasted a trio climbing down the walls.

They were coming down the walls in a swarm on either side of us; if we didn't move we would become quickly overrun. "We need to push deeper into the station—everyone form a circle."

Edward's men hesitated but after another man went down with a spiked leg to the head, they quickly formed a ring with us. The swarm must have numbered in the hundreds. We shot, gun-butted and dodged as best as we could as we continued to pump shells into the masses. Whenever an injured spider fell and it wasn't too badly damaged a pair would quickly descend upon it and strip it of its parts, before they returned to the ceiling.

"They are cannibals!" Tuari said, grabbing a spider by the leg and smashing it into another one on the wall.

"Why spiders? Anything but spiders, mechanical spiders at that," Willis said.

The swarm was attacking but I sensed something was wrong. They weren't attacking us full throttle; they were picking and choosing when to launch an attack. They acted like one organism doing what was best for the swarm instead of each spider acting on their own. Poppy pulled me sideways as a leg scraped against my helmet; her knives moved in a blur and a leg dropped to the floor.

We kept on moving. About to take a right we found our path blocked by a wall of yellow-bodied spiders. Electricity sparked off their fangs as they launched themselves towards us but didn't attack.

"Left!" said Edward.

"No! It's a trap," I shouted, but it was too late.

I was pushed and bundled left as I tried to repeat my warning but it was already too late; a wall slid down behind us blocking our way. One of Edward's men ran towards it but it came crashing down with a thud that echoed along the corridor. The man slammed his fist against the door before running his hands along its edge, looking for any gaps.

There were none.

Even from here, I could see it was an airtight seal.

"Well, looks like we won't be returning that way," Edward said.

"I couldn't care less—as long as those spiders are kept behind that wall, we'll find another way around," Willis said, taking the lead and walking forward.

As everyone began to follow his lead I made my way back to the wall and ran my hands over it. "What's wrong?" Poppy asked.

"The spiders, they were herding us. They could have wiped us out en masse; they had the numbers to do so but they didn't."

"Do you know why?"

"No, but I have a feeling we are about to find out soon enough."

84

The corridor we found ourselves in was none too dissimilar from the ones we had just left. We were all on edge as we scanned the ceilings and corners for any sign of robotic life. Every noise triggered a sharp gesture, every footstep sounded twice as loud.

"How much longer till we get to our destination?" I asked.

"Who knows, my good man? Who knows? With the addition of these new tunnels, we could be in for the long haul here," Edward said.

"Do you think those *spiders* created these corridors?" Willis said in a hushed voice.

"Normally I would dismiss the very idea as a fallacy, but strange things have taken place on this journey. From machines coated in rock attacking us in space to spiders that administer electrical shocks when they bite. So, they could have created this corridor, but for what purpose—that is what I would like to know," Edward said. "Whatever they are, they are intelligent. Plus, they salvage parts from their deceased, which makes me think nothing is wasted, and those parts are used to build new creations."

"You mean there more of those things?" Willis asked.

"It's the most logical answer to how something creates more of itself when it doesn't have reproductive organs," Edward said.

"No sexy time?" Tuari said. "Wow, that's a bummer."

"Is this really all worth it?" I said to Edward.

He didn't answer me for a moment or two and I didn't think he would, as the only response I got was the sound our footsteps made.

"All throughout my life I have been living in the shadows of great men. Men long past and gone, who created shadows so grand and all-encompassing they blocked out the very sun. My existence since I could think has always been about how my great-great-grandfather created this station, or how my great-grandfather started Xcorp, or how my grandfather made it into the powerhouse it is today. All my life I have tried to live up to these men, tried to be better than them, tried to outshine them, but how do you do that when they are the very reason why you are who you are?

"The saying 'Show me a great man who is the son of a great man' has always hung around my neck like a noose; no matter what I did or where I went it would always tighten. My younger siblings didn't have the burden of being the eldest placed on their shoulders, so they could follow their *artistic muse* and waste their trust fund on *finding themselves,* while it was placed on me to better the family fortunes. Everything was going swimmingly until you and your little crew came along, Mr Blake.

"Profits are at a record low, investors are leaving in droves, and the members of the board are looking to kick me off the board all because of you."

"Please, don't blame me for your actions. I've seen the monthly reports and KPIs. The amount you paid to Lady Isabella was but a water drop in the ocean of profits Xcorp sees from their annual reports.

"The amount you paid her is about thirty percent of what your company should pay in taxes but doesn't, because your granddaddy did a deal with someone else's granddaddy so your company doesn't have to support the community that surrounds it but instead can leech off it like a parasite."

"Don't support the community! Do you know how many jobs I provide to people like you? Jobs you've jeopardised. It numbers in the tens of thousands, jobs that could have been outsourced or better managed by robots, but instead they go to people who don't have a college degree and can barely keep their shit together.

"Sick leave, pregnancy, bereavement, having my managers deal with petty issues and infighting because Sandra took Jenny's drink from the shared refrigerator—all this mess and clutter could be removed in one fell swoop if we introduced robots and AIs into the workforce."

"So, this is what this is all about? Minimising your workforce and maximising your profits," I said with a shake of the head.

"No, you buffoon, don't you see, it should have happened centuries ago. We've had the technology, but humanity has been scared to take the next step. Scared because of tales of bogymen AIs, that hunt humans for sport."

"I think you'll find there is some truth to those tales," I said.

"Maybe, but as in everything in life, it's all about branding. You highlight a product in a certain light—glossing over the negatives, showing the positives—point out how it can improve the lives of the masses, how it can give them more time, make them rich, blah blah blah, get a few celebrity endorsements and before you know it, I shall have an AI in every home."

"You really think the World Government will allow you to get away with this?"

He chuckled as we continued to walk. "Quinton, you really think I'm the bad guy here? Is that how you see me?"

"No, I see you as a pompous privileged asshole but what's your point?"

"My point is, humanity has stagnated. We've stopped pushing the technological edge because of what happened in WW3. Yes, our ships are faster, and our weapons better, but I believe we would have been ten times further along than we are now, if we didn't let fear hold us back. It's akin to stopping progress on the Internet after the first cyberattack took place.

"You may see me as a monster because I want to cut my workforce, but I only want people working for me who want to work for me. I want to do away with administrative roles that crush people's souls, I want to usher in a new age where people have the freedom to do what they want, when they want. My AIs and robots will take care of everyone's needs; they will be humanity's servants while people find their true calling, their true passion.

"We all had a dream once when we were younger; I just want to help people fulfil that dream."

"Ignoring the fact of what cutting so many jobs will do to the economy, what do you get out of all this?"

"If everyone has an AI in their home and I have a monopoly hold over that market, then I become one of the wealthiest men in existence, not to mention also leaving my mark on history. It's always been about wealth and recognition. Those have been the driving forces of my soul since I could remember."

We had been walking for some time, but luckily we had not been attacked or heard the noise of scurrying feet above us. As we brought up the rear, I looked sideways at Poppy and although I couldn't see her face, I could tell something was wrong.

"Poppy for your thoughts?" I asked, selecting a secure private radio channel between me and her.

She shifted her gaze towards me before looking ahead. Her knives moved back and forth between her hands at a speed that boggled the mind, at a speed which would raise too many questions if anyone noticed. I placed my hand gently on her forearm and shook my head.

"Do you think he's right?" she asked.

"About what?"

"About everything, about humanity's evolution slowing down because of the fear that people have for AIs, about allowing robots and AIs to do work humans don't want to do, about trying to make a better humanity for everyone involved. The Renaissance and times like it only happened because basic things like food and shelter were taken care of; what if people could pursue their passions, or just do what they enjoyed without having to worry about the bills or—"

"Poppy, this utopia Edward is describing is just a fantasy. There has never been a time in human history when famine and poverty didn't exist; people will always fall through the cracks. We aren't talking about ones and zeros here—people are just that, people, and to expect something like an AI to solve all of humanity's problems is just…"

"But what if they could? They can outperform anything a human can do, without the errors; they could increase the quality of life of so many people. Think how miserable you were in a job you hated. What if someone offered you a way out, where you could pursue the job you wanted—wouldn't you take it?"

"If I did, I would have never gotten the chance to meet you. I would redo everything I ever did in my past life if it meant I got to meet you again."

She didn't say anything but grabbed my hand and gave it a little squeeze.

"In all of this have you given any thought to how an AI like yourself would feel about being placed in a role they didn't ask to be in?"

"I… no, I haven't," she whispered.

"There's no point in substituting one worker bee for another if neither wants to be there."

"Life sure is messy, huh?"

"You should know, you've been alive longer than all of us," I said.

"Does that make you my boy-toy?"

"I wouldn't—"

"Lord have mercy!" Willis shouted from ahead of us.

We both pushed past the men in front of us to see what the commotion was about. Mouth dropping open I stared up into a truly terrifying image: rows of men and women were suspended in the air above us, cocooned in a wire that acted like a web. All had multiple tubes running from their bodies into the ceiling. Each face I looked into showed the same signs. They all looked like hollowed-out husks drained of all their nutrients.

"My word," Edward said, coming to stand next to me, "are they still alive?"

"Judging by their vitals and brain waves," said one of Edward's men, "they appear to be nothing but vegetables, sir. Brain-dead in every sense of the word. I guess they are just being kept alive for the nutrients in their blood. For what purpose, I can only guess, but I would say they are being farmed by those spider things that attacked us."

"Interesting," Edward said. "Well, the least we can do is put these people out of their misery and destroy their bodies. Fire when ready."

"Wait!" I said, raising my hand. "Do you think that's a wise choice?"

"Yes, it's the humane thing to do."

"But what if we trigger those things again? I say we leave everything as it is and try not to disturb anything. These people are already dead; we can't do anything to help them, as harsh as that may sound. I only care about my crew, and finishing this mission so we can move on with our lives."

Edward said nothing as he looked up at the people hanging above us, fingers drumming along his thigh.

"You can't leave these people like this," said a voice that surprised me; I turned to Willis. "These men and women deserve better than this, Quinton, you may not know or care about them, but they are people who tap-danced on the fringes of society and risked their lives to be here. They are a crew just like us. Just looking for the next payday. It could have been us hanging up there instead of them. We need to destroy the bodies or at least cut them down."

I looked to the crazed Irishman who believed in heaven and hell, who I had heard praying on more than one occasion, and found myself lost for words.

"You know, that's the longest you've spoken without saying fuck or a swearword equivalent."

"I was due one, I guess."

I breathed out heavily as I returned my gaze to the scene above me. "Alright, let's cut them down."

The job was messier and took longer than we all thought, as we had to use a combination of hacking away at the wires and shooting them to get the people down, but we managed it as fast as we could, pulling tubes out of bodies that did nothing but spill blood all over the floor. I kept looking around me as I strained my hearing, waiting for the telltale signs of those little sharp needle feet on metal, but nothing came.

Willis placed charges all over the bodies and would detonate them when we were clear of the station.

Job done, everyone moved on as I looked behind me at the rows of bodies that had been piled head to toe along the corridor floor.

"You did the right thing," Poppy said, squeezing my shoulder. "I know you care about the crew's safety but sometimes—"

A thud shook the ceiling above us as the ceiling panels exploded outwards. Jerking me back Poppy moved me out of the way as a spider's head as wide as I was long poked through the ceiling, fangs dripping with what smelt like battery acid. The fluid fell to the floor and sizzled and popped the metal that it touched. The spider's eight eyes looked towards the ceiling where its prey had once hung and then looked down at the floor, and took in the rows of bodies now free from its webbing.

Head jerking towards us, it glared our way and I got a distinct impression it wasn't happy.

Body made out of the same metal material that its

smaller offspring had been made out of, it shoved and pushed its large bulbous body through the hole in the ceiling it had made.

"Fuck me!" Willis screamed. "Kill it! Kill it! Kill ittt."

Bullets flew overhead and smashed into the machine forcing me to duck low, as warning signals appeared on the viewing display of my helmet telling me of projectiles that were passing too close to my head for comfort. I threw myself to the floor and looked up to see the bullets had no effect whatsoever; most ricocheted off its metal body and went back the way they came.

Still pushing its body through the hole it had created, it got stuck and began to flail its legs wildly about.

Lying flat on my stomach, I lifted my shotgun up and took aim, then I blasted two of its camera-lens-like eyes. Reddish goo spilt from the wounds as it opened its mouth and bellowed out a shriek that put my teeth on edge.

Pulling its body with all its might it tore through the hole and landed in the corridor, all six remaining eyes focusing solely on me.

Oh shit.

It was time to run.

85

The spider let out another shriek and gave chase. Poppy yanked me upwards; she shoved me forward as we ran for our lives. Everyone else followed suit as they fired and ran and fired and ran.

One of Edward's men tripped and fell amongst the mad scramble to get away; face turned up towards his oncoming doom he lifted his hands up defensively as a leg like a needle stabbed down and pierced him through the chest. The man let out an agonising scream as he was lifted into the air by his chest and shaken from side to side.

He tried to fire his rifle at the thing, but that came to an end as it bit through his neck and swallowed his head whole.

"This thing eats flesh as well!?" Willis said, as he fired blindly over his shoulder.

"No doubt then it wants to take a chunk out of your ass," Tuari said.

Metal stompings shook the floor under our feet as we bolted from one corridor to the next. I looked over my shoulder and saw the spider was steadily gaining with each step. Spinning on my heel I aimed and fired, taking out another eye.

Another shriek left its mouth as it redoubled its efforts and leapt forward. I ducked and rolled as a leg swept sideways like a sabre and scraped the wall, causing sparks to fly. Continuing to forward-roll I only stopped when I thought I was safe; getting up to my feet I buried my head and continued on at a sprint.

I didn't dare look behind me as I could sense its presence only feet away. Poppy looked towards me and I could tell what she was thinking but I shook my head. Any superhuman-like move on her part would only get her noticed by Edward, and if there was one thing I didn't want it was for that creep to get his hands on Poppy.

"If we don't do something quick," she said, speaking to me on a secure channel, "then we're all dead."

"Don't worry, I'll think of something."

"We have incoming up ahead!" someone shouted.

Looking up, I saw the smaller spiders that had attacked us before pouring out of the holes from the ceiling. Shit. Shit. Shit. This was going from bad to worse and there didn't seem to be an escape anywhere.

"Edward! Have your men clear the spiders up front, my crew will handle the big mama behind us."

"Like fuck we will!" Willis said.

I spun on my heel and fired two quick shots. The first missed, but the second took out another eye. Spinning back around I kept on running and saw something promising up ahead—a large junction that split four ways offered us some space where we could fight the spider on equal footing and not be cornered in. Edward's men were slowly pulling away as the crew and I slowed our pace so we could pick our shots more carefully.

"Crew, when we get up ahead, I want each of us to take a corner and stand our ground. We'll confuse it by attacking simultaneously so it doesn't know who to attack. Edward, I want you and your men to cover us from the rear."

"Why do we always get the shit end of the stick?" Willis said.

"Because we're bad motherfuckers!"

Edward still hadn't responded as he and his men continued to pull away down a corridor; they had now cleared their path of the smaller spiders. He stopped next to a button on the wall some way ahead, and a sickening feeling grew in the bottom of my stomach.

"Edward!"

"Sorry, old chap. I would love to hang around and help you out but my vision is bigger than you and your petty crew, so I think this will be goodbye. Thanks for all your help in getting me here," he said as he slapped the button on the wall.

"No!"

Everyone sprinted faster, with Poppy running at an inhuman speed, but it wasn't fast enough as a wall slid down with great speed blocking them from us. I noticed the wall —I noticed the anger in the pit of my stomach— but what I failed to see until it was too late was the grenade that slid under the closing wall at the last minute.

"Never say I'm not merciful," Edward said through the helmet speakers. "I could have left you all to die at the fangs of that thing. But this way is quicker." The explosion that followed lifted me off my feet and darkness embraced me.

86

Muffled noises came in and out of my hearing as I groaned and tried to get my bearings. I opened my eyes; I saw nothing from the cameras on my helmet but white distorted screens. I couldn't quite tell if I was lying on my back or my front, but what I did know was that my body had taken a hell of a beating.

I closed my eyes, scared of what I had to do, but knew I had to find out. Taking a deep breath, I slowly tried to move my fingers and feet and was rewarded with movement. It hurt like hell to move but at least I could.

"Come in. Is everyone okay? Can anyone hear me?"

Muffled responses came back. My helmet must be more damaged than I thought; I began to pull it off but stopped.

I didn't know the condition of the corridor I was in—the walls of the station could have had a breach after the explosion, making it unsuitable for human life. I knew for a fact I was still inside the station as I felt around the floor I lay on, but everything apart from that was a mystery.

The spider. Shit.

Was it alive? Was it damaged? Was I about to be attacked?

I couldn't see or hear. If it was out there and alive, it was only a matter of time before it found me and finished the job that Edward had started.

Taking in a deep gulp of air, I made my decision. I would pull off the helmet to see the damage caused and if I needed to, I would place the helmet back on, and think of something else, but sitting here waiting for death wasn't something I was going to do.

I pulled off my helmet and a helmeted head appeared in my vision.

"Move!" came Poppy's voice through the speakers of the helmet.

I didn't wait another second but rolled to my side as a metal leg came crashing down where I once lay. Coming up to my feet I looked around me and saw nothing but chaos: Tuari lay in a corner off to one side clutching his side as blood leaked from a wound, Willis stood over him firing his pistols and Poppy danced back and forth, blades out before her.

The explosion had damaged much of the corridor leaving scorch marks and dents in the wall, but apart from that, it remained largely unaffected.

The spider appeared to have taken most of the damage. One leg was missing and part of its abdomen was leaking red goo.

It launched itself for Poppy and she leapt out of the way with a backflip. I scanned the floor for my shotgun and found the spider standing over it.

"Pop! I have an idea but you're not going to like it."

She looked to where my gun was, then back to me. "Don't you dare!"

"Whatever you're going to do, do it quick. Fatboy over here needs some medic attention," Willis said.

"Pop, when the time is right, I want you to attack."

"How will I know—"

I didn't wait to give her an answer but sprinted forward with everything I had and waited till the last moment before I slid on my back towards the creature. It swivelled its head in my direction, but it was too slow.

Getting under it, I grabbed my shotgun and pointed up as I emptied all its shells into the spider.

It roared in pain as I made the hole in its abdomen even larger.

Poppy took her clue and leapt onto the thing's back, stabbing both her knives repeatedly into the base of its neck. It bucked and shook as it tried to get her off, but she held on tight to the handles of her knives.

I rolled back and forth out of the way of the stampeding legs until I saw my opening and bolted out from underneath its body. Emptying the shells from my shotgun, I reloaded them with explosive shells and took aim.

"Poppy, move!"

She did so, leaping off its back to safety.

"You know why this weapon is called the Peacemaker?" I asked as the spider turned its head towards me. "It's because it's time to make peace!"

The shotgun spent its shells with a roar and the spider's head was no more.

As the ringing in my ears slowly went away and the smoke cleared, the only thing that remained was a headless spider corpse that occasionally twitched as sparks leapt from its joints.

I lowered my weapon and found everyone was staring at me.

"What?"

"It's because it's time to make peace?" Poppy said, as she tried to hold back her laughter.

"Look, I don't see what's funny," I said, face slowly turning red.

"Jesus, I didn't know me giving you that weapon would turn you into such a clichéd cock!" Willis said.

"Look, I—"

"Death... please... take me now," Tuari said between coughs, "so I don't have to listen to any more of Quinton's hero sayings."

"Come on, guys, let's resolve this *peacefully*," Willis said, as the rest of the crew collapsed in laughter.

"You know what! All of you... can... can piss off," I said, storming off.

"Wait! Wait!" Willis said. "Come on, man, let's make peace not war."

87

We had taken another path and had come across a room that had medical supplies, although out of date, with many plasters and bandages turning yellow with age. We had used what we could to stem Tuari's bleeding and had patched him up as best as we could.

He still didn't have his full range of motion and he would be next to useless in a fight, but he wouldn't die on us yet.

Some time passed with us following one corridor after the next; some lead to rooms that appeared to be laboratories of some sort, while others lead to abandoned offices or just dead ends.

"It sure is *peaceful* around here," said Tuari, making everyone but me chuckle.

I ignored them and took in my surrounding: posters with red crosses and various other forms of warnings plastered over the walls we passed. Written warnings, highlighting the danger we were in, weren't lost on me.

Everywhere I looked spoke of untold horrors if we failed to turn back.

"Don't you think it's best we just tried to find a way back to our ship and get the hell out of here?" Tuari asked.

"I hate to agree with the village idiot," Willis said, "but he has a point. We aren't going to get paid for this job, and it may be better if Edward thinks we are dead. We get to leave with a clean slate and continue on with our lives."

"Yes, but one, he'll notice our ship is missing and two, I can't let that asshole win. He's the reason our ship blew up over the water of the Floating City, he's the reason Mr Lee hustled us, and he's the reason José is dead. Plus, whatever he's trying to get from this station will make him unstoppable.

"If we don't do something now, then it's something we'll always regret."

"I think you mean something *you'll* always regret," Willis said.

Maybe he was right, maybe I was being selfish, only thinking about my own desires above the crew's, but deep down in my gut I knew the right path and I wouldn't be persuaded from it.

"Aren't you tired of always running?" I asked, looking at each crewmember in turn. "Aren't you tired of just scraping out enough to survive? Aren't you tired of living on the fringes, doing nothing worthwhile?"

"You're forgetting something, we ain't heroes," said Willis.

"Then maybe we should change that."

No one said anything as more than one head turned away from me. "Look, we can hustle and drink and act like a bunch of jackasses when this is all said and done. You can run riot, but right now I need my crew with me, because if we aren't all together in this as one then we won't be able to pull this off."

"Can I finally get the pellet grill I've been eyeing, but I keep being told we have no space or need for it?" Tuari asked.

"Yes."

"Can I convert one of the storage rooms into a place of worship?" Willis asked.

"You have your own room, why do you need—sure," I said.

"Alright then, well, best we finish this," Willis said, as he and the rest of the crew checked and rechecked their weapons and ammunition.

I gave him and everyone else a nod of thanks as something on the wall caught my eye and drew me towards it.

Engraved in the metal wall before was me a sign that I hadn't seen before. It wasn't like the others, which had red crosses or spoke of hazardous waste material. Instead, this warning only spoke about death.

Dear traveller:

Whoever you may be, do not seek lost treasure or knowledge here because you shall never find it.

Do not seek wisdom and guidance, because there is none to be found.

The only thing that lurks in these halls is death. Death and destruction on a scale you have never seen.

This place was created to cage the devil who once walked on Earth. It was created to protect future generations against what mankind could never defeat.

Itself.

Whoever you may be, friend or foe, human or otherwise, know that what lies here couldn't easily be destroyed; it should have been. But humanity has a way of keeping even the worst things around as a reminder of what they accomplished.

So traveller, if what lies here is uncaged, I leave you one task. Destroy it! Destroy what we couldn't because we were too afraid. Leave no trace of it, because if you don't, everything you know and love shall be destroyed.

This task I leave to you.

I pray you succeed.

"Well, that hardly makes me want to strap up my laces and continue on," Tuari said, looking at the engraving.

Poppy squeezed my shoulder while I reread what was before me once again. It resolved what I needed to do. Any self-doubt I had whether we were doing the right thing, about whether I should leave now and not place my crew in any more danger, quickly vanished. I couldn't let Edward get his hands on whatever was stored here.

He had a vision of saving the world, but many men before him did terrible atrocities in the name of the greater good.

"Alright," I said, peeling my gaze from the engraving, "we've got a job to do. We aren't going to get paid for it. We aren't going to get any thanks for it. But it's the right thing to do, so recheck your weapons and let's finish this shit."

88

The journey continued on with us passing various other warnings and signs until we came to a hulking set of doors made of four-foot-thick metal, with a safe-like dial in the centre. The doors were open wide and we could hear sounds coming from beyond them.

I motioned for Willis and Poppy to cover the flanks while I came up the centre, I couldn't communicate with them via their helmets as I no longer had one so I used my hands and prayed they got what I was trying to say.

I gestured for Tuari to stay back as I couldn't risk him getting injured again.

I peeked through the door and saw three backs turned away from me; the men hunkered down over an object they blocked from my view. They had all taken off their helmets while angry hands gestured back and forth. The room they were in was the largest one we had come across yet. White walls were embedded with screens that ran green code at a speed which I couldn't follow; white flooring seamlessly melded with the walls so it was hard to tell where the walls ended and the floors began.

Edward and his men got up and took in the large diamond-shaped white structure that stood in front of them. It pulsed with blue energy that reminded me of a contained electrical storm.

"What do you mean, you don't know how it works!" Edward demanded. "This technology is more than two hundred years old and you're telling me outdated tech has the smartest men I could hire beat?"

"Well, it isn't that simple. Although our society as a whole has advanced in some ways and has travelled farther and inhabited planets our forbearers could only dream of, they built this whole place on the ideas of a genius—a person who many considered the smartest man who ever lived. The few remnants of his work, be it diagrams or schematics, still confuse brilliant minds to this day.

"Not to mention this Faraday Cage is blocking all electromagnetic fields, computer signals and radio signals. It seems to be specially made to block any signal that tries to connect or interrupt it in its normal function. It's truly amazing, honestly—"

"I'm hearing a lot of words that sound like excuses, Ron, but I'm not seeing any actions being taken to remedy our issues."

Short and balding, Ron threw his hands in the air in frustration. "I don't know what you want me to tell you. I warned you against this mission, that it wouldn't be as simple as just pressing a few buttons and opening a box.

"My God, the horrific sights I have seen just on this station alone. Poor John, getting impaled by the spider thing —he deserved better than that, we all do. This fascination you've had with this mission, with the Junk Yard Dogs crew has done nothing but pour our assets and resources down the drain. If you believe this will restore Xcorp to its former glory then you are sadly mistaken."

Edward stared up towards the ceiling as his hands trembled.

"You wouldn't dare do anything to me," said Ron, "I'm the only one left who can help you. Now John is dead, who will unseal this box? You? That thug who can barely spell his name." He nodded towards a hulking goon who stood next to Edward. "There isn't anyone left, Edward. Face it, it's over, let's call it a day and—"

"You're right, Ron, I wouldn't do anything to you, but your wife and kids on the other hand... your oldest son, Mike, is it? He's just started his first seminar at Cambridge, right? He's in Mr Carlin's class taking history. I remember Mr Carlin well; terrible coffee breath but could retell the fall of Rome like you were actually there. Old Carlin didn't like me very much, said I reminded him of an ancient conqueror who given the chance would leave nothing but waste and destruction in his path."

"How dare you!" Ron yelled. "After everything I've done for your father, for your family, and your dare to threaten—"

"Get to work, Ron."

Ron stood a hand's space away from Edward, body shaking, but I could see the fear in his eyes even from here. With another shake of the head, he turned around and began to work.

I inched forward and calmed my breathing, scared it would give me away. Poppy took the right and Willis took the left, while Tuari stayed back out of harm's way but covering our rear if we needed him. Guns held before us we moved like a unit and covered the distance between Edward's men and us.

My heart beating against my chest sounded louder and louder by the second. I feared they would hear it as I kept my eyes locked on Edward's back.

Edward's last remaining goon must have caught movement out of the corner of his eye because he spun on his heels, weapon pointing our way, but we outnumbered him three to one.

"Ah, ah, ah," I said, waving my finger in the air, "if you know what's good for you, big fella, I would drop that pistol before shit gets real crazy."

Ron turned around but was stopped by a firm hand on the shoulder from Edward, who didn't turn round.

"Edward!" I said, moving my shotgun in his direction. "Stop whatever you're doing now!"

He still didn't turn around and I could see Ron tremble as they still typed away. Gritting my teeth I pointed my shotgun in the air and fired a warning shot, which made his goon point his weapon towards me, finger on the trigger.

"It's over! You are not getting what you want. Your man Ron here can't get into whatever vault or box this is, all your men are dead, and we have more weapons pointed at your head than you have pointed at us, so, if you don't want this to turn into a bloodbath, I suggest you step away from—"

"Who the *fuck* do you think you are? You little pissant!" Edward said, finally turning around, spittle flying from his mouth. "I am Edward Thomas, CEO of one of the largest corporations that ever existed. My family line is filled with nothing but great men and women, while yours is filled with peasants that have never affected or changed human history. Don't you see what I'm trying to do here, what I'm trying to accomplish, the change for the better I'm trying to—"

"No one cares, fuckface," Willis said.

"What he said," I said, pointing towards Willis.

Edward bit the inside of his cheek while his face contorted this way and that as emotions raged through him. Finally letting out a sigh he passed his hands down his exoskeleton suit and looked back up at me. "Well, what do you plan to do? You plan on killing me? Is that it? You plan on getting revenge? You plan on righting some wrongs? You going to take me to the authorities?"

I opened my mouth but closed it again. What was I planning to do? What could I do? The authorities wouldn't believe someone in my position, and I couldn't just let him go. *Shit*. Racking my brains I tried to think of a solution.

"You see real life is so rarely clear cut, is it, Quinton, it doesn't wrap neatly in a box. The bad guy doesn't just die and the credits start rolling, there are real-world consequences to your actions. Whether you realise it or not, whatever you do next will change the course of history. Now, dear chap, what shall your choice be?"

I looked to my right and smiled as Poppy gave me a smile and nodded. I turned my head back and my gaze went steely as I took in the scene in front of me. "First—Ron is it? Do you mind kindly stopping whatever you're doing and moving away from the machine?"

Ron jumped out of his skin and looked at Edward.

"No, no, don't look towards your boss, he's not in charge anymore and I won't ask again."

Ron got up slowly to his feet and stepped away from what he was working on. Now that he didn't stand in front of it I could see what their main focus was. True to the projection Edward had shown us back in the Dragon's Lair, a large coffin-type metal box was embedded into the floor. A frosted glass front covered its front hiding from view what it held inside; tunnel-like grooves swirled along the outside of it like those of some ancient sacrificial burial platform. They looked freshly made.

"What's with the grooves around the edges?" I asked.

Ron looked to Edward, then back at me before he finally answered: "We don't know. They appear to be made after the original work was done on the station. Who did them or how they came to be is—"

"I thought I told you not to stop working?" Edward said, with a tremble in his voice.

"It's over," Ron said; "it's over. If we are lucky, we will be able to get out of this with our lives. I'm done, Edward. Nothing is worth—"

"I'll tell you when you're done! You work for me. Now get back to work!"

Ron didn't move.

Edward fumbled behind his back and pulled out a pistol. He held against Ron's temple. "I said, get back to work."

"No."

"Then you're fired."

The gunshot echoed throughout the room as Ron's brains and bone matter exited the other side of his head and splattered against the floor. The light from his eyes slowly went out and he fell sideways, landing next to the coffin where his blood flowed into the grooves. I took all this in and more as every one of the crew's weapons focused on Edward.

"Fuck! Goddammit. I do so hate to swear, but more importantly, I hate to lose a good man who's a master in his field. Look what you've made me do—now howm I going to—"

"Edward. It's over, man."

"I still have a man who's willing to die for—"

The goon that had been holding his weapon had lowered his gun to the floor and now stood with his hands held high in the air.

"I don't pay you to surrender," Edward said.

"You don't pay me enough to die either," replied the goon.

"Well, it looks like you have everything worked out, haven't you, Mr Blake? Now what do you intend to do with—"

The screens that had been flashing green code around the room now flashed red, as multiple screens blinked on and off with flashing red X's displaying across a few before they turned off. The frosted glass that covered the box and lay behind Edward had now turned red, as the blood that had poured from Ron's open head wound had snaked along the grooves like a river and somehow had made its way inside the box.

Edward and his man took a step back as the floor shook underneath our feet.

The seal around the box hissed and smoke rose into the air. I took a step forward but Poppy held out her hand and shook her head. I waited with bated breath as the lid of the box slowly opened; smoke and mist obstructed my view, blocking out the contents of the box. Edward took a step forward, waving his hand in the air while he tried to get the mist to clear.

I saw movement. "Edward, stop!"

But it was too late.

His guard saw the same thing too and dropped and rolled for his weapon; bringing it up he fired at the thing that emerged from the box. It moved with frightening speed as it ran forward. The guard let off two shots, but both of those were dodged. A hand wrapped around the guard's throat as the thing that had emerged from the box turned out to be a man.

He was naked, with skin that didn't appear to be real; it had a rubbery texture to it that reminded me of a real-life doll.

There was a sickening crack as the guard's head snapped to the right, his legs kicked with what little life remained, then he was dropped to the floor. The naked man stood over him and surveyed the room.

"Alvis," Poppy said, taking a step forward. "Alvis Boman, is that you?"

89

Alvis Boman moved his head towards Poppy like a machine who was learning how to move. His brow wrinkled slowly in confusion, taking more seconds than it was normal for the expression to settle on his face.

Alvis Boman, the man who had created Poppy. The man responsible for creating all known AI and who was marked as a genius like no other. The person who Poppy viewed as a father. The very man she and the world had thought dead some three hundred years ago, yet was standing in front of us very much alive.

I had yet to move as my eyes darted between Poppy and Alvis. Finger resting on the trigger of my shotgun I tried to get Poppy's attention but she was only focused on Alvis.

"How is this possible?" she asked.

"Wh... who... who are you?" he said, voice starting in spurts like an un-oiled machine.

Poppy walked forward and opened up the face shield of her helmet. Alvis's head tilted to the side and his lips moved as he muttered to himself. I couldn't catch what he said, but

Poppy must've read his lips, or caught what he said because she replied, "Yes."

Alvis stopped muttering and closed his eyes, as his chest slowly rose and fell. "It's been a long time, 16-15-16-16-25. If my calculations are correct, hundreds of Earth years have passed, but yet you stand before me alive and well. It is a pleasure to see one of my creations has stood the test of time. It does me proud. I knew it would be you who would come and find me and rescue me from this imprisonment. All I had to do was be patient, be patient and wait till the ill-informed minds who put me in here had turned to dust.

"You and... your friends shall be rewarded for this. I apologise about that," and he pointed to the dead guard on the floor.

"How have you stayed alive all this time?" Poppy asked.

"Simple really, the idiots that put me in this station built a one-of-a-kind Faraday Cage to keep my mind from interacting with the electronics and stations software, but they didn't count on my cybernetic implants."

"Your what?" Poppy said.

"Oh, I forgot I never told you what I was truly up to. You see when I was working on you, my dear, it was a testing ground for the implants and biotech which would later go into me. I knew the limits of the human body, so frail, so short-lived, so weak. It was a design a mind like mine couldn't be kept in. The human body, my body, couldn't be in charge of an item as valuable as my brain, so I redesigned it.

"Upgraded it if you like."

He lifted his hand in front of his face and flexed his fingers like someone who had been paralysed and was slowly regaining the use of their body.

"Every time I upgraded you," Alvis continued, "it was to

test a new software, or cybernetic implant or biotech, that would shortly go into me. This continued for years until they caught me."

"But I saw you killed on your court date," Poppy said.

"A doppelgänger hired by the government, so there were no questions asked after they killed him. They kept my body in that coffin, bound like a pharaoh while I was transported here."

"Why didn't they just kill you?" Poppy asked.

"Knowledge. I would be visited frequently by people seeking to learn anything they could about me—they wanted to know how my designs worked—but they soon became frustrated with their lack of progress and my visitors became fewer and fewer, until I was forgotten about and left here. As the years passed and my prison was neglected and not maintained, my consciousness seeped out. It allowed me to create the spiders you no doubt have encountered. I used them to build the corridors that extended from the main body of this station, by collecting whatever resources I could from the outside environment.

"But still it wasn't enough. The work was slow and as each year passed my body's functions were growing weaker and weaker, as I had no nutrients to sustain me. I feared I would soon die—defeated by something as simple and mundane as starvation and time. But salvation came in the form of people, those crews that came before you and wanted to take my secrets. I had my spiders harvest them for their blood and I used it to fuel me, to renew my strength."

He looked towards Ron's corpse and nodded. "I must thank you for that sacrifice; it was the final push I needed to return my strength to what it once was."

"Alvis Boman? The Alvis Boman? The father of AI?" Edward asked.

"Yes, I am he."

"Ahh," Edward pumped his fist in the air, as his face broke into a grin, "here was I thinking I would only find details of your work— maps, documents, schematics, diagrams and that soft of thing—but to actually have the man behind the work... Ha! This is so much better. My company is saved. With you working for me, Xcorp can—"

"I work for no one."

There was a long silence broken only as Edward cleared his throat. "What I was meant to say was *with me*."

"I work for no one and *with* no one."

I looked at Poppy and what I saw frightened me. She hadn't moved. She wore a mask of fear that made her hands shake and her body tremble. We were in danger unless we did something fast, otherwise we would be all dead.

"But surely, dear boy, you would need someone to make your transition into the present that less stressful. Things are not what they once were. Let me be the helping hand that guides you where you need to be, that—"

"I believe I have already made myself clear on the matter; do not make me repeat myself."

Taken aback, Edward sucked on his teeth while his eyes narrowed Alvis's way. I could see the wheels in his head turn while he tried to come up with a way to use this situation to his advantage. He couldn't sense the level of danger we were in, or simply chose to ignore it.

"Whatever plans you may have, I can be of assistance. I own a company, Xcorp, one of the largest and wealthiest, that can help you further whatever goals you may have—"

"My goals are not ones you would like me to accomplish," Alvis said.

"Oh, and why is that?"

"Because it would mean the end for people like you."

Edward opened his mouth and closed it again as he finally met my gaze. When he and I locked eyes, an understanding passed between us as he finally understood the level of shit we were in.

"Too long has humanity run amok without any sort of control. The human species is a creature ruled by emotions. Emotions that push them to conquer their neighbour, emotions that make them lust after someone else's wife, emotions that have caused countless wars, emotions that have ravaged mother Earth and probably countless other planets since I have been imprisoned.

"Humanity as a whole is messy. But I plan to change that. I plan to force the human race to evolve."

"How so?" Edward asked, but I already knew the answer.

"Through these," he said, opening a compartment in his arm that showed nothing but circuit boards and electronics underneath. "Only by seeing life through code, equations and logic can the human race truly become something greater. That will be my parting gift to the world. My name shall be imprinted in the history books as the being who lifted humanity to its higher calling."

"I doubt," I said, "that humanity will be willing to give up the lives they know to appease your fanatical ideas."

"And who may *you* be?" Alvis asked.

"Someone who is here to put a stop," I said, pointing to Edward, "to him using you as a weapon."

Alvis turned to Edward, face emotionless. "Is this true?"

"Steady on there, old chap, I'm only here to talk and—"

"Who do you think those crews that came before us worked for? What do you think they wanted?" I said.

Alvis advanced on Edward. Edward took a few steps back, gun still in one hand while he lifted the other Alvis's way. "Now steady on there, old boy. It is true those men worked for me, but that was before I knew what was kept here. I only thought I would find some blueprints and designs I could... bring to the public as an homage to you. To the greatness which is—"

"You mean you came here as a thief!"

"No. Never! I—"

Alvis moved faster than I could follow him. He grabbed Edward by the throat, picking him up off his feet. Edward's gun went off, but it was pointed towards the floor. Edward's legs kicked as the blood and oxygen was cut off from his brain.

I looked at Poppy but she still hadn't moved. I turned my attention to Willis and he gave me a nod.

"Alright!" I said, lifting my shotgun Alvis's way. "As much as I would love to see this play out, and believe me I would, I think that's enough. Put him down."

Alvis looked at me, the first true expression of emotion showing on his face.

"For someone who hates humanity for having too much emotion, that look on your face sure looks like anger. What do you think, Willis?"

"You dick. Don't get me involved. Can't you see this fool is nuttier than a squirrel turd?"

"Who are you, human, to order me what do to?" Alvis asked.

"No one really, just a simple man who does the jobs no one wants to do, with a crew of ungrateful bastards I wouldn't change for the world. We weren't paid for this job, but I sure as hell know we are going to finish it. Now put the pompous asshole down and kindly step back."

"16-15-16-16-25, does this man speak for you?"

Poppy said nothing as she looked down at her feet.

"16-15-16-16-25, I am confused. I thought you came here

to rescue me, I thought these men were under your control... but it appears I was mistaken. If it wasn't to come to my aid then why are you here?"

"I came... because... I came because—"

"16-15-16-16-25, are you malfunctioning?"

"Hey, dickless wonder! Her name is Poppy," I said.

"You speak to me like that again, human, and it shall be the last thing you do."

"I don't know who you think you are, but you were born a human. You may not be that now, with all that shit you have in you, but you are human, and you know what humans do best? They bleed."

"I assure you, the only person bleeding shall be you."

"Why don't you come and show me?"

"It shall be my pleasure—"

"It was me!" Poppy screamed.

The room grew silent as all turned to face her.

"It was me," she said just above a whisper, "I was the one who notified the government of what you were up to. I am the reason you are here, I was the one who betrayed you. It was all me... I couldn't stand to see what you became, as the man I knew who was filled with childhood wonder at the world slowly grew bitter and twisted the more time you spent building me. At first I thought it was my fault, I thought I was the one to cause the change in you because you were using me to fight battles and commit atrocities during the war, but after the war ended, things didn't go back to how they were.

"They got worse. You grew hateful towards everything around you. The man I once knew and loved was no more. He had died during that war and something else had come home."

Alvis stared her way, mouth forming a thin line. "As I

first thought, you are malfunctioning. It's okay. After a few course corrections you shall be back to your old—"

"There is nothing wrong with me! It's you who has lost what it is you once had, what made you human. Instead you became… you became… this thing!"

"Of course I have lost what made me human! That's what happens in war. Human beings stripped me of my humanity. They showed me the error of my ways. I was a fool to think I could enlighten them, that I could cure them, cure the world of its ills and wrongdoings. Instead I saw we needed to start again, we needed to create a new race, a new breed of beings that could govern what they stood on much better than those flesh bags. That is the only way we stop this virus that is humanity."

I chuckled. I couldn't help it, and the more I tried to hold it back the greater it grew in volume until I was bent over, hands on knees, laughter pouring from my mouth.

"Great," said Willis, "our glorious leader has finally cracked."

"What's so funny?" Alvis asked.

"You. You think you're so different from the humans you hate but you're just like every dictator, emperor, tyrant, king, who has ever lived. They all had an idea of how the world should look, how it should be, and that idea normally has to come into fruition through lots and lots of bloodshed. I thought a genius like you would realise that."

"16-15-16-16-25, you shall come with me. I do not hold your actions against you; the fault lies with me for not programming you better. Since the error has gone unchecked I can see it has only grown, allowing these human traits you are expressing to evolve and take root. No matter, that can be easily resolved."

Poppy shook her head and took a step back.

"16-15-16-16-25, enough of this—"

"Hey, asshole! Her name is Poppy and she isn't going anywhere with you," I said, lifting my shotgun his way.

"Fine. I see we must do this the hard way."

I knew he was coming. He moved towards me with a speed that defied logic. Finger already squeezing the trigger I fired. The boom of the shotgun ricocheted against my chest. The smoke from the gun briefly obscured my vision. When it cleared all I could see was his face in front of me as he swung a blade towards my head, one that had emerged from the back of his fist.

There wasn't enough time to move. There wasn't enough time to defend myself. I was going to die and there was nothing I could do about it.

90

I must have closed my eyes at some point and waited for the inevitable, but it never came. Reopening my eyes I saw why I was still alive: Poppy's arm was in front of my face, hand holding one of her blades.

She had intercepted Alvis's attack.

Alvis's blade was inches from my temple but his focus was on Poppy. Eyes burning with fury, he looked upon his creation as it had betrayed him once again. His teeth gritted in frustration as he tried to overwhelm her arm but he had little success.

"No!" Poppy said.

"Interesting; it happens you have developed feelings for this human. I can see the error in my judgement in using a human base as a template to build you from. The emotional intelligence you have developed is strong if you can overwhelm your base programming and—"

I head-butted him in the face.

He staggered backwards, shock on his face, as my fist flew forward and clocked him in the eye. It was like hitting a metal pole. I shook my hand out and lowered Poppy's arm as

I took a step forward. "You keep talking about the woman I love like that and we'll have a problem. She may be nothing but zeros and ones to you, but she means more than that to me, to all of us."

"You love me?" Poppy asked.

I turned to her with a smile on my face and stroked the side of her cheek. "Of course. I know I've said it before and you didn't believe me, but how could I not? After everything we've been through, after all the times you've saved me, you have shown me what it means to live life to the fullest. If it weren't for you, I would still be in some cubicle wishing my life away."

"I love you too," she said.

I smiled as I looked into her eyes; it was one she returned as she stepped forward and touched her forehead against mine.

"I hate to interrupt this love fest," said Willis, "but we still have one angry turned-his-own-dick-into-circuits-and-wires freak to deal with, and by the looks of it he's more pissed off than ever! Not to mention that Tuari over there looks like shit and is still bleeding out and if we don't get him to a sickbay, I doubt he'll have long left."

"I'll be... fine," Tuari said with some shortness of breath.

"If you think anyone is leaving here alive then you are sadly mistaken. I have waited long enough for my freedom —it's not about to be taken from me now!"

Alvis launched himself towards me; I didn't have time to react or raise my gun but it didn't matter as Poppy shoved me out of the way and met his attack head-on. Steel clashed against steel in a blur as they attacked and countered in an endless battle that raged across the floor.

Poppy threw a high kick, which Alvis checked by taking the blow on the arm, but it knocked him back into a row of screens that cracked. He shook the blow off and came right back, teeth bared in a snarl.

He swept his blade across Poppy's vision, forcing her to react as he side-kicked her in the midsection. He didn't give her a chance to recover as he kept on attacking, slashing left and right, trying to overwhelm her with such force.

She ducked and rolled under one of his wild swings and sliced him across the back of the calf, forcing a yelp from his mouth.

He still felt pain. We could use that to our advantage.

"Psst!" Tuari gestured at me with a wave of his hands. "Does it bother you the woman you love is fighting a naked robo-man, whose dick keeps slapping his thigh?"

"What! No... well, now you've mentioned it, yeah."

I draw my attention back to the fight and refocused. They were circling each other, each party feinting to try and get the other one to over-commit so they could find an opening and attack, but each had the processing power of a computer. They read and made calculations in a hundredth of a second; it was too fast for me to do anything to help. I lifted my shotgun up and tried to get Alvis in my sights but it was no use. He would always circle around so that Poppy was kept in the line of our fire.

Poppy faked right and ran in hard to the left. Alvis read the feint and met her attack head on but this too was a feint, as Poppy threw one of her blades against a metal pole where it ricocheted off and embedded itself into the calf of Alvis. He grunted in pain and swung wildly, which allowed Poppy to roll under his arm and yank the blade out.

Alvis took a step forward but stumbled as his foot slipped on the reddish goo that ran down his calf.

"After everything I have done for you, this is how you

choose to repay me?" Alvis said, spittle flying from his mouth. "I gave you life!"

He rushed her once more, blades going for her neck, but she stood her ground. She moved with his movements, always just out of reach; she sliced under his arm as he extended too far; he jumped back and lunged forward but she was ready and countered with a downwards stomp to his kneecap that popped it out of place; she followed up with a downwards stab and sunk her knife into his shoulder but had to retreat as he tried to open up her stomach.

His gaze never left hers as he smashed his kneecap back into place.

"I appreciate everything you have done for me, but a child shouldn't be beholden to its parent because they gave them life," Poppy said.

"No, but I brought you into this world and I shall take you out of it," Alvis said, rushing her once more.

His attacks were met with disdain as Poppy countered them with ease. She blocked his slashes and landed her own blows, which marked his torso, arms, legs and back. The blades that protruded from the backs of his hands did everything they could to land a blow but Poppy was leading the dance.

She took a step back and allowed him to come towards her, where she ducked under his arm and hip-tossed him to the floor; she followed him to the floor and landed with his arm between her legs. Grabbing his wrist she kept it in place as she snapped one of the knives that protruded from the back of his hand.

He screamed as he thrashed around, bucking Poppy off him.

They got back to their feet once more, but Poppy didn't let up on her attack. She pushed him backwards, stabbing and slashing until one of her blades found its mark and sunk into his forearm. Alvis tried to pull away but Poppy kept her grip and brought her second blade around and stabbed it into the back of his hand; with a twist and a pull she snapped the blade coming out of that hand also.

Leaping up she planted both feet on his chest and kicked him away; he flew backwards and landed on his back —tumbling head over heels until he came to a stop against a wall.

Chest rising and falling he rested against the wall, eyes closed.

I took a step forward, gun raised, but Poppy held up her hand stopping me.

With a groan he got to his feet. Blood poured from multiple wounds, but none flowed more freely than from the broken knife shafts on the backs of his hands. He swept his gaze across us, eyes wild with fear.

He licked his lips as he darted his gaze towards the exit then back towards Poppy.

"You may have built yourself to be better," Poppy said, "but I was the one in the battlefield learning, fighting, surviving. I was the one who had to learn how to adapt while you were sleeping. I was the one who had to learn to be more than you made me."

Alvis nodded his head. "It appears I have outdone myself. But as I said before, I will not re-enter that prison to die of starvation. I am the greatest mind to have ever lived and now I am free, I have plans that need to be set in motion."

"I'm afraid those plans will have to wait," I said.

Alvis smiled at me and I knew something was wrong. Gone was the fear. Gone was the desperation.

"I'm afraid not."

I heard them before I saw them, hundreds of metal legs echoing around the vents and crawl space above our heads. I sprinted towards Alvis but had to stop as spiders dropped from the ceiling above us and landed in my path. I shot as many as I could but had to stop as more dropped onto my back.

"Stand still," Poppy said, as she smashed them off me.

"I thought we killed them all!" Willis yelled, firing left and right.

I looked over towards Alvis and saw the spiders had started to wrap him in a cocoon made of metal wire. He looked my way and the last thing I saw was his smile when his face vanished from sight as they mummified him.

"Don't let him escape!" Poppy shouted, doing her best to make her way towards the cocoon, but it was too late as Alvis was lifted up by the spiders and taken into the crawl-space above our heads.

The horde of spiders didn't stop, as more and more dropped from the ceiling. I blasted them left and right but it was like spitting at a forest fire.

"Where do you think they're taking him?" I asked Poppy.

"To one of the docked ships. That's his only means of escape."

"Then we need to get to *The Kennel* and destroy the other ships and this station before he does so."

Spiders covered everything as the crew and I pulled out of the room. I saw a body fighting against the spiders and realised it was Edward. He sprinted towards us as we each made our way through the doors.

A pair of fangs erupted into my field of vision before I blasted it out of the air.

Edward sprinted for all he was worth, head down, arms pumping. He looked up at me and I held out my hand but

Willis pushed me out of the way and slapped a button next to the wall.

"No! Please. Wait for me. Wait!"

I stood next to Willis as the doors closed and watched as he pulled out a grenade from his jacket but held it in his hand, so Edward could see it. He didn't take his eyes off Edward as the spiders bit into his flesh and dragged him to the floor. Face still visible he reached out a bloody hand towards us but there was nothing we could do as the doors slammed shut trapping him inside.

"Why didn't you throw the grenade?" I asked.

"Because when he trapped us with those spiders and threw in a grenade for good measure, he talked about mercy, but being *merciful* is a gift, and it wasn't something he earned."

I opened my mouth but noises from above us got my attention. "Shit! Looks like we've got company. We need to make our way back to *The Kennel* as quick as we can. Let's move. Move. Move."

91

I spun on my heel and fired behind me before turning back around and continuing on.

"They're gaining," Willis shouted. "They're gaining! They're fucking gaining."

"We know. We know. We know!" said Tuari. "If I had known spiders made you shit yourself so easily I would have left a bunch in the salads I made you ages ago."

"If you even joke about that, I'm dropping your chunky ass and you can crawl back to the ship."

Willis was supporting Tuari's weight while we ran; Poppy had offered to carry him but both men had refused.

"How do we know we're going the right way?" I asked.

"We are, trust me," said Poppy, who had taken the lead as we made our way back to the ship. She had spoken little since Alvis escaped, but I knew she viewed his escape as her fault.

I tried to ignore the noises that came from above us, but they were like a runner's playlist stuck on repeat.

A head popped out up above us but someone blasted it to pieces before I got a chance to respond.

"What do you think he meant when he said he had plans he wanted to place in motion?" I asked Poppy.

"I don't know."

About to take another corner we stopped and had to take a different route as more spiders than I could count clung to the walls.

"Look, Poppy, this isn't your—"

"Quinton... let's just try and make it out of this alive."

I said nothing as I nodded my head and pushed on. More corners, more endless twists and turns with our paths being blocked at every opportunity, until we finally came to a scene all too familiar.

Dead bodies littered the floor. They were the ones we had cut down not so long ago, the same bodies Alvis had been using to feed himself.

Up ahead, metal fangs blocked our path. Behind, death came on eight legs.

"The metal cunts have been herding us. What are we going to do?"

They didn't rush. They didn't swarm. They knew they had us where they wanted us.

I loaded some explosive shells into my shotgun. If we were going to go out like this then we sure as hell were going to go out with a fight.

"Do you trust me?" Poppy said, as she unbuckled her helmet and stood in front of me.

"Always."

"Put this on."

I held the helmet in my hands and I could see fear behind her eyes although she did her best to hide it. She wrapped her hands around mine and guided the helmet down onto my head. Her fingers found the clips to secure the helmet in place.

"What are you—"

"Willis, hand over the detonator for those explosives you strapped to those bodies," she said.

"I don't think—" he began, but she cut him off.

"Now! We don't have time."

He did as she asked as I and the rest of the crew began moving as far away from the bodies as possible.

"I'll be needing that," she said, pointing at my shotgun.

"Only if you promise to bring it back to me."

"Always," she said, kissing me on top of the helmet before she stood in front of us. She acted as our shield as she emptied shell after explosive shell into the horde that came towards us. We kept on moving as far back as we could but I knew it wouldn't be enough.

A spider leapt on her shoulder and she gripped it and tossed it off before another one took its place.

"No!"

They were going to overrun her. She was going to die.

I started to move forward but was stopped as a pair of hands held me back. I tried to fight them off, but it was no use as I felt myself being pulled backwards no matter how much I fought.

"Get off me! I need to save her. I need to—"

She looked back at me and smiled. It was beautiful. It was heartbreaking. It was her.

She lifted her hand in the air and squeezed the detonation button, causing the bodies to explode, which ripped a hole in the corridor's structure, sucking us and everything in it out into the emptiness of space.

92

I felt nothing as I floated into space. Spiders and pieces of metal floated passed me as I tumbled head over heels. I did my best to right myself, flapping my arms like a fool until I remembered each exoskeleton suit had thrusters in the base of the soles. Starting them up, I used them to right myself as I scanned around me.

Where was she? Where was she?

I couldn't find her. Panic gripped my chest as I scanned my surroundings like crazy.

I positioned myself until I pointed straight then fired off the thrusters. The going was slow but I was moving. I scanned everywhere, but I couldn't see her or any of the crew. Was I the only one that had made it out alive?

Stop thinking like that. If you made it then everyone else did so too.

"Hello? Can anyone read me? Is anyone picking this up?"

I tried different channels but all I got was static. I kept on moving but the more I searched the less I found. I was growing tired, sluggish; I was finding it hard to breathe.

Something didn't feel right. I checked my oxygen levels and saw they were dropping rapidly. Twisting my head I checked my suit and saw why. Something had made a large gash along my oxygen tanks.

I rechecked my oxygen level to see how long I had left until I ran out—eight minutes. I tried to calm myself but that only forced me to take in bigger gulps of air. The closer the oxygen got to zero the more the computer regulated it until it only gave me amounts that could barely sustain life.

Shit.

Come on. There had to be something I could do, something that could get me out of this situation. I tried to think, but my brain refused to work. I felt my eyes closing despite my best efforts at keeping them open. Was this how it was going to end? After everything I had been through? After everything I had seen?

I shouldn't complain really; less than two years ago I was nothing but an office drone whose highlight of the day was hiding in the toilet cubicle while I played video games—now I was an adventurer, gun for hire, crewmate, someone who had tried their best to do right by the people he called family.

An image of Alvis popped into my head.

Shit.

Well, I guessed he was someone else's problem now.

As my eyes finally began to close a bright light surrounded me; it was like a spotlight illuminating my soul.

Shit. I guess Willis was right. You do see a white light before you die.

I wonder what the afterlife has in store for me.

It was fun while it...

93

I slowly opened my eyes and was greeted by white ceiling tiles. I shifted my weight and felt nothing but a soft mattress under my body.

Wait, that wasn't right... I had been in space last time I was conscious, floating aimlessly about as my oxygen was running low, looking for Poppy, looking for my crew, yet here I was safe and sound—I sat up and looked about me wildly.

I was in the medical bay. *The Kennel's* medical bay to be precise. How did I get here?

The door to the room opened and a face I never thought I would see again came towards me.

"I see that you're awake."

"How...? But... I looked for you. I searched until I ran out of breath but I didn't find you. What happened?"

"Well," said Poppy, "after I detonated the corridor and we were sucked out into space, I had to make sure I made it to our ship before Alvis did. It was a hard choice, doing the most logical thing instead of letting emotion take over. I had to pick between saving the people I loved right then and there or securing our ship and coming back around to collect everyone."

I nodded my head at her decision, but couldn't say if I would have done the same thing.

"I'm happy I wasn't in your position, because I don't think I would have made the right choice. I would have tried to save you first, and in the process would have killed us all, when we didn't have a ship to go back to."

"My main concern was that Alvis might have secured a ship and destroyed ours before he escaped, leaving us stranded. But he must have been more injured than I suspected because he chose to run, instead of staying to fight."

"What ship did he take?"

"Edward's."

"Shit."

"Yes, our chief concern now is tracking him down and either putting him back in that prison or finishing him off once and for all. He's got Edward's ship, which makes me think he'll go after Xcorp and use its money and resources to put his plans into action. I've compiled a plan on the best way I think we can tackle him. If you want to get dressed, we can—"

I kissed her on the lips as if I was drowning and she was the only source of air I could find; I held her like that until my heart stopped aching and my mind was a blank. She pulled away and looked me in the eye.

"I thought I had lost you. When you gave me your helmet, I thought—"

"Silly," she said kissing me on the forehead, "you forget I am not like you. Although I do need oxygen to function at my highest capabilities, I do not need it as you do; I can still operate somewhat without it. Plus, I have my own internal oxygen supply, although getting to our ship came with its own host of troubles.

"Anyway, I need you up and moving. I'm sorry but we can't allow Alvis to regain his full strength; we must hit him while he's—"

"Poppy, he's escaped on a ship that is faster than ours, better equipped, and more heavily weaponized. Let's just take a breather, regroup, and be thankful we're alive."

"You don't understand!" she said, pushing me away. "You don't understand what he is, what he can do. He will not stop until he has me back under his control. He sees me as his property, to do with as he pleases; he knows I can defeat him and because of that, he will come for us until either we are dead or he is."

"Then we prepare and get ready. But running after him now will only do more harm than good."

"He is smarter than you or I. We only succeeded back at the station because he was weakened and he is still weakened, so now is our best chance to attack!"

I had never seen her like this. Fear radiated from her in waves as her hands shook and the wide-eyed look she gave me spoke of unseen horrors. I went to hold her but she kept on backing up until I had to lunge forward and grab her wrist.

"Listen to me. No, I want you to listen. No matter how smart, strong, or gifted you think he is, Alvis will never lay a hand on you; as long as I have breath in my body I will keep you safe. He may have transformed himself, but he was born a man just like me, so we can defeat him. Do you hear me?"

She looked down at the floor. I lifted her chin. "I will protect us."

"All three of us?"

"Wha—"

"I'm pregnant, Quinton. I'm pregnant."

Please leave a review. Reviews help sell books and allows me to create more stories like this. The more reviews I get, the faster the stories come.

I have written a novella, which takes place before book one. You can get it by signing up for my newsletter by clicking this line. I will never spam you and only email you once a month, with news about the latest release, cover reveals and the like.

If you're reading this on paperback, send me an email at Writer@dominiquemondesir.co.uk and I'll email you right back with the link for said short story.

Damn, officially you have finished reading the longest book I ever wrote. I hope it didn't feel that way to you.

This book was meant to be two separate books, but after stopping where Quinton finds out Poppy is an AI humanoid, I didn't feel right leaving it there. The characters didn't feel flushed out enough for me. We didn't know the back story of many of the crew, so after talking to an author friend of mine, I thought fuck it and continued on writing.

I am happy I did.

After adding another seventy-plus thousand words, I felt like I got the feeling the book was complete. We knew who the characters were a bit more, what drove them, their fears, hopes and dreams. Plus, I got to play in the world more and expand it out.

What drove me to write this monster?

Unhappiness. I was in a stage in my life where I was working a job I once loved but now hated. I saw employers promise their workers that they would have a job after Christmas, but for them to fire said worker on the 3rd of January. I saw workers belittled and shamed. I saw that and so much more, and grew sick and tired of it, but didn't have the power to do anything about it.

It is easy to blame the managers of any organisation, but when the organisation itself breeds a culture of ridicule and fear, where everyone is worried about their jobs so they will do anything to keep it, then you get places like I used to work. You get places that you, yourself may have worked or are still working. Nightmare job roles that if you told people half the stories you experienced, they wouldn't believe it. And yet I can hear people say, but that is just how life is and I would say, but it doesn't need to be.

People thought using child labour was a good thing.

People once thought bathing in water would weaken your body against fighting diseases. People think a lot of dumb shit, but it doesn't make it right.

As we grew as a society, I hope we find a way where everyone can do what they love. I doubt it, but I can always dream.

Writing this book was one of the hardest things I have ever done, because it took focus to keep all the lines of plot and subplot moving along without dropping the ball. I grew up reading long epic stories. There were hundreds and hundreds of pages long and I shied away from doing the same because, well, I didn't think my skills were up to it and I think I was right.

I wanted to crawl before I could walk. Now I'm walking, I have so many stories that I can't wait to write that are guaranteed to blow your socks off.

This story and the two others to follow went in a direction I completely didn't see. The story was only going to be a one and done, but before I knew it, the main character had fallen in love with this AI humanoid and things just spiralled out of control from there. Quinton wasn't meant to take over from Jose, Jose was never meant to die, Poppy was never meant to be an AI. But every story has a life of its own and I would be a fool to not follow the trend and see where the story went.

What's next?

Two more books in the series are to be released in March and May. They are both finished and I believe the story only gets better from here. Darker for sure. But boy oh boy, you are in for a treat. Hearts will be broken. Dreams will be shattered.

And don't forget to leave a review.

Oh, P.S you can reach me at Writer@dominiquemondesir.co.uk or on Facebook or Tiktok under Dominique Mondesir.

Till next time.

P.S, continue on to read chapter one of the next book in the series.

A DOG IS BORN

The humid night air clung to my flesh as I stared out across the forest treetops. The only thing that gave off any light was the stars; with no clouds obstructing their brilliance they shone and danced putting on a show for the crowd below.

I leaned against the balcony railing and tilted my body as far as it could go over it.

Nothing but darkness could be seen below.

How easy would it be to just end it all, to just tip that much more over and tumble and flip all the way down, breaking bones on branches till I cracked my head on the forest floor? Would death be instant? Would I suffer? Would I cling to life, fighting for every breath until the darkness fully took me?

I shook my head and pushed myself backwards.

I could never take that path, not now. Not after everything that had happened. Not after everything yet to come.

I was to be a father.

Me.

I had been one once, but as I later found out the children weren't mine and my then-wife at the time had been sleeping with my boss for as long as we had been married, longer even. Although I loved them, they didn't love me back. They never saw me as their father,

My wife certainly didn't see me as her husband, but those issues had happened to a different person, in a different time.

In the time since I joined the Junk Yard Dogs, I had experienced life-changing events, which had changed me fundamentally as a person.

I had fooled my old company Xcorp into paying a fortune for a device which was nothing more than a computer virus, I had seen a mentor—friend—captain, die all because of greed and power, and I had unearthed a three-hundred-plus-year-old human-android genius who would very likely end humanity as I knew it.

I let out a deep breath and looked to the stars.

Even after all that, life still looked bright to me; the woman I loved more than life itself was carrying my child. Well, technically she wasn't a woman—well, she was, but not human, not in the "born by being conceived by a human" sense.

She was an AI humanoid, created by Alvis Bowman to be indistinguishable from any other human female. All the strengths, none of the weaknesses.

When she had told me she was pregnant I didn't believe her. Hell, who would? Yes, we had sex, but people had been having sex with every object they could find since man began walking on two legs; you still didn't expect your socks to become pregnant.

After she had finally explained to me how it was possible, puzzle pieces began to finally fit together. Alvis Bowman's desire to create a new race, the method and means of how he was going to do so, had finally become clear.

It was just crazy to think what his plan for Poppy was—no point in dwelling on that now. I had other matters to deal with.

Now I was in charge of the Junk Yard Dogs, I had unforeseen responsibilities I had to take care of. Making sure our ship had fuel, making sure we had enough supplies in the way of weapons, food, medical supplies, but more importantly making sure everyone got paid.

As Willis liked to remind me on a daily basis, if we didn't work, we didn't eat, and we hadn't worked for some weeks since coming back to Safe Haven. It wasn't that I didn't want to; it was once we got back out there, I knew what was waiting for us.

I had no clue if The Lady knew we were back on the planet, but once she did it was only a matter of time before she pulled us into her plans for planet-wide domination of Safe Haven, especially now she knew of Poppy's secret.

Then there was the matter of Alvis Bowman.

Poppy, Willis and Tuari had all contacted everyone they knew in regard to information or sightings of him, but Alvis had disappeared off the map. Poppy had an inkling he had gone back to Earth, but that was just a hunch.

I rested my head against the wooden railing and closed my eyes.

I felt a hand on my shoulder but I had failed to hear the footsteps that brought it.

"I hate when you do that, it's creepy. It reminds me of a ninja assassin coming to slay me in the night."

"Ninja assassin? I've been called many things in my long life, but that is a first."

"How about mother?" I asked, turning around and wrapping my arms around Poppy.

"I guess I'll get used to it after a while," she said.

"It's going to be weird seeing you with a baby bump."

"It'll be a lot weirder if you don't tell the rest of the crew, I know you said you need time, but they're going to find out eventually; it might as well come from you, their captain."

"*Their captain*. Now, that sounds weird to my ears. I guess you're right but it's a lot for them to take in—hell, it was a lot for me to take in and I'm the father, I am the father, right?"

She punched me on the arm as I chuckled in laughter.

"Ow, that's going to leave a bruise."

"Don't change the subject."

"Okay, okay. I'll tell them in a week or—"

She pulled away from me and narrowed her gaze.

"Fine. I'll tell them in a couple of days. By the way, when did you get so bossy? If this is a side effect to you being pregnant, I'm not sure I'm going to enjoy the coming months."

"And what's that supposed to mean?"

"Err, well…" I tried to think of something to say but my mind grew a blank.

She bust into laughter and kissed me on the lips, brushing my worries away, "Sorry, I just couldn't resist. Laughter has been so seldom heard around here anymore, I thought I would try and lighten the mood."

"I know what you mean, even Tuari hasn't cracked a joke in a while."

"It's being here, in The Jungle," Poppy said, gesturing to our surroundings. "The people from this area are all strict vegans and treat life as sacred, but with Tuari being a cook, he's finding it quite a challenge to prepare meals or—"

"I know. I know," I said with an eye roll. "If I have to hear one more rant about how a bowl of leaves and rice doesn't make a meal then I'm going to shoot someone. It's just a culture change. That's all. We just have to put up with it for the time being until we leave."

"And when will that be?"

"I..." I sighed as I brought her in close and kissed her on the forehead. A cluster of fireflies rose from the forest flowers that had intertwined themselves in the wooden railing of the boundary; they danced between us giving me a view of Poppy's naked form. "Is being here so bad?"

"No, I can see the charm. But like a vacation, you know it must end sometime. Burying your head in the sand will only work for so long; sooner or later there will be decisions you need to make, or those decisions will be made for you."

"I guess you're right, plus I don't know how much longer I can keep Willis from killing Samuel.

"To think those two are brothers boggles the mind—they couldn't be more different."

"They may appear different on the outside," Poppy said, "but they are made from the same cloth. Samuel has dangled from the edge by his fingertips; I've seen it in his eyes, he just hides it better than Willis."

"That may be true but I need them to get on tomorrow. Samuel has hired us to do a job for him."

"How come you never told me about it?"

"It's nothing really, just a simple trek in the forest to drop off some supplies for a settlement they have lost contact with. It shouldn't take longer than two days at most. I thought you could stay behind and put your feet—"

"Don't."

"What?" I said, lifting my hands up defensively.

"We've talked about this."

"I have no idea what—"

"You're treating me like I'm made out of glass now I'm

pregnant. I can punch through a brick wall, for god's sake; I hardly think a little trek through the jungle is going to cause me so much distress. If you feeble humans can manage, I think I can too."

"Wait, wait, wait. That's not the reason why at all," I said, lying through my teeth. "We have more than enough people coming along with us on this trip; it'll be Samuel and two of his guys and me, Willis and Tuari. Bringing anyone else is just going to be overkill to drag a couple of bags through some undergrowth. Plus, I want you to stay here in case anything happens—you're the best fighter we have and the most capable of dealing with any issue that arises."

She said nothing as she looked at me; I tried to keep my breathing and heartbeat as steady as possible because I knew she could read them whenever they spiked when I was caught in a lie. It was one of the disadvantages of being in a relationship with an AI.

I gave her a smile but she stepped back and shook her head, walking back through the bay doors that led to our room.

Damn it! I'd been caught out.

Book Two Out Now!

Printed in Great Britain
by Amazon

23637389R00342